ETERNAL NIGHT SHIFT SERIES

RHYS

LENA NAZAREI

Editing, design, and distribution by Bublish
Published by Nurse Lena Books

ISBN: 9781647048402 (Paperback)

For the real "Olivia" & "Ellie" – as you leave the nest and begin your lives, I give you this advice: follow your passion, don't live for anyone but yourselves and never let anyone tell you what you're supposed to be. I love you more than words can say.

For Emily – thank you for supporting all my crazy ideas and dream chasing. I can't wait to see what the universe has planned for us.

For Jeremy & Logan – thank you for being a safe landing pad and lifting me up when I was down. Thank you for being as excited about these books as I am and never laughing when I tell you my dreams.

For Summer – thank you for your amazing support and encouragement. You make me feel beautiful and that's more important than you know. I can't wait to see your dreams come into reality.

For Julie & Tori – thank you for letting me pull you into this crazy world. I'm so grateful that I walked into that café on a night you were working. Now, we're friends… soon we'll be neighbors.

For the real "Alex" – thank you for your encouragement, positivity, acceptance and friendship. Thank you for all the laughter, for being an ear to listen and for being a puzzle piece match in all this chaos. Pretty soon we'll have clean aisles to walk in. Can't wait to celebrate.

Most importantly – For the real doctors, nurses, social workers, RTs, HUCs, chaplains, phlebotomists, therapists, pharmacy techs, transporters and housekeepers that are still doing the hard work in healthcare…. I thank you. Only we know just how hard it is sometimes; only we know the darkest moments we have to smile through. I will forever be grateful for the parts you play in the whole system. Just know that I appreciate you.

I love you all. Xoxoxoxoxo.

PROLOGUE

November 2020

My Dearest Katie,

You will have to bear with my clumsy attempt at a journal. As you know, it was your idea. Anyone who has read your journals understands how much we've been through. You've assured me that writing everything down helped you immensely. Alex also writes in his journal and seems to find comfort in it. You've both encouraged me to write since I'm not much of a sharer. It's not that I don't want to tell you all about my life. It's that I just don't know how to start, nor do we have the time to unpack all of my 200 plus years.

As your wedding approaches, I'm inspired to do this for you. My marriage gift to you is my life — for you to know the one who came before you and what fated events brought us together to be family.

If you should choose to share this with the world, I give you my blessing.

If I'm honest, as I should be or this exercise is wasted, the pressure to do this came from another place as well. The night you fought Jeremy, the night you faced danger for the third time, was too much for me. For days after we put Tamela in the ground, I could not let you out of my sight.

You are my daughter.

Watching Sorin mourn his only progeny filled me with the need to hold onto you tighter than ever. It occurred to me that fear has stopped me from allowing you to truly know me - fear that you may not look at me the same.

But should anything ever happen to either of us, I want no secrets between us – only love and acceptance.

It is hard to believe 14 months have passed since I shared blood with you. While the first half of that time was fraught with danger, watching you the last five months has brought me great joy. You are adored by so many; Alex and Sorin are excellent mates for you. The powers you possess are wondrous. To think that I brought someone so good into eternity gives me such pride. Turning you is my greatest accomplishment. Everything else since that moment has been like gifts from the universe.

You will do great things for this world.

Being uncle to your daughters is an honor and brings a happiness I still don't believe I deserved. As I tell this story, you will learn why it means so much to me. Sharing your children with me takes great trust and I will be forever grateful.

As I tell you this story, I'll try my best to remember it all. It has been so many years. Some of the memories are faded, lost to time.

I will, for you and whoever else may read this, not use the old ways that we spoke. Rather I will write it in a way that you can understand. I don't want to confuse you and too much will be lost in the retelling. Only know that it was a different time in a faraway land. It's important to me that you comprehend only the point of the words and not that it is authentic. I cannot promise I'll not slip into it as I write but will work to keep it understandable for a modern reader. However, if you would later enjoy – I'm happy to give you a realistic demonstration of the speech. It has been a long time, but I used to do a very good impression of my father. Perhaps, I can do it for you some day.

We must start with some history.

In 1707, Scotland entered into a union with England. The country was poor; suffering was widespread. Finding peace with the English and joining forces with them was the only way for our land to survive. However, not all my countrymen felt this way. They held onto the past horrors at the hands of the English and would rather die - watching their families starve - than join with them. The Jacobites, a group of my countrymen, fought against this treaty only to fall in 1746. Many good men were lost.

My great-grandfather was clan chief in the Highlands when a time known as "the clearances" began. He was offered some land in the lowlands in exchange for relinquishing this position and allowing the clan to fall apart. He laid down his tartan and took the offer. To hear my father tell it, he was a coward. I think differently. I believe my great-grandfather was wise enough to know that he could give it up and save his wife and son or it would be taken by force. He swallowed his pride and walked away.

My grandfather would be raised on that land in a small house that he helped his father build. They grew food and had sheep. My great-grandfather had been in the land for a short time when he was approached by the English for political position, but he declined and stayed a quiet farmer, hated by many for not dying in battle to protect the clans' ways.

But others must have seen the wisdom in this way of life because other families would ask to build on his land, and he let them. Before long, a village sprang up. My grandfather grew and married a young girl who had moved into the village with her family. They built their own home and had their own sons – including my father – who married a girl from the village – moved into my late great-grandfather's house and worked the land. This was a legacy my father was proud of.

In 1784, I came – the next son in the Selkirk line. My mother suffered greatly during my birth and the midwife explained that her womb would never hold another. My father would later tell me that my mother wept but he was glad for the one son they had been blessed with.

My mother told me that he had gotten drunk, gone to the barn and his wails could be heard across the valley.

My father and mother were well respected in the village, as they were the descendants of the man who gave all those families a safe place to live. If the English ever visited, they were offered food and shelter, which they enjoyed and left. The village was never a target because of this.

As I grew, to my father's dismay, I did not embrace this simple way of life. I wanted more. I foolishly felt I was better than the people of that village and destined to do more than raise sheep and put a child in a local lass. Glasgow was a perilous two-days ride and I wanted to be in that city more than anything. As a young boy, when visitors came to our land, I would beg them for tales of the city. To me it sounded like a fantasy, this bustling town of opportunities with new faces and limitless options for me. Countless nights I laid in bed and dreamt of running away to start a new life in Glasgow.

As my eighteenth year came, my father started to pressure me. I think he knew that my heart was elsewhere, and he was desperately trying to extinguish the fire he saw inside of me….

PART ONE:
GLASGOW

I

March 1802

"You will grow to love this life, my son." My father had subjected me to this lecture so many times over the years that I could say it along with him in my head. I sat quietly as to not bring on his wrath. "When I was young, I too wanted for more. I dreamt of kingdoms and wealth, wished for a war to fight in - so I may be a brave protector." He ensured I was looking for the next part, the one he wanted me to hear the most. "That is the fancies of children, lad. I grew up. When not much older than you are now, I married and became a father. Becoming a man means laying those fantasies down and doing what is right for this village and your family."

I waited patiently for the end of the words so I may be free to find something more interesting to do.

"Now," he boasted. "A warm fire, food in my belly and my wife at my side is all I need. I have pride in my land and what I have to show for my hard work and steadfastness."

This was the last line of the speech and my cue to do what I must to earn my leave from the home. "Yes, father. I know you are right," I lied.

"You must start to think of a woman to call wife," he continued; this part was new. "Is there any in the village that you fancy? There are many fine, strong lassies to choose from. I will need to start talking with a father of a daughter soon to secure your marriage."

A rare loss for words overcame me. My father had not been so blunt before, only hinted at the desire for me to marry soon. Time had emboldened him to push harder.

"I have not thought of it." I had an idea to get out of this and be free to do what I had planned with this day. "Perhaps, I should go into the square and start to look?"

He seemed pleased. "That is a fine idea."

I ran for the door before he could draw me back into any more of his ramblings about pride and the pleasures of a farmer's life. I was determined to not settle for such mediocrity and certainly would choose no girls from this village for wife. It is not that they were ugly, many of the daughters were fair of face. But they were all simple and raised like my mother - to be no more than wives and mothers.

Running for the loch, I hoped Collin remained. A glance skyward to the sun revealed that I was later than we had planned. Thankfully, the sight of him throwing rocks into the water assured me he had waited. He turned when he heard my approach.

"Late as always, Rhys." He slapped my back as I reached him, pausing to catch my breath before speaking.

"My father," I explained. "Now he is telling me to find a wife. He wants me to choose a girl from the village so he may ask her father and start plans. He'll see me wedded sooner than later."

Collin laughed. "And who would you pick?"

I reacted with disgust. "Ach. None," I exclaimed. "I have better conversation with the sheep."

We both fell into laughter at the thought of taking one of the local girls into our beds. We knew well what a man and woman did in their room. Admittedly, the thought of doing that with one of the females I saw at church each week filled me with curiosity and excitement, but I was not willing to go through a wedding to have the wedding night.

"Come," Collin said. "Let's get to the alehouse. I heard a stranger is there. Perhaps we can hear some stories."

Following the path made from the many feet that had traveled from the loch to the center of the square, we chattered about what must lie outside our little town. The smell of the livestock let us know we were back. When I was young and adored my father's stories, he had told me how this place had started with one small home and had grown into what it was now. The sounds of people moving about their daily lives hit our ears as faces we knew passed in front and away from us. Everyone was known to me. I'd been around them since the day I left my mother's breast. Some had moved in over the years, built homes, but none had left. To my knowledge, the only way someone had left this village was to ascend to Heaven.

For the thousandth time, I promised myself I would be the first to leave this life behind for something grander.

"Where are you two going?" the little voice came from behind us and was well known.

"Ugh," Collin groaned as we both turned to face his little sister. "Dierdre, go away."

She took a defiant step towards us. "I won't," she stated with a confidence beyond her years. Her ebony hair was a tangled mess, as it usually was. The dirt across her face made her sapphire eyes almost sparkle in contrast and the anger was clear in their gaze. "You will let me join or I will tell ma."

"Tell her," Collin said, crossing his arms. "And I will tell her you've been climbing trees again."

She was shocked. "How do ya know?"

This time I crossed my arms. I had known this child since Collin and I first became friends and she was a babe in her mother's arms.

"Because you are covered in dirt, girl. You better wash yourself before you are seen and get a switch to your backside."

"Why can't I come with you?" she whined.

Diedre had been following us around since she could toddle. She'd been like a shadow, lurking behind us at every turn. More times than I could count, we'd run off, leaving her crying with her hands outstretched for us. But the last thing we wanted was some little girl slowing us down or telling her ma what we did.

"Because, we're men," her brother asserted. "It isn't proper for you to be around us so much. Go find the other lasses to be with. Leave us be."

It was her turn to laugh. "You aren't men," she spat. "Not until you have wives and houses. And, no lass would marry you, not even a blind one."

I think she believed that would hurt us. When it didn't work, she accepted defeat. Grunting, she turned and ran.

Collin shook his head. "Something's wrong with that girl. She is like a wild beast, not a female. I think she'd be happier in the pen with the animals than in a pretty dress."

I watched the little thing run and knew she was likely headed to the water to wash the incriminating dirt off her before she was spotted. The mothers reveled in telling one another that their child was "less than perfect." A 14-year-old girl climbing trees and playing with animals would be a scandal. "I pray for the poor bastard that must marry her."

Collin laughed. "Could you imagine? My father will have to give away all his sheep to get someone to take her hand."

Minutes later, we were in what served as the village's tavern. A crowd had already formed around the new man in the village. He was not much older than myself, perhaps 20. His face was gaunt, letting everyone know he was not getting enough to feast on at regular intervals. The plate in front of him was heaping. I was certain none would ask for payment in return. It was the way of our locals – do for others and God Almighty would bless you.

"It grows so fast," he was saying through mouthfuls. "English and Scots live next to each other without quarrel. Tobacco and sugar are plentiful. New factories are built in only a matter of months, then making cotton fabrics to send to all the lands, even the New World."

Stories of America were my favorite. A land across the ocean built up by those who wanted freedom. They had fought like us to be an independent land, to not need England for help. It was strong and run by its own laws. I dreamed of seeing it someday.

We were enthralled by this man, listening to him until his plate was empty and the sky was growing dark.

Collin pulled on my sleeve. "We better get home or we will both be going to bed with no food. I don't know about you Rhys, but I need to eat."

I didn't want to leave but I knew my friend was right. Walking home, we talked again of our plans to run away. We would pack only what we needed and walk until we reached the city. There we would wash the sheep stench off ourselves, find jobs, make lots of money and start the lives we were meant to have. We'd be free from our parents and never be forced to do anything again.

When I entered my home, dinner was being placed on the table. My stomach clenched with hunger when the aroma hit my nose. "Welcome home," my mother chirped. "Sit down and I will bring you a plate."

My father swallowed the mouthful. "Did you find one that you like, lad?"

I had completely forgotten that I was supposed to be on a wife-finding mission. I had not prepared a lie. My mother sat supper in front of me and I filled my mouth with food to buy some time. My father didn't continue to eat; he stared at me with hope in his eyes.

"I did look, Father," I answered. "I dinna find one that I would take as a wife. Perhaps tomorrow." His gaze faltered and he took a breath. I knew a long-winded speech was coming.

My mother interjected. "Archie," she chided. "He's just a boy. You cannot expect him to find the love of his life on the first day of looking.

He has time to find the right one." She kissed the top of his head. "Not everyone can get as lucky as you did."

He tried to look stern, but my mother had a way of softening him. "You over-mother him, Elinor. He must be ready to take on his duty as a man, husband and father. The Selkirk name is with him. This land is to be his."

She kissed the top of my head and went to stoke the fire. "Oh Archie, he will but let him do it in his time. Let him find the right lass and start his life his way."

I loved my mother. She knew that I did not take well to being pushed, that if given my own space I find things on my own. But she did not know what was truly in my heart. She still believed I would find a nice village girl and live near them in my grandfather's house. She dreamed of holding her grandchild someday. I knew it would break her heart when I left but that sorrow was not enough to throw me off course.

Since I had my mother's support, I felt brave enough to say more. "Many of the other families do not ask their sons to marry until twenty-five, Father."

"They are not my sons, you are." He wiped at his mouth.

We finished that dinner with the agreement that I had until my twentieth birthday to choose a bride. If not, my parents would choose for me.

So, the date of my departure was set. I didn't know it that night, but a series of events had been set into motion that would determine my fate.

2

March 1804

"We will need to set the packs in a place that we can reach in the dark, a place that no one else would find it," Collin whispered.

"Aye," I agreed, looking around to ensure no one was close enough to hear. The space behind the church was the safest for making such plans. Villagers only came back there when they were going to visit the grave of a loved one. Most did that after a church gathering. On this day, the church sat quiet so it was unlikely someone would choose now to pay their respects.

"Your grandfather's house sits empty, waiting for you to move in with a wife," he acknowledged. "It would be fitting to hide the things we take into our freedom in the place you are meant to settle down."

I nodded. "It would and no one goes in there. So, we pack tonight and take it there. Then tomorrow night," I smiled. "We run."

He also smiled, slapping my back and nodding. "We're doing it, Rhys. We are going to the city."

"We are," I exclaimed proudly. Walking to the corner of the church, I looked into the town I hated. "I'll put this place at my back."

Watching the same people move about the same square, doing the same things they did each day made me shake my head. I felt pity for these people – stuck to live an unimportant life. I was about to say it to Collin when I saw the head of black hair headed our way and dropped down to a squat. "Your sister is coming," I hissed.

"Did she see you?" he asked.

"I canna be sure," I answered. "Let us move out in case she did."

We stood, making our way around the church and out of our hiding place. We were almost into the crowd when she found us. "Hello, Rhys," she beamed.

"Hello, Deirdre. What are you doing this day?" I didn't know if she'd spied where we had been but acting like we had nothing to hide seemed the best approach.

"Looking for you," she answered. "May we talk?" I noticed her hair was brushed and had never seen it so clean or kempt. I do not think I'd known before then that it had soft curls. Until this day it usually was wild and I'd seen it with leaves scattered through it more than once. To the contrary, at that moment it shined in the sunlight. The dress she wore matched her eyes.

I looked to Collin, questioningly. He shrugged his shoulders to indicate he had no idea what she was up to.

"Say what you need and then Collin and I must continue. We have important tasks to complete," I put my hands on my hips to punctuate how serious I was.

She looked to Collin. "Without him please."

Now Collin really looked confused. "I will find you later," he said. "Stay in sight of people," he cautioned. "That last thing you need is talk." Then he left me to a very awkward situation.

Diedre dropped her head and walked to the right of the square. She sat on the wall around the well we all fetched our water from. Her intense stare at her lap and silence meant I was going to need to move this conversation along, so I sat next to her.

It was then that I saw her trembling and was filled with dread. "Deidre," I spoke. "Did something happen? Has someone hurt you? Tell me." I was surprised by the protective need that suddenly overwhelmed me. It was one thing for her brother and I to make her cry but if anyone had touched her in anything but love, I would kill them.

She looked up and fixed her gaze on mine. "No," she reassured me. "I am not hurt but nervous."

I relaxed. "Thanks to God," I sighed. "I thought someone had-" I shook my head to clear away the thought. "Do not mind it. What is it then? Why are you nervous?"

She squared her shoulders. "Just listen and when I am done, give a simple answer. I canna take more than that."

"Aye," I answered, then remained quiet as instructed.

"I know you are to choose a wife in three days. That if you have not, one will be chosen for you." She laid her hands on mine. "Choose me, Rhys. I would be a good wife to you, give you children. My ma will teach me to cook."

Shock had taken away my ability to speak or move. Replaying what she had said in my head, I was certain I had not misheard it. Her eyes pleaded with me. I opened my mouth and let the words tumble out without thinking. "You're only 16, Deidre."

"Other girls have married at this age." She scooted towards me. "And if you choose now, it will take some time to arrange it all. My da and yours will talk. My ma will teach me all I need to know. I will be 17 when it is time and that is a good age to become your wife. You will grow to love me as I already love you."

I pulled my hands away and stood, looking down at the wide eyes. She was the sister of my best friend, a little girl that had followed me around and annoyed me. Despite the dress and brushed locks, she was just a girl to me.

"I canna," I said. "Diedre, I do not feel for you that way." Pain washed over those lovely blue eyes, but I could not stop. I had dreams that did not include her. "I am sorry. You will find a man who deserves you, cares for you." She was silent as I spoke. Only her tears rolling down her face let me know just how bad I'd hurt her. I had to finish this. "But that man is not me."

Then I turned and did not look back. I just left her alone, weeping enough tears to fill the well she sat in front of.

On the next moon, we continued that cowardly behavior, sneaking away in the night. In our foolish youth, we believed we were leaving behind a place that was not good enough for us. We believed we were finding the exceptional life that we deserved.

It would be too late once I realized what we had really done that night when we stole food from our home and disappeared down a path that we believed was our right.

3

June 1807

The travel to Glasgow had been much harder than our naïve minds had anticipated. We had run out of food in two days and water was not always easy to find. As the days progressed, we became weaker and needed to stop to rest more often. We had to take turns sleeping through the night as we heard wolves often and knew that we were no match for a pack.

A week into it, we were seen by a man with a horse and cart. He took pity on us, gave us apples and a ride the rest of the way. I still believe that we would have not made it another day if that man had not found us.

As we approached Glasgow, we believed we were reaching utopia, that this city would open its arms to us and offer us riches beyond imagination.

Instead, for the first two months we lived on the streets with the other fools who had wondered into the city with no money, food, or plans. There was no need for sheep farmers in the city and we had no skills to offer. We snuck around at night looking for trash in the hopes of food scraps to fill our bellies. We slept in alleys and watched the disgust on people's faces as they looked down at us. We even discussed returning home with our heads hung low to beg forgiveness from our families.

On the third month, I was awakened by a man's foot in my back, jostling me. "Boy," he barked. "Boy, wake up."

Confused and groggy from malnourishment, I looked up at the man and waited for my eyes to focus. Jamming my elbow into Collin woke him up so we could both jump up to face whatever was happening. "Are we not allowed to sleep here?" I asked the stranger. "We can go somewhere else."

The man was shorter than I by several inches but broad and very well dressed. A sharp nose was made more prominent by his small, brown eyes. Streaks of grey mixed in with the dull blonde of his hair and pieces of it had fallen from the low ponytail. I guessed him to be in his 40s. He cocked his head to the side. "How old are you boys?" He was English, the first Englishmen I had ever spoken to. When they arrived in our village my father has always told me to stay away, for fear I would somehow offend them.

"Twenty," Collin answered without hesitation.

"You are thin," he poked a cane in my direction. "But you both look strong."

I was not sure where this was headed but I did know that fighting was not the best option if you wanted to stay out of jail. This man looked wealthy so I was certain that whatever occurred, Collin and I would take the blame. "We were raised on farms," I offered. "Worked the land."

He nodded approvingly, looking up and down each of us. "Would you like work now?" he asked.

"Yes," we said in tandem. I knew that appearing desperate made us vulnerable. However, it was futile to tell someone who found you sleeping in alley that you did not need money.

He waved his hand in a beckoning motion, turned, and walked towards the street. We followed, looking to each other for assurance that this was not a horrible idea. My mind was telling me that if we were together, we would be safe. When the man reached the entrance to the alley, he turned right and picked up his pace. Lacking of food had made us slower than we used to be but we managed to keep up as the man began to speak.

"The wages are low but I give you a room to sleep in and two meals a day. If you work hard and are promoted, in time, you will get a nicer room and three meals a day plus one day off. This is what you should work towards."

I could not believe our luck. While I knew nothing what the job entailed, I did not care. Short of butchering children, there was not much I would've said no to. A small piece of my pride had left me each time I had to eat garbage.

I focused on what the man was saying as we walked. "You will work seven days a week at first. From seven in the morning until ten at night. You will break only to eat dinner and only for fifteen minutes. This is also the time you will relieve yourself, so I recommend you limit your water during working hours. You may drink as much as you want when you are off. Do you understand? I do not repeat myself."

"Yes, sir." I answered.

"What will we be doing?" Collin asked.

As if timed, the man turned down a small street and pointed to a large brick building. "This is my business – fabrics mostly," he announced and made his way to a side door. "You will work in the basement. It is hot and hard labor, but I trust you boys are able to handle it." He turned to us. "If not, say it now and you may return to your alley to sleep."

"We can handle it," I eagerly told the man.

"Wonderful," he opened the door we had approached to reveal stairs leading down and the sound of machines. "I am James. And, you are?"

"Rhys Selkirk."

"Collin Argyll."

He arched an eyebrow. "You only need to go by first names now. Let go of whatever it is you left behind." Abruptly, he headed down the stairs and we followed.

Reaching the bottom revealed a massive room with machines as large as houses. Half a dozen men worked, each one manning a machine. None of them looked up at us. The sound was deafening so we didn't try to speak. James motioned to an open door on the right and we continued to follow him through it. Shutting the door behind us did not do much for the noise, only showed us a long, poorly lit hallway. Keeping up with James was getting harder as we were now exhausted on top of hungry. We'd been woken from much needed rest and it was weighing on me.

Thankfully, after a few turns and a few more hallways, we reached another door and it was quiet enough to speak.

"This is the workers' quarters. I will show you your room. We lost two men off our morning shift so you will replace them and take their room." He pulled open the door to reveal a hallway of even more doors. Only one was open. This is the one he stopped at and the room he disappeared into.

A twin bed sat against the wall to either side of the small, windowless room and was topped with a blanket each. One dresser sat between the beds with two drawers, one for each of us. Above that, a small mirror was the only thing on the wall. James turned to face us with delight across his face. It was brief and the first time we saw real emotion from him. "Enjoy your sleep. Tomorrow at 6:30, breakfast will be ready. It is up the stairs, in the kitchen. Follow the smell of food. At 7 sharp, I expect you in the machine room to start your training." Just as suddenly as he'd arrived, he was gone from the room, leaving us to sleep on a bed for the first time since we left home.

That small, hot breakfast the next morning was the best thing I'd eaten in my entire life.

Our training was quick and we caught on fast. The men did not speak much and we did not care. We spoke to each other on break, spoke at night by candle light in our room, and worked hard. We rarely saw James. The men said that was good as you only saw James when you were being let go. One man cryptically explained that the two men we replaced had gotten on James' bad side and gone missing. When we asked for more detail, he just walked away. But it was enough to tell us to do what we we're told and stay out of our employer's way.

A year later, we would be rewarded with promotions, an extra meal and break, and every Sunday off.

We used our day off to explore the city. With the little money we had made in the first year, we found drink and women.

Bear in mind, it was not the end of our journey; we still spoke of riches. We dreamed of going to the newly independent America and starting our own business, then hiring unfortunate souls off the street and making them do all the hard work. But for that time, we had beds and food and coins in our pockets, so we were happy.

We continued this habit for two more years. While we did not grow a fortune, we held onto our hopes. The money we didn't use on female comfort or liquor was saved for our future. The women of the night loved us as we were young, virile, and well-muscled from work. We were a respite from the overweight, old men that they often had to pleasure. Because of this, we felt like kings when we entered their establishment. We smiled as we watched them fight for the chance to be chosen by us.

It had made us full of unearned bravado and gave us a sense that we were somehow special.

On a Sunday afternoon, two months after my 23rd birthday, it would all change. As we chattered about the women we would choose that evening, we heard a knock on our bedroom door. Opening it revealed a woman. I knew she worked in James' fabric shop upstairs, but her name had escaped me. We never went up there as James was clear that he did not want customers to see us. He asserted that his clients were sophisticated and would not want to be around unmannered brutes like us.

"There is someone in the shop for you. I told them to wait outside and you would come around to meet them," she said dryly and shuffled away before we could ask for more.

Moments later, we turned the corner of the building to glance a seemingly young woman with her back to us, just outside the shop's front entrance. The air left my lungs when she turned and I saw those sapphire eyes.

"Dierdre," Collin cried out and ran to embrace his sister. He was pulling back to take in the sight of her when the shock wore off and I shuffled forward to stand at Collin's side.

"Hello, boys," she said. The smile on her face was blindingly bright. Her dark hair was piled on top of her head in a mass of curls and pins. She looked back and forth between the two of us. "No greeting from you, Rhys? Has the city taken your tongue?"

I was not certain how to act, so I leaned in and placed a light kiss on her cheek, taking in the smell of her. When I pulled back, I found my voice. "What are you doing here? How did you know where to find us?"

She laughed and it made my heart swell. "Please," she playfully slapped Collin's arm. "I have been chasing you two since I first walked. Finding you has always been my greatest power." She paused to turn those blue eyes on me. "I knew when you ran away where you were headed. I had overheard you two whispering your plans so many times I could have repeated it in my sleep." She held up a hand to stop me from interrupting. "I kept your secret by the way." She turned to Collin and I felt a loss when those eyes weren't on mine. "Everyone knew when you disappeared where you'd gone. Everyone knew it was only a matter of time before someone left that village. I always knew you'd be the first."

I wanted to ask about my parents but was too cowardly to hear what I had done to them, so I kept silent and listened.

"The village continued on. People still talk about you two sometimes. They wonder what happened to you and if you have become rich or turned into highway robbers."

"So, why do you come now?" Collin asked. "After all this time?"

Her eyes moved back to me and she grew serious. "I am to be married." For the second time in minutes, I felt as if I could not breathe. I could not understand why I would react this way. Of course, she would be promised to someone. She was the right age and had become very beautiful.

"To who?" I asked before I could stop myself.

"Angus," her response held no emotion.

"MacPherson?" Collin laughed. "The boy who used to cry when his ma left his side?"

She smiled and it filled me with warmth. Her eyes stayed on mine. "He has turned into a fine young man. He is good to his parents and works hard. He has already begun building us a house. He insists I am too good to live in an old home but should have a new one."

"Do you love him?" I asked.

Silence hung in the air. "I could," she answered.

So much was unspoken between us. I wanted to tell her not to marry Angus. But why? I did not want to marry her. She had given me the choice and I had told her no. I wanted to live a free life in America.... did I not?

Or, had something changed? Was it still what I wanted?

My thoughts were halted when Collin whooped beside me. "Well then sister, congratulations. This is cause for celebration. Let us take you to eat. Wait," he exclaimed. "How did you get here? Where are you staying? Do you have no chaperone?"

"An old man stopped in our village on his way here. I asked him to take me so I may invite you to the wedding. He agreed and is taking me home in two days' time when he starts his next delivery. It has taken me a day to find you so," she looked down. "I am afraid I must leave tomorrow."

"Did you come alone?" I asked, filled with a mixture of frustration and fear. "That was dangerous, Diedre."

"I did not," she answered, still looking down. "Your ma came with me, Rhys."

I took a few steps backwards to steady myself. "Where is she?"

"We are staying at a woman's boarding house. She waits for me to return," she finally looked up to see how I was responding to the news. "She will not see you, Rhys. I am sorry. Your father has forbidden it."

I nodded. "Of course," I conceited. "Will you tell her I'm well? And, that I'm sorry."

"Of course," she answered, stepping into me and laying her hand on mine.

"Enough of this sadness," Collin shouted, pulling his sister from me and wrapping his arm around her shoulder. "Let us take you for whatever feast you want."

She laughed and leaned her head into his. "Yes," she said. "I could eat a horse."

"Well," he pretended to think. "I do not think they serve horse here, but I can fill you to bursting. However," he arched an eyebrow. "I suggest you do not get fat until after the poor boy has taken you as wife."

"Very solid advice," she squealed and they headed down the street together towards the center of the city. I followed behind, trying to sift through all of the thoughts in my head.

Was I sad that my mother would not defy my father to see me? I did not think so as I understood her obedience to him. Yet, I knew he would not truly know if she did see me. I also knew that my mother was an honest woman, a quality I admired in her.

Was I sad that Diedre was marrying? That did not make sense to me as I did not harbor those feelings towards her. She was merely a girl from the village, the little sister of my friend, a pest that we had spent our lives trying to rid ourselves of. But, listening to her tell Collin all of the events that had occurred in our village since we left, I knew those feelings were changed. I knew that she was no longer a little girl scrambling up trees to throw rocks at the boys who picked on her, but a beautiful woman with eyes deeper than the loch.

She was betrothed, I reminded myself. She was promised to another.

I imagined her in a wedding gown, promising to Angus that she will be his for life, to share his home and his bed. She would bring him children and did not every woman deserve to hold a wee one in their arms?

And, had I not told her I wouldn't give that to her, broken her heart for the sake of my dreams? I'd fled in the night to give myself what I always wanted – a life without any woman or child holding me back.

But, Diedre….

"The day has gotten away from me," Diedre said, breaking through my contemplation. "It is dinner time?"

"Yes," Collin said. "Which is why I am taking you to dinner."

"I cannot," she cried out in frustration. "I'm to be back to the boarding house by supper. I cannot be out any later." She threw her arms around her brother. "But I have just found you."

The thought of her being gone from my life again was unbearable. I knew she must return but I was not ready yet to say farewell for good.

An idea came to me. "Are there any men in the boarding house?"

"No," she answered. "The woman who runs it is a widow."

"Have you seen any of her husband's clothes about?" I was relieved that she did not ask questions, just answered.

"Aye," she said. "She has all his clothes in a hall closet. Says she cannot part from them. Do you need clothes?"

I thanked God for our luck. "When they are asleep, take trousers, a coat and a hat. Hide your hair inside it. Then, come here. We'll wait for you. Be sure to walk with your head down and try to walk like a man. If they do not believe you to be one, this will not work. Can you do that?"

Her smile was mischievous. "Aye," she asserted. "I played with the boys until my chest grew round and I was no longer able. I know how you walk."

Collin was onto my scheme. "As a man, you'll be able to stay out with us all night and no one will bat an eye. You can return before they awake. It will be one last night of fun before you become a wife and mother."

She was bouncing with excitement. "Aye. I'll see you here after sundown. It may take some time but wait for me."

"We will," I assured her. We each got a kiss on our cheeks and as she walked away, I felt that kiss like an electric wire against my skin. I knew I would wait for days to see her again.

4

We had returned to our room to grab more of the money we had saved. It was for our trip to the New World but this night was important and we wanted to celebrate Diedre.

We waited outside the tavern as promised. For hours we watched people approach with anticipation only to realize it was not her. Full dark had set in and the sounds of drinking were erupting from inside.

"Perhaps we should not take her in there," I said to Collin.

"Rhys," he patted my back. "She'll be safe. We'll not let her out of our sights and sit on each side of her." He was making me feel better about this plan. "I know my sister - the little spy. She'll love to see what us men do on our nights off. She'll have a few drinks and hear the boys when they do not know she is there. This is the best wedding gift we could give her."

"You are right," I relented. "We will be with her."

A man turned the corner and approached us without haste. The coat was dark and long, meeting pants that matched. But it was the hat that gave it away if you were looking closely. It was a little too high. I knew it was because a mass of raven hair was stuffed underneath it. Other than that one detail, Deirdre was true to her word. She had taken on the believable gait of a man, chosen clothes big enough to hide her curves but not so large that they looked ridiculous. Her head was down and several lads passed her without looking twice.

When she reached us, she looked up and those sapphire eyes were alight with glee. "Hello boys," she said, purposefully making her voice deeper.

"This is going to be fun," Collin said and opened the tavern door to let the roar of Sunday night drinkers out onto the street. Once inside, we found a table far off in the corner. Dierdre walked between the two of us to improve her chances of not being noticed.

Once sat, Collin offered to buy drinks and made his way to the bar, leaving us sat next to each other.

"So," I started and cleared my throat. "You will be Diedre MacPherson? When is the big day?"

She also cleared her throat, answering in the deep grave that she felt made her sound manly. "In one month."

Ice filled my veins and I was sure my heart stopped for a moment. "That soon?"

"Aye," she answered, whispering as to not be overheard. "Many of the girls my age are already having their first or second child. I could not wait any longer."

I turned to her. "Is that what you want?"

She faced me. "I do not have a choice. I must marry. You know this. It is the way."

"But-"

"Drinks," Collin exclaimed when he returned with three glasses of pale brown liquid and placed them triumphantly on the table. He sat across from us and leaned in. "Have you ever had whiskey, Diedre?"

She shook her head, having already adjusted to the new topic of conversation and dropping the one we had just started. "I've not."

"Then," he winked. "Start slow."

She did not start slow, of course. She drank deep and wiped at her mouth with the back of her hand. "That is quite good," she said.

For hours, we laughed and drank. We told stories from our childhood. She told us about the village: those who had died, those who had married, the new babes and a fire in a barn.

As she spoke, I could smell the village and hear the sounds of the people I had known for so long, then just forgotten.

I did not want the night to end but knew that we must say goodbye at some point. I didn't want her to be caught sneaking into the boarding house. If Diedre was found to be drunk and sneaking in, my mother would know I had something to do with it. I'd already broken my mother's heart enough for one lifetime. And, I didn't want Diedre to be accused of not being pure for her husband.

I stood. "I think we should be getting you back."

Diedre pouted. "No. I am not ready."

"Well, sister," Collin stood. "This is my last act as older brother before your husband has dominion over you – you are going back to the boarding house to sleep. That is an order."

"Fine," she relented.

We stood, each one of us on each side of her, and walked out of the tavern. The night air was crisp and fresh. I took in a deep breath and let it out. I loved nights like this. I looked over to Dierdre and she was doing the same – lids down, breathing deep and feeling the air on her skin.

She opened her eyes when Collin pulled her into a hug. "Sister. I must go attend to someone," he peeked over the girl's shoulder and winked at me. I knew exactly where he was headed. He met her eyes again. "Rhys will walk you home."

"You would leave me?" she asked.

He smiled. "I will find a way to be at your wedding."

"You will?" she squealed.

"I will. Facing Ma and Pa is worth being there to see you on that day."

With one last hug, Collin turned and disappeared down the street to find the brothel. Diedre faced me. "It's just you and me, Rhys. Shall we?" She held out her arm and offered my elbow.

The street was quiet. I so rarely enjoyed the stillness of the night. On Sundays, Collin and I were so focused on drink and women that we did not take time to appreciate the blessed moments we were given. I thought of the many times we could have faced death because of our choices but somehow it all ended in our favor. And still, we never took the time to just appreciate being alive.

"What are you pondering?" Deidre asked.

I patted her hand. "Life. How lucky we are to have it."

She stopped and faced me. "You have changed greatly," she said. "You are so different from the boy I knew."

"Is that bad?" I worried.

"No," she answered. "Just different. You feel so much older than your years to me."

I thought about that. "Well, we lived a hard life when we first arrived. Slept on the streets, ate from the garbage."

"You did?" She gasped.

"We did," I smiled. "But a man found us and gave us a way to earn money, a place to sleep and food."

She started to walk again and I continued at her side. "Things always did work out for you two. It is like an angel is looking over you. You were never caught despite always doing things you should not. You made it out of the village, just like you said you would. People spoke of you. They thought there was no way you two would safely make it here, but I knew you would. You do anything you set your mind to. You're so smart."

I stopped. "Not smart enough to have taken your offer."

She froze and turned. "What do you mean?"

"I should have said yes." It was out before I knew I was even thinking it. "Should have married you. I never should have left you by that well, crying and alone. I'm a fool and a horrible man."

She didn't move and I was afraid to break the silence so I waited for minutes, letting her make the next move. When she did, it was to step into me. The slap across my face stung but didn't hurt as bad as the tears streaking down her face. "You are a fool, Rhys Selkirk. You broke my heart and then left me alone in that town. I had to listen to the villagers whisper about you and Collin. I had to bear the wails of my parents and your parents, had to comfort them while inside I was broken and dead. I had no one to talk to about my sorrow, no one to help me put those pieces back together. Slowly, I found the strength to move on, to forget you, to tell myself you were happier. I believed that you had found your dreams and I was in awe of your determination. I told myself that you had to sacrifice me to have your wishes come true and that gave me comfort." She didn't wipe at her tears but let them flow. "I found a man who I do not love but will be good for me. He will never hurt me the way you did, would never choose himself over me."

She laid her hand on the cheek she had struck. "And now you tell me that you wished you'd said yes, that it was all for nothing, that my heartache was for nothing?" She turned her back to me. "What am I to say to that? What is it you want? For me to come here and live in poverty? To break my parents' hearts? To shame Angus by breaking a promise?"

I had not thought this through. She was right. What did I offer? Would I go back with her? Ask her to come here? But for what? A small room that she would share with her brother? A job in the shop?

She whirled around and faced me. There was no time to react when she closed the distance between us and looked up at me. "Because I will, Rhys. I will come here to be with you. Because God help me, I still love you, have always loved you. Even as I plan to marry Angus, I dream it is you that will take me to bed on our wedding night."

I didn't know what to say, only what I wanted. I pulled the hat off her head and let the black curls fall down and around her. Then, I lowered my head and laid a kiss on the lips of the little girl who used to follow me around.

Her arm wrapped around the back of my neck to pull me closer to her and hasten the kiss. My tongue urged her lips to open and they did, allowing me to deepen the embrace. Our pace turned frantic and my head was screaming for me to stop but I didn't think I could.

Then her lips and arms were gone.

I felt a strong grip on each of my forearms and heard her cry out.

To my horror I looked up to see a man behind Diedre, his arms wrapped tightly around her waist. His smile showed rotting teeth and his eyes held evil intentions. I struggled against the grips of the men holding me, one on each side. A fourth man came from my right slamming his fist into my stomach. The pain folded me in half while I was dragged down into an alley. Deidre's grunts and cries told me she was fighting.

"Why would a beauty like you dress as a man?" The voice held a gravel quality and is one I can hear in my mind to this day. Fighting through the pain in my gut, I stood up straight to a sight that would be forever branded into my brain. The man pressed himself against Diedre, her back against a brick wall.

"Get off of her," I bellowed and was rewarded with a fist against my jaw. I tried to yell through the blood filling my mouth but was treated to another blow to the face. I fought to lunge forward, to save Diedre but the men pulled me back over and over. Another fist to the stomach brought me to my knees.

The man on my left arm bent to speak into my ringing ear. "We'll each have a go," he rasped. "If you stop fighting, we'll leave some for you. She will be nice and warmed up for ya."

"No," I raged, fighting to my feet.

The one holding Diedre had stripped off her coat and was working at her pants while she fought against him. She slammed her knee into the man's crotch, but he was only stopped for a moment and maintained his grip on her. He grabbed her hair with one filthy hand and used the other to drive his fist into her mouth. The wall behind her meant there was nowhere for her head to go so her delicate face took the full force of his hit. Her eyes closed and she went slack. I prayed that she would remain unconscious.

My injuries were too great. I saw the blackness starting to slide in from all sides. Fighting to remain awake, I screamed into the night, raging against these men and their brutality. I cried out to God to save us. This brought on the laughter of the men and another blow to my jaw. "There is no God," the graveled voice proclaimed into the air.

Again, I fell to my knees. This time, the men came down to the ground with me. One grabbed the back of my head and slammed it down to the stones underneath me.

The blackness overcame me as I heard Diedre cry out my name.

She was awake.

The rain on my face woke me. There was no need for my brain to try and recall what had happened. As soon as I was aware, I knew exactly what I needed to do. I looked up and ahead of me, pushing up to all fours and scrambling to the heap. My head screamed with pain but was no match for my racing heart.

She lay motionless, naked as the day she was born.

Cradling her head in my lap, I lightly slapped her cheek. "Diedre, please. Wake up. Diedre, wake up. Wake up." But the blood seeping from the back of her head was pouring to the ground, mixing in the rainfall. There was too much and I knew in my soul that she was gone.

That is how the police found us - drenched, beaten and broken. One of us alive. The other dead.

Collin arrived not long after, dropping down to his knees next to us. He pulled his sister against him and rocked. The wails that came forth from him echoed into the sky. For minutes he begged her to wake and told her he loved her. "You must go be married," he wailed. "You're to be married. You must wake. You canna leave me; I just got you back"

The police finally pulled us from her and told us we must go answer questions. Everything I did was like I was outside of myself, watching me talk to an officer, watching me be told to go take care of myself but not leave the city.

I watched wordlessly as Collin was questioned. As he was not there, he only spoke of what led up to the attack. Then, he gave answer to where the body was to be sent.

This is when I heard the voice of my mother, asking where we were. This brought on a small clarity and a relief to the fog I had been walking through. I shot to my feet and ran to the front, following the sound of my mother's voice.

I expected her to run into my arms for comfort, to tell me she thanked God that I survived. She came to me slowly, with empty eyes and struck me across the face, the same place Diedre had slapped only hours before. Shock held me on place.

A single tear rolled down her face. "You asked that girl to meet you when you knew it was wrong. Women are to be home at night for a reason Rhys, because this world is not safe for us." Hatred filled the void that had been an empty gaze only seconds before. "But you wouldn't know or care because you are a man. You can do as you please and you did, didn't you? You wanted a night of fun and cared not what would happen to that girl." She shook her head. I had never seen disappointment in my mother's eyes but that is what I faced now. "You should have protected her." Her tears flowed more freely but her voice did not waiver. "I knew you were a free spirit, son. But I never thought you to not be a good man."

As I watched her leave the building, I fought to stand still and not run after her. She had spoken truth. I had not protected Dierdre and was not worthy of love or forgiveness. My mother had every right to hate me, considering what I had put her through. Deep down, I believed I was being punished by God himself.

And, that would be the last time I saw my mother.

Collin and I walked back to the factory with no words between us. The rain continued to fall but I did not notice. I was moving but had no control over my body. Some other force seemed to walk me to our little room. I wanted to ask my friend what would be next, wanted to beg him to forgive me for not saving his sister. But I could not speak.

When we returned, a woman sat on my bed. It was the same woman who had told us that someone waited for us outside. Could it truly have been less than a day since we saw sweet Dierdre on the street above?

She stood, her eyes wide when she saw my face before she looked down. "James has heard of the attack and your loss. He's told me you have as many days as you need with pay. He is away on business but will see you this night." She shuffled from the room, her gaze focused on the ground.

Collin sat on his bed, staring at the floor between his feet. I approached the mirror above the dresser to face what had terrified the woman. I looked as if I'd walked out of a river, fully clothed. My right eye was swollen shut, dried blood covered my forehead and cheeks. The jaw was as swollen as my eye but this was also decorated with a bruise that colored the bottom half of my face. I knew I should find water to wash the blood from myself but only had enough energy left to sit on my bed, opposite my oldest friend.

How long we sat like that, in silence, I do not know. Collin's far away voice was the one to break it. "I am to go with her to the village. I will have to tell my parents, tell Angus and stand by them as I see her laid to rest."

"I'll come with you," I said reflexively.

"You canna," he answered in that same monotone voice. "Your ma says you will not be welcome in the village."

Words of argument dried up in my mouth as I truly understood all the consequences of my selfish choices.

He continued. "I will come back after she is covered in dirt and I'm able to find transport." He finally faced me. "Will you tell James? We're to leave soon."

"Will they not need her to find the men who attacked us? Use her for clues?" I was shocked that it was happening so fast.

"I was told they will not likely find the men, that these attacks on women are too plentiful." A tear sprang from his left eye and made a trail down his cheek. "They will not waste their time on a poor village girl, Rhys. She is just another dead lass to them."

I stood, pacing the room. "No," I growled. "They must."

"They won't," he roared and I sat, afraid to bring on more of the wrath I heard in his words. He calmed. "I will go today. The women will clean her and make her ready. She'll find peace in the cemetery of our home."

Nodding quietly, I thought carefully of what to say next. "I am sorry, Collin. Sorry I could not protect her."

Silence hung in the air and my words appeared lost in his sorrow. Not addressing my apology, he stood, looking back at the floor. "I must go. I will help your ma and carry Diedre to the cart, then leave with them. I will return."

Before I could say anything else, he was through the door and I truly did not know if I would ever see him again.

Lying onto my side, I faced the wall and pulled my knees to my chest. My stomach cried out with this movement, the damage in my torso being made known. When I had urinated earlier, it was more blood than other fluids. I knew that I still may not survive this beating, that I may fall asleep and the damage to my insides or my head may take me in my slumber.

As I let sleep overcome me, I hoped I would die.

6

To my dismay, I did not die in my sleep. Instead, I was awoken by a strong hand shaking me. "Boy," James urged. "Boy, wake up."

Rolling to my back, I blinked with my one good eye and tried to adjust my vision to the figure in the dark. The candle that once lit the room had burned out while I slept. I heard the match strike and saw James' face in the flame light. He touched the match to a wick, shook the flame out and sat the new candle on the dresser. "Your heart was dying."

I stood, facing my employer. "What do you mean?"

James pressed his hand to my shoulder, urging me to sit back down, which I did. He sat on Collin's bed. "Your injuries are great; no man can survive that level of abuse."

My brain was fighting to understand the words. I realized the blows to my head must be worse than I imagined for the sentences he spoke made no sense.

"I see you are confused," he continued in that clipped English accent I had never gotten used to. "Let me make this easy for you." He leaned forward and placed his forearms on his thighs. "Lie down."

The sensible part of me was telling me that this was a bad idea. The rest of me did not care what happened to me. I only wished for death to take me faster than it was. Clearly my wounds were not grave enough as I was still alive. I laid down, turning my head to the left to face James.

As I stared at him, sitting on the bed in front of me. Then, with a blink, he was gone from my sight. His movement was too fast for me to see him cross to me. I felt the weight of his chest pressing into mine, pushing me into the bed, just before I felt the sharp pain in my neck. I believed it to be a small knife and didn't question why James would be murdering me. Truly, I didn't care. I only fought for a second, then gave into it. I hoped this attack would be enough to end my suffering. I silently begged God to allow me into Heaven but knew deep down I would not be welcomed, nor did I deserve it.

My consciousness was slipping away when something was jammed into my mouth. My broken jaw was forced open and searing pain ran down my neck. Liquid filled my mouth and slid down my throat. I knew not what it was but knew I wanted more. Gulping down the warm drink, I drank and drank until the thing was pulled from my mouth.

By candlelight, I saw James holding his wrist to his chest and wipe something from his mouth. "I suggest you be in this room before the sun rises. Lock the door. Should you survive, I will see you after the day is gone."

He stood and abandoned the room, leaving me to search the space for signs that the previous few minutes were only a dream. Was my brain so bruised that it was confusing fantasy and reality, showing me things that were not real?

To my surprise, I felt unexpected energy and knew I should take advantage of this moment to wash the blood from my face. In my current state, I would surely scare those who laid eyes on me.

When I stepped outside, my bare feet upon the cold street, I found that the rain had ceased. I squatted down, filling my cupped hands from a puddle and splashed it onto my face. Rubbing the water over my jaw, cheeks and forehead, I braced myself for the pain of aggravating my wounds. But no pain came. Perhaps, injuries can be so grave that you stop feeling. Looking around, I saw that no one walked the streets. Peering up to the sky and seeing the moon's position, I knew I had slept through much of the night. People would rise and join the street soon so now was a good time.

Finding a particularly large puddle, I stripped down and used the rainwater to wash my body. When I was finished, I pulled only my trousers back on. The shirt was covered in blood. My heart ached looking at the remnants of the girl I would never hold in my arms again. Vowing to burn the shirt, I rolled it up into a ball and held it tightly in one hand.

It was then that I was aware I could hear single drops falling from above and onto the ground next to me. Each landing was like a thunderous drum beat. I was certain that my ears had taken damage along with my brain and worried this new way of hearing sounds meant I would eventually lose sound altogether.

Around me wind rustled the trees. The sight of the leaves dancing in that breeze was suddenly beautiful to me. Sitting onto the still wet ground, I lay back, closed my eyes and listened. The symphony of the night brought me an unexpected and welcomed peace.

For a beautiful moment, I forgot that I was in mourning and my wish for death began to fade. The reprieve was ripped away when the pain tore through my body. My muscles spasmed as fire lit up against my feet.

When the seizing relented, I sat up to find the flames that were burning my soles but saw only a small amount of dawn light across my toes.

Instinctually, I crawled for the side door. The stones of the alley dug into my knees as pain rolled through me again. I dropped to the ground, letting the next round of spasms hit and release. Then, I pressed up to my feet and stumbled for the entrance. Wrenching the door opened, I fell forward and down the stairs, landing on the hard floor of the machine room. Several men looked up, but no one came to my aid. To them I must have looked drunk. I cared not what they thought, only knew I must get to my room.

Using what little energy I had to stand, I lurched forward to the hallways, bracing myself on the wall as I stumbled down each one. The next round of seizures hit when I was only feet from my room. I was no longer able to stand, my legs no longer listened to my brain's commanding. Using my forearms to pull me towards sanctuary was taking too long but it was my only method of movement. Once in between the two twin beds, I let the contents of my stomach escape my mouth in a black tide. I rolled to my back and kicked the door shut. I knew I was supposed to lock it but could not. My arms had joined my legs in succumbing to these fits. My stomach wrenched and twisted – I prayed for it to end. Over and over, I begged God to kill me.

Then, a kind of icy stiffness overtook me and I felt as if I was being slowly dipped into cold water. As it reached my chin, I sighed.

Finally, I thought. Death is here.

I expected death to be black, but it was like dreaming. The room around me changed, became my childhood home. I stood, walking through the familiar rooms to find the one my parents shared. A wee baby laid in a basket, sleeping. Scanning the room, I saw my pale, trembling mother. My father stood by her bed, towering over an unknown woman next to him.

"She will not be able to carry another child, the damage is too great." She sat on the bed, addressing my mother. "Be grateful that you have one and survived his birth. Many women cannot say the same." She laid her hand on my mother's and sat there as she cried. My father left the room, passing me without knowing his grown son was watching. I turned to follow my father in the past, expecting to walk out into the room we shared meals in. Instead, I stepped into the village square. The bustle around me was well known, as were the faces.

"Found ya," I heard the anger in the boy's voice and knew what I was turning to see. Charles was our age but a brute for a 10-year-old. He was as wide and tall as a grown man. I turned to young Collin and we knew we could not win against Charles, just as we knew the approaching bully had discovered it was us who let his sheep free. At the time we had thought it good payback for the torture he had put us through for years and that we would not be caught. But, the time to pay for our prank was coming fast.

"Run," Collin said as he threw his shoulders back, raised his chin and announced, "It was I alone, Charles. I'd hoped chasing after your sheep may help you lose a little of that belly."

My 10-year old brain knew the right thing would be to stay and fight at Collin's side, knew it was better for the punishment to be shared by two. But I ran and left sounds of my friend taking my beating at my back. He would have to take to bed for days to heal what had been done to him, then face punishment from his own father for risking a man's livelihood with our stunt. Yet, Colin never told a soul I had played a part in the scheme.

As my little ten-year-old legs ran for the loch, and away from Collin's brawl, I recognized it was the beginning of my life-long cowardice. I expected to reach the water but instead came to a halt when the well appeared in front of me.

I saw myself, days before I would flee, sitting next to a raven-haired girl who begged for me to love her. "No," I screamed to the boy but my throat made no sound. "Please do not say it, you bastard. Tell her yes. Do not leave her." Alas, there was no other sound than the conversation I knew too well.

As Rhys stood and unknowingly walked past his future self, I watched Dierdre weep the sorrow of a hundred lifetimes. She cried for a boy that was not worthy of her love. I begged her to stay in town, marry Angus, have babies and live a long life. But even as she fell to the ground and sobbed, I knew I could not change the fate of that girl.

"I am in Hell," I thought.

And, Hell I was in - as the scene in front of me fell away to reveal a dark, alleyway on a rainy night.

"No," I bellowed to the sky. "I cannot. Please don't make me watch this. Please. Take me to Hell, burn me, beat me but do not make me do this."

But I had no rule in Hell. Only the Devil can control this and he knew how to torture me. I squeezed my eyes shut but couldn't block out the sounds of whimpering and grunting. I had to hear the unmistakable sound of a head hitting the street and a girl whisper, "Rhys, please help me."

I was drenched by the rain, cold to the core and shaking so violently I thought my bones may snap.

Opening my eyes, I expected the sight of Diedre, pale and unmoving in the night. Instead, she stood out in front of a home. The rain had disappeared with the alley and the village had grown up around me. Her hair was glorious, curled around her beautiful face, falling around her shoulders. Following my gaze down, I saw her belly was swollen with child. Her smile was warm and that warmth filled my chest. She beckoned me to her, turning and opening the door of the cottage. She invited me to join her.

Yet, I felt a pull at my back and turned to see what was calling me. It was the road that left our village, the same path I had taken to leave before my 20th birthday. It called to me, promising me something but I was not sure what. Somehow, I knew I had only seconds to choose – Deidre or a journey.

Returning to Deidre, I called out to her. "Find peace, dear lass. Be safe, warm and happy in this place. But I do not belong here. It is not my home nor what I deserve." Her face fell and she retreated into the house. I spoke to the spot she had been. "I love you."

Then, I faced the road ahead and walked for the second time out of the village, to the mystery that awaited. Night fell around me as I ventured into the darkness.

My eyes opened to that same darkness yet I could see just fine. The beds, the dresser, the door – all visible as if a window let in moonlight. I sat looking around to affirm that no window had appeared while I slept.

Climbing to my bed, I curled up into a ball, trying to process what I just been through. Had it been a dream? If so, I never wanted to sleep again. Or, was I in Hell still? Would this be the cycle I was doomed to repeat? I'd start in this room, fall to sleep then be cursed to live those moments again and again with no way to affect them, only to wake here again. I believed it was what I deserved as sleep threatened to overtake me and I fought it. Like a boy, I whispered into the empty room, begging my mother to come comfort me, for my father to scare away the monsters under my bed, for Collin to come fight for me.

They were the words I repeated until a blessedly dreamless sleep would take me. Little did I know, I would never dream again.

The dead do not dream.

7

My eyes snapped open. It took no time for reality to hit me. I realized that I could see from both eyes, not only one.

Standing with surprising ease, I found the shiny glass on the wall. Both eyes looked back at me. Fumbling to find a match and light the candle, I held the flame up as I believed this must be a trick of the darkness. The fire danced in my green eyes, which had taken on the quality of an emerald. My skin was without flaw or scar, like a babe who has never seen the sun or felt the sting of a cut. The red of my hair seemed to be pulled out of the brown and shone as if not real.

The door opened behind me and James stepped in. "You did not lock the door but at least you were smart enough to not be in the sun."

I turned to face him, confused that he did not mention my new appearance and the healed injuries.

"I must say," he crossed his arms. "I'm surprised you made it. Stronger men than you have not." He turned to the hallway and waved for me to follow. "Blow out the candle and leave it. You do not need it. I will have a woman scrub the place you vomited."

Curious but cautious, I followed his order and his path upstairs to the shop. It was dark as business was done for the day, but it was not where we were ending. I followed him through a door behind the counter and down yet another hallway, ending in a room that could fit three of my rooms. A large bed to the right was neatly made with a blanket of all colors. The colors seemed to dance and twirl. I stared, not trusting what I was seeing.

His voice came from my left. "You will get used to it. Come, sit. We are wasting time." Tearing my gaze from the bed, I saw him sitting in one of two chairs. They were covered in a fabric I had not seen - shining and soft. I sat in the one that he did not occupy, entranced by the feel of it against my bare back.

"I have given you a gift of sorts." He began, opening a small box on the table next to him, retrieving a crystal decanter and a glass. Pouring the red liquid into the glass, he reached it out me. The smell hit my nostrils sending searing pain through my upper teeth. My hand shot to my mouth. I thought, perhaps my broken jaw had not fully healed. What I found was two sharp fangs had erupted on each side of my teeth. Laying my thumb against the point of one broke the skin easily. I assessed the puncture on the pad of my thumb, only to watch it disappear. The skin was unbroken in seconds.

"Those will be better controlled as the nights go by. I suggest keeping your head down and your mouth closed when around humans for the next few nights." James shook the glass, making the liquid slosh. Grasping at the glass desperately, I gulped down the cold drink before registering that it was clearly blood.

"The thirst will be fierce for a few days but should die down." He leaned forward and took the glass from my hand. Once it was filled again, I expected it back, but he sat it on the table next to him. "So, here it is. You are a vampire. This means a few things. First, you will need me to make sure you stay fed and have a place to sleep away from the sun. Disobey me and you will find yourself on the street. Two, you will work for me without question."

"I already work for you."

He wagged his finger back and forth. "Not that, boy. I have humans for that. You will do whatever I ask of you. If I need you with the machines, I will put you there." He leaned forward again. "But if I need you for other things. You will do those, too. That is-" he retrieved the glass and held it in front of me. "If you would like to eat."

I nodded and was rewarded with the glass. As I gulped and shuttered, he continued. "You will tell no one what you are or what I have done for you. You will not feed from anyone in the city, do you understand?"

Confusion over what he was saying left me without a response. He grabbed my chin and squeezed, pulling me into him. "Do you understand?" I nodded, fighting the grip on my face. He let go. "Repeat it back."

I swallowed. "Do not feed from anyone in the city. Tell no one what I am."

He leaned back. "If you are discovered, you will be destroyed. You will not tell them that it was me that made you, do you understand?"

I nodded again, still trying to wrap my head around what he was saying.

"If you are not stupid, no one will find out so you will not have to worry." He rubbed his chin, contemplating and I felt like he was trying to decide whether or not to share the next piece of information. Then, I saw resolve in his face. "What was done to you and that girl is unforgivable." He paused. "We are not the monsters, men like that are."

I felt a tear threaten to wrench from my eye and blinked to fight it back.

His gaze was filled with something like fury. "When you are ready, find those men and make them pay." Taking the glass and setting it down, he grabbed my face again. "I give you this one chance to kill. Only the men who took her are you allowed to kill and you must make it look like an animal attack. Tell me you understand."

"I do," I said and I did. In that moment, I knew exactly what he was telling me.

When he let go and rested back into the seat, his gaze went to the wall next to him. "You mustn't let that kill make you wild. You must be strong and stop when the men are dead."

A thought crossed my mind and I was not sure if it was wise to ask. Yet, I was sure I would not forgive myself if I did not. "What about Collin?"

James met my eyes. "What about him?"

"He has the right to join in making those men pay. He is a good man and deserves this." I might have pushed it too far. James may send me into the street for being ungrateful. I let him think on it.

"If he returns," he said. "I will turn him as well. But, you will both owe me a great deal and I am not kind if my debts are not repaid."

Relief washed over me. "Thank you, James."

He waved a hand. "Do not thank me yet. You have heard very little."

"What else do I need to know?" I asked, worried about the mystery of the unknown considering what I had already learned.

"Listen close because I do not repeat myself," he waited for me to nod that he had my attention. "The sun will kill you. So will being beheaded. I suggest you let neither of those happen. If they do, you will be dust and there is no coming back from that." He paused for questions, but I had none. "If you avoid those two fates, you will live forever. You are stronger than ten men and faster than any other creature. Eventually, you will have a magick of sorts," I opened my mouth and he raised his hand to silence me. "I do not know what kind of magicks, they are different for each. I do not know when it will arise, but you must control it." He stood and paced the room. "You must drink blood to survive. You can eat food, but I don't suggest it and it will do nothing for the hunger. I will provide you with blood as long as you obey me. Tonight, you had two glasses because you are newborn but from now on, you get one a night."

"Where do you get the blood?" I asked.

"It is not your business to know," he said, stopping to face me. "Be happy that you get blood without the work." He started to pace again.

"You will want for release soon. The change makes everything in us stronger, including the need for pleasure." He walked back to me. "This is important. If you are not fed, you will find it hard to resist feeding when you are in the throes of lust so go to the brothel after you have fed, not before. Do you understand?"

"Aye," I agreed.

He waved his hand for me to stand and I did. With a hand on my shoulder, he spoke. "I will send you tonight to a woman and give you the money you need. But after tonight, you work for the blood, the room and the women or you go out on your own. I do not operate a charity."

"Aye, sir."

He pulled coins from his pocket and slammed them into my hand. Then, crossed to a dresser, opened a drawer, withdrew a shirt and tossed it at me. "Cover yourself and go. Get it out of your system so you can be useful to me tomorrow night. This is your only night off until I feel you have earned more so enjoy it."

Then, he pushed me to the door and I left to find the street and a woman to satiate the need that was growing stronger by the minute.

8

The sounds of the city at night overwhelmed me. I heard every conversation, toppling over each other. The noise of glasses clinking, a rowdy piano, rats moving through alleyways and feet on the street was roaring in my ears.

"Quiet," I said and to my delight, the sounds decreased to a dull rhythm of sound.

As I approached our favorite gentleman's house, I smelled the perfume of the women and the liquor on the breath of their clients. When I entered, I had to blink against the bright lights. Women who were familiar to me sat all around the front room like inventory to be counted or purchased – which is what they were. As each turned to me, their eye grew wide.

Off to my left, I saw one stand and approach. She was one I knew. If memory serves, her name was Anne. Though truly, none of them gave their real names.

"Rhys?" Anne whispered with a mixture of awe and want. Her red hair fell down to the swell of her backside. I smelled the heat on her as her rising temperature flushed her skin and felt as if I could not contain myself.

Wrapping my arm around her waist and pulling her into me, something like a growl rolled from my throat. She was pliant in my grasp, eyes locked on mine. "Come with me." Lifting her with ease, I carried her on a path I knew well to the backrooms. Which one was hers, I did not care. I chose the first open door, went through it and used my back to close it. Throwing her onto the bed was easy as she weighed nothing to me.

She was filled with excitement. No fear was found in that gaze and it assured me that she was unaware of my changes. I stalked to her and she rose onto her knees, holding each side of my face. "You are beautiful, Rhys. What has happened to you?"

Perhaps she did notice. However, it did not appear to be enough for her to worry as she was hardly shying away from me. "It is looking at you that makes my eyes bright."

She laughed. "Sweet words."

I crushed my mouth onto her before she could ask any more questions. The need in me was on the brink of being too much to bear. I knew I must not lose control but every cell throbbed for her. She pulled the shirt over my head and our kiss broke only long enough to get it to the side of the room. I tore at her corset, ruining it to free her breasts. She drew away, backing up the bed on elbows, spreading her legs. I spied that she had nothing under her skirts and freed myself from my trousers, taking in the scent of her.

What ached in me was something I had never experienced. I wanted to sheath myself in her but it was more than that. I wanted to devour her. The electric shot through my jaw, telling me my fangs had descended. However, caution was lost to lust and I did not care if she saw them.

Reaching out I grabbed each leg and pulled her to the edge of the bed to rip off her skirt. Her squeal of delight turned into a gasp when I drove myself into her. Gripping the sheets with each hand, she tried to steady herself against the strength of my thrusts. I fought to hold onto my control. Reason forced me to slow myself as to not hurry the moment or hurt the girl.

Pulling out, I flipped her over, allowing her to rise and position herself so I may enter her again. Once inside her warmth, Anne came up on her knees, arching back against me so I may fill my hands with her heavy breasts. This position brought on new sensations but also put her throat dangerously close to my mouth. The image of me clamping my mouth around that tender neck was vivid. I could almost feel her blood flowing down my throat. I turned my face away from her but did not stop my thrusting. I could not have.

When release came for both of us, she screamed with pleasure. Reaching back, she wrapped her arms around the back of my neck to steady herself and postpone us coming apart. With the lust fed for the moment, the hunger had nothing drowning it. Her pulse thrummed loud in my ear.

I pushed her roughly away and she rolled onto her back with the look of a punished child. I pulled up my pants, fastening them and found the shirt. Her voice was worried. "Did I do something wrong?" she asked.

"You did not," I said to the wall, afraid that if I faced her again, offering herself to me, I would not be able to stop myself from ripping into her throat. Pulling the money from my pocket, I tossed it backwards at her. "This will cover your fee and your ruined bodice."

I hurried from the room and ignored the approaching girls in the front room. They clamored to proposition me, most promising to do it for free. But they did not know the hunger that filled me had nothing to do with their services and everything to do with feeding.

When I returned to the shop, I found James in an office next to his bedroom. He glanced up from his desk with annoyance.

"What have you done to me?" I challenged.

"Are you serious?" he slammed his fists onto the desk top. "I made myself quite clear. You are a vampire and I do not repeat myself. Now, be away from me. I have business to attend to and do not need a pup mewling at my feet. I expect you in this room tomorrow, as soon as you arise. I will have blood for you and tell you what I need of you."

"I need more blood," I growled.

With movements too fast for me to see, he was in front of me, my throat in his grasp and lifted from the ground. "You will get none," he snarled. "I have given you two glasses and a whore for the evening. This is me being very kind. It does not happen often." He opened his hand and let me fall to the ground. "Stop being a child and start being a man. Soon the hunger will subside. I do not want to see you again until tomorrow night or you can sleep outside. You choose." He returned to his desk, picking up a pen and scribbling on the papers in front of him.

I retreated from the room, unsure what to do next. My feet carried me without thought, to the side door and out into the alley I had spent my last night as human. Leaning back against the wall of the building, I looked up at the night sky.

There had been tales in my village of creatures such as this – things that look like a man, come out at night and search to feed off the living. Visitors had brought stories of a mad prince to the east who impaled his enemies on spikes, drank their blood and continues to live four hundred years later. My grandfather had told me a story that his father told him, of beautiful women who roamed the Highlands at night, drawing men to them, only to feast upon their blood. As a lad, I was frightened. As I grew, I believed our parents and grandparents had told these tales to keep us from sneaking out of our homes at night.

So that night, gazing up at the stars, it was not that I didn't know what I was. It was that I did not know if I could exist as this for eternity.

Could I truly live on the blood of others? Could I face Collin when he returned and offer him the same? Could I find and punish the men who had ruined my life?

Or should I stay in that spot and let the sun take me?

Warm tears sprang from my eyes and I sank to the ground.

Something caught my eyes, a bundle off to my side. Reaching for it, I pulled it close, realizing it was the shirt I left behind the previous night – had dropped in the middle of my convulsions. The smell of blood came off the dried stains of the shirt. It was the memory of Deirdre's sweet face that brought me out of my morbid reverie. She was dead and the men who did it walked the streets free. They lived to eat, drink and laugh while Deidre's weeping mother washed her for burial.

The rage that filled me, dried my tears. I threw the shirt away from me, into the shadows of the night then balled my hands into fists. Slamming them downward, I braced for the pain in my knuckles but felt none. Examination showed no damage to my hands. I stood, turning to the brick wall and driving my fist into it. Still, my hand was without injury.

I remembered well the faces of my attackers, as they would know mine when I found them. To my amusement, I realized they did not know something much more than a man was looking for them, bringing death with him.

The roar that ripped from my mouth shot out in to the night, sending birds aloft and rats scurrying away.

All my life I had been smaller than my peers, slender. They had tormented me for my thin arms and scrawny legs. But age had broadened my back and tireless work on the machines had brought lean, hard muscles.

And, James' blood had brought me speed and might.

I had been given a chance - a chance to be a new man. I vowed to be the Rhys I had wished I was – strong and unrelenting in the face of danger. I promised Dierdre, I would avenge her. I promised mother I would be a good man. I promised myself I would use what I had been given to right a wrong.

I let the newfound purpose propel me down the stairs and to my room. I would sleep and go to James as requested. I would do what he needed of me. Then, I would start to hunt my prey.

Killing those men would not only avenge Dierdre but would feed the hunger that gnawed at my gut.

9

I awoke, gasping for air - flailing into the dark of my room. Sitting up, I clutched at my chest and felt nothing, my heart lay still. The hunger hit within moments. I must eat or I feared I would tear at the next man I saw.

James was where he said he would be, patiently awaiting my arrival. His fingers were laced in front of him and resting upon his desk. The box that I knew held blood sat to his left. I said nothing, only stood in front of him.

He smiled, motioned for me to come forward, opened the box, retrieved the decanter and poured a full glass. My fangs erupted into place. My arms stay at my side, aching to reach for the blood but I stood my ground. When he offered it to me, only then did I close the distance and take my meal. Using all of my strength, I did not gulp but took my time finishing the drink.

"You learn quickly," James said when I had finished. "I'm pleased."

Laying the empty glass on the corner of the desk, I nodded. Peace came with the blood in my stomach, as the hunger was gone for the moment. I did not know how long it would last but I was grateful for the lull and felt as if my head was clear for the first time in two days.

"Do you have any magick yet?" He asked me, scanning my face signs of secrets.

"Not that I am aware of," I answered.

He seemed to believe me. "You would know," he said and before my eyes I watched the man change. Prior to this, his hair had been a dull yellow and grey, his eyes an unimpressive brown. His skin showed signs of age and damage from being outside. As I watched, an unseen paint brush had run over him, fixing flaws in second. His locks were the bright color of fresh wheat in the sun. His eyes were a brilliant hazel - the eyes of a young man - surrounded by the same perfect skin that I saw in the mirror.

"How?" I asked, forgetting myself.

"Magick," he answered and as quickly as he was revealed, he went back to the older man I had first met. "That is my power, to mask myself and appear more human. I have another but that is for another time." He changed the subject, as if telling me I was allowed no more questions. "I had a task planned for you, but a man has not come to work so you will be back in the machine room I'm afraid. It is a waste, but I will have to postpone your errand." He swept his hand to dismiss me. "You will feel when it is time for you to retire to bed. Be back here at the same time tomorrow night."

I knew well to not challenge James. He had shown me that he was stronger, faster and more skilled than I. Certainly, he would stand by his threat and send me out into the day on my own if pushed too far. So I obeyed, manning a press that night as I always had. I knew the men I worked with and if they noticed changes in me, they said nothing.

My new condition made the work easier than I was accustomed too. I was so much stronger than I had been as a mere man and did not need breaks. Sometime in the night, the hunger returned. I ignored it, forcing myself to focus on the job and not on the beating hearts of the men around me. Hours later, a sickness overcame me and I knew I must away to my room for the day.

Waiting for sleep to take me, I was dismayed with the events of the night. I wondered if James would be true to his word and allow me to track down my attackers or if I was merely a way to have an unquestioning employee forever.

To my continued disappointment, the next four nights were the same. I woke, went to James for blood and was sent down to the machines. The missing worker had been found in his home, dead and cold. It is believed that his years of heavy drink and working the machines had led to an early grave. James did not seem to mourn the man. He only cared that I work in his place until he could be replaced. So, I took his blood, worked his fabrics and went to my room. Only to rise and repeat the same night.

On the sixth night of my new existence, I woke to darkness as I knew I would, ravenous for sustenance. Each night it was less of a shock when I arose. I sat up, swinging my feet to the side of the bed and placing them onto the floor, feeling the hunger fill every cell. As James had told me, the hunger was better than it had been on the first night. The blood I drank was lasting more of the night and when the ache in my stomach returned, it was now only a dull cramping. In time, it should no longer bother me.

I found my reflection in the mirror, seeing the face I expected. How any human could look on me and not see that I was different was baffling. I wished to look more like I had when I arrived in this damned city.

Before my eyes, the reflection changed. The eyes dimmed, losing their emerald shine and brown overrode the green. The skin under the eye swelled slightly and bagged down. The scar on my chin returned and the skin took on a hue of a boy who had been raised on a farm, under the sun.

My mouth fell open in disbelief. I touched my face, then the mirror and then my face again. Had I gained magick as James had foretold? Could I, like he, change my appearance?

I ran for the door and up to the office to find him.

When I burst through, he jumped to his feet. "You imbecile. You cannot move that fast when others might see you."

I was not sure what he was saying but only wanted to ask him my question. "Do I look different to you?"

James came from behind his desk to face me. "Ah," he nodded. "You can mask. Very good. That will be helpful for tonight."

After pouring my meal for the evening, he snatched a small paper from the mess atop his desk and handed to me. Finishing the drink, I set the glass in its place and read the address on the note he'd given me. "What is this?" I asked.

"That is your task for the night," he cleared his throat and crossed his arms in front of him. "The man who lives there owes me money and his time to repay has passed. You will go. If he does not give it to you, you will break a bone. To not feed from him or kill him, only break a bone and tell him he has three days or you return to break another. Then leave."

I shook my head. "I do not know if I can do that."

James uncrossed his arms, gripped the desk edge behind him and leaned back. "I thought you understood this arrangement, Rhys. You will do this." He smiled. "Think of it as practice for when you find the men who took your girl. If you cannot break a man's bone then how will you kill four?"

I was left with nothing in response.

"You may choose which bone you break, only make a point. Then, you may spend the rest of the night as you please. See a woman or look for those men, I do not care." He turned, poured more blood into the glass, then drank it himself. With his back to me, he finished his request. "Just be back here tomorrow night. Either bring me the money or tell me which bone you broke."

As I turned to leave, he spoke to my back. "Oh, and you will need him to invite you in."

10

After walking much of the city, I found the street I was meant to hurt a man on. Before me, brick houses lined each side of the lane. They were thin and jammed together, each an exact copy of its neighbor. Laundry hung from some of the windows. I could hear marital relations in one home and marital fights in several others. Softly, a baby's cry was on the wind.

The one I was aiming for was halfway down and on the right.

I focused and heard only the man shuffling about the rooms. Knowing that a wife or child would not wander onto the scene gave me some relief as I knocked. The man who answered was inches shorter than me. His width came not from hard labor but from too many meals.

"Good evening," he said.

I attempted to enter the home but found that I could not. A resistance was between the man in front me and myself.

"Invite me in," I commanded, not knowing why I must insist this but somehow understanding it was part of being a vampire.

"Are you in some kind of trouble?" he asked.

"Please, invite me in."

He seemed hesitant but manners won and he stepped back. "Do come in."

With one swift motion, I entered, shut the door, moved behind him and wrapped my arm around him to slam my hand over his mouth. "Do not make a noise. Nod if you understand."

He did.

Removing the hand was a risk but he did not scream, only turned to raise his hands and show me he held nothing. "Please don't hurt me. I have no money, but you can have whatever you like in the house."

I shook my head. "I did not come for trinkets. I came for the money you owe James Spencer."

"Oh," the man's eyes widened and all color left his cheeks. Others would not have seen the slight trembling, but I did. It did not bode well for the poor chap.

"I take it you do not have it?" I asked, praying he'd say that he did and I could leave.

"I need more time," he stuttered, patting himself down like he may miraculously find shillings in his sleeping gown.

Three options lay before me. I could break a bone and leave. I could leave, tell James I broke a bone, be found lying and cast out only for James to break the man's bone or worse. Or, I could tell James I would not do this, be cast out only for James to break the man's bone or worse.

It was best I do it quick.

Grabbing a wrist with one hand and an elbow with the other, his forearm snapped like a dried twig. Then, I had my hand off the wrist and over his mouth before he screamed. "Listen," I whispered. "Spencer will make me do worse next time. Find someone to set the bone and find the money. Then," I leaned in. "I suggest never borrowing money again."

He was hyperventilating but no longer screaming.

I left him, holding his ruined forearm, making it all the way out to the street before I vomited up the blood in my stomach.

Errand completed, I had no desire to start my search for the attackers or to find a woman to bed. Instead, I wandered the streets of the city I had spent my youth dreaming about, wishing I could go back in time and tell young Rhys not to run away. While I knew I had no choice in tonight's events, I was sickened with myself. Suddenly, this vampire gift seemed less like a miracle and more like a punishment from God.

I I

Opening my eyes, the next night was disorienting. Not because I was confused but because there was candlelight.

I shot up to see a man sitting on the other bed, staring at me.

"Collin," I cried, jumping to my feet, arms outstretched. He did not cease his staring or move. I lowered myself back to sit on my bed and waited for him to speak.

"What did I miss?" he asked.

I was not certain how to answer. "What do you mean?"

"Well," he stood. "I arrived this morning and was told by that horrid shop woman that I was not to go our room per Master James' orders. I was sent to a different room to sleep and told to fetch you at sundown." He looked down at me. "Imagine my surprise when I find you, sleeping like the dead, looking like you've aged backwards and with no signs of injury on your body. So," he grabbed my arm and pulled me up. "I ask again. What did I miss?"

"We must go to James," I knew it would anger Collin but did not know how to explain the last week. Before he could argue, I urged. "Please, friend. Trust me for a few moments and all will be explained."

The struggle was clear in his gaze, but he relented and followed me up.

James instructed us to enter after I rapped on the closed office door. As had become habit, he was behind his desk. What papers he shuffled or words he scribbled, I did not know. But it was the same this night as each night before.

"Ah," he said, when he saw the two of us come in and shut the door. "I heard you had returned. Truly, I did not think you would."

"I would not leave Rhys alone," he stated as if James should have known this. I heard the caution in his voice. He was still waiting for answers.

"Did you tell him?" James directed at me.

"No." I answered. "I thought it best we do it together."

"I see," he folded his hands in front of him. "First, I would like report from your assignment."

With Collin's arrival, I had forgotten the unpleasantness of the prior night. It came flooding back to me. "The forearm."

James nodded. "Good choice. Makes a statement without crippling him." He stood, coming out from behind the desk and motioned to the seat he had occupied. I thought for a moment that Collin would insist on information, but he followed the hand and sat in the fine chair.

James and I stood next to each other, facing my confused friend. "I am a vampire," James said dryly. He had chosen a direct method. I froze, waiting for Collin's response. His face was blank as James continued. "I have made Rhys a vampire. This is how he is healed and not in the ground where you know he was likely headed when you left."

I turned to face James and then Collin. Was it true? Had he left me here, believing I would succumb to my wounds alone?

"I am offering you the same. Immortality, strength and a chance to kill the men who murdered your sister," he crossed his arms. "Or, I can wipe your memory and send you back to where you came from, never knowing the truth."

He could erase memories? If that is so, why had he not offered me this?

Collin's heartbeat showed no signs of stress, but his breathing increased. "How dare you?" He said quietly. "How dare you mock me in this time of grieving?" He set that heated gaze on me. "Why would you play along with this?"

I feared he would set off James' temper so I spoke. "Think about it, Collin. I am healed. My very appearance has changed. You could not enter my room until sundown. You have never seen James in the day."

Slowly, realization was replacing the rage. I kept going. "Together, we can bring justice to those monsters and vengeance for Diedre."

"What is the price?" he asked.

James answered. "You will work for me as you have been doing. I will provide you with sanctuary from the sun, money when I feel you have earned it and blood to drink."

Collin jumped up, moving to the side of the room away from us and looking at me. "You drink blood?"

"I do," I answered, honestly. As much as I wanted him by my side, I wanted him to know what he was being offered. "And you would have to, as well."

As if on cue, James pulled over the box, pulled out the decanter and poured my meal into the glass. I took it on instinct, but paused to spy my friend. He was watching intently. When I gulped it down, he gasped. "Monstrous," he whispered.

"We wipe his memory then," James advised.

In a blink, I stood between my maker and my friend, arms out to each side. "Give me a few hours. Then, you can turn him or send him away."

James was annoyed and I braced myself to be thrown out of the way. Instead, he cocked his head. "You have until an hour before dawn. Either way, we need time. But," he smiled. "You owe me for this extra time."

If last night had taught me anything, it was that being indebted to the man in front of me was not a good choice. However, the man behind me deserved this chance.

"Aye," I agreed. "We will return to you at the instructed time."

Collin's breath on my back told me he was about to argue. I turned, threw him over my shoulder and was out the door, away from danger, in seconds.

12

The side of the building was as good a place as any to return my friend to his feet. He took several steps back immediately. Frozen, I allowed him whatever distance he needed between us to feel safe so he could listen.

"What are you?" he whispered

"You know. You just do not want to believe it." One step towards him. He didn't step back. "Our parents spoke of them as demons. But I am no demon. I am the same Rhys." Another step closer.

This time he did take a step back. "You drink blood."

"Aye and it is no different than eating the meat of something that was once living," I reasoned.

"Where does it come from?"

"I do not know." Again, only honesty. "James provides it so we do not need to go out for it or put ourselves at risk of being discovered."

Collin shook his head. "This cannot be."

I took a step forward. "It is. And, it can be for you. Living forever, never aging, strong as an ox, magick inside ye and the look of an angel."

"Magick?" he asked.

"Aye," another step closer. "Each of us is given a magick of sorts." I wished to change my face back to the Rhys he knew, bringing up the mask, and he crossed himself. I closed the distance between us, grabbed each of his upper arms. "Collin. Think of what we can do." I dropped the masking and allowed him to gaze into my vampire eyes. "Dierdre cannot rest until those men pay. We can take them off the streets, save the lasses they will hurt in the future and give your sister peace."

And there it was, the moment he gave in. I had pressed the right spot and taken away all resistance.

"Will it hurt?" he asked after several minutes of contemplation.

Letting go of his arms, I stepped back to give him space to breathe through the next words. "Aye. It is a pain you have never known and it will last for an eternity. You will wish for death then fall into visions."

"Visions?"

"Aye," I thought of the best way to explain. "Pieces of your life played before you. Then, you wake as this." I spread my arms for effect.

"And the blood?"

I shook my head as if it was no great thing. "Tastes like the sweetest wine and quenches like fresh spring water."

He looked up to the sky and I followed his gaze. Wispy clouds obscured the stars. "The sun?" he said more to himself than I.

"To be true, I do not miss it much. Had enough of it on the farm." This was the first time that night I had not been completely honest with him. I was beginning to mourn the warmth of it but it felt trivial in the grandness of it all.

I heard his weight drop down to the street and found him lying on the ground, still gazing at the sky so I joined him.

We lay like that for hours, talking of our boyhood and the dreams we had. We spoke of the children we had grown up with and how we would still be young when they were holding their grand and great-grandchildren. I promised him we would work for James until our debt was paid and then continue our path to America, where the life we yearned for would be ours for the taking. That we, like our employer, could use our abilities to gain wealth and power.

When it was time, I stood with ease, holding out my hand to help Collin up. "Ready?" I asked.

He paused only for a moment, then nodded.

So, I led my friend back to James and sealed his fate.

13

I was not to be present when Collin was turned. James sent me to my room, telling me I would either see my friend the next night or not – that my presence would not affect the outcome so was useless. Glancing back before the door shut, I saw fear in Collin's eyes but knew he must endure this part and it was not for me.

Lying in my bed, I strained to hear any sound that would tell me if Collin had taken James' offered blood or been sent away with no memory of us. Only the machines, nocturnal animals and occasional words from the night shift workers met my ears.

That was until foot falls outside my door sent me to open it.

Crimson was smeared around Collin's mouth and his eyes were the most brilliant blue I'd ever seen. He stumbled into the room. "I swear I can hear rats from a mile away."

I whooped and slapped his back. "Aye and this is only the beginning."

Lurching to the mirror, he touched his perfect face and smiled. "Oh, the ladies will love this."

I laughed. "Of course, you would be thinking with your cock at a time like this."

He turned. "It dinna much hurt, though. Just when he first bit me."

"Sit down," I instructed, locking the door and sitting on my own bed. "This is not it, my friend. Only the beginning. As the sun rises, it will start." I reached and laid my hand on his knee. "But I will not leave you. I will be next to you when it happens and here when you awake."

Collin didn't entirely grasp what I was saying but I knew he would soon. "James said I may not survive."

"Aye," I leaned back, making sure he saw how unworried I was. "He said the same to me but I am here. And, you are the strongest of us both. If I can make it through, so can you."

"That is very true," he jested. "The times I have saved your hide, the beatings I have taken for you so those wee arms of yours weren't broken."

I flexed my bicep. "You mean these wee arms?"

He laughed. "If the village could see you now."

A smile crossed my face. "Perhaps we will visit someday."

The feeling in the room changed and his face fell. His gaze dropped to his lap. "Rhys. Your father-" his words were cut short when he jerked and threw himself backwards on the bed. The violence of the convulsion propelled his body to the floor. Shaking, he rolled to his side, slamming his arm over his stomach. I dropped to his side, gripping his shoulder to let him know I was there.

"Shhh," I soothed. "It will be over soon. Do not fight it, just relax and sink in."

He arched back so hard that I worried his spine may break. I jumped up, not knowing what to do and wishing I could take this pain for him.

When he rolled to his knees and hands, black filth poured from his mouth.

Then, the blackness took me as the sun broke over the crest.

14

Awareness snapped me awake and I threw myself forward out of bed. At my feet was what had erupted from my friend's gullet just before I was taken into sleep. Terrified to find an empty shell in Collin's bed, I wrenched my gaze from the floor to the mattress.

Collin lay there on his back, motionless. Vomit and blood caked the space around his mouth. The paleness of him was hard to believe and a grey hue lie just under the whiteness of his flesh. I locked my gaze upon his quiet chest and saw no rise or fall.

Cold realization took me to my knees, a scream threatened to rise up my throat.

Then, the ashen hue fell away and Collin sat up, gasping for air and flailing his arms about.

The scream I was about to release from my lips transformed into a cry of celebration. Jumping to my feet, I lunged for him, wrapping my arms around him. He returned the embrace, thumping my back twice. "You dinna think I would leave you so easy, did ya?"

Breaking the hug, I laughed. "You crazy bastard, I knew you could do it." Rising to my feet, I pulled him with me. "Come. Let us wash your face and go to James. If he is sending you to where I think he is, you will want to hurry."

He peered at the mess on the floor. "What do we do with this?"

"Do not worry about that. I will clean it before sunrise. Tis my gift to you."

"Was there so much inside me?" the amazement clear in the tone.

"Aye," I answered. "Don't know what it is but it came from me as well."

"Cannot wait to see what my piss will look like," he laughed.

"No more of that," I informed him. "No more relieving yourself."

He looked up, incredulous. "You lie."

I put my hand to my heart. "Truth. It has been a week and nothing. Come. We must not keep James waiting."

When we crossed the threshold to face James, he did not need to glance up. "I see you survived. Guess I should not underestimate boys from the village."

"Aye," I said, proudly.

He waved his hand over the box. "Pour a glass each, I am quite busy tonight."

Once the meals were poured, I watched Collin gulp it down. I took my time, savoring the taste and knowing I would have no more until the next night. "May I have more?" Collin asked.

"One more," James said, finally looking up to see us. "The rest of the nights you will be given only one. I trust Rhys will teach you all you need to know. I will not be raising you as a mother does. I suggest you learn as fast as your friend has."

I poured James his second glass and dutifully put the decanter away.

"Shall I take him to the whorehouse?" I asked and Collin choked on the bit he was drinking.

James retrieved coins from his top drawers and tossed them in our direction. "There is enough for both of you. Collin, because this is your first night and you must. Rhys, because you convinced Mr. MacMillan to bring me the money he owed."

In my periphery, I saw Collin's face turn to mine and knew he would question what that meant. I took the glass from him, set it in its place and ushered him from the room.

"What was that?" Collin asked when we were on the street and walking.

"What?" I was determined to make him ask outright.

"Well, our employer just told us to go find women to satisfy us and gave us the money to do it. Not that I am complaining. I tell you I could satisfy fifty lasses, the way I feel right now," he growled. "I have never been filled with a need so great."

"That is why," I interrupted before he could tell me more of his desires. "The blood makes everything stronger – our bodies, our senses and our needs." I stopped, grabbing his arm to stop him as well. "Collin, listen to me well. You feel like a man, but you're are not a man. You must control yourself. You never go to a woman before you feed or you risk the hunger taking a life."

Confidence made his eyes shine brighter. "I can control myself Rhys. I was satisfying lasses before you knew what a prick was for."

"This is no joke," I cautioned. "My first time after I changed," I grabbed his chin to make him focus on me. "I almost broke the poor girl's hips and wanted to rip out her throat when I was done."

At least that brought on a bit of worry in his gaze. "I hear you."

Releasing his chin and arm, I continued. "They will be drawn to you now. Not just because you're fair of face and strong but because I think something in us calls to them. They do not know how close they are to death so you must be the one in control, do you hear me?"

"Aye," he agreed but I was not convinced.

Collin had always been the better man but had also been chasing girls by the time he was twelve. He was randy as a human and I hoped the vampire in him could keep that lust for lasses separate from the lust for blood.

We could not avoid the brothel as not doing this would only make him more dangerous, but I would be sure I was close to the room he was in.

When we entered, the women begged.

To my relief, Collin chose a woman who was larger and looked as if she was strong of mind. I knew she would stop him if he got too rough and that gave me some peace. I looked for Anne, knowing she would do well for me and it would give me a chance to apologize for the brutish way I had acted. But she must have been with another.

To my right, a girl whispered "Choose me." Facing her, I was met with blue eyes and ebony hair. Without thought, I stepped away from her.

"Not you," I said, resulting in a pained look from the girl.

In the end, I took a female with brown hair and eyes. Though my heart was suddenly aching, the need that was triggered by the smell of the women was threatening to take my will from me.

I am ashamed to admit it, but I turned the girl away from me as I bedded her. Unable to see her as a woman in that moment but only a means to feed a craving, like the blood I drank.

In the other room, I heard Collin grunting and the woman screaming with pleasure. I waited for sounds of a struggle or danger but none came. When he left the room, he had the smile of a cat who has had his fill of mice.

15

Once the hunger for blood and need for sex was fulfilled, I knew it was the best time to teach my friend what it meant to be as we were now. We had coins left and he hinted at another lass but I led him out of the brothel and a safe distance from the smell of the women. During the times I had wondered the streets since arriving, I had found a spot I loved. While the city offered several churches, the smallest of them had become a place I found peace. I had never walked through its doors but instead sat on a stone wall surrounding the small cemetery at its side. The spot offered me comfort as it reminded me of the village graves Collin and I used to hide among. As I sat, this night, he joined me with our backs to the rest places of strangers.

"I feel as if I could wrestle a bear," he exclaimed proudly.

"Aye," I agreed, slapping him on the back. "Tis a powerful thing we have been given. But it comes with a price." Pausing, I waited for a question, yet Collin just continued to stare out to no place in particular. I continued, "We cannot be in the sun, as you know. And chopping off our head will kill us, leaving nothing but ash."

"Are the stories true then?" He asked. "Do we live forever?"

"Aye," I answered. "James says if we keep out of the daylight and don't get ourselves caught, then we will never die."

"So," he laughed. "What is the down side?"

"We drink blood, as you know." I wondered how to say the next. "And, let us be honest. James owns us. He is stronger than us and faster, too. He would send us to the daylight without a single care."

"So," Collin said. "We continue to work for him as we have and save our coins. Then, when we have the money, we run away from him as we ran from the village. Once on a ship, he will not follow."

I thought about it. Could it be so simple a plan? "How do we eat on the ship?" I asked. "Avoid the sun? Do you not think people will notice that we sleep in the day?"

"We walk on as ourselves, during the night boarding. Then, hide in cargo. Take blood with us and use rats when we run out. When we are close to America, we hide in a box, let them unload us, then awake on the docks and walk into the New World." He reported it as if he had always planned it.

Was I a fool for not having used the last week to plan this very thing? I'd always known that Collin was braver than I, but it was not until that night that I realized he was smarter too. In that moment, I accepted that Collin was the reason I'd ever made it that far. Dierdre had told me I had an angel watching out for me. That was the second I realized that Collin had been my angel. Nevertheless, I had convinced James to give him this gift, had refused to leave him behind. So, could it be – that in this new life - I would now offer Collin as much as he offered me?

However, there was more he didn't know. "Collin," I paused. "James does not just ask that we work as we have before. He has made it clear that we are to do whatever he needs of us."

"Fine," he relented without thought.

"It is not just working fabrics, Collin. He asks for more of us, things we would not ask of others."

That was when the delight finally seeped from his face and he looked to me. "What has he asked of you?"

I sighed. "For some nights it was just the machines and I tell you, we can work without needing to stop now. I can do three times what I did before. Then," I couldn't hold back now. "he sent me to break a man's arm."

"What?" Collin jumped to his feet.

"Aye," I locked into his eyes so he could see I was not lying. "A man who owed James money. I entered his home and broke his arm, then just walked away. That is how I earned the whore this night."

Collin returned to his spot on the stone wall and I left him to think. After some time, he spoke. "We can do this, Rhys. Whatever he asks, we do. We do not argue. And once we have the sum needed," he faced me. "We go. And, forget everything that happened here."

Meeting his eyes, I found determination. He truly believed we could do this and that made me believe. "We forget," I agreed.

"And," he was resolute. "Whatever we do to the men who took Deidre, is locked away in the same place."

"Aye," I relented.

"What men?" We followed the voice to the top of the church steps and found a priest. How we had not heard him emerge, I do not know.

We had been trained well as lads and instinctually moved to stand for the man of God. As he descended the steps to meet us on the street, I took him in. The brown hair was painted with streaks of grey, which made me put his age at fifty, yet his face was one of a man ten years younger. The green eyes were so like mine that for a moment I thought he may be one of us. It was the sound of his heart beating in my ears that told me I was wrong. He was a human man with the eyes of an immortal.

"Boys?" He addressed us once in front of us.

"Yes, Father?" We answered simultaneously.

"You are out very late. What brings you to us at this hour? Are you in trouble?" His voice was soft and held the kind wisdom of an uncle or grandfather.

We looked to each other for a story but were tongue-tied. It was I that spoke first. "As boys, we would sit outside our church, among the grave and talk for hours. This place reminds us of home."

He nodded. "I see. Well, it is to be your home too then but why come now?"

"We could not sleep," Collin answered and I breathed out a sigh of relief at his quick thinking.

"So," the priest arched his eyebrow. "You are not vampires, then?"

16

I do not think, at that time, or any since, I have been so shocked. Moments went by with the man staring at us and us staring back. Collin broke the silence with a forced laugh. "Father," Collin started and even to me it sounded unnaturally relaxed. "I have never heard a man of God make such a joke."

The priest was clearly not falling for our ruse. "Boys," he held up his hand, palms out, in a gesture of peace. "I know the truth and I am a friend. Come in?" He gestured to the church's entrance.

"Can we?" Collin asked.

"You're new, then?" The priest asked, in a fatherly tone.

"Aye," I answered, still unsure if I was making a mistake. James had been clear that I was to keep this a secret. But the man knew already, so I felt it foolish to continue to lie.

His smile was warm. "Yes, you can enter."

We followed him up the stairs and into the Church of Scotland. The priest entered first and I'm embarrassed to say that we hovered at the threshold. Collin and I held onto the beliefs of our village, that things like us could not enter a house of worship. I know that I was worried I would burst into flames after my first step into the sanctuary. Even so, it was I that took the risk and crossed over, only to find I did not perish. Collin followed and we sat next to the priest.

He nodded his head. "Father Thomas."

"Collin," my friend responded. "And, this is Rhys."

"How are we able to walk into the church?" Collin asked.

"You cannot enter a private residence but may enter the houses of God," he answered with no hesitation. "For these are open to any, like a business is open to any. But," he cocked his head. "That cemetery you sat by?" We nodded. "You cannot step foot on. It has been consecrated and spelled. Those such as you cannot enter it. You will find other places spelled in this way. It is magick older than those like you. They block your entrance, no matter who may invite you in." Father Thomas treated us to that same warm smile. "How old are you?"

"Both 23," I answered.

He nodded. "I meant how long have you been turned?"

It was the first time I had heard it referred to as "being turned" but I knew instantly what he was asking. "Him only a day," I said. "And, I a week."

The priest seemed to ponder for a moment. "I see. And, the one who turned you?"

I knew instantly not to say anything about James. He had been quite clear that I was to never reveal his name as the one who made me this way. I had to think fast. "We were both attacked and awoke like this. Each do not know who it was but have found each other this night."

Silence hung in the air as we waited for Thomas to respond. I thought I may need to add to the story when he finally spoke. "You do not have to tell me the truth. I understand that you need to keep some secrets, as the others before you have as well." He laid each of his hands on each of ours. "Just know that you are safe here. Whatever you tell me, I will never repeat. This is a sanctuary for humans," he smiled. "And, otherwise. I pray for you as I pray for all who find me." He pulled away his hands and leaned back against the wood of his seat. "Now, do you have questions?"

"What do you ask?" Collin inquired.

"About what you are," the father answered bluntly. This left us unsure how to continue. Could this human offer us information on what we were? If so, how?

"What are we?" Collin spoke up.

"I trust you have heard the name vampire. But it is more than that. I think you are a different version of us," he responded. "Like a mirror."

"A mirror?" I asked.

"Aye," the warm face of a parent was back. "When you see yourself in a piece of glass, something looks back. Perhaps, it is another version of humanity. That is what creatures like you are."

"Creatures?" Collin responded.

"I apologize," the father laid his hand back on Collin's. "Not creature but not truly man. As the sun has the moon, darkness has light and the same day a person dies, another is born. It is a balance. And, perhaps, those such as you are the balance to man."

"I dinna understand," I shook my head.

"You are only in darkness, never to die." He paused to be sure we had the time to digest what he had said. "So, perhaps, there are things like you that live in the light to bring life."

"Angels?" Collin asked.

"Perhaps," Thomas answered.

"So, we are demons?" I spoke without thinking and it was more of a statement than a question.

Now, he moved his hand from Collin and rested it on mine. "I do not think you are," he assured. "I think people have taken the scripture and made broad assumptions from it. They use the word of God to defend their hatred of others and things they do not understand." He looked between the two of us for the next words. "Perhaps, man does not truly understand angels, demons and all those in between. Perhaps, it is just those who live in darkness and those who live in light. All of which are from God and seek to bring balance."

I found an unexpected comfort in his words. Until that moment, I did not realize the weight I carried on my shoulders. Hearing this man say that our nocturnal existence did not necessarily mean we were evil, brought me a relief I did not know I was seeking.

"So," seriousness crossed his face. "Who are these men you were speaking of when I came out of the church?"

We glanced at each other for assurance that we should speak honestly to this man. It was I who spoke. "Four men attacked myself and the woman I was with a week ago." I saw Collin in my periphery and the nod that told me to continue. "The woman was his sister and an untouched young woman of 19, promised to marriage in one month." I swallowed and cleared my throat. "They beat me, violated and murder her. And, the police are doing nothing to find them. They will not see punishment unless we bring it to them."

Again, silence hung in the air and we waited for the priest to respond. "I'm sorry for what happened to you and her, sorry for the loss you feel." He leaned back. "But what you are planning will haunt you for eternity, my sons. Why not let them face their God at the end and suffer His will onto them? Let Him take this weight off your shoulders."

It was I that stood, slamming my fists against the wooden seat. "They do not deserve mercy, Father. You did not witness what they did, did not have to hear her cries. I did."

Collin looked to me, then the priest and back at me. Ultimately, he chose to stand at my side. "If we find them, they will pay." His voice was quiet but full of rage.

Father Thomas stood as well, facing us without condemnation in his gaze. "Please understand that I understand, as a man, what you must feel. But, as a man of God, I know the price you will pay for seeking what you think is justice. Whatever you choose, children, I will be here whenever you need me." Then, just as abruptly as he entered our night, he turned and walked away from us, behind a curtain.

We looked to each other, both unsure how to respond to the last hour. Quietly, we walked from the church and into the night. Whether we would eventually kill those men or not, we knew we must return to our beds and out of the sun. Vampires are not free to carry out tasks in the sunlight – no matter how righteous they may feel.

17

For the next two weeks, we would not know the vengeance we had chosen this existence for. Instead, we drank our one glass of blood and were sent to the basement to work the machines. James offered us no timeline to when we would be able to start tracking down Diedre's murderers. He just gave us blood and told us to go work. In the few moments between ending our shifts and falling into our daytime comas, we'd whisper angrily about the unfairness of our lives. The time was not diminishing our need for revenge, but increasing it.

Thankfully, the blood lust was not as voracious as it had been the first few days. Now, the glass of blood given each day was quenching our thirst for most of the night. Although, to be truthful, the thirst was always present, like a dull toothache.

More dangerous, there was another burgeoning need being untreated as well. Along with not giving us time to search for killers, we were given no chance to go to the brothel. Our desire for release was quickly becoming more fierce than the need for justice or the hunger for blood. It sat on the edge of my mind and threatened to take my sanity. By the start of the third week, Collin and I were snapping at co-workers and our control was slipping. I knew that it was a matter of days before our grip was gone and we exposed our true nature to a human.

It was that night, with our sanity so unstable, that James sent us on a new errand for him. "You will not work the machines this night," he said as we drank our rations for the evening. "I have a task for you. If you do it with enough of the night left over, you may go find a woman."

I was ready to say yes to whatever it was when Collin inquired about the specifics.

"Go to this address." James handed a folded paper to my friend and sat to peruse the papers on his desk. "Find a man named Oliver and break his neck. Make sure you have no witnesses and do not drink from him."

I was speechless.

Collin was not. "Kill a man?"

"Yes," James answered, still looking down and beginning to scribble on a blank sheet. "He walks with a limp so I can't imagine it will be difficult for you." He laid down the pen and made eye contact with me. "Once done, go to the whorehouse and tell them that you are my employees. You may have one woman each and they will send me the bill." Then, he waved his hand to dismiss us.

I knew the conversation was done and found Collin's wide eyes. Gesturing to the open door, I left the room and hoped my friend would follow me. It wasn't until I was in the dark alley that I spoke.

"We must do this, Collin." I saw he was about to interrupt I cut him off. "He will send us into the sun. We have nowhere to go. We must do what he asks and continue to collect our pay."

"Our pay is shite," Collin raged.

Shushing him, I grabbed his hands. "He'll hear you and I tell you truth, I believe that he'll have no problem killing you or starving you." Collin calmed and I let him go. Turning to the brick wall, he slammed his fists against it and leaned into the building's side.

Silence hung in the air. I fought the urge to fill it and let him run each option though his mind. When he turned to me, the defeat in his eyes was heart breaking. "It is one thing to dream for the death of those men, but to kill a man in cold blood who has done nothing to us -" he trailed off. "I don't think I can."

"I will do it, Collin. You do not have to." And, I meant it. I would do this for him. I would pay him back for all the beatings he'd taken for me, pay him back a small portion of what I owed him for not protecting Diedre.

"I canna let you," he started.

I laid my hand on his shoulder. "You will let me do this for you, Collin. You will." I forced a smile on my face and hoped that I looked like it would not bother me to take a life. "Then, we find a woman and make her scream with pleasure." That coaxed a grin from him. "Then, we lock what we have done away in a place in our minds that we never visit."

"Aye," he agreed and handed me the paper that sealed a man's fate.

18

The address was a dock. Fish, whiskey and the stench of working men hung in the air, overwhelming our vampire senses. Dozens of males shuffled about the area, loading and unloading, pulling nets onto boats, bringing barrels off, scrubbing, gutting, packing and drinking. There were conversations mixed with grunting and a few were singing.

They did not notice us as we moved about the commotion. To them, we must have looked like anyone of the dock workers. Our clothes had not been washed or changed in two weeks and carried the odor of machine work.

I was contemplating how I would find this Oliver, who I would ask and how I would ensure we would not be remembered, when Collin slapped my back and pointed to his left. Following his finger, I knew the universe had shined upon us. The man was large, bent slightly at the neck from years of hard labor. His beard came to his belly, a filthy hat sat askew on his head and slid slightly as he stiffly limped from task to task.

Approaching him was not difficult; the noise of the dock would have masked a great deal. So, when he turned to see us, he startled a little then settled back into his normal bent posture. "What?" While he was likely in his forties, his voice was that of a man twice his age. The tobacco smell wafting off him explained the damaged vocal chords.

"Oliver?" I asked, not wanted to set my sights on the wrong victim.

"Aye," he barked. "And you are?"

"Never mind that," I answered with the same level of unkindness. "We need to talk," I looked around, conspiratorially. "Somewhere private."

Amusement filled his gaze. "Oh, do we?" His laugh was harsher than his spoken word. "I'll go nowhere with you two. I've work to finish and whiskey to drink." He attempted to push past me, but was unable to. Shock replaced the amusement in his eyes when he hit the solidness of me and I did not budge. I knew he was about to panic and draw attention to us. His mouth opened and he took a deep breath.

I locked eyes with him. "Don't speak," I said reflexively, feeling a heat rush up my throat and out of my mouth as I spoke. Oliver froze. His mouth remained open and his breath was held.

Collin grabbed my arm. "Did you do that?"

"I don't know" I answered truthfully.

"Try something else," Collin urged.

Gesturing to a dark corner of the dock, away from the hustle, I spoke. "Go behind the warehouse." The man didn't move. I made sure to catch his gaze with mine and repeated the command. This time Oliver turned and made his way to the shadows. Collin and I followed, making sure that none of the other dockworkers were paying attention to this scene.

"When will I get magicks?" Collin asked when it was safe to talk.

"I don't know," I answered. "Have you tried?"

Collin thought about it. "No," he answered. "We've been trapped in the factory." He looked at me and I watched his eyes grow wide.

"What are you doing?" I asked.

"Trying to change my appearance like you and James can." He said, his voice straining.

Shaking my head, I disappointed him. "You look the same. Not all of us get the same abilities. Try to command him." I nodded towards the still staring Oliver.

Collin took the man's face in his hands and turned him to face the vampire. When they were looking into each other's eyes, Collin spoke. "Sit down." Oliver dropped to the ground on his bottom, his legs splayed out in front of him.

Collin whooped in celebration and I shushed him. "I have mind control," Collin whispered.

"Aye," I slapped his back. "Good for you. Now, we must kill this man and then we can go celebrate." And just like that, the mood changed. Collin and I looked down at the dazed man at our feet. He looked confused and I worried that our abilities were wearing off. Did we need to keep eye contact? Did it only last a moment? I didn't know but I was sure we didn't have time to test our new power. The other dock workers were not far from us and eventually one of them would wander back to this spot or go looking for the missing Oliver.

"How do we do this?" Collin asked.

"*We* won't do anything," I answered. "I'll do it. You dinna have to even watch."

He rested his hand on my shoulder. "I will not leave you to do this alone." He moved to squat down in front of Oliver and found the confused eyes with his calm ones. "My friend is going to stand behind you. You will not move or fight."

Finding my spot behind Oliver, I leaned down to grab each side of his face. I had to close my eyes, not look at either of them, if I was to do this deed. Tapping into my rage at Dierdre's death, our new lives with James and the constant nagging hunger in my belly, I twisted quickly. A crack rang into the night as the man fell limp.

I had only a moment to process my first kill before Collin became a blur and left the dead man. After the briefest of pauses to wish the man's soul find rest, I fled, following my friend to the only place I found sweet release.

The noise of the women hit my ears before the sight of the brothel. We slowed and walked as human men the rest of the way. The dock felt a million miles behind us; I was already locking away the memory of my dark deed. Lost in the thought of what I was about to do, I separated the killer in me from the good, young man I still needed to believe I was.

Seeing us walk through the entrance sent the ladies into a flurry of excitement. Cassandra, the one who ran the house, stood straighter when we told her that James had sent us. "In that case," she smiled. "I have something special for you." To my dismay, and the disappointment of the girls in the front hall, Cassandra pulled us towards a red curtain and to the other side. The hallway that was revealed was dimly lit, leading down towards a red door. She gestured for us to go and we did, so she could follow us from behind.

When we reached the door, a voice called from the other side. "Come in." It was the most beautiful thing I'd ever heard – like music. Those two words slid down my spine and into my gut, filling it with sweetness and warmth like an aged whiskey. Collin shivered, telling me that he felt it too.

Inside the room, a large bed of red satin filled much of the space. As I look back in my mind to this memory, I can tell you that its color was that of the finest rubies. Although, in 1807 I had never laid eyes on any real gem before. Either the color or the fabric itself made the linens seem like they sparkled in the flames of the few lit candles. But once I laid my gaze upon the woman in the center of the bed, I forgot all about the rich bedding.

Her hair was the vibrant red of fire. The waves of it tumbled down around her face, her shoulders and onto that ruby satin. Its masses hid her breasts, but I could see the swell of them and knew she was nude. Part of the sheet lay over her middle, covering only the most precious portion of her. The rest of her was exposed for us to take in and that perfect body was the palest I'd ever seen. Her milky white skin held not a single scar or blemish. She rested with her hands behind her, holding herself up in a sort of reclining lounge like an offering to us.

"She's mine," Collin's voice broke my reverie, and I fought the urge to fight him for the goddess before us.

She laughed and the sound made my legs weak.

"She is for both of you," Cassandra declared.

We turned together to face the madame. "Both?" we asked in tandem. "No," I continued. "We canna do that. It will be too much for her."

The woman in the bed laughed again, drawing our attention. "How sweet of you to worry about me." I heard now that she was Irish and wanted to fall into her. I barely heard the shutting door at my back, barely registered that the madame had left. The woman's words continued and the effect on my body was powerful. "I can take more, do more, than you can imagine, Rhys."

"How do you know my name?" I asked.

"I have heard you in this place before, heard your name on the lips of the other girls." She turned to look at my companion. "Yours too, Collin." I think I was halfway in love with her. "I have waited patiently for my turn with you. Considering what the other ladies have said about you, I cannot wait to lie with you myself."

Collin was walking towards the bed like a man in a trance. I fought through the desperately growing need and grabbed his arm. "Wait," I spoke with a strength even I didn't know I possessed. "We canna do this. I am worried that only one of us would damage your fine body. Two of us together, we must not. You canna know what you are inviting. We are too strong and our need is even stronger."

Her smile was one full of a desire like my own. "Which is why only another vampire can satisfy you both this night."

19

Only then did I focus on the sounds in the room and discovered no heartbeat. She sat silently, allowing us to fully comprehend what she'd revealed. "You're a vampire?" I asked.

"Aye," she answered. "As are you." Her voice, while beautiful, no longer made me weak or pulled me into her.

"Does Cassandra know?" Collin asked.

"She does," the woman answered. "Worry not. She is very good at keeping secrets. None of the other girls know about me or the two of you." She lifted herself to sitting, and pulled out each hand to pat the spaces to either side of her. We followed, Collin sitting to her right and I to her left, slightly in front so we could all still look at each other.

"Why does your voice no longer affect us as it did?" I asked.

"Because I am no longer using my power," she answered, as if educating a pupil who struggles to understand the simplest of ideas. "I don't think I need my powers to make you want me." She gestured to my lap and the bulge within it.

I had no time to be bashful. My need for her was dimmed only by the initial shock of her revelation and was returning with a vengeance.

"I know that there are men who lie with other men, but I am not one. And if I were, I could not with him." I nodded towards Collin. "He is my oldest friend."

She lay one of her hands on my thigh and the other on Collin's. "You are no longer humans. You need not concern yourselves with who you find pleasure with. You will live an eternity and to rob yourself of any pleasure in all that time would be a waste of what you've been given." Collin opened his mouth to protest and she lifted her hand to stop him. "However, you are new and I'm not one to push anyone into something they do not want. You may each take your time with me separately or choose to do it at the same but not touch each other. Whatever you want this night, I'm happy to give you." She leaned back to rest on her hands again, this time allowing her hair to fall back and expose her ample breasts. Her nipples reacted to their freedom, hardening like they were reaching for us. Her next words were spoken with that power back in her voice and filled my chest with a crushing need. "What happens in the room is for us three only."

I didn't know what Collin was contemplating or if he would hesitate. I leaned in to fill my mouth with her left nipple and find the weight of her full breast with my hand. She moaned, giving me the permission I needed to lose myself. I sucked as I ripped at my shirt, pulling my mouth away long enough to throw the garment into the room and return to taste at her mound. I felt Collin next to me, filling his mouth with her other breast and squeezing its fullness. She arched forward and her cries rolled down my back like a massaging hand. My fangs erupted, causing me to throw myself back and away.

"Don't stop," she begged. "You will not hurt me. You cannot. You do not have to be gentle with me." Only then did I fully realize the opportunity we'd been given. We would not break this female as she was not human. We could truly lose control and she would be able to handle our strength. Given our newness, she was more than likely stronger than us.

Since this was my first time with another vampire, I felt much like a virgin, venturing into something unknown but full of the possibility of new pleasures. But I possessed the carnal knowledge of one who had experienced intercourse enough to know what to do. This meant the nervousness that accompanies a virgin on their first night was not present to restrain me or dampen my excitement.

I tore at my trousers, freeing myself. Collin rose to his knees on the bed and did the same. For a moment, we paused. All of us were now not only nude, but did not have to hide what we were. The promises in the air were intoxicating, the options endless.

She slid her hands to each side of her, lowering her back onto the mattress to lay flat and waved for one of us to come to her. Collin obliged, until he was straddling her chest, a knee on each side of her. He leaned forward and growled into the room as she pulled the hard length of him into her mouth. He began to raise and drop his hips, moving in and out of her as she sucked. As friends, we had spoken of all things and I knew this was the first time a woman had pleasured him with her mouth. Until that moment, we had only thought this a lie and no woman would truly do such a thing. His cries told me that it was something to experience and then I was lost in my own want again.

I did not need to think about my next move. She opened her knees to each side, pulling the garnet satin off her and exposing the fiery hair that protected the place on a woman that held her true power. Moving to the bed, I crawled up to her, spreading her legs apart and sheathing myself with her in one thrust. Collin was just pulling out of her, so she was able to supply the air with her own scream of pleasure before her mouth was filled again. She moaned while she sucked and Collin's breath was quickening as I struggled to control my own pace inside of her.

He cried out with his release, every muscle within him quaking. She pushed him from her chest and grabbed onto my ass, squeezing my muscles, and almost pushing me over the edge. I froze, fighting to regain my hold and not wanting this experience to end. Collin came to her side, languishing against her and running his hand over her swollen breasts. She grabbed that hand and slid it down to a point within her hair that she knew well. Guiding his finger to move in a way she liked, he continued with the motion. I did not know at the time what she was teaching us, I only knew that it caused her to clench around the part of me within her heat. "Start slow and gentle," she whispered. "Then quicken when I tell you."

Collin followed her direction as she began to lick up his neck and suckle on his ear. He closed his eyes, the growls beginning in his throat again. I slowly moved out of her and back in as her muscles quivered around me. Collin's breath came out in sighs, his fingers continuing the slow circles requested. I knew my grip was weakening and I would soon lose myself. I increased my pace. "Faster," she sighed into his ear and his fingers followed their command. She slid her hands up her stomach to grasp her breasts, massaging her own body. The sight of a woman bringing herself pleasure, revealing in her own form, was heady. It pushed my sanity to its brink and my thrusts were fueled by a strength well beyond what I'd had as a mortal man. She moved her hips to meet my thrusts and Collin quicken his circles against that secret spot she'd shown us. She screamed only moments before I did. Her body gripped me with her orgasm and sent my own throbbing into release just as my vision was threatening to leave me.

I collapsed onto her in time to feel the last of her shaking. For moments, we all lay there and waited for our facilities to return to us.

Finally, Collin broke the silence. "Can a woman bring pleasure to herself as a man can?" His voice was above me. I raised up so I could see her response as I was also curious about this. She was smiling and clearly as satiated as us.

"They can," she revealed.

"Do they all know that?" I asked and felt a little foolish. The last thing I wanted was for this goddess before me to know just how inexperienced I was. While I was far from a virgin, I realized at that moment that I knew nothing about sex for women or anything beyond a male penetrating a female. I had a feeling that there were many more options to explore.

"I don't know," she answered. "I have taught many of the girls here. I want them to find pleasure for themselves and not only to be ways for men to find pleasure."

"But," Collin paused like he was deciding whether or not to ask, then continued. "Do women who are not whores know this? Do they do such a thing?"

The woman below us laughed again. Even without the magick it was a beautiful laugh, a sound I enjoyed. "I do not know. I do not talk to many women who are not in this business. I hope they do. I feel quite sad for them if they do not."

"What is your name?" I felt like a brute for not having asked this woman her name before we fell on her like beasts.

Until that moment, I thought her smile to be wonderful. But her previous grins were nothing compared to the one she gave me now. "Liadan. But you can call me Lia." She sat up. "Now, we have about an hour more until you need to leave and be indoors before the sun. So," she wrapped her hand around Collin's member and he sucked in air. "What would you like to do with it?"

20

That night, I laid in my bed and mourned quietly. I didn't want Collin to hear, question my grief and ask me to divulge what I was feeling. He had already fallen into sleep, but I was not so lucky. I was plagued with thoughts: thoughts of the man I'd killed, thoughts of the woman we'd used that night and thoughts of what could have been. I hated myself for finding such ecstasy only hours after I'd ended a man's life. More than that, I hated myself for finding pleasure in a woman while Diedre lay cold in the ground. Only a month before, she'd been murdered. I should have been grieving and finding her justice, not in a brothel. And what hurt the most was the knowledge that I wanted to return to Lia, have more of her and learn more about her.

I was a terrible son, a horrible friend, and the worst man to walk the Earth. I did not deserve to find any happiness. I did not desire to have a woman look at me in any way, let alone the way Lia had looked at me.

I rolled to face the wall, my back to the best friend any one could have and knew that one day I would need to tell him everything. He knew what had become of his sister, but not that we were discussing the break of her promise to Angus, not that she loved me and not that I had kissed her. He did not know that my kiss upon her lips is how those men knew that she was female, how she was made vulnerable to attack.

How would I ever tell him?

This as the thought haunting me as I fell to darkness for the day and the same thought that filled my consciousness when the next dusk brought me back.

Rolling back, I found my friend sitting up and smiling. "Hello, there." He stood and made a show of stretching himself out. "Is this not a glorious night?

"What are you babbling about?" I groaned. He grabbed, pulling me from the bed to stand and slapped a hand on each of my shoulders.

"We were taught the secrets of a woman last night, Rhys." He pumped his hands into the air like he'd found victory in a particularly hard battle. "We can bring woman to their knees with pleasure. They will worship us." I shook my head; only Collin would think such things.

I was glad that he was in such good spirits but resolved to sit him down some time that night and tell him the truth. Whatever it did to our friendship, I wanted it over. I could not carry the burden anymore and he deserved to know the truth about the man he shared this new existence with. If he forgave me then perhaps, I could forgive myself.

We followed our usual steps up to James' office for our nightly rations. Knocking did not result in the usual invitation to enter. We waited a minute or two and knocked again.

"Behind you," James spoke from our back, eliciting jumps from both of us. We turned to face our maker and saw he was already walking towards the shop. Following him, he led us to the front door and out into the night. For a moment I hesitated, filling my gaze with the spot on the sidewalk that we'd first seen Diedre. Then, I shook the memory away and met my maker outside.

"First," he commanded. "Well done on the assignment. He was found behind the warehouse. Most believe it to be a drunken accident but the men who needed to receive my message did and have already made arrangement to pay their debts."

"Second," he crossed his arms. "I understand that you met Lia last night."

I didn't know why but I saw a flash of unhappiness in James' eyes. While the reason he was unhappy was a mystery what I did know is that lying to James was futile. "We did," I answered.

"Normally, I would protest such a thing as she is very expensive," he held his hand up before I could apologize and argue ignorance of cost. "However, I also understand that you shared her which I appreciate. Just know that should you want her in the future, it will come from your own pockets. I have instructed Cassandra that any time I offer to pay in the future it is to be one of the common girls from the front room."

I could not comprehend someone talking about a person like they were property but knew better than to show James my disapproval. Had I not treated those girls like property every time I'd used them for my own release? I hung my head to look at the ground. "Of course," I conceded.

"Will we be getting blood this evening?" Collin asked. I tensed, awaiting James' response. I didn't want to anger him but also wanted to feed the hunger in my gut so we could go to work and I could eventually talk to Collin.

"No need for glasses tonight, boys." James continued before we could ask why we would not eat. The sternness in his voice was confusing. Had we angered him in some way? He held up a folded piece of paper and my heart sank. He was sending us after another man. "This is your last night off. I have been nothing but giving to you."

Collin and I looked at each other, hoping the other knew what our maker was talking about.

"These are the names and location of the men who killed your girl." He let go, allowing the paper to flutter to the ground. Instinctually, I reached for it, grasping it in my fist before it found the street. "You have the whole night to kill them and feast on their blood. Tomorrow night, you belong to me completely.

A quickly as he'd appeared he was gone and it was just Collin, me, the paper clutched in my fist and the promise of vengeance.

21

Four names presented themselves in sprawling script: Clive, Fletcher, George, Benjamin. Below that was an address not far from the church. I didn't know the exact location but knew it was an area that many avoided. We stared at the letters for a moment. Vibration filled every cell within me.

Collin had stopped breathing. Palpable energy vibrated off him, telling me that he was as shaken as I. Thoughts raced through my brain, thoughts of blood and brutality. Violently, a gust of wind burst around me, pushing at my body and running through my hair. Turning to Collin, I saw the space next to me was empty and took off with the same speed to follow my friend, not caring if we were seen.

The address provided seemingly arrived with only our thought. Stopping with the same intensity we'd began, we found ourselves on a corner. Collin tore the paper from my hand and read the words again. The sounds of revelry slammed against my ear drums, surrounding us. The sharp sound of breaking glass was followed by the roar of drunken men applauding something. We followed it to the kind of bar we would've never dared entered as men and had no need for now as immortal beings. It took us only seconds to see that the address of the bar matched the black letters on the nearly destroyed note.

Before he could enter, I clutched my friend's arm. "We have one chance; control yourself. If we are to have the time we want, we must find them and get them alone. Do not let emotion take this from us or put us at risk."

His barely perceptible nod was all I needed.

The chaos of the tavern erupted around us as we entered, moving with purpose and our heads down to the back of the room. A table in the rear was empty of men but full of garbage. It mattered not to us what was on the tabletop, only that it allowed us a vantage point. We each found a chair. Putting them with backs to the wall, we sat side by side with the massive crowd ahead of us.

The din of the packed room was deafening. I worked to control the sound in my ears and turn it down. While it no longer threatened to burst my eardrums, it was still too disordered to pick out single conversations. I worked on scanning faces instead of trying to pick out words. I knew that Collin was relying on me to find the attackers as he had not seen the men. The size of the crowd made it difficult, as did the fact that every man seemed to move about without pattern. Odors threatened to overwhelmed me. Mentally pushing back sound and smell, I fought to focus on each face. I knew this must be what it was like to be a predator, hiding in a bush, each muscle frozen, waiting for the lone prey and perfect moment to show itself.

As I look back to tell this tale, I cannot truthfully tell you if we waited seconds, minutes or hours. My mind only knows it didn't see my targets and then it did.

They were not together at first glance. I saw the man that held my left arm as Diedre was attacked. He was on the outside of the mass, spitting into a corner. I felt something inside me instinctually lash out at this man before I knew what was happening. He froze, only his head turning to lock eyes with mine. I nudged Collin and tilted my chin in the man's direction. There was no time to say anything as the man stood upright and walked towards our table. Whether it was my power or the universe aligning, a quarter of our prey was making his way to us and saving us the chase. My muscles tightened to a point that I feared they would snap when the man reached our table and spoke.

"Do I know you?" His voice rumbled in my chest and the scent that came off him told me he was diseased in some way. I fought the urge to pounce on him when I heard my friend next to me speak.

"What is your name?" Collin asked.

The man snorted like he may resist than answered simply, "Fletcher Graves. And you?"

Collin's power pushed against my side when he spoke again. "You do not know us, Fletcher. You believe we have just arrived to Glasgow this night, are very rich and very dumb. So, you will go get your friends Clive, George and Benjamin. You will allow us to buy you a round. When we leave, you four will follow us until we reach a secluded place and then you will jump us to steal our money."

Fletcher listened intently to Collin's words, his eye fixed upon my friend's the entire time. He didn't respond immediately, appearing to need a moment to process the direction. When the words registered, the bulk of a man stood up straight and laughed. "Thanks for the kind offer, young lads. I'll get three of my closest friends and return to take you up on those drinks. Welcome to our city."

Only when the brute lumbered away and into the crowd, did I relax. "Good thinking," I slapped Collin's back. Every nerve in me vibrated with anticipation. I silently lectured myself. Reminding my body and brain that we had a mission and that these men needed to be stopped. I cautioned myself not to act in impulse and ruin this one chance. I vowed to myself I would remain cool and collected. And it worked… for roughly a minute.

My resolution was shaken as I saw Fletcher return with his three companions. Only one truly held my rapt gaze. It was the rotted teeth that I saw first, and the night of Diedre's attack returned in achingly clarity in my mind's eye. As the four stood before the table, it was only him that I watched. The gravelly voice of my nightmares slid from that fetid mouth when he spoke. "I understand you lads have just reached town and are buying ale for anyone willing to tell you where to stay and where you may find work?"

Collin remained in the lead. "That is correct, Mr-" he both answered and asked.

"Call me Clive," Diedre's attacker responded, sticking out a bony hand. I managed to pull my gaze from his face to that skeletal extension and notice the greying of his thin skin. Illness and decay danced along all four of the men before us, but Clive's was the worst. Somehow, the knowledge that they'd not only soiled sweet Diedre but had done it with diseased bodies sent my rage to dangerous levels. Collin managed to wrap his hand around Clive's to shake and I was astounded by his ability to remain so calm.

Clive's hand ventured sideways into my view for a follow up shake, but I let it remain in the air until the man finally dropped it to his side. His brow furrowed and for a fleeting second, I thought he remember me, but he instead grabbed a chair from the side of the room and pulled it to sit in front of us. His three lackeys remained standing, behind and to the side of him, showing us that this greasy, long-haired hooligan was in charge.

Once we'd signaled the barkeeper and ordered a round, pretending to drink at the same pace but only touching the ale to our lips as we tipped the glass back. We need only remain silent and allow our prey to drink themselves into a stupor and regale us with their stories of the women they'd bedded and the amazing work they'd promise to get us. Only once did they ask a question of us, wanting to know where we'd travelled from and where we planned to end. We didn't lie, telling them the village we'd come from and the plans to go to the Americas. They laughed at that, insisting that we didn't want to go over the seas but would do better to stay here.

After the fourth round, Collin stated he was going to pay the barkeep and we would need to head to lodgings so we may rise early to find work.

The men promised to meet us outside the small church after breakfast and take us to the wharf where they would connect us to "very fruitful employment." When Collin returned to the table, he gave a small nod to me and I stood.

"Thank you for the company, gentlemen. We will see you in the morning."

With that, Collin and I made our way out of the tavern and into the dark night. We did not look behind us. We knew they would follow, even before their diseased smell hit the air around us. Everything in me screamed to turn and snarl at our would-be muggers but I knew I must control myself only a few more moments.

We were not far before a dark alley presented itself. Not a single sound floated up from the shadowed dead end. Collin stopped, pointing down it. "I think this is our turn," he spoke loudly into the darkness.

"Are you sure?" I asked. "You can't see the end. It could end in a wall for all we know."

"I'm sure it is," he responded. "If it isn't we can just come back to the street."

My friend made a show of stumbling down the path into the alley and I followed in the same theatrical way. Shadows enveloped us in a way that would have hidden even a human but made an immortal truly invisible. To our dismay, only three of the men crept down after us, one stayed at the street to watch. We had to postpone our revenge a minute longer, waiting patiently for our followers to squint into the dark and call their friend down to help solve the mystery of the disappearing travelers.

Finally, the four men reached the brick wall and we emerged from our spots to stand between them and their escape.

22

What we must have looked like to those four men in that moment I will never know but I saw the expressions that slid across their faces and knew it was only the beginning of their Hell.

"What do you two think yer doing?" Benjamin growled with a confidence that wasn't entirely showing on his face.

"We're bringing the punishment you deserve," Collin roared, leading to George and Benjamin backing into the wall itself, like they could push through it.

Clive stepped towards us, producing a knife and showing it to us with the certainty that it would send us running. Instead, I stepped closer to him. "Do you remember me?" The quiver I expected in my voice was not there; to the contrary, I felt like my nerves were on fire and the excitement building in me added a growl to my words.

"Should I?" He snapped back.

"You should. For it would be a shame for you to not know why you're about to die."

His laughter was a barking sound and it echoed off the alley walls. His friends joined his laugh and stepped forward to flank him. The confidence that Clive was projecting was making them feel safe and they were using his energy to rebuild their tough exteriors, falling back into to the vile habits of criminals.

"You may not remember me," I slowly closed the distance between us. "But, you'll surely remember the girl I was with, the girl you violated and murdered."

His eyes grew wide and the paleness I expected to cover him was instead a flush. "Ah yes," he snarled. "Now I know your face. You cowered and cried." He looked down then back up at me. "I don't know what made it better, that she fought or that she was untouched before I broke her in." His wildly beating heart was like a drumbeat in my ears. The memory of Dierdre's last moments did not shame him but thrilled him.

In a flash, my hand was around his throat and he was lifted into the air. His feet shot out chaotically, trying to find ground or connect with my body. Collin had thrown one man into the brick wall and the snap that filled the air assured me he was dead. Another screamed while the sounds of tearing flesh and wet gurgles hit my ears. I could not wrench my gaze from the man I held in the air to see what Collin was doing or if he needed assistance. My vision was only for the hideous creature I was desperate to bring suffering to. Something primal rose inside of me, begging for blood and meat.

When his movement began to slow and his heart beat threatened to cease, I dropped him into a pile at my feet. Taking only the briefest of moments to assess the scene around me, I found what used to be a man at the base of a wall, bent at an angle that nothing could survive. Another brute was under my friend, seizing as his throat was ripped into. The third would-be attacker was curled in a corner, crying and mumbling what sounded like a prayer. I'd no time to focus on the words because Clive was regaining consciousness and attempting to stand. I let my prey get to his feet, wavering and looking around for support from him gang. The realization that he was doomed showed on his face.

"The things you're feeling now," I snarled. "The hope that there is still a way out, the fear that this is truly how you'll die and the confusion about why this is happening to you? That's what Diedre was feeling." The growl in my words only spurred me on as it reminded me that I was no mere man but a beast.

I shot my fist into his chest and sent him into the wall behind him, only to swiftly follow him and press myself into him to stop his crumble to the ground. I wanted him to know what it felt like to be trapped between brick and death as Diedre had been. "This is for what her parents must live through." I grabbed one arm and snapped it, feeling nothing but elation when he screamed. "This is for the children she will never have." The crack from his other arm breaking did nothing to satiate my rage. "This is for her brother, who must live forever with her loss." My hand drove into his stomach, ripping through the skin and grabbing at his intestines to pull them out and let them spill forth. "And this is for her… and everything we could have been." I bit into his neck and pulled back, feeling it give way and allowing the hot blood to spray onto me. Only then, when the blood hit my mouth, was I pulled from my need for vengeance and reminded of my great gnawing hunger. I wrapped my mouth around the wound and drank deep.

While the blood I'd been drinking in glasses was delicious, it was like stale cider compared to what slid down my throat that night. It was sweet and I couldn't get enough. When there was nothing left, I stood and look down at the ruin of a man. I'm ashamed now to say that I did not see a human but only an empty pitcher of drink and wanted so much more of it.

Turning to find Collin, we locked eyes and I could see that he was having the same thirst as I. With three of the men dead, both of us focused on the whimpering man in the corner. He prayed to the heaven, hands clasped so tight that they were white. Odors of emptied bladder and bowel filled the air as we approached. He didn't acknowledge us but continued his pleading to his God for mercy and forgiveness. But it fell on deaf ears that night as we pounced. When we we're done with him, we moved to the first man that had died, the one folded in half.

Only when all four men had nothing left to offer us did we regain enough reasoning to flee the alley.

23

Stripping down at the river bank, we rinsed the remnants of the attack from our clothes and laid them out to dry. The water sparkled like jewels when we broke its surface to enter and wash. Waves against my skin were like caresses and pushing through the water massaged my dancing muscles. I'd never felt such sensations. Everything before this moment had been a muffled existence compared to what I experienced after a hunt and feeding. My spirit seemed to arch with sheer pleasure and release, as if it had finally been given what it craved.

Collin's smile was one of satiety and complete lack of shame. He was the cat with a belly full of canary, the happiest I'd seen him since Dierdre's death. My joy was heightened by the knowledge that he'd found a moment of peace at last.

We moved like this for what felt like hours, washing our bodies of the blood and languishing in our ecstasy. He broke the reverie, "I cannot believe I'm saying this, but I don't think I need a woman this night."

"Nor do I," I agreed. "I feel fulfilled in a way I never have."

"Aye," he nodded and laid on his back to float.

"The sun will rise soon," I sighed. "We must return to our rooms."

Collin groaned with disappointment, but I knew he could also feel its approach. We need to find shelter from its rays but also needed to get away from the river before someone found us bathing in such a way. With damp clothes on, we could walk back appearing as two drunkards who'd fallen into the water and we're stumbling home to face the consequences of such a night.

Once back in our rooms, we lay in the dark and listened to the sounds of vermin in the walls, the shifts changing, the breakfast being made upstairs and the city awaking.

"Rhys?" Despite whispering, Collin's voice was so loud in comparison to all the other sounds. I waited for the next question. "I know what we did was wrong, but I don't feel like it was. I would do it again."

I let that confession rest on the floor between us, pondering if he wanted reassurance or just to have said it aloud. I'd known him my whole life and knew he did not waste words. "Aye," I offered. "I would too."

I thought he was done but he surprised me with more. "I liked killing. I don't know if it is because it was them or because I truly enjoyed it."

It was so simply stated but so like my own thoughts that it startled me. He'd put into words my exact feelings in that moment that I felt somewhat comforted to not be alone in this. "Aye, I as well."

Silence then remained our companion until sleep overtook our fading rush.

As we enjoyed a dreamless slumber, a pedestrian stumbled across four bodies in an alleyway. The police knew these men well and had known it was only a matter of time before they turned on each other or tried to rob the wrong people. After the altercation, it was clear that stray dogs had fed on the dead or dying men to fill their empty bellies. The paper would print this story and warn the people of Glasgow to watch for packs of wild canines who may now have the taste for human flesh. Then, the case was closed and the men were being thrown in an incinerator to ensure their decaying bodies didn't spread whatever diseases they definitely had.

No one ever claimed their belongings. They had no money to leave behind to kin. They had not sites to visit or kin to grieve them. They were forgotten quickly and only two vampires would ever remember their names.

24

When we arose the next night, we went to James as if nothing had happened. We followed our nightly protocol: knocking, entering when told, standing before his desk and awaiting orders. While he scribbled and we waited, I glanced the newspaper and the headline proclaiming that four bodies had been found. I held my breath, certain we had been too sloppy and James would dole out our penance at the finish of his writing.

Instead, a rare smile crossed his face when he looked up. "How was it?" he asked.

Exchanging glances, I answered truthfully as I knew he could tell a lie. "Quick."

This brought out a laugh in our maker, surprising us both. "I can imagine. The first time I killed," his eyes seemed to drift away then return. "Well, I also did it too quick. I learned to savor the experience and be in the moment. I trust you feel grateful."

I'd felt many things since we'd hunted and ended the lives of the four men who would haunt my thoughts for eternity, but grateful was not one of the things I'd experienced. However, I knew James expected a certain response and was about to oblige when Collin took the cue.

"Quite grateful, sir." He managed to put a hint of gratitude in his voice making me glad he'd been the one to speak. "We thank you for the opportunity."

James was clearly pleased. "Well, you are welcome and you did well. The police believe it to be a brawl and a wild dog attack. They've already sent the bodies for destruction. I'm told you didn't go to the brothel. What did you do with the night?"

I answered. "We swam in the river and washed our clothes."

I was afraid he wouldn't believe we'd done nothing after such an experience. "Yes, good choice. The women would surely have noticed the results of the feeding."

His words struck me. What results of the feeding? I knew I'd felt differently but had I looked different as well? I scanned my body, looking for any change and found nothing. I thought back to the previous night, remembering the river and the sensations, our admittance that we wanted to do it again. If we'd had changes to our bodies or powers, we wouldn't have known as we didn't really test it. I wanted to ask him what he'd meant by that but knew that question James or showing any sign of ignorance was not wise.

If Collin was confused, he didn't show it. He asked James about our tasks for the night and our glasses. James scoffed. "After draining four men, I do not think you need blood tonight. You will work the machines. Two men were found stealing and dealt with. Get used to that basement. You'll be down there until I need something only you can do. I will see you tomorrow night."

My impulse was to be angry but in truth I was not hungry. He was right that I didn't need more blood after my fill the previous night. However, it didn't lessen the sting that I felt knowing that we'd be treated this way for however long it took us to save the money to leave. As we made our way to the machines, I realized that the promise of vengeance had been like a light at the end of a dark tunnel and it was now over. I had nothing to look forward to, no fire to keep me pushing ahead, no mission to focus my thoughts on those long hours in the factory. What did it say about me that I was disappointed that I'd already murdered four humans and could not hope to do it again? What did it mean for the future?

I'd become vampire to right a wrong that'd been wrought on an innocent girl. Now, those men lay cold and the joy I'd felt the night before was gone. Ultimately, I felt no release or reprieve from my sorrow. In truth, the weight in my chest seemed to grow heavier. What did I have to keep me going? What light did I walk towards in this very long, dark tunnel? Not even death could be a comfort to me as I would never die, only ask James for a glass of blood and what he would have of me – night after night, year after year, decade after decade.

As I began my work, I found my focus slowly sliding from my thoughts to my body. The work felt like little to me. My body was strong as a vampire but so much stronger that night. Within my periphery, Collin worked at the same incredible pace. I marveled in my ability and tested my potential when free to do so – finding an iron bar in the scrap pile and bending it into a circle only to return it to its original state. Was this the result of the feeding that James' had spoken of? I knew I had to get through that shift and into my room to speak with Collin and test my theory.

When the dawn approached and we ended our work, I followed a quiet Collin into my room. Only when the door was shut and we could whisper did I speak. "Are you stronger?" I asked.

"Aye," he answered. "What else do you reckon we can do?"

I stood before the mirror and called on the part of me that glamoured. First I saw my reflection shift into the more human looking version that I used when I left the building. Then, I dropped it to show the bright green eyes, shining hair and flawless skin of the vampire I now was.

"That's not new," Collin scoffed.

His laughter died when the reflection in the mirror shimmered to show his own face in the glass. He grabbed my shoulder to turn me his way and stared into his twin. "Lord Almighty Rhys," he gasped. "You even have the wee scar above my lip that faded when I was turned."

As I let his image drop from my face and returned to myself, I trembled with excitement. "What can you do?" I asked.

"I don't know. I mean, I can't really go testing my mind control on the boys at the machine. James would have my head before sunrise."

"True," I relented.

He balled his fists and punched one into the air. "I wish I could just bring the power to me. You know? Say 'come here' and it would come."

A squeak behind us pulled our attention from the moment and onto a small mouse in the corner of the room. Where he came from, I didn't know. In truth the whole building was infested with mice, rat and other creatures. We heard them scurrying about in the walls at all times. But this wee one had come into our room and seemed to be greeting us.

Collin's soft spot for animals had been present since birth so I wasn't surprised when he dropped to his knees and started to coax the rodent. "Hello there," he sounded as if he was speaking to a baby. "What are you doing in here? Are you lost or just need a friend? Come here and-" Whatever my friend was about to say, it died on his lips as the little grey thing ran to him and stopped at his knees.

"It's listening to you," I said in disbelief but then felt the warmth in the air that I knew was magick. "Collin, what were you thinking when you said 'come here'?"

He thought and answered. "I was thinking about how I could bring on my magicks."

"I think you have," I whispered for fear we'd be heard. "We haven't much time before dawn. Tell it to do something."

"Spin around," Collin said and the mouse turned in a circle then looked up at him. "Climb onto the bed," he instructed. The mouse scurried up the bed post and onto my mattress, turning to Collin and awaiting his next command. "Jump up," Collin asked and the mouse made no sound as it leapt upward and landed back on the blanketed top.

"You can control animals, Collin." My voice was filled with the wonder I was feeling. If this was a vampire power, I didn't know. I knew we should tell James but was starting to worry that he had too much control over us already. There was a part of me, even then, that told me to keep our maker at arm's length and not trust him. I didn't know who we could talk to about this but felt it was better to keep it between us for now.

"Send him away," I instructed and Collin did, telling the mouse to return to his family and be safe.

As we lay in bed that night, we both agreed that the human blood we'd drunk the night before had been the reason for our strength and the powers we seemed to possess. Collin admitted that he felt the same way about James, not wanting to share his new animal abilities just yet. If somehow the older vampire became aware, we could feign ignorance and state that we thought all vampires could do it.

We'd admitted to each other that we'd both felt the disappointment of avenging Diedre's death and not experiencing some form of complete healing because of it. We both still grieved for her and it was not diminished by our actions. And now we faced an eternity as James' servants.

It was that night that our desire to go to America became our only focus. We vowed to work quietly, remain humble in front of our maker, save our money and only spend when we absolutely had to. Since we did not need to eat, it was only women that we needed to use our humble earnings on. So, we promised to only go when our need was on the verge of being dangerous. Once we'd saved enough, we'd await an assignment outside of the factory and use the freedom to run. It would be the next night before James realized we hadn't returned and by then we'd be far from Glasgow.

The next night, our new strength and powers began to dwindle. The need for blood was back; the glass given to us by our maker did nothing to take the hunger away. As I worked the machines, I felt an itch under my skin as if it was alive and wanted to tear itself from my muscles to be free. My temper was short; any small thing would set me off. The cracking sound of a man dropping a bar caused me to punch a brick wall. The resulting mark in the stone should have raised some suspicions in the workers but they chose to ignore it and only made an obvious point to avoid me. For nearly two weeks, I fought the unpleasantness of the post-hunt detox and only found comfort in the fact that Collin also struggled. Our need to feed on fresh blood was like a constant screaming in our ears.

As the effects faded and I found new peace in our mediocrity, I vowed to never hunt again, never drink fresh blood again. As intoxicating as it had been, I knew to keep it going I must constantly kill and could not reconcile it in my heart. As the results of the hunt faded, so did the desire to satiate the beast I now knew lived within me. I locked that part of me away and began to wrestle with a question I'd been afraid to ask.

A month after the hunt, James gave us the night off. It was so unexpected that I questioned the motivation but was wary to press our luck. Collin headed straight for the brothel and I did not fault him for this. But on this night, I'd had only one need that I wanted met and it was for answers.

25

I knew the walk to the little church well and made my way there without thinking. I worried that its proximity to the tavern I hunted four men in would make it no longer feel like a refuge but was relieved to find the same calm wash over me that I was used to when seeing it. I stood at the bottom of the stairs, looking up at the door. Staring at its solidness, I pondered whether I deserved to walk thought that entryway. Did Collin and I deserve absolution or were we beyond any hope of goodness?

The creaking of the door was like an invitation as it was pulled inward and Father Thomas stood in its opening. My head hung so low that my feet were all I viewed on the walk up and into the quiet, sacred space. Only candlelight interrupted small pieces of the dark chapel. It was comforting to me, like the shadows could hide me and what I'd done. But I knew, if there was a God, he was quite aware of what I'd done and it could not be undone.

We sat in silence for minutes. Only the Father's heartbeat, breathing and birds sleeping in the rafters alluded to anything being in the church. It was I that finally spoke. "Are we damned?" I asked.

"In what way?" he responded, showing no shock from my query.

I cleared my tight throat. "Are we evil things? Do we belong to the Devil?" The vulnerability I felt with this open question was clear in my words.

Father Thomas inhaled deeply and let it out. "You were human. And now you are not." I opened my mouth, but he stopped me with a hand. "I mean that while you are not human now, you once were. Which means you were made in His image and therefore have His love. So, I believe all things that begin naturally have the ability and possibility of choosing the righteous path and therefore being entered into Heaven. He leaned forward, placing his hands on his knees. "Now, do we sometimes make mistakes and do evil things? Yes. But it is not all that you are."

"But," I started, then took a minute to gain courage and continued. "Are there acts so evil that it does become all you are?"

The priest crossed his arms across his chest, leaned back and looked up in thought. It was so much like an action I'd seen so many of the village men do – that my own father had done countless times – that it warmed my own chest. In that moment he felt so like a father that I desperately wanted his approval and his assurance that I was not a lost cause. "I do not think it so," he answered. "I think that if you truly have remorse over an act and truly ask for forgiveness, then it is yours to have. But," he looked at me, pausing to ensure I was listening. "If you continue to engage in evil acts and do not learn or grow from these things.... know that God can see into your hearts and your true thoughts."

Silence fell over us again. I contemplated asking to go into confessional, telling the priest the whole story, begging for absolution. But in truth, I was not fully remorseful for what we had done. I still believed that those men deserved death but wrestled with the knowledge that we'd been the ones to bring that sentence.

Father Thomas spoke instead. "You may feel that you balance the scales by answering violence with violence or death with death but in the end, I think you will find that nothing will truly make it right. Now you carry the weight of vengeance on top of the grief of loss. Try to learn from this and use your eternity, strength and gifts for good, not evil. I think you will find that it sits with you much better."

Then he stood and left me in the chapel to understand the meaning of his words. While I wouldn't comprehend their full meaning for a century, I knew that night that he was aware of what we'd done and was going to keep that secret for us.

26

I spent another hour in that chapel, rolling around in my head all the things that had happened from the moment I'd left my village until now. I wondered about the life I would've had if I'd said yes to Diedre at that well. She'd be alive, my parents happy and my life would include the warmth of the sun. But I also knew it was pointless to ponder such things. My desire for freedom had been too strong and I would've eventually left. Does that mean that all our futures are set and our destiny cannot be changed?

I wondered what kind of God would have created a destiny for Deidre with such darkness and pain in the short time she'd had on this Earth.

When my thoughts became too dark, too abstract and unanswerable, I stood and stormed out of the chapel. The energy inside me felt larger than my physical body. I couldn't have named all the emotions that swirled inside me at that time but anger, sadness and hopeless were in the mix. I needed desperately for the peace that I'd sought in the church and hadn't found.

The brothel was uncharacteristically calm that night. I heard Collin somewhere in the rooms and found a small amount of rest with the knowledge he was safe somewhere, finding his own form of brief reprieve from our current circumstance.

Lia emerged from the backroom as if I'd called her and she answered. A sort-of understanding filled her eyes when they met mine. The subtle nod of her head led me back into her chambers without a word. Her presence was at my back, assuring me she followed.

Heaviness overcame me and drew me to my knees on the carpet as we entered. She shut the door behind me and drew me into her arms. She was so much stronger than I and the knowledge of it brought about a feeling of safety.

Weeping felt like taking in oxygen after being smothered. My sobs echoed in the room. She rocked me, gentle shushing into my ear and whispering that she would hold me for as long as I needed.

When my energy was gone and my sadness dried upon my skin, she stood to find a basin and fill it with water. I laid onto my back on the carpet, exhausted from the grief and could not have stopped her even if I'd wanted to. She washed the remnants of my blood tears and started to answer questions without them being spoken.

"You will find solace someday in the knowledge of eternity but only with a purpose. You had a reason to go on, an aim to reach but now you have accomplished it. You question your function in this world and see forever as a burden, not a gift. You find yourself the puppet of another and cannot swallow the idea of that being your new unending existence. You feel trapped and foolish for allowing yourself to be put into this position. How can you ever be free? You think about death as your only exit but worry about what lies on the other side of death while knowing that it may be better than what lies before you now."

I stared up at her, her face framed by the waterfall of ruby hair that fell to each side of my face while she spoke. Her emerald eyes were so like my own, yet she seemed somehow ethereal. This fantastical creature washed me as a servant would a master and spoke truths from my own mind.

She locked her gaze onto mine. "You must find a purpose, Rhys. It's the only thing to keep you sane. Find a reason to continue and picture it so well in your mind that you feel you may touch it. Some nights it will seem so close and other nights you will worry that it will never be reality, but you must hold tight. I have seen many vampires lose their grip when they have nothing to want for."

I sat up and she continued to stare into me. "Some of us are well and truly stuck but you mustn't allow yourself to be one. Play the game you must to keep moving forward. And when the time comes, take it and be free."

How did she know so much?

"While you bide your time," she stood and returned the basin. "You are safe here."

"I thank you," was all I could muster to meet her kindness. "Let me pay you for your time."

She laughed and that tinkling bell was back in her voice. "You'll do no such thing. Friends do not charge for friendship."

The smile that crossed my face was both a shock in the circumstances and quite genuine. "Friend," I grinned. "I like that."

"So do I," she answered. "Lovers and enemies are quite easy to make but we do not get many true friends, even when we have an eternity to find them."

A knock at the door ended our conversation and Collin peeked his head in. "Put on your pants, Rhys. We need to get back."

"Was just coming to find you," I lied.

With a kiss on her cheek, I said my farewell to Lia and followed Collin to our small room in the factory. As we lay and awaited slumber, I thought about what Father Thomas had said, then what Lia had said. I needed a purpose and it should be one for good.

"Collin," I prodded to see if he was still awake. He answered with a grunt, so I continued. "We must get away from here, focus again on our trip to the new world. When we are there, I wish to help people. Let's open a business such as this and employ those who need it most- those with no home, no family, no hope. We will be kind to them."

"Aye," he responded. "I like that, Rhys. We'll call it Argyll & Selkirk."

We calculated until dawn, making plans for what we could save and how long we felt it would take. If we saved the brothel for only when we truly needed it and chose girls who were less expensive, we felt we could be gone in a mere ten years. For someone whose life had no end date, we felt a decade was like a blink of an eye. A renewed hope filled me.

Ten years until I could be free and fulfill our destinies of helping victims of unfortunate circumstance.

27

April 1915

It was not ten years like we'd foolishly planned in our early days of existence.

With the small amount that we were paid for our work, the rising costs of things and our vampire libidos, we found ourselves squirreling away a tiny sum only to need it for both of us to find release. We were forbidden to touch a woman outside of the brothel, to find free pleasure, so we were forced to spend our wages on women. They were the only thing we had outside of James' tasks for us and we often found the idea of spending what we had preferable to saving for a trip we were starting to realize would never happen and suffering the pains of unmet lust. So, much like you may find momentary reprieve from your life in a glass of wine or a chocolate cake – even though you know you shouldn't – we often went back to the one joy we had and gave our coins to the ladies of the night.

For the purpose of this journal, there is no need to go into great detail about my existence from 1807 to 1915. It was the same – work, sleep and the occasional visit to the whorehouse. I can give you a brief summary of that century.

With James, we spent much of our time working the machines. While the technology changed, the need for fabrics did not. We continued to work his factory and produce very costly items for James to sell while making only a fraction. The company was presented as being handed down from son to son to son with the exterior changing to match the growing city and the storefront adapting to the times but the basement remaining much the same. While the men who worked at our sides came and went, they were the same type of worker – quiet and unquestioning. Only Collin and I remained the same.

The business of female companionship also adapted to the era it found itself in. As the 1800s turned into the 1900s, the business of pleasure had to be more discreet. The brothel would go through managers like undergarments, being called a gentlemen's parlor or cigar club but the idea was always the same. The women were now pretending to be serving the men or making drinks or being companions for the evening but always ended up in their rooms. Lia remained in the establishment. At first, she would be presented to the new person in charge as a new hire and then mesmerize them to not notice her lack of aging. The girls came and went so fast they would not be any wiser. Eventually Lia bought the business herself and stopped taking clients.

Except for me, of course.

Collin liked the variety. He would sometimes grow fond of a girl and pay her for several visits but inevitably, he would grow bored and choose a new one, always leaving the previous girl heartbroken.

But I stayed with Lia. I found comfort in not having to hide what I was. I found comfort in the familiarity of her. The nights of passion were never lacking. They varied from lovemaking to physical exercise and were always what we needed in the moment. Over the years, it'd become like a dance. We knew each other and our bodies so well that often we didn't need to speak our desires.

Some nights, we'd only talk. We spoke of our homelands and what we'd thought Glasgow would be like. We talked of business and she would often use me to explore ideas for growth, ways to attract new and valuable clientele. She wanted her girls to be treated well and looked to bring in exclusive customers who were high quality. When she took over, the instances of abuse almost disappeared. A few times, I would need to help a man out of the establishment and make it clear he would not be welcomed back.

Lia and I had created something deeper and more precious than romantic love. We'd grown our friendship into an unbreakable sort of bonding, finding a complete acceptance and sanctuary in each other. She knew things about me that I never could have divulged to Collin. After 50 years or so, she divulged to me that she was turned against her will as a means for money. A vampire came across her in her village and was taken by her beauty. He knew what someone who looked like her could fetch, especially if she could take abuse and be an endless supply. He turned her and took her in the night. She left behind a 4-year-old son and 8-year-old daughter. She'd told me once that my stories of boyhood reminded her greatly of her own boy. He'd had a wild streak and had wanted a life of grandeur. Her daughter had been more reflective in nature, wanting to be in the quiet of a field staring at the clouds and who told stories of her own making that would rival the greatest authors. She spoke of them infrequently so when she did, I remained silent and let her speak, then wiped away her blood tears when she was done. And, in our way, we would move on and pretend the stories of now dead children hadn't been told.

As much I know about her, I never did hear the names of that little boy and little girl.

Collin and I continued to visit the church. Not long after the night we'd killed Diedre's murderers, Father Thomas would take on a 20-year-old apprentice named Father Michael. He was trained in the religion, the services, the city, and us. Father Michael accepted us like he'd always known vampires existed and truly treated everyone as equals. It was

Father Michael who painstakingly taught Collin and me to read and write. When Father Thomas died in 1830, we wept crimson tears as they loaded him onto a cart to be brought to his home village. Father Michael would bring in his own apprentice in 1846, a young man named Fergus. As his teacher had, Fergus would eventually learn of our true nature. He was quite nervous around us at first, needing a few years to warm up to the men who only visited at night. By the time Father Michael passed away in 1867 and Father Fergus took over the church, he would look forward to our visits and ask many questions about us. He was a man of research. Looking back now, Father Fergus would have loved the internet and all that knowledge at his fingertips.

Father Fergus' apprentice came in 1907. His name was Alden. Like many of the apprentices before him, he was barely out of his teens. But unlike all that came before him, he did not need to be introduced to vampires. Fergus would tell me one night that Alden was not like the other priests, who went into the priesthood to fight a theoretical darkness but joined after facing darkness at a young age. The exact story would be up to him to tell me some day if he was ready, but he knew of vampires and would have no issue with us visiting if Father Fergus assured him, we meant no harm. I would instantly adore this new priest. When talking to him, I sometimes forgot I was more than a century old and would feel 23 again. He felt like an old friend.

Father Fergus was showing signs of a diseased mind months before he was gently removed from his position at the church. Father Alden had done so much in the previous years to help Father Fergus maintain his position and hide his worsening forgetfulness. But when he walked into a parishioner's home asking for his mother so he may get dressed for school, we all knew it was time for him to be taken somewhere to finish his days in peace and with supervision. The carriage came for him in the day, so Collin and I were unable to say goodbye. We had told him the night before that we loved him and Father Alden told us that he remembered our conversation but I knew it to be a sweet lie.

Alden was only 28 when he was asked to take over, so young for such a responsibility, but he was determined to fill the very big shoes left for him. It was the same year his old village would fall to smallpox and the lone survivor - his sister Nettie - would arrive to stay with him.

While I felt for the young girl and respected her brother greatly, her arrival barely registered. It coincided with a time when I was lost and a kind of depression had taken hold. While I found solace in my time with Lia and my pre-dawn talks with Collin, I was growing spiritually weary. A century of the same routine, the same machines, the same people, the same unreachable dream and the same room to sleep in was becoming terrifyingly similar to my idea of Hell.

Something needed to change soon or I was going to walk into the sun and hope that, whether Heaven or Hell, whatever lay beyond was just different.

28

It had been three weeks since we were allowed out of the factory. I knew I should go see Father Alden and officially meet his sister. He'd spoken with such joy about her coming while also showing great sorrow for the loss of his parents and their village. Small pox and fevers were tearing through the lands and taking human life at a staggering rate. I knew I was blessed to not be susceptible to such medical horrors but my compassion for life was slipping away and I found myself faking concern when humans spoke of such things.

The need for release had been building in me, consuming my every thought and I told myself that I would sake my thirst this night with Lia then do the right thing and see Father Alden after, if there was time, and if there wasn't then I would go at next opportunity. Even as I thought it, I knew that the next night of freedom could be a week later or a month, depending on James' whim. Collin kept pace with me, caring not about Alden and his sister and only thinking with his prick. If he was in as bad a mood as I, he did not let it show. He burst through the doors of the salon with little decorum, wrapping his arm around the nearest girl and picking her up. She was squealing with delight as he carried her up the stairs and to whatever room he'd choose. Knowing him, her hand was already up her skirts, showing her everything he'd been taught in the last hundred years.

I found Lia in her back room, counting money and writing sums into her books with her tight, tidy script. I knew to wait until she'd finished as she was easy to distract and would be frustrated to lose count. If I frustrated her, I ran the risk of not getting what I needed from her. So, as trained, I stood in front of her little desk while she counted twice and wrote it all in.

When she looked up from her completed task, her smile was genuine. "I was afraid you'd found another girl." While I knew we were not human, I rarely glanced at myself in the mirror. It still amazed me that she looked and sounded the same after all these years. I didn't really notice it with James or Collin since I saw them daily but with her, I would go weeks, only to return to the same lovely skin, garnet hair, verdant eyes and melodic voice. I found solace in that – the sameness of her.

There was a safety in loving someone that could never die.

"James would not allow us out," I answered like she should have already known that. "If he had, you'd be my first stop." I went to her, bowing dramatically and looking up sheepishly. "But I dreamed of you."

"Of course," she giggled. "I'll pretend that's true because it's sweet and nice to hear."

I took each hand and she rose to lay a light kiss on my lips.

The first night I'd met her, when she presented herself to us in that grand ruby bed, she'd seemed bigger than life. But I would learn the next time I saw her, that she was small. The top of her head stopped inches below my chin, making it easy for her to lay her cheek against my quiet chest as we stood. It was one of my favorite things she did, lay her ear against my sternum and wrap her slim arms around me. The strength in her hug was always more than that tiny body should be able to conjure, like she was trying to meld us together. When she stepped out and looked up at me, her eyes held the question of what I would need that night.

I answered that question by lifting her up and feeding greedily with my mouth on hers.

She'd told me often that she was raised in the woods, often running through the tress with no more than a shift, barefoot and loving the feel of nature around her. When she told me stories of her youth, I'd often joked that I think she may be a fairy and she answered the same, "Perhaps I am."

When she wrapped her legs around me, I could feel that she had nothing under her simple dress and her womanhood was there for me to take. I turned towards the wall of the bedroom, taking great strides until her back was against the solidness of it and braced. Letting go of her back, I pulled at my trousers and let them fall to the ground. She broke the kiss to pull down the shoulder of her dress and expose the milky breasts that I could draw from memory. I made quick work of my shirt to press my skin against hers and continue that ravenous kiss. When I shifted to find my destination inside her warmth, I growled without breaking that desperate dance of our tongues. She moved expertly, gliding herself over me to bring us both to climax simultaneously. As the waves subsided, we broke into a comfortable laughter.

"Forgive me," I grumbled into her chest. "I was in such need."

She playfully slapped my back. "Don't you say a word, Rhys. You've nothing to be forgiven for. We both had our pleasure. Whether it comes fast or slow should matter not." She wiggled so I would place her down on her feet and I pulled my trousers back up as she sat on the end on the bed, patting the spot at her side. "Now, tell me how you've been."

The sigh that escaped me was stronger than I meant it to be. "It's the same, Lia. The same machines to make the same linens to sell to the same customers after I drink the same blood given to me by the same man and before I sleep in the same room by the same person." I stood and paced the room. "How do you do it? The same building, the same bed, the same business. How do you do it without going insane?" I looked at her. "I think I may go mad."

"Simply put?" she asked and I nodded. "You focus on what is not the same." I waited for a continuation, but she sat quietly, waiting for me to speak.

"I do not understand," I finally admitted.

"The stars are different each night. The smells in the air change, as well as the sounds. New people come into the city with stories of other cities. Those we became used to will die or leave. Even our time together is not the same. We tell new things to each other." She opened her hands. "This conversation has never been had." She gestured for me to return to the spot by her side. "Focus on those differences and you will start to find wonder again in our long existence." She turned to take my face in her hands and made me look into her gaze. "Over the centuries, I have seen too many of our kind lose their minds from what you speak of. Please, Rhys. Do not head down this path. I could not bear it if I lost you."

"How old are you?" I'd never asked her directly. She'd hinted at a time long before my own but had never told me actual numbers. She'd known when I was made vampire and how old I'd been in human years, but I knew nothing about her time on this planet.

Her laughter was filled with the sound of tinkling bells and a feeling of bliss washed over me. "A girl never tells her true age." I knew three things in that moment: she would never divulge her age to me, I would never again ask and she was much older than I'd guessed.

When her power over me shifted from bliss to lust again, I'd forgotten about my line of questioning or my encroaching depression. All I could think of was losing myself inside her and I vowed this time it would last much longer.

29

To my relief, we did have time left in the night to see Alden and properly welcome his sister. Collin was pulling on his trousers and rushing down the stairs as I was calling his name. He looked guilty and though I didn't want to waste the time, I had to ask. "What did you do?"

He waited until he could whisper in my ear to answer. "She's just told me she loves me and wants to be my wife."

Slapping his back, my laugh was one that came from my core and hurt a little with its intensity.

"It's not funny, Rhys. I liked that one but now I have to choose another."

This just made me laugh hard enough that I had to escape into the street before the crimson tears gave me away as not human. He followed me, obviously annoyed by my lack of empathy for his plight. Angrily, he stomped towards the church and made a point to not look back at me. To his dismay, the sight of a vampire having a temper tantrum only increased the hilarity of the situation and I could barely remain upright as I followed him and continued my laughing.

The walk was the exercise I needed to calm so by the time we reached the now familiar building, I'd stopped my guffawing. "Let's just get this over with," Collin snipped, still upset with me and over the loss of his current favorite girl. He led the way up the stairs and into the chapel while I wiped away my tears and composed myself.

Father Alden was inside the room and seated in a pew halfway back from the pulpit. Next to him was a girl. Her brown hair was a mass of wild waves and obscured any semblance of shoulder or head. It didn't appear to have been combed recently, if ever. I'd not often seen a woman who didn't care for her tresses like a cherished accessory. But it wasn't the hair that held my attention, instead it was a sense in the air.

A fragrance filled the small room and was something new. The usual incense of the church was present, but a new scent was mixed in and just subtle enough that I couldn't place it. And it had a chill to it, like the smell was accompanied by a breeze from an open window on a winter's night. It emanated from this girl, I was sure of it, but in 100 years I hadn't come across it before.

"Boys," Alden bellowed when he stood, turned to us and opened his arms. Despite our vast age difference, the Father always called us boys, as all the Fathers before him had. He shimmied past what must have been his sister to come out and up to us. The usual embrace and back slaps were followed by him turning to the unmoving girl.

"Nettie?"

She stood, head bowed and exited the pew. When she turned, it was with a grace that must have come from years of dance but at the same time felt otherworldly. Her plain brown dress was clearly handmade and bare feet peek out as she floated towards us with the softest of foot falls. Brown eyes met ours when she reached us and raised her gaze. The hair and eyes matched her brother's but that is where the similarities ended. Alden's jaw was strong and chiseled with cheekbones to match on each side of a wide nose. His sister was the opposite with soft features surrounding a sharp, aquiline nose. That mass of chestnut waves had been pulled back and knotted purposefully in places to keep it off her face. As she approached, that chilled perfume increased and lifted off her skin in ebbs and flows.

"What are you?" The words slipped from my mouth before I knew I'd formed them. It was terribly rude, but it could not be taken back.

Her pupils reacted to the question by growing to almost swallow her chocolate irises with their blackness. I heard her stop breathing and her heartbeat raced. She looked to her brother in fear and he calmed her with a hand on her shoulder. "I thought they may sense it," he assured her. "And, if I worried about them knowing, I would not have allowed you to meet."

A fine trembling had spread across her limbs and I felt immediate regret for frightening her while still not understanding what was happening. I froze in an attempt to not scare her any further, like you may do when you come across a deer in the woods and want it to know you will not hurt it.

Alden motioned for us to follow to his chambers, a small office behind the dais. As we crossed over the stage, past the pulpit and large crucifix, I had a moment of worry that I should not be near such holy items but quickly pushed those thoughts aside. If God were going to cast me down for being in a holy place, he would have long before this moment.

Once in the office, Collin and I sat on the small couch. Alden pulled two chairs over to face us and awaited his sister to sit in one before he sat in the other. "What I am about to tell you must stay with us," he folded his hand together in front of his stomach. "I would never tell anyone about your existence, never put you at risk." He looked to the girl, "And I must insist you do the same for her."

"Of course, Father." It was Collin who answered. I had still been robbed of speech by confusion and worry about what we were about to hear. She was not a vampire, I knew that for certain. While we didn't meet many, we'd met enough to now be able to spot them. Her brother was human, this was one other fact I was certain of.

The priest tapped his sister's leg, communicating in a way that only siblings can. She took a deep breath and let it out. With a small, soft voice that contradicted the wild energy radiating off her she spoke and changed my reality. "I'm a witch."

30

Collin bolted up to his feet. "A what?" Fear slithered off him and his discomfortable was palpable.

She stood in tandem, fists at her side and shoulders squared. "How dare you? You know what you are and you have the nerve to look at me like that?" She crossed her arms. "Let me guess, you've been warned to stay away from witches, that they're grotesque things that steal babies and make men unfaithful to their wives?"

This stopped any words that Collin may have foolishly been thinking to say. That was exactly what we'd been warned about in the village. We'd heard tales of women in the woods who made potions with the hearts of animals and the moss of trees, using these spells to curse towns and bring illness. Whenever crops failed or a sheep died, it was always blamed on witchcraft. Looking back, I'm ashamed in what we used to believe. And considering that I was now one of the nightmare creatures we used to warn children about and discuss in the shadows of taverns, I knew most of our gossiping was based on fiction.

Collin sat. "You're right," he wisely conceded. "I'm sorry." I don't think I'd ever heard Collin apologize to anyone outside his kin.

Nettie also sat and it appeared as if a delicate truce had been established. She continued reluctantly, "Witches are born, you ninny. It runs in the blood but some of us are born into a family that, to their knowledge, never had a witch before. We can teach some things and some women have a knack for magick but for the real work, you must be born with the abilities."

So many questions filled my head. I wanted to know what she could do, if only women were witches, if she knew what we were without being told, how many witches were out there and more- but knew to be silent. She waited to see if we would react poorly before she continued. "I've always been different. Only when my magick began to show did I understand. When my ma found out, she began to keep me in the house, only taking me into the woods in the night to help me control it all."

Alden picked up the narrative. "Our mother's sister had been a witch and was burned at the stake for it. So, understandably, she was scared for Nettie. But she did her best to help her learn and not make her feel ashamed. When I was 18 and Nettie 13, my mother told me the truth. It was then that I joined the church."

"Why?" I blurted out. It seemed such an odd response to him finding out his sister was a witch. Did he want to stop her?

"To protect her," he answered. "In our village, and many others, it is the local church that finds and punishes witches. While public execution may no longer happen, I assure you that killing a witch is still done quietly and quickly in many towns and what they call a trial is just a formality. The accused woman is doomed and often not even really a witch. I knew that being in the clergy, I could keep her safe. No one suspects a priest's family and if they did, I'd be the first to hear of it. Now," he raised his hand to stop my next question. "Do not think I do not believe in God or have faith and that my days are a charade. I do have a great deal of faith and believe in what I do. It is an extra reward that I was able to also protect Nettie." He looked to her and his love for her was evident. "I don't believe witches are from the Devil," he looked at us. "Just as I do not believe vampires are. I think both of your kind can choose to do good and both of your kind have some bad people in your flocks."

I pondered that. Nettie, more than myself, had no say in what she was. She was truly born this way and at the mercy of those who did not understand her. I felt a great sadness for her, having to hide what she was from such a young age. "Your mother sounds like a wonderful and strong woman."

"She was," Nettie answered and discreetly wiped a tear from her eye. "But she is not here and my brother is the last of my family. So, I have come here until I know what to do next. I cannot marry as I will not pass this on and my brother is married to the church. So," she squared her shoulders, "the magick dies with us."

Again, I was speechless. I found a profound respect for her strength to sacrifice love and children to save next in her line from danger. But at the same time, I found a bleakness in the thought of it. While my existence was not everything I'd dreamed it would be, at least I had the comfort of physical release and a love with Lia that put no one in harm's way. Nettie did not have that option as anyone connected to her would be at risk.

"Do not pity me," she spoke to my thoughts. "I have chosen this and it's what is right."

I raised my hands in surrender. "I'm sorry. I cannot help what I feel." Lowering my hands, I attempted one of my myriad of queries. "Is there no sanctuary for your kind? A place where witches can go?"

She arched an eyebrow. "Is there no such place for vampires to go be safe?"

"Good point," I relented.

"And," she cocked her head to the side. "There are many more of you than us for we are a dying breed and not immortal."

I wanted to continue the questions, but Alden stopped me. "I must ask one more thing of you two before you go."

Only then did I noticed the weight of the approaching sun and know we must get back. "Yes?"

"If something should happen to me," he laid his hand over his heart. "Please keep her safe. We have no one else we can trust."

"Of course," I answered without thinking. So many priests over the years had kept our secret, allowed us sanctuary in this place and protected us. While I never wanted anything to take Alden from his sister, if it did, I could offer this to him as a payment for all those years.

She stood. "Well then," she outreached her hand for me to shake. "I consider you family and will treat you as thus, Uncle Rhys."

31

It was another month before we were allowed to leave the factory. We didn't see James much. At this point, he'd trusted us enough to go into his office, pour only one glass each and then get to work. We knew well the lengths that James would go to when he wanted to make a point. Whether he would be able to tell if we took more blood or didn't work one night, we didn't want to find out. He had such a hold on us that merely the fear of his wrath kept us in line.

I spent much time thinking of Alden and Nettie. Their commitment to each other, the priest's mission to protect her and the idea that their bloodline died with them haunted me. Whether blood or not, Collin was my brother. And both of us would be the end of our bloodlines. I found such similarities between their bond and ours, it gave me comfort. I think it was the idea that our brotherhood was a very "human" thing and that we still held onto that human part of ourselves by having each other. I wanted so badly to go talk Alden and Nettie again. The factory seemed more like a prison than ever.

At this time, the first World War was raging, and the fighting pulled many Scottish men away from the country and work. We were expected to do more than ever to make up for the dwindling workforce. Between the war and the increasing prevalence of tuberculosis and plagues, women would start working with metals to make the supplies needed. While James refused to put women in his basement, we heard from others that they were working many of the factories in Glasgow.

When I wasn't thinking of Alden and Nettie, my thoughts were of Lia. I wondered what she was doing and could muster the sound of her laugh in my mind. I looked forward to the time we could see each other. I wanted to tell her about Nettie and learn what she knew of witches. I wanted to hear what she may have heard about the war from the men who visited the gentleman's club.

If Collin thought of anyone I didn't know. All he spoke of in this time was his renewed desire to go to America.

When we were reticently given our next night off, I was torn between the church and Lia's. I equally desired both. But my inner battle was stifled by shock when I reach the main street. I'd known that more workers were coming to Glasgow in light of the war but couldn't believe how quickly the city that I knew so well was changing.

In response to the masses flocking our city, the rents were being increased on housing, leading many to choose the streets. The sleeping bodies in alleyways and on corners reminded me of Collin and I when we'd first arrived. I could vividly remember what it felt like to have no way to get our next meal and no bed to sleep upon. While seeing someone live on the street was not new, in 1915 the numbers were increasing daily.

As we walked to the church, we talked about how our night would play out. Collin and I agreed to see the priest first with the intention of a quick visit, then to finish our night with women. We wanted to be closer to the factory at the end of the night, instead of risking the sunrise further away as we had a month prior. It felt like the wiser way to use our night.

It's funny how you don't know when you're going into a series of events that will change your life forever. You just go about your plans like you have any control over fate and think these next few hours will be ordinary, only to look back later and know you were fools.

32

We found Father Alden and Nettie sitting outside on the steps. June was approaching and the air held the promise of summer. The priest was visibly tired. His sister was twirling a flower in her fingers quietly while he enjoyed the moment of rest. They looked up as we came upon them and their smiles were genuine.

"Father," I asked. "Are you well?"

"Oh, I'm fine," he answered. "We've had more parishioners then ever lately. More people in the city, more prayers for men at war, more need for food and warmth. I'm just recovering from a long day is all."

"Well," Collin jumped in. "We will not take up much of your time. We only wanted to see how you were."

"We've missed you," Nettie added. "Can you not come more often?"

"We canna," I answered. "Though we wish we could. I must confess I have many questions for you. My curiosity has overtaken my thoughts recently."

"Can you write then?" She asked. "Send letters to us and we to you?"

Alden laid his hand on her back. "It is not safe," he answered, stealing my own thoughts. "If anyone should read the letters-"

"Do you not have mind control, then?" The question was abrupt and without concern for who would hear that it took me aback. "Tell the deliverer to never read the letters," she said as if she was telling someone to pick up what they had dropped.

Looking around, I ensured no one was nearby and answered as plainly as she'd asked. "I actually do but it's not as strong as you may think."

This brought a delighted chuckle from her. "It's the animal blood."

Alden gasped and jumped to his feet, grabbing his sister by the arm to pull her into the church. We followed, worried that his actions meant danger. When inside, he spun her to face him as we shut the heavy door. "Nettie. What are you thinking?"

I expected fear from the smaller sibling as he'd gotten quite rough with her and was clearly unhappy. Instead, she faced him with anger. "They've the right to know. You canna keep it from them. It's wrong."

"Keep what from us?" Now, I felt anger. It was obvious that Alden had told Nettie something that affected us yet not shared it with us. The betrayal stuck me like a dagger. He was one of the few people I believed would never lie to us, not even through omission.

His eyes darted between the three of us, the only human in the midst of vampires and a witch. I could his brain furiously calculating what his next action should be. His fatigue was evident and what may have ultimately pushed him to give up the fight.

He gestured to the pews and we sat, like pupils waiting for a lesson. He sat in the one before us, giving us his back. Nettie stayed standing behind us.

When he spoke, it was to the general room. "Every priest who has known you has passed your existence and story down. I know that on the night of the," he hesitated, not knowing how to say it. "-vengence, you felt more power and strength than ever before. I also know that it was weeks of agony after you hunted and went without the fresh blood. I know that as a vampire uses bottled blood or the blood of the ill, it can weaken their overall powers and strength. This is even more so for those that feed each day off animal blood and even more if it is bottled animal blood."

He was silent, letting us process what he'd said.

Continuing, he remained looking ahead. "Over decades or centuries, animal blood – let's say a single glass of cow blood from the butcher, would keep a vampire from going insane with blood lust but also make him weak among his kind and easy to control."

Again, he gave us the silence we needed to understand what he was divulging to us.

Nettie stepped forward and picked up with the story that was being told. "When vampires first roamed, they'd feed from humans and kill them; it was easier to murder in those times. As killing someone became harder, vampires realized they could live off the animals, but it came with the consequence of losing power. Over time, they didn't want to pay that price anymore, so they learned to feed off those who had too much ale or were not mentally sound so that the ramblings the next morning about a man who drinks blood was not taken seriously. And, for a long time, this was how it was. But as the times change, so must your kind adapt. But they all remember what different kinds of blood will do for a vampire."

I knew what they were saying without outright saying it but was struggling to piece it all together.

Alden turned to face us and continued. "Some vampires use that knowledge, and the fact that the younger ones don't know this, to their advantage."

Collin said what I'd been thinking. "James-"

"Shhh," Alden interrupted. "Do not say his name."

"If," I started. "We were given a single glass of old animal blood every day for over a century, our powers would be so weak that anyone could best us." Alden nodded so I continued. "But, if we were to get fresh blood, theoretically, would our powers return to full or is it too late?"

Alden bit his lower lip. I saw the way within his eyes. He didn't know what to say, struggling between honesty and what he'd been told to never reveal.

Nettie had made no such promise. "You are vampires," she answered. "You rebuild damage that would kill others and don't fear death. A night of fresh blood and you'd be finding what's lost."

Collin and I faced each other, trying to read our thoughts in our gazes.

Alden attempted to stop the plans we were formulating. "Boys, listen to me. If he knows that you know, he will not risk an uprising. He will kill you. Do you understand me?"

Concern filled every word he spoke and turned me back to him. "Do you know him?"

"No," Alden answered. "But each of us is told of him. He is not like you two. He does not show you his full nature and I pray you never see it. If half of what I have been told about him is true, you mustn't incur his anger or give him a reason to be rid of you."

"But Father," Collin scooted forward. "How do we just go on like before? Drink his offerings and allow ourselves to remain weak?"

"You must," Alden pleaded. "Every priest that has been where I am has searched for a way to free you from him with no answer. Even now, I continue to search but you must be patient."

"No," this was from Nettie. "Let me spell him so they may be freed."

Alden stood. "Absolutely not," he bellowed. "I shouldn't have even told you. You will not get involved. There is already a chance that he knows what you are. Let us not give him a reason to seek you out."

"Alden," she argued.

"Go to your chambers, Nettie." It was a sternness I'd never seen in the man; he was clearly upset and not to be argued with. I felt Nettie gathering her energy to fight only to decide to leave. We heard her door softly close a minute later and Alden continued. "Let me be clear. He cannot know that you know or he will have no more use for you and send you out into the sun, never to think of you again. He will find two more to make like you and do his dirty work. Please," he sat again. "Let me work on a way to free you. Forget what you've been told. Go back to your routine and do not do anything foolish. If not for me or for yourselves, for Nettie. She is now tied to you."

With that, he sighed in a mix of resignation and exhaustion then excused himself.

33

Once outside and a block away, we began to discuss what we'd learned. As we talked through it, it all began to make sense. We'd known how we felt after our one and only hunt. We'd known how it felt to go without that fresh blood. We'd seen our powers dwindle. But we'd been so focused on James' tasks, or next trip to the brothel or our talks of America that'd we'd never noticed what was right in front of us. The sameness of our nights had become like a hypnosis, sending us into a trance-like state of acceptance. And we'd been so naïve when we'd been turned, so grateful for the place to sleep and the work, so focused on avenging Deidre, that we'd never asked any questions.

Rage started a slow boil in my gut. How could I have been so blind? How could I have replaced one trapped existence for another. It was the village and my father's insistence that I fall into his plans for me all over again – only now it was Glasgow and James. I'd allowed over a hundred years to pass without ever standing up for myself.

Collin babbled next to me, expressing the same sentiments. Only he added one. "Let's just try it."

This pulled me back into the moment. "Try what?" I asked.

"Drinking from a drunkard," he answered. "A small amount, just to see the difference."

Freezing in place, I stared at him. "Are you mad?"

He matched me and stared back. "What?"

"James will know," I exclaimed. "What did Alden just say?"

"Think about it Rhys," my friend was giddy. "He's almost never there anymore. And when he is, his face is buried in papers. We're nothing but his dogs. He wouldn't notice if we came into his room walking on our hands."

I thought about it, half-swayed to his point. If we took only a small amount from someone who was lost to drink, perhaps we would have some of our power back. "I don't know."

Collin started to walk again and I followed as he continued his persuasion. "If something were to truly happen to Alden or Nettie or Lia and we needed to fight - we could not. Every other vampire is stronger than us."

This did make a good deal of sense. All these years I'd found solace in the fact that I was a strong, powerful vampire and it turned out, I really wasn't. In the world of vampires, I was a weakling. If someone I cared about was in danger and the opponent was one of my kind, I'd be bested in a fight.

"A small taste?" I asked.

"The tiniest," he promised. "And, this is a perfect time to find one."

And, he was right. Not long after we agreed, we glanced down an alleyway to find woman, sitting on the ground, back against the brick and snoring. The sound of her drunken breathing bounced around the alley and assured us that she'd had quite the night. We approached her as quiet as possible but it was not necessary. A rat ran up her arm and onto a nearby trash can without her so much as twitching.

There was a voice inside me screaming not to do this. She was helpless and alone. I knew I was crossing a line I could never return from. The other side of me, the beast that had been in hibernation for a century, pushed me to try. That beast reminded me that I was not a human and this was my nature.

My fangs erupted from my gums with the thought of biting her and her jugular leapt rhythmically from her neck. As I sank my teeth into her, she remained asleep. I had a brief hope that she was having nice dreams when the blood hit the back of my mouth and I was lost to the taste. Rolling down my throat, the hot essence of her brought an immediate rush of ecstasy. I fought the frenzy that rose within me and pulled back after two swallows. Collin lunged to do the same, pulling back after a moment to groan in pleasure.

My body screamed for more, watching the blood roll from our fang marks and become lost under her blouse. I wanted to lick it off her, wrap my mouth around her again and suck until there was nothing left of her. I cared not who she was or who would mourn her. Collin grabbed my arm and pulled me to the street. A high began rolling over me in waves, a high much different than the one before. The night we'd killed the men had been sheer rage and brutality, but this had been a simple feeding, with no fury to take away from the experience.

Without needing to speak, we made our way to the gentleman's club. I wanted nothing more than to take this newly fed beast into the bedroom with Lia and learn what I truly was capable of.

34

Lia was sprawled across her ruby bed like an offering of the richest pudding to a man who was starved. She bolted upright as I came into the room and slammed the door behind me. The sheets fell from her to reveal the pale, perfect form that I knew every inch of. Tearing at my shirt, I stalked towards her.

"Stop," the sound of her voice brought on her request, halting me in my tracks. She rose from the bed to pull on a robe and came to me. "You've fed, you stupid fool."

Her hold on me let go, causing me to stumble into her. She wrapped her arms around me and pulled me in, her ear against my chest. She whispered at a decibel only I'd register. "If he finds out, Rhys."

The lust that had threatened to consume me only seconds before was washed away by the awareness of how scared she was. "He won't know," I answered. "It was only a sip, only a brief taste."

"But, why?" she asked. "Why now after all this time?"

"Because I didn't know," I finished my previous planned path to the bed to sit and run my hands through my hair. "All this time he's be controlling me, keeping me weak, and I didn't know. How he must laugh when he thinks of the ignorant, farm boy he's using as his attack mutt."

I stood, crossing to the side and drove my fist into the wall, easily going through it and into the brick behind it. The fury I felt was edging on madness. It threatened to rob me of sight and my facilities.

Lia came behind me, pressing herself into my back and wrapping her arms around me. "You must be quiet, if he were to hear you."

"How would he?" I bellowed. "Everyone speaks of him like a boogeyman, in all places at one time, with ears all over and knowledge of all. He is only vampire, like us."

She caressed up and down my torso in an attempt to calm me. "He is not like us," she whispered. "He is ruthless, has not the heart that we do, does not care for anyone or anything. And, I worry about you speaking so freely here because," she paused. Her fear to continue made me suspicious. I'd already learned so much this night, was there more to know?

"Because, he comes here often."

I whirled and pushed her away. "What do you mean? Speak plainly."

"Your maker," I noticed no one used his name. "Used to own this business. Did from the time I first arrived until he sold it to me. As owner, he came and left as he pleased, taking whatever girl he pleased. He chose every manager and they were his unknowing eyes and ears. When they didn't fall in line, he rids himself of them and finds another." She turned to face the wall, unable to face me for the next. "His temper has gotten the best of him too many times and too many girls have been lost to his thirst and irritation. Some were very young. I've helped him get rid of too many bodies to ever find peace again." She faced me again. "I cannot lose you to him, Rhys. Cannot help him hide your lifeless corpse."

Darkness had taken the sparkle from the emerald eyes I cherished. Her light was what I loved so much about her and it was gone. I'd promised anything to bring that light back, but I wrestled with my anger and need to understand. Every priest I'd ever trusted in this city had kept secrets from me. Lia had kept secrets from me. The little pieces of happiness I'd found for myself in this horrid life had been lies. Could I trust anyone?

"Tell me all, Lia." I tried to keep the coldness out of my voice and failed. I didn't want to scare her but knew I must hear it all or risk leaving and never coming back. I knew myself well enough to know that continued betrayal may break something I couldn't repair. It was best to know it all and then try to reconstruct our friendship. But, another night of lying from her would be too much to take.

She dropped to the ground, legs tucked below her, garnet hair cascading around the now bare shoulders as the robe slipped down.

"He is my maker and my husband."

35

I don't think a single sentence has ever rocked me like that one did. She was in front of me on the floor but felt miles away. My vision swam and the blood in my stomach roiled. The energy that I'd planned to spend with lovemaking still boiled inside me. I wanted to rage, tear apart the room and bring the building down around me. I wanted to grab her and beg her to explain her omission in a way that made sense. What reason could there be for not divulging this to me in all those hours of telling stories and revealing our pasts? She'd told me of her children, her barefoot times in the woods, her mother, her little house and her dreams of helping girls through her business. How had she never mentioned that the man who held me captive was also her husband and the one to bring her into darkness?

I replayed the story of her turning in my head.

"You said a vampire came across you in your village, stole you in the night." I challenged her to unravel the web of lies.

"That is mostly true," she answered, still looking at the carpet.

"Well then try completely true this time," I snapped.

"It was an arranged marriage," she pulled back her shoulder and rallied her strength. When she looked up at me, I could see the shrewd business woman who was used to shutting down when giving men what they wanted. "I was promised to him by my father. My father had fallen for his English charm and believed him to be a noble man. When we married, he was 38 and I 16." Something flashed across her eyes, but she continued. "I was a mother 9 months later, still a child myself. He was cruel to me, but I knew nothing of marriage and believed this was a woman's lot. I loved being a mother and a home maker, took great pride in the food I made and the house I kept. He was not home much as he trapped animals to sell for their furs. When he was away, my mother would come to help with my daughter. Some of those times, I would escape into my beautiful forest and lose myself in the trees, talking to the birds and dancing for the deer." She stood, no longer cowering on the floor or abasing herself. She faced me without wavering, ready to face whatever reaction I had. "Several years later, I had my son. My father died and my mother lived with us to help. When he wasn't home, it was a rather lovely life and I was happy." She crossed to the closet, calmly pulling out a nightgown and allowing her robe to fall to the floor. As she covered her perfect body with the ivory silk, she kept up with the retelling of her history. "He'd been gone for so long that I thought he must have fallen prey to thieves or beasts and would not return. I sold dried herbs and baked breads for enough to get by and thanked the goddess that he would not return." She turned. "But, he did. One night, he came into the home while the children and my mother slept. I was sewing a hole in a dress when he entered and knew he was different. At first, I thought him a ghost because of the paleness of his skin. But he assured me it was him and that he'd fought to return to us." That night he was more forceful than he'd ever been. I feared I would have broken bones and bruises come morning, planning how to explain these to my mother. Before dawn, he told me he must leave but would return that night."

She sat at her mirror and stared at her reflection like she didn't recognize the woman in the glass. "I said nothing to my family that day and they did not ask why I was having trouble walking. That night, I sent them to a neighbor, telling them that I feared I was becoming ill and did not want them around me for a few days, that I would come for them when I knew it was safe. They took a loaf of bread to offer to our fellow villager in exchange for a bed. The one they visited was a widow and I knew she could use the bread and the company equally."

A single tear rolled down her cheek. "I was never to see them again."

I was stock still where I stood, afraid to draw her attention. My ire had been replaced with heartache listening to her tale and seeing the pain in those eyes. I wanted to apologize and beg her to stop but I had to hear the end, had to know there were no more mysteries between us.

The next was recounted without any emotion. "He arrived not long after the sunset and revealed what he was. Without ceremony or explanation, he attacked and turned me. When I arose, he simply told me we were leaving. After taking me into the woods to kill and feed from an animal, we threw me onto a cart and we left. In my daze, I didn't even think to look back at our cottage or take a memento. I have no child's blanket to hold or dress from my mother to cherish. He took me with merely the clothes I wore, from the only home I'd known and the children I will mourn for eternity. We rode at night and hid in the daylight, feeding from the creatures of the forest that I'd once danced for and considered mine to protect. We boarded a ship in the night, and he gave me to some of the men during the voyage. It was payment for our transport. When we reached this area, it had not been settled long. He made quick work of charming the people around him and gaining their respect. Before long, he'd established a small, secret business for those who wanted the company of a beautiful, young, flawless girl who could withstand force and could not say no. We've been here since, as the city has grown and the people change, the needs for release has never wavered."

She stood, reaching her hand out to me and I came to her. The last was said with my hand in hers. "He grew bored with me a very long time ago. His factory became his home and this remains a second source of income. When he does come, it is for a new girl, never me. He has not touch me in 500 years. He only allowed me to buy this from him to protect his assets, I know that. But it is mine on paper and that is enough. While our marriage is long dead in the eyes of the law and he no longer employees me, he is the one to mesmerize the people who grow suspicious of me and has his dirty hands in law enforcement and politics. And, he reminds me often that he can take everything away from me in one night with only one police officer."

She smiled in a sort of peace offering and I answered it by pulling her into me. "If he knew I told you all of this," she whispered. "You and I would be beheaded before dawn."

"Why does he allow me to be with you?" I asked. In the chaos of my mind, many questions fought for attention, but that was the one I most wanted an answer to.

The tinkling bell laughter gave me relief as it meant my friend was back to herself. "He does not love me, Rhys. He feels nothing for me. I am like one of his machines, producing money and bringing in profits."

"But," I couldn't put it into words and speech failed me.

She patted my chest as you would a pupil who has tried to answer a riddle but never will. "Take some time to let all of this settle in your mind. You will have many questions for me and I promise I will never again withhold information from you or lie to you again."

I pulled back to make her look up at me. "Promise me." I needed to hear it again.

"I vow it to you. No lies," she raised her chin and offered her lips. I answer with a kiss and the forgiveness between us was understood. "And, I to you. No lies," I assured her.

Collin called from the other side of the door. "We must go now," his muffled voice came. "I mean, right now."

He was right. I felt the sun creeping in and knew we'd cut it too close again.

"I will see you again when I can," I said.

I hadn't known it then, but I'd just done the one thing I swore I wouldn't and lied to her.

36

Our powers had returned. They were nothing like they'd been the night after we'd killed four men, but they were there. Collin had tested it when we returned, calling out to the animals and bringing two mice and a cat to us, sitting side by side like they we're not natural predator and prey. He'd sent them away with the command to return the next night and they had, sitting outside our door when we opened it.

We found James' office empty and knew we must drink our glass or risk him suspecting us. It was like drinking from a rain puddle, it helped with the thirst, but you knew there we better options out there to be had.

Finding our assigned stations in the basement, we both itched to get out of there and re-experience the previous night's tasting. I snuck to my room, attempting to use my masking to transform into Collin again but my power was not strong enough yet. Upon my return, I did find that I was able to mesmerize the man next to me. With a wink to Collin, I told the men in the room one by one that we we're working by their sides and they would see us at our machines all night. I also told them to pick up their paces in the hopes that a dozen men working faster than usual could make up for our missed work. And with that, we fled from the factory like two school boys skipping their classes to find trouble to get into.

The warnings of Alden and Lia played in my head on a loop. I could see her face, begging me to be safe, see the priest's face as he assured us that he would find a way for us to be free. But, the roaring in my veins for more blood was too strong. The need was all I could feel and any semblance of rationality, any pleading from my friends was lost to that desire.

We rushed for the tavern, not caring who may see our alacrity. No inebriate conveniently waited for us to drink from them in an alleyway, so we had to be patient. We sat inside, against the back wall, watching for anyone who could be victim to our thirst. Within an hour, a man stumbled out of the bar and we followed. When he'd turned the corner and found himself on an empty street, we struck. He fell under the weight of us, hitting his head and losing consciousness. Locked into the sound of his heart, I made sure to stop before death and pulled Collin off of him. The man would have a terrible headache the next day, be anemic and very hungover but should live.

As we fled the scene, the high was already taking over. Colors grew more vibrant, the stars brighter and the night air intoxicating. The streets felt new to us, holding possibilities for pleasure and wonder.

The sound of laughter stopped me in my tracks and I looked up for the source. An open window on a second floor held a single light. Perfume rolled down from it and wrapped around me while the giggle filled the air again.

With no care for who may hear, I shouted up. "Madam?"

The laughter stopped and a woman came to the window. She was somewhere in her twenties with blonde hair piled atop her head. The light behind silhouetted her, making her nightdress almost transparent. What lay underneath was full and I wanted it. "Yes?" She asked.

"What are you laughing at?" I asked.

"My friend is making me laugh." And a second blonde girl appeared next to her.

"Is it just you two?" I continued to push my luck, shouting up at two young women in a state of undress but the blood was making me bold.

She hesitated, then answered. "Yes. We're in town to work."

I looked back at Collin and smiled. To the girls, I said one last thing. "Invite us up." And, they did.

Collin had become well versed in pleasuring a human woman and finding his own pleasure without hurting them. But I was much out of practice as I'd only been with Lia since the month of my turning. I had to focus my new energy on control in order to sate this lust without using my vampiric strength. The result of the struggle was that I lasted longer than I expected, bringing her to orgasm several times before emptying myself into her.

When we left, the girls were sleeping soundly. We didn't feel the need to mesmerize them as we doubted these women would tell anyone about inviting two strange men into their flat for passionate, unattached sex. It was not something women admitted to in those times.

I knew we must get back to the factory, but I had one last idea before the night ended. Since we'd already crossed so many boundaries, it felt much like we were invincible. I wanted to test this, see what I could accomplished unfettered.

One shop was still open, a store with necessities such as baking goods and the like. The local shops, like the bars and brothels, had started catering to the factory workers, remaining open as late as possible to meet the needs of shift employees. When I entered this shop, only one man was present. He was clearly the shopkeeper as he was behind the counter, fighting to keep his eyes open. When I approached, he startled and chuckled. "Sorry, son. Guess I didn't get enough sleep today. What can I do for you?"

I found his gaze and called on my power to lock his eyes with mine. He froze. "You can give me the money you have," I spoke, hearing Collin gasp behind me.

Without hesitation, the man opened the register and handed me what was inside. I stuffed in into my pants and held his gaze. "You do not remember where the money went. Now go to sleep."

He closed his eyes and was snoring before we were back on the street. Collin let a triumphant roar out into the night. It reverberated and bounced down ahead of us. "Do you know what this means?" he asked as we walked back.

"What?" I asked, though I knew he was thinking the same thing I was. We were nearing the factory, so I thought about telling him to stop talking but was elated from the night and felt untouchable. I let him continue.

He turned to walk backwards so he could face me when he answered. "If we have women without paying and take money from the shops, we could be out of here in no time at all. We will be in America before you know it."

His certainty was contagious. I felt a kind of hope I hadn't experienced in a very long time. For once, we had a solid plan for getting away. It wasn't without risks, of course, but it was better than anything we'd had until that point. By the time James realized what we'd done, we'd be on a boat to the new world and far from his clutches.

37

The next night was the same. We mesmerized the men in the basement, waited in a local tavern for a man to stumble out into some shadows, pounced, drank and ran. The women we found were sex workers who had turned to the streets instead of working inside an establishment. When we were done, they were well sated. Expecting to use my power to convince them we'd already paid them, they instead surprised us by telling us to forget their fee as we were a welcomed break from their usual quarry.

This only served to bolster the high we were riding from the blood and sent us to find a shop to rob, believing we deserved everything we took as payment from the universe for suffering all these prior years.

When the money was stuffed into my pockets, we returned to the factory. We had enough time to help the men with the work we should have been doing but gave no care for them and ran to our rooms to count our ill-gotten earnings.

A small cigar box served as our bank and was already fuller than it had been in the hundred years we'd been attempting to save. We'd been naïve boys when we'd arrived in Glasgow and had been heavily sheltered since. We hadn't a clue about how much we would need to get to America, find a place to live and start a business. We decided we would stash away money until the time to run presented itself. Once we arrived in the west, we could always use our powers to steal more if we needed to.

Suddenly, America felt closer than ever, and I want to go that night. But we knew we must be strategic about our departure, and I needed time to say my goodbyes to Lia.

Would she come with me if I'd asked? This is what I thought of as I lay in my bed. If she came with us, her girls would be without protection and James would be furious. Collin and I could be easily replaced but Lia was a different story all together. But, could I just leave her there? Leave her to end her days with no one to talk freely to? The thought of her crying alone in that ruby bed broke my heart and was the mental image I fell asleep to.

The next night, we skidded to a halt at the sight of James behind his desk. He looked up in surprise. "So eager to work?" he asked.

"Aye," I answered, staring hard at the ground in the hopes he did not sense the changes in us. I felt his stare for only a moment and then it returned to his work. He waved his hand. "Then by all means, drink and go."

Collin poured the glasses, and we gulped down the liquid so we may flee the room. It wasn't until we were back in our room that we whispered. "What now?" I asked.

His face fell. "We must work. It is too risky."

"Aye," I agreed. "But I'm already aching to go out."

"I as well," he groaned. "If we are caught then all of this is for not. We must remember our goal and not allow our pricks to do the thinking."

"You're right," I sighed. "We work and the next night he is gone, we go out."

Unfortunately, James was in his office every night for the next fortnight. He must have been distracted by great business dealings to have not noticed our states.

As the nights without fresh blood stretched on and on, the aching in our guts became unbearable. If I'd been human, I would've worried I'd die from the agony. However, death would not come for me and the suffering was far greater than the one we'd experienced before. I thought only of ripping out the throats of the men in the basement with me as I worked the machine. What stopped me was not my fear of James but the knowledge that Lia would somehow pay the price of our actions. If I killed one of his men and he realized I was in a blood frenzy, he'd know I'd drank human blood recently. Since he knew how close Lia and I were, it was only a matter of time before he asked her if she was aware.

This was the knowledge that played over and over in my head whenever I envisioned the delicious blood that ran through the veins of my co-workers. It was so close and yet could not be mine.

At dawn, we'd lament in our room, sometimes grasping the blankets for relief and screaming into pillows. I asked Collin to call animals for us to drink from, but his powers were gone.

After a while, the withdrawal eased and the glass of blood started to help the hunger again – not sate it, mind you – but help.

It was around the same time that James gave us a night off. We knew better than to feed with the likelihood that our maker would be in his office the next night and we would need to suffer the lack of feeding again. We thought about going to the church, saving our money and not seeing the women. But in truth, I missed Lia terribly.

Collin found a new girl and was gone before I could remind him to not pay for more than one time. Lia greeted me in the front room with her professional smile and asked me to come to her rooms with her.

Once in, it was clear she was well aware of what I'd done the two nights after I'd last seen her. It wasn't the ire I'd expected but a calm that overtook her. The calm was worse; I'd much rather face the temper.

"You've fed on locals." It wasn't a question but a statement.

"Aye." I saw no point in lying but waited to see if she knew the rest.

"Why?" She asked it so bluntly that I needed a moment.

"What do you mean?" I honestly wasn't sure what she was asking.

"Why do it when I told you the consequences? When you promised?" She was still calm but I saw a hint of frustration seeping into that perfected façade. "Why risk so much?"

What filled my chest wasn't the shame I thought I'd feel if she found out; it was indignation. "Why not?" I returned. "I'm a vampire. I need blood. And what I'm being given isn't enough. He's keeping us weak and it's not fair."

She cocked her head, matching my indignation with her own. "Who told you that you're owed fairness? What made you think that fairness was ever an option?" Her power started to build in the room. It dawned on me that, until that moment, I didn't know the extent of what she could do. I'd felt her melody, experienced her using her voice to sway me or delight me. But it never occurred to me that she may be hiding more.

What was building in that room was far greater than tinkling bells in a laugh.

"You risked yourself, your friend, me and my girls with your recklessness." She was maintaining that eerie calmness, pushing back the frustration in her features and only showing me her wrath through magick.

It felt like being thrown into a boiling pot.

"I wasn't caught," I challenged, trying to call on my own power but finding nothing to pull in. The weeks of animal blood had already washed away my two nights of human feeding.

"Yet," she rebutted. "You weren't caught yet. But you will be." A wind blew through the windowless room and caused her hair to dance around her. "Because you are young and cock-sure and do not know that you are doing."

"How dare you speak to me like that?" I physically pushed through her power, stepping into her.

The magick retreated back into her. The resulting calm and chill in the room was a shock to my senses. She shook her head, disappointment evident in her gaze. "You are a fool and tonight only proves it. I could have snapped you in half, but you care only about being right instead of saving yourself. You could have strategized, tried to assure me, run, anything. But you instead let your tongue get the best of you and further offended me. When he finds out, and he will," she lay a cold hand against my cheek. "You will stand no chance against him."

38

My showdown with Lia should have knocked some sense into me, slowed me down and taught me the error of my ways.

It didn't.

Instead, I was enraged and full of pride. I felt as if she, like James, was trying to hold me back and control me. I whole-heartedly believed that I could only count on myself, that she didn't know me, and that she was trying to make me go against my vampiric nature for her own selfish purposes. What these purposes were, I didn't know, but I was certain she didn't want me to have power like she did.

I had a renewed determination to take what I felt was my destiny by using strangers for their blood, to satisfy my needs and steal from hardworking people. Collin and I bolstered each other's selfishness by reminding each other that the end would be worth it when we were happy in America. We repeated that we would help unfortunate souls in the new world and thereby make up for our bad deeds in Glasgow.

We knew full well that hunting and drinking would eventually be stifled by James' return and we'd have to undergo the withdrawal each time but we didn't care. We'd rather have the intermittent ecstasy of fresh human blood and the resulting agony of going without than never taste it again.

After my fight with Lia, it was only one more day before James was gone and we were back on the hunt for our next meal. When the blood hit my throat, I forgot all about Lia and cared only for this feeling. The subsequent robbery did not gain us much but the girls we encountered after were very eager for our time and expertise.

The next dawn, I mesmerized the young girl in James' fabric shop to take a letter to the priest and his sister when she walked home. I explained that she must never read my letter or the ones that came to me from the church since God would know and punish her. Being a devout woman, she took this to heart and I trusted that she would rather die than read our words.

In this letter, I told Alden and Nettie about our inability to leave the factory as James had us working a grueling schedule and we did not know when we would be free to see them again. I asked how they were and thanked them for their honesty during our last visit. I assured them that we were not avoiding them. I asked for them to write us back as we missed them and wanted to know they were well. I assured them that the girl who carried our words was a woman of faith and held the secrecy between a priest and a parishioner as sacred.

For the next year, we kept this up. Our letters started general. As we grew to trust that the shopgirl did not read them, we spoke more openly. I did not divulge our nights out to the priest but did talk of our plan to save for a trip to America, our longing to be out from under James, our difficulty with drinking the animal blood offered by our maker when we knew it kept us weak. I asked thickly veiled questions about Nettie's nature. Asking things like when she knew, how she knew, if she could change it if given the choice, what other things existed and what her abilities were. Some she answered – she would not change who she was, she knew very young but didn't have a label until she told her mother, she knew because she was able to hear and know things she should not. The rest, she explained, I must wait for and could not be put on page.

She wrote much about missing home and hating being "locked up" in the church. She felt her brother was too much of a keeper and should allow her more freedoms. She spoke of dreams she would have and how she felt sad for us that we no longer dreamed.

These letters were comforts to me when I was in the throes of blood withdrawal. I would read them over and over as my stomach twisted and my throat screamed. I would fantasize about a separate realm, adjacent to this, where I was a man and fed on venison and mead and had a house full of children. I would swear I was done with the blood and could not continue to put myself through this, swear to come clean to Alden and Lia – begging for their help.

But then James would leave, and we would fall into our patterns of hunting, feeding and robbing.

I had not seen Lia since the night we fought. Often, on my nights out, I would feel a pull towards her establishment, tell myself I needed to fix our friendship. Then, pride would take over and I would tell myself that she could have come to me at any time and chose not to. My power would come over me and I'd be drunk in the blood and magick, forgetting my dear Lia for another night.

As the autumn of 1917 arrived, the city was filled to bursting with people working the munitions, metals and fabric factories. The war was raging, and Glasgow was not unaffected. Finding someone to feed on had become almost too easy and our nights were losing their luster.

It was crisp night when I decided to forgo the feast and visit the church to surprise them. Collin chose to go on a hunt without me and it was not the first time. We'd picked up the habit of finding separate humans to feed on and separate girls to bed. He too had the power to control minds but chose to not waste the energy and instead stole from pockets after he fed. This meant, on those nights apart, we'd return with double the earnings.

We said our farewells and I made my way to the church. As it came into my view, it felt changed. It was once a huge part of my existence, a place I sat in frequently. But I had not crossed its threshold since the night Alden had released a secret that so many before him had held tight. On this night, it felt foreign – like stepping back into a life that no longer was. The vampire who'd visited so often before had been a fraction of his potential. And now, I came at full power and a wider knowledge than I thought possible.

Nettie leapt up from the front steps and ran to me. She squealed as she embraced me. Her brother waited on the stairs for me to come to him. His embrace assured me he was not unhappy to see me. Perhaps he'd been too tired to walk. "Join us," he returned to sitting. "It is a beautiful night."

"That it is," I agreed.

"We've missed you terribly," Nettie sat to the other side of me, looping her arms around mine and laying her head on my shoulder. "I've loved your letters but did hope we'd see you walking down that sidewalk someday. And, you have."

"I should have visited sooner," I relented. "We don't get out often but when we do, I must admit, it is a different kind of company I need."

"Well," Alden patted my thigh. "You're here now and that is what matters. Can we do anything for you?

"Actually," I lay my free hand on Nettie's arm. "I'd love to ask you some of those questions, if it's all right."

She sat up straight and stood to her feet. "Sure," she smiled. "Come to the graveyard?"

I startled, looking between the priest and the witch. "I can't."

She reached her hand to me. "You can," she giggled. "I can remove the spell that keeps you out."

39

I searched Alden's face for confirmation. Every priest had told me that my kind could not walk that ground. I had believed them and never attempted. Now, this girl was telling me I could.

"The ground is spelled," Alden answered. "To keep that which is not human out. Nettie is able to remove and reapply the spell. The church does not like to announce this to the public, but is has always been the work of witches. This is why people feel peace in the cemetery as they bury and visit their loved ones."

I followed them to the edge of the graves, still not believing I would be able to walk the ground. I could feel the power pushing against me as I approached, felt the need to walk away from it. That is, until it was gone – gone is not the right word – lifted. It was lifted above us, and Nettie indicated I should move forward, which I did.

The power hung above us like clouds, not visible, but tangible nonetheless. As I moved through the stones, I pondered aloud. "I understand giving the grieving a feeling of peace when they're here but why block vampires?"

Nettie stopped and faced me. Her brother remained silent at her back. "Not just vampires." She raised a finger, "Wait a moment." Raising both hands above her with palms to the sky, she looked to the sky. Her fingers curled as if she'd been given a bowl of soup in each hand and was offering it to the stars. Streaks of colors, faint at first, began to dance above each palm. The vividness of them grew, like being pulled from around us and into these rainbow clouds. As they coalesced to one swirling waltz, she brought her hands down to throw them onto the dirt below her. As the colors hit the soil, they burst up and around us to disappear.

"We cannot be seen." She said it like she was reporting what she'd eaten at supper.

Alden clarified. "She's called magick to protect us from sight. No one can see or hear us in this place."

Nettie's smile was one of pride. "Now, ask what you will."

It was a few moments before I could process my thoughts into speech. "Why keep vampires out of the cemetery? Is it all cemeteries?"

"Not all," she answered. "Many churches were, and are, used as the judgement and executioner of things they deemed unnatural. Like vampires-" she pointed at me. "And, witches." She lay her hand on her heart. "But others, such as fairies or shapeshifters." She dropped herself to the ground, sitting with legs crossed like a girl much younger. I joined her on the ground and her brother walked amongst graves, likely already knowing this.

She continued. "The churches would have their grounds spelled against these things so, when an unnatural thing is punished and put in the ground, their kind cannot come for them later."

Shaking my head, I interrupted. "But why?"

"Many churches and hunters believe that we can come and pull our kind from the ground to bring them back to life." She was being so patient with my questions.

"If they kill witches, how can they have witches spell the grounds?" I asked, hearing the frustration in my voice.

She smirked. "Good question." She ran her hand over the grass and small white flowers erupted from the ground. "You see, there have been witches over the years who will do the bidding of the church to save themselves. They help to hunt down others, help with punishing and give the clergy whatever they wish to remain off the burn pile."

"Disgusting," I spat.

She arched an eyebrow. "Do you not think there are vampires that have betrayed their own kind?"

I thought about that and knew she must be right. Betrayal to save one's skin has been a theme throughout human history. It only stands to reason that supernatural creatures do the same. "But, why keep this spell in place here? There are no trials held or punishments doled. Nettie can just lift it for good."

"I can answer this," Alden returned. "The church will send their representatives from time to time to ensure I'm meeting my duties. I'm to keep the secrets of the church and maintain the spell on the grounds. With them, always, comes a witch to check. It is why the spell must stay and why I must have a quick way to hide Nettie. If the church's witch were to recognize her, they may take her away."

"Where do you hide her?" I asked.

"There is a door under the pulpit, it leads to a space under the floor," he answered. "She hides there."

Guilt overwhelmed me. While I'd been running the streets, thinking only of myself, she'd been living in fear. Her brother had been on guard day and night, knowing that his sister may be in danger any second. And while they sought to protect each other, I spent my nights hurting and stealing and weaving a web of lies. I had the urge to confess all to the priest, beg him to help me be better but was pulled from my thoughts by Nettie. "I'm okay," she said, as if answering my thoughts. "They've only come twice since I arrived and both times they stayed only a few hours."

"Would they kill you?" Something churned in my gut at the thought, but I had to ask.

"I do not know," she answered honestly. "They'd definitely kill you."

Her lack of hesitation at sharing this truth brought a laugh from me. It was amazing the way she dealt with her plight, never showing self-pity or anger, just accepting it and facing it head-on.

"Any other questions?" She asked and I knew she'd always give truth.

"What are your abilities?" It was something I'd wondered since she admitted her nature and I didn't know if I'd ever have another chance to ask.

"As I understand," she widened her eyes to indicate that I was able to rebut if necessary. "Vampires manifest only one or two powers." She paused and I nodded to validate the statement. "Witches are not like this, once in our power, we can learn and grow magicks. We can spend our lives generating more as we learn more. Do you understand?"

"I think," although I was not sure.

"The way you learn speech," she reframed. "First a word, then more words, then sentences, then reading and writing. That is our magick. First a small thing," she waved her hand over the patch of flowers she'd created and they retreated into the ground. "Then, more complex." She waved her hand over herself and as the hand passed, she was lost to my sight. She was there and then not. I heard laughter behind me and turned to see her amongst stones 20 feet away.

Standing, I applauded and she bowed. Walking to me, the delight on her face was lost to a sorrow. She sighed, "What good is it, though, if it is feared and cannot be shared?"

Realization overtook me. She had already declared her intention to never have a child, for her magick to die with her. Was that the right thing? For magick to be lost? Sadness filled my gut and ran cold across my skin. I pulled her in for a hug. "I am sorry for you, Nettie. It is not right."

She nodded into my chest. "It is not. None – not you or I or wolf or fairy – should have to hide. We should all be safe to be true to our nature and find love." She pulled back. "However, it is not the way and we mustn't be lost in a fantasy of change or we may miss the life we have."

"Such wise words from such a young one," I patted her head as a teacher may a good student.

"Nettie," Alden began. "We must return the spell and go to bed." He addressed me. "As much as we love your visit, we are not nocturnal and need rest."

"I understand and am grateful for the time." As she worked to return the magicks to the way the church expected, I thought about the evening. This girl had been so honest with me, telling me things that could endanger her very life. And, I'd hidden so much from her. I spoke nothing to them about my change since seeing them last, my hoarded money or my falling out with Lia. The omissions were the same as lying and I knew it. She'd given me all truth and I'd repaid them with dishonesty.

When back in front of the church, Nettie grasped my hand. "Don't stay away so long this time."

"I won't," I assured her.

But that was just more lies.

40

When I met up with Collin at the factory, I did not share what I'd learned that night. He had stopped speaking of the church and no longer wanted to visit. He didn't write letters to Alden and Nettie and didn't care to hear what they wrote to me. I think he'd lost the need to know anything outside of himself in those days. He sneered at the faith we'd been raised on as boys.

As I look back, knowing what would happen the next night, I believe that Collin was starting to believe he was a god of sorts.

When we lay in the beds that night, I confessed to him that I'd grown weary with our activities. I no longer got the same high off of feeding that I did in the beginning. Even sex was becoming rote. It gave me physical release, but I was no longer thrilled by the bedding of a different girl each night. I did not look forward to the withdrawal that was inevitable on James' return and our hunts no longer felt worth the suffering. But I also didn't want to return to living off of our maker's minimal offering. What I didn't say aloud was that I missed Lia and feeding on drunks was no longer good enough to pay the price of nights without her.

Even if I returned to her, would she forgive me?

Collin listened in silence. When I finished my confession, the pause was so great that I thought he may have fallen asleep while I rambled. But he'd been waiting to be sure I was done before speaking. "I know what you need."

"You do?" I asked, not believing he could truly fix it.

"I do," he demanded. "We will speak tomorrow, if James is still gone. I do not want to say it here."

This assurance that he had the cure for my despair was what rolled around in my head until sleep overtook me. What had he discovered? Had he been doing someone on the nights that we separated that brought zeal back to his outings? If so, why wait so long to tell me?

When awaking, we ran to James' office. To our delight, he remained away and we could continue our outings. After mesmerizing the machinists, I kept silent until we reached a quiet street. Collin pulled back into the shadows and I met him, backs against a wall. He whispered in the way that only we can, so mortal ears cannot detect it. "Hunt as we are meant to," he hissed.

Disappointment pulled a groan from within me. "We have hunted, Collin. It does not please me anymore. I merely do it for the blood now."

"That is not what I mean, brother." He looked around. "I mean, hunt like a predator and don't show mercy to your prey."

"Killing?" Certainly, that was not what he was saying. I needed to clarify.

"Feeding to fill," he answered. "And leaving no witness to tell tales."

"I canna," I asserted. "I'll not cross that line." The truth of his words hit me. "You have?"

"It was an accident at first," he shrugged. "I didn't stop in time." A wicked smile crossed his face. "The last drops of the blood as the heart stops, are almost the sweetest you can taste."

"What do you mean by *almost*?" I didn't know if I wanted to hear his response.

"The sweetest," he leaned in. "Is when they are afraid."

"Why are they afraid?" I asked.

"Because," he responded. "I let them see their death before I give it to them."

Horror and curiosity swarmed my mind. He was admitting to killing humans who were aware enough of him before death to be terrified. Did that truly change the taste of the blood? Was it better than what we'd been doing? I struggled to picture the man I'd known for over a century, the boy who took a beating for me, terrorizing humans with the intention to kill them. He was talking about cold-blooded murder and smiling.

Could I do such a thing?

"I canna," I repeated. The man before me resembled someone I cared for but was a stranger to me now. "I'll not betray you but cannot do this with you."

"Enjoy your night, then." And he was gone, not caring who may see his speed. A trembling overtook me. It was the result of a strong need to follow and experience what he'd promised. The beast in me was furious at my lack of action. It wanted to do what it was meant to do and stalk prey. I had crossed so many lines I never thought I would. Taking this next step would be something I could never return from. While we had convinced ourselves that feeding on and robbing humans would help us reach America, I had no way to rationalize murder.

My legs were walking without my conscious decision to move. I only knew I needed to get away from the spot where Collin had revealed such dark things.

I was in front of Lia's before I registered the path I'd been travelling. Opening the door was one of the hardest things I'd ever done but it was merely the beginning of the difficult task of rebuilding our kinship and bringing her back into my life.

She stood halfway between the entrance and her room, back to me. I froze, afraid to summon her and start the series of events that would play out once I spoke her name. Would she forgive me, embrace me, throw things at me or – the worst – cry?

I didn't need to speak because she turned. Upon finding me, her eyes grew wide. She reached out a strong finger towards the door. "Out," her voice bellowed. "Now." It was as if several unseen men were pushing at my chest at once. Withstanding the force was not an option, so I ran from the brothel and away from the pressure.

Once on the street, I roared into the night. People who walked the night, those sleeping in corners, even animals paused briefly to eye the man screaming like a lunatic then went back to their business. Rage enveloped me. She would not even hear what I had to say, would not allow me the chance to speak. She allowed James to use her for half a millennium and continued to cater to him but would let a hundred years of friendship, love-making and support die over a single fight.

The anger propelled me to the tavern and the man I hoped to find, who lounged in a back chair and smiled when he saw me.

"I knew you'd see reason," Collin smirked. "Let's find you a meal."

41

After much talk, Collin decided that my first kill should be an easy one. We left the tavern and went on a search for the right victim. It wasn't long until we found her.

Down an alleyway, seated upright against the wall, was a sleeping woman. It was so similar our first fresh human feeding that it struck me as fate. The smell of liquor was strong enough that I was shocked when her eyes fluttered open and she slurred out the words "What're you thinkin'?"

I crouched before her and found her eyes with mine. "Shhh," I whispered. "You're so tired. You need to sleep." Heaviness overtook her lids, and they fell again. She would die in her sleep, and it felt like mercy on my part. I asked myself one last time if I could kill a human that had done nothing to me.

Collin leaned into me, his mouth an inch from my ear. "You are a vampire, Rhys. This is what we are meant to do. No one tells the wolf to not be a wolf."

There was a kind of reasoning in his coercion, something that felt true. His words invited me to experience what lay before me. Had I been denying my true self this whole time? Not accepting my nature?

When my fangs sank into her neck and the blood rolled down my throat, the usual delight came over me. It was not new to know the blood of a living human. But, when I would've previously pulled away from her and stopped, I did not. As I continued to drink, that delight turned into the ecstasy that had once enthralled me but been lost. Wrapping my arms around her, I pulled her to me in a cradle, like a lover. I drank and drank, feeling her heart thunder against my still chest. She began to twitch, her body instinctually fighting to survive, but it was too late and I was too strong. As the drumbeat against me slowed, her muscles relaxed. What rolled down into my stomach was molten sugar and the richest of wines.

Releasing her to fall to the ground, I threw myself backwards onto the ground. I was swathed in pleasure, bathing in a sensation greater than any orgasm. Collin whopped into the starless sky. "What did I tell you?" he crowed. "We have been severely missing out, Rhys."

Grabbing my hand, he pulled me to sitting and then up onto my feet. "Now," he slapped my back. "Go home. Enjoy your walk and get some rest. I have not had my own fun."

"I-" my attempt to stop him or garner more information was useless. He was gone from my side. Frankly, I did not care at that point. Power rolled through me and around me. It felt like purpose had been restored to my existence and I had no further thought for the corpse at my feet.

While walking back to the factory, I smelled more in the air than ever before: flour from bakeries, perfume from women, those unwashed and those freshly washed, the river and the trees. The heat that the bricks had held onto from the sun rippled off them like waves of color. Sounds fought for control of my hearing: a bat screeched, a couple fighting about money, bawdy laughter in pubs and a piano. Mentally, I turned down the noise as I'd learned to do.

As much as I didn't want to return to our little room, I knew that the night was not endless. Plus, it was the first time in too long that I did not want for anything or worry about the future. I was truly and thoroughly content, all my needs met.

What did it mean that murder was what finally quelled the storm raging inside me?

Once in my room, I found paper and began to write. This time it was Lia that I penned a letter for. She may have been done with me, but I was not ending this without speaking my side of things.

After 14 attempts to write words that expressed how I felt and 14 wadded up balls of paper in the corner, I resigned to her never knowing how I felt. I'd tried pleading and admitting fault, I'd tried telling her everything that Collin and I had done, I tried angrily telling her how wrong she'd been to throw me out. However, none of those approaches gave me solace or felt right. So, I'd given up. In truth, nothing would make me feel as good as I did at that moment and Lia would only tell me not to do it again so, why fix our friendship? I accepted that Lia's time in my life was done, and I should end the chapter, move onto the next part of my story. Holding onto something for longer than you should will only bring your sorrow and pain.

You can hold onto an apple, but it will still inevitably rot.

42

When I awoke the next night, Collin was not in his bed. Panic set in immediately. I told myself that he arose first and was in James' office checking to see if our maker had returned. But when minutes ticked by and he didn't return to the room, dread ate at my stomach. When I didn't see him in our boss' chambers, I began the plan of where to look first, and drank two glasses as to not raise suspicion if the content was checked that night.

Checking the cigar box showed that all our money remained so he had not taken it to flee. Truthfully, I did not believe he would but was searching for any clue of his whereabouts. When the mouse pushed its way under our door, I let out a sigh of relief. The mouse and he had become close. It tended to meet him in the room when we returned from the night. Not seconds later, Collin came in with the smile of a naughty child who had a dirty joke to share.

"You prick," I snapped. "Where have you been?"

"Cut it too close," he answered, throwing himself onto the bed so the mouse could climb onto his chest and have its head scratched. Collin obliged as he continued. "I was with a young lady until near dawn. Her husband arrived from his night shift not long after I'd finished with her," he wiggled his eyebrows "and almost caught us. I hid in the basement, hoping to slip out when he slept but he stayed awake too long. Thank the stars, the cellar had no windows and no one found me while I was out." The mouse had enough and ran off the bed, under the door and to wherever he goes. "When I came to, I returned to you. Is James here?"

"No," I slammed the cigar box shut and shoved it back into its hiding place. "And you're damned lucky he isn't. I had to drink two glasses of that shite to cover for you. Don't know what I would have said if he'd been in there."

"Well," he jumped up. "He wasn't so end your wallowing. If I'd wanted to be griped at, I'd have found a wife. Ready?"

"For what?" I asked, still pissed that he'd been so reckless and cut it so close.

"For the hunt," he clapped his hand together and rubbed them. "You're first night as a true predator."

Sensations from the previous night returned to me like a ghost in the room. The sheer thought of another kill electrified my body and heat rose up my throat. "Aye."

Expecting another alleyway or tavern, I was delighted when Collin led us to a park of sorts. With our speed, we could reach the outskirts of the city quickly. Taking back streets meant we were not seen and had ample time to return once finished. I'd spend so long on the same city blocks that I'd forgotten anything lay outside of Glasgow, forgotten that someday, as I had with my village, I would be able to just walk out of its boundaries and leave it at my back.

I found that I didn't need much instruction. The park offered us thick tree lines to hide among and there we sat, unmoving in a way that only our kind can be, waiting for the right circumstance. The beasts and birds of the forest rang out around and behind us as they too went about their nights and searched for safety, food or shelter. This is what we listened to until new sounds joined the chorus – the sounds of people. Specifically, it was a man and woman. Their conversation revealed their need for a remote spot in which to have a clandestine liaison. The man was already running his hands over her despite not having the coverage of the trees yet and she was playfully pushing him away.

We backed further into the woods when it became clear our spot was in their direct path. Shadows favored us and the couple passed within inches of our faces on their way to a thick tree. She twirled to back against its solid trunk, throwing one arm above her and the other hand pulling up her skirt to expose her shapely legs. The man was clearly going to accept what she offering, dropping to his knees and burying his face between her thighs. His sight was lost to her womanhood, and she had closed hers in passion, so neither saw us approach.

It wasn't until I'd pulled him away from her and into the air that he'd realized something was wrong. Her eyes flew open as Collin put his hand over her mouth.

When I dropped the man back down to his knees in front of me, I struck from behind to rip open his throat and began my feast. I heard Collin whispering to the woman and her screaming against his palm but was too lost in my own feeding to register fully what was happening.

Collin had been right when he said fear sweetened the drink. Pulling great gulps down from the man, I felt like I'd never get enough of this and drank until nothing remained.

Wiping my mouth on the man's shirt, I let go of his lifeless bulk to assess Collin's success. He no longer needed to cover her mouth as she was never going to scream again. When he backed away from her, she too became a mass amongst the dried leaves of the forest floor.

We cared not if they'd be found, what the death would be attributed to, who would mourn them or what years we'd robbed them of. We only cared about the high we got off the hunting and feeding, thinking only of the next time we could do it.

James returned the following night, and we were forced into withdrawal again. This time was far worse than previous, the agony of the bloodlust threatened to break my mind and spirit. Working the machines, I kept one eye on the man nearest to me, watching the vein in his neck dance in time with his heartbeat. I do not know what strength I tapped into to stop myself from slaughtering him or how I remained sane. That time, and every time I went without blood after that, is lost to me. It was like walking through a fog and living in a space outside of reality for days on end. The physical pain was numbed by the screaming inside my head to find blood from any source.

We survived it and found peace after a few weeks, only to start the cycle again two months later when James left.

We'd hunt and murder, empty the pockets of our victims or store we'd not hit before. We had a different woman each night as the stronger we became, the more drawn to us they were. Collin would sometimes not return to the factory, always finding places to hide and never getting caught despite his recklessness increasing as he began to believe he was unstoppable.

When James was in town, we fell into line and played the part of dutiful minions. And, when the war ended towards the end of 1918, the streets became full-blown outdoor parties as men returned and the humans believed a peacetime was ahead of them. It made it easier to hunt, all that chaos, and felt like even vampires had something to celebrate.

It was only a few months later, as the city started to learn what it meant to be in a post-war era and started to rebuild, that our fun would come to end and my whole world would crumble.

43

March 1919

I awoke to the door shutting and found Collin standing over me. "He's gone," Collin slapped his hands together with glee. "I thought he'd never leave."

I shot my hands in the air with triumph. "Thanks be. I couldn't stand another night at those machines. So many men have returned and are looking for work. I don't know why James canna give them the jobs and let us do otherwise with our time."

"Fool, James pays us a wage that no man would take for this work and he knows it." Collin slapped my stomach. "Now, up with you. I have special plans. It's not often a man turns 135 years old."

"Christ," I groaned. "Why do you insist on keeping track of birthdays, man? It's ridiculous."

"'Tis not," he countered. "We have little to celebrate so let me have these tiny things."

"Right, brother" I conceded. "You win. What will we do?"

He jumped up and down like a child receiving a gift or candy. "Come with me and you'll see, old man."

We pulled on our clothes and I noticed again how thin they were getting, knowing that we'd soon need to spend some of our earnings on a cheap outfit. I'd wanted to charm some shopkeeper into giving us garments but knew these could not be explained on our meager wages.

Pulling enough power to mesmerize the men in the basement was a valiant fight. I was weakened from weeks without fresh blood and mentally reminded myself to solidify the mental control upon my return post-feeding, lest it wear off from my lack of magick.

Stumbling into the street in reels of laughter and plans of our night. I slammed directly into a body I knew well but hadn't seen in years. She appeared as if from nowhere and took the impact of our collision without adjusting a single muscle.

"Lia," I gasped. "What? I mean…how-"

"Lia," Collin snapped, clearly not happy to see her. "Nice to see you but we must go."

"Rhys," she addressed me, ignoring Collin to my right. "Please, let me explain. Follow me to my parlor and listen to what I've to say. If you do, and never wish to see me again, I will respect this. But, please-" although she showed no emotion, I noticed a fine quiver in her lips. "just hear me this night. I risk much just coming here."

Collin pulled on my arm, but I held my ground, eyes locked on my former lover. Collin yanked again and I wretched it from his grasp. "Go ahead, Collin. I'll find you." I expected a fight, but his need was too strong and with a blur he departed, leaving Lia and I to walk the streets.

Anyone who saw us pass by likely thought she was a lady of means taking a poor homeless man to some kind of charity work. The people of wealth in the city had made it a habit to help those returning from the war with no family and no money. It was the popular cause amongst society's upper class, and they made a game of showing off how much they helped the less fortunate.

No one would have looked at us and said *there go two vampires who once loved each other and are now strangers.* But that is what we were.

I believed it would be a quick exchange; I couldn't fathom any words she could conjure to undo all the years of hurt. With hindsight, I too had things to apologize for but could not remember them in that moment. I could only recall the way that she'd tossed me aside and broken my heart in a manner that only someone you trust completely can.

In her room, a strange piece of furniture met me. She'd replaced the bed that had held my happiest times, echoing with our whispers and sighs. The mattress, headboard, linens were all new, like she had erased every reminder of our time together.

Aware of the emotion that may well up and my inability to control them, I kept my back to her. The last thing I wanted was for her to see was how she impacted me still. A subtle click let me know she'd locked the door, a useless gesture and one she never did on our previous encounters. Then, she crossed in front of me to sit on the end of that imposter bed to look up at me. "I know you are angry," she began. "You must put that aside to hear what I say clearly and be logical."

Her telling me how to feel only replaced the small amount of sorrow I had with more irritation, leaving that to be the sole emotion I now experienced. I wanted to hold onto that familiar anger, use it as an anchor to stop me from drifting into the forgiveness that her face urged me for.

It was her eyes that started to cool my temper. Inside them, once I calmed enough to examine them, was genuine fear and pleading. "I'm listening," I whispered.

"The night you came to me," she grabbed hold of my hands. I left them stiff but allowed her to hold them. "James was here, in this very room." Chill marched from head to toe, a knot growing in my gut as she spoke. "He was suspicious that you were sneaking out when he was away and waiting to see if you showed. If he'd seen you-"

Reality overtook me. My foolishness had put me seconds from discovery and her quick actions had saved me. I thought of my activities that night, the cold-blooded murder, knowing now that James had been in the same city.

She squeezed my hands. "He's done this many times since, sat in this room, waiting to see if you would show. He believes you defy him for my company. Should that be affirmed, he would punish us both."

"I-"

She interrupted. "I believe he is truly gone this night, but I must tell you more despite his command that I never go to you or reveal what I know." She stood to level her eyes with mine, my hands still in hers. "He believes you or Collin are murdering people to feed, collecting power and money to leave his employ. He knows, Rhys; he knows everything." I sank to the ground, and she followed me down. "What have you done, Rhys?" She implored. "Tell me."

It rolled from me like a recitation, no thought or emotion. "We've killed, drank, robbed, slept with women in the city."

Silence lingered and I awaited her response. It was all out between us, and it was abundantly clear that she owed me no apology. I saw well that I was the only one in the wrong, the error of my ways and how selfish I'd acted.

"You must run," she stated plainly.

Shocked, I found her emerald gaze. "What?"

"Run," she demanded. "If not tonight, then tomorrow. I do not know how long he is away this time, but you mustn't hesitate. Do you have enough?"

"Perhaps," I answered, still processing the idea as she stood and crossed to the mirror. She removed it to expose a hole in the wall that her hand darted into. Out of the abyss, she pulled a stack of money to lay on her desk. When the mirror was back in its place, she came to me, reaching her hand down to take mine and pulled me to standing. "You will take that. It's one of the few secrets I'm able to keep from him." She stopped my protesting by raising a hand. "Is there a place you could hide until tomorrow's sunset? You must find Collin and retrieve your things. You will not have enough time to flee tonight."

"The church," I shouted.

"The church?" she asked.

"There is a small hiding space below the dais." I didn't know if it was big enough for Collin and I, but I knew Alden would hide us if asked. I also knew it was putting him and Nettie in danger, but desperation overrode my concern.

"Don't tell me any more," she demanded. "It's better if I don't know."

"Come with us," I begged, pulling her into me. "Come with us and be free."

She tilted her head to the side and a sad smile pulled some of the sparkle from her eyes. "I cannot. You he will eventually stop looking for. I-" she didn't need to finish the words. I knew well that she was irreplaceable. We stared into each other, knowing this would be our last time. I searched for what to say. What words could show her what she meant to me, tell her that she was the reason I'd made it through my time in this godforsaken city? Nothing my simple mind could construct felt big enough for what I was feeling.

She rose onto her toes and laid a kiss upon my lips. I answered that kiss, trying to express all that I could not say. In every touch and whisper during our final time together, I gave all that I was to her and she to me. We knew we were saying goodbye with our bodies and tears.

As we lie next to each other, I begged her a final time to come with me and she only laid another sweet kiss on my lips in declination. "I'll always be with you," she smiled. "Always."

She rose from the bed, and I knew the moment I must leave her side forever was fast approaching. She pulled a small silk bag from under her bed and stuffed her money into it. As I dressed, she listed instructions. "Do not fight me. Take this and leave without sorrow. Find Collin and get your things from the factory. Hide in the church until sunset tomorrow, then run." She faced me sternly. "If you need power to flee, take only what you need from someone and leave them believing it to be a whiskey dream. Use you powers for good, Rhys." She dipped a rag into a water basin and crossed to me, slamming the bag into my hand, catching my sight and washing the blood tears from my face. "You do not need to kill. You are not that man."

"Aye," I whispered, full of shame and gratitude equally. The woman before me knew all my darkest deeds and was giving up so much to help me, without judgement or chastisement or expecting payback.

"I ask this of you," her voice wavering. "Have a good life, be happier than any man has ever been, be kind and help those in need." She lay a hand on my now clean cheek. "Think of me but do not let those thoughts hold you back from living life to the fullest."

Laying my hand over hers, I smiled. "I promise."

Pulling back and facing away from me, she spoke into the room. "Now go."

And, I did – heading into freedom and leaving her imprisoned.

44

I searched the streets, the bars, the shops and could not find Collin. As the minutes turned into hours, I knew I must return to the factory to pack our things. Eventually, he would arrive and I could tell him the plan. I only hoped it was with enough time to make it to the church.

In the room, I found not even the mouse. I lay the bag of cash on top of the cigar box and returned it to the hiding place. There were no mementos to pack, no keepsakes from our time in Glasgow. We needed only the clothes on our backs and the money to find freedom.

I found a match, bringing it and Nettie's letters to the alley outside our factory. As they burned, I felt nothing. I knew every word and would be taking those thoughts with me in my mind. I did not need the papers and would not risk James finding them.

Lying on my bed, I stared at the ceiling with every nerve in my body alight with excitement and apprehension. Without Collin, I couldn't take my next step but ached to run from this place now.

What would America be like? What business would we start? We knew the making of fabrics well but not the business side of selling them. Perhaps, we could start a gentlemen's club. I'd helped Lia with her business so often that I knew well what it took to run such a place. We could easily control disorderly visitors and have women nearby at all times. Did America have such establishments? Were they as welcomed as the ones in Scotland? I didn't know but the more I thought of it, the more it seemed like a brilliant idea.

I thought of Alden and Nettie's reactions when we ran into their church, asking to be hid. Would they question it or just put us in the secret underfloor chamber? Would we even need it? If Collin waited much longer, we would need to sleep in the factory that day and merely start our escape at sundown. Would we stop to say goodbye to the priest and his sister? Risk the time it would take? We must, I concluded. But it needed to be quick.

I thought of the goodbye I'd had with Lia. Had it been enough? Did she truly know what I felt for her? That my love for her was deeper and purer than simple romantic love? That she'd been more soulmate than friend or lover? I had to believe that she knew, had to hold onto that to be able to cut ties with this city. And, I had to believe she would find me someday, that she'd find her own escape and follow me to America.

But even then, I knew she never would.

She was not one to waste words or say things she did not mean. She wanted me to have a full life without her, wanted me to leave and never look back.

Could I do that?

And, could I keep my promise of never killing again? I was through the withdrawal and on the other side but that was just the physical need. The dark part, the beast in me, would always think about it. There was no time period I could fathom that would be long enough for that piece of me to never sink its teeth into a screaming victim. It had been awakened and experienced the ecstasy of hunting. It couldn't be told to just crawl back into the shadows of my mind. How would I satiate that animal without taking life? How would I go back to merely a taste from a drunkard?

As that beast in me insisted it could not be done, my heart vowed that I must.

Looking back, I could plainly see every small concession, every white lie I'd told myself, every step across a line that had led me to be the monster I'd become. The figure I'd seen in the mirror that night resembled the man who'd arrived in Glasgow but was difficult to recognize anymore. I truly didn't want to continue in the ways that I'd become accustomed to.

"When we get to America," I vowed into the night. "I will start fresh."

As sleep slipped in, I meant those words but was aware that I had a long hard road ahead of me and prayed I was strong enough to fight for my soul.

45

Fire ripped across my scalp and a solid weight slammed against my legs. I was on the hard floor of my bedroom with a strong grip holding tight to my hair.

"Get up, you ungrateful, deceitful bastard." There was no need to open my eyes to know it was James who spoke. The voice was familiar but the roar underneath the words was new. His hand forced my head back at an angle that tested the strength of my neck. A sneer twisted my maker's face. Rage was contorting his features. "Your play days are over." His free hand rose to show me the cigar box and silk bag.

Releasing my hair, he backed up. "Stand."

I did, just as a fist slammed into my jaw, rocking me off my feet and into the wall behind me. I managed to stop myself from slumping to the floor, but my vision blurred for a moment. My mind raced. How much did he know? Was this punishment for the money only or more?

Where was Collin?

"Looking for your friend?" he raged. "I see he isn't here. Where is he?"

"I don't know," I mustered and was relieved it was the truth.

James stalked towards me, and I braced for another blow. Instead, he leaned in, stopping his eyes just before they touched mine. "Liar."

When he pulled back, he held my shirt to ensure I followed him to his office. Once there, he threw the box and bag to his desk, whirling around. "You have one chance to tell me everything."

"What do you mean?" I asked, hoping he'd indicate what he wanted to hear so I had an inkling of the extent of his knowledge.

"What have you boys been up to while I've been away?" He spoke slowly, making each word like a stab.

"Nothing," I answered. "You'd be aware if we had." I hoped flattery would soften his mood.

"Would I?" he asked, eyebrow arched high. "I've been quite busy and lost interest in you decades ago." He raised his chin and looked down his nose at me. "I foolishly believed you to be so well trained that I didn't need to pay attention to you." He dropped his gaze and I felt power growing around us. "I was wrong."

"Sir-" my words ran dry. My thoughts raced too fast for me to speak coherently. I thought of the money and tried to figure out how to explain it. I thought of my missing friend and tried to figure out how to explain that.

He turned away from me, slamming his hands against his desk. Sounds of wood cracking under his force sent a jolt through me. When he faced me, his eyes appeared to have a light behind them. "You will follow me, without a word." He sneered. "Or tonight, you die."

The trembling in me was so great that I feared my feet would not land on the street with each step I took. I filled my gaze with the back of James' shoes and the ground I walked upon, for fear that meeting anyone's gaze would alert them and pull more into this very dangerous situation.

I was certain of our destination and wondered if Lia knew we were coming and how angry James was. Did he know the bag of cash was hers? Would he hurt her?

To my shock, when we stopped and I raised my head, it was the church that I gazed upon. A haze surrounded it, like heat was rising off the ground in waves but only around my little sanctuary. Confused I looked around for Father Alden or Nettie, only to find both not on the steps but in the graveyard. It was difficult to see them clearly through the waves of magic, but they stood amongst the graves. Next to them, a woman in a cloak stood and the ruby hair that spilled out of the hood told me exactly who it was. But, before I could wonder why Lia was in the graveyard with a priest and a witch, my eyes fell on the man kneeling before them.

Collin had been found.

46

I saw the power that encircled the church and cemetery, but it didn't
prepare me for the feeling of walking through it. I had to physically
push against it to cross the barrier. Once through, I could see the tableau
more clearly.

Father Alden stood with Nettie to one side and Lia to the other. On
his knees, back to them and facing us was Collin, his head hung low. I
called out to him, but he didn't move.

Rushing over, I dropped down and realized he was in a sort of trance.
Looking up to Nettie, I saw the tears in her eyes. To each side of her,
the other two parts of the trio had no expressions, stone-faced to hide
their thoughts.

I stood as my maker approached. I turned, backing up to stand
next to Lia and join the line of witnesses. James commanded Nettie to
awaken Collin, which she did with a wave of her hand. He took in a
sharp breath to wildly looked around him.

His fear was palpable as his gaze landed on James.

"Stand," our maker barked, and my friend did as he was told. "You
thought yourself smart, didn't you?" James asked but clearly didn't want

an answer as he continued. "You had few rules: do not feed on the living and work when told to. In exchange, I gave you blood, time off, sanctuary from the sun and pay." He grabbed Collin's face. "You have been not only feeding but thieving and hunting and killing. You've put us all in jeopardy with your actions." He threw Collin to the ground, who wisely remained there, looking up. Standing up would have appeared confrontational and Collin was attempting to ride out his maker's wrath. "I've not only found your hoard of cash," he spat at Collin. "But I watched you kill and feed." Collin let out a gasp. "Try to tell me lies now, boy. Try to tell me you haven't been doing what I plainly saw you do."

Collin scrambled to his feet and seemed to calculate his next move. He looked back to me, questions in his eyes. I tried to tell him with my gaze to beg for forgiveness, to offer anything for mercy. He gave a small smile and a nod. I thought he might have understood what I told him.

He turned back to James and squared his shoulders. "I did."

James approached slowly. "Alone?" he asked.

"Alone," he answered.

I warred within myself. Did I tell James that I joined Collin on those nights? Would the punishment be less severe if shared across two? Or should I remain intact to help my friend after his price was paid? Did I implicate Lia if I confessed my crimes? As I thought her name, I felt her hand against mine and knew well that she was telling me to remain silent.

James nodded. "Get on your knees," he whispered, and Collin again did as he was told. When James reached behind his back, my friend took this moment to look back at me. My gaze was upon his face. He gave me a single wink and smile. I thought if he was not worried then neither should I be. I felt the wink was signaling to me that he had a plan. All these thoughts took no more than seconds, just enough time for James to lift the sharp blade in his hand and swing it down in a fatal arc with vampiric speed. Collin was still smiling as his head slid from his shoulders and landed on the ground behind him.

Nettie let out a single wail as I lifted my eyes to James and saw the bloody saber in his hand. Lia remained frozen. Alden took a step forward.

"How dare you?" He cried out. "On the Lord's soil you act with evil and make us all watch?"

James answered the priest's revulsion by stepping forward and pointing the blade towards the quietly crying witch. "Say another word and I tell your superiors what you have hiding here. I'm sure they'd do much worse to her." James wiped the blood of my dearest friend off by sliding the side of the blade over the priest's shirt. "He was mine to punish and I showed him a swift death. He did not do the same for all those that he killed. Where is your indignation for his victims?"

Alden stepped backwards, putting space between him and the armed vampire. "You do not get to decide the punishment for sin. Only God may do that."

James barked out a single laugh. "Your God is not our God, Father. He turns his back to us the moment we turn." He spun to face me. "Do you also have issue with my decision?" He raised the knife casually. "Would you like to confess anything?"

Shock had cemented me in place with no ability to speak. I stared at the two pieces of my oldest friend, disconnected and a foot apart.

One moment, I'd had a best friend and then I didn't. No final words, no ceremony, no warning. He was there and then he wasn't.

My usual cowardice won out. I shook my head, unable to talk.

He slid his eyes to Lia. "Anything?"

She also shook her head.

He addressed Nettie. "Hide him" he barked.

I saw her shakily step forward, tears waterfalling from her eyes. She was looked so much younger than her twenty-seven years, with the weight of the world upon her shoulders. Trembling hands rose parallel to the ground. She spoke something inaudible into the air and the earth below us shook. The empty vessel that used to house Collin's spirit, sunk into the dirt, as if being pulled down. When all traces of him were gone from sight, she stepped back into the line, turning into her brother's embrace. He held her, a stern gaze still upon the vampire that had used her to cover his acts.

"When we leave," he instructed, as if she a pupil and he a professor. "You will spell the ground so that no vampire may visit. And," he snapped. "If you allow another vampire to walk this soil, I ensure that you and your brother face the church. Am I clear?"

Nettie nodded her head against her brother.

James waved his hand towards Lia and I, unceremoniously walking from the graves and out into the street. We followed diligently, not looking at the humans on our way out. I didn't know what Lia was feeling but I knew that one glance to the priest and his sister and I would likely fall to the ground with grief. I had to focus on the space ahead or risk losing myself to the sorrow that was still held back by disbelief.

Once in front of the gentleman's club, James placed a small kiss on Lia's check. "I will see you tomorrow," he spoke without a hint of emotion.

She disappeared into her establishment without a look back and I didn't blame her. I'm sure she'd seen worse from James than his display that night and knew well not to push her luck. She'd only had to be witness this time, instead of punished.

This left myself and my maker to return to the factory. The silence of our walk made it hard for me to not start processing what'd just happened and what may lie before me. I couldn't fathom returning to that room, knowing the bed next to me would never be slept in again, couldn't picture the eternity that lay before me without Collin at my side. Since the days of boyhood, every plan I'd made included my best friend. We'd never dreamt a dream that didn't involve us being side by side.

But the reality that slowly slipped in was that Collin was truly dead and never to return.

As we approached the same door James had led us to the night he'd offered us jobs, I was irrevocably broken. I wished desperately that I could turn back the clocks to that first night – tell James we didn't need his job and send him away from that alley. Collin and I would have remained human and been long dead, but we would've died together.

Instead of entering the basement I knew so well, James continued down that alley, past his factory and to a small building behind it. I knew it to be his storage. I'd entered it only when needing to carry something heavier than a human could carry. This night, I carried nothing but the weight of extreme grief and the uncertainty of the future.

Once in the vast space of discarded things, James crossed to the back where a large steel door stood. The weight of it was clear as James pulled it towards him. The sound indicated that the hinges were not used often. He disappeared into the shadows of the room, and I dutifully followed. The walls were solid grey brick and met a cold floor the same shade. Dark stains dotted the ground but were far from the most unsettling thing present. Two thick chains were attached to an even thicker arch of iron that erupted from and disappeared into the concrete floor. As my gaze fell onto the shackles, I knew my nightmare was far from over.

He pointed at the chains. "Put them on your feet and put the locks in place. I will check so I suggest you do it correctly."

"I won't," my voice sounded foreign to my ears. The fear had changed my tone.

His power grew once again, filling the room. As his power increased, his volume dropped. "Don't think me stupid, boy." His laughter was vile, full of malice. "What you have done to rid yourself of the letters from Nettie, the crumpled letters for Lia, does not matter. I've read them all already. You have no secrets from me."

A fine quake filled my core and descended my arms and legs. I was wrong when I thought that Collin had been given a harsh punishment. He had died fast and been shown mercy. It was I that James was angrier with. Watching Collin die had only been the start of my torment. There was more to come.

James slowly prowled a circle around the chains. "You let your dearest friend – your brother – take the full blame. All the while, you committed those acts by his side." He looked up.

"Why let me live then?" I was finding my voice, recognizing that it was better to push back than be a part of whatever he had planned for this room.

"For two reasons," he bent over, lifted a chain and extended it to me. "Because you are a coward and therefore are likely breakable and trainable. Without Collin filling your head with his own defiance, I think you will eventually fall in line. He was never going to."

Rage was slowly replacing my fear and threatening to take over my reason. It would be better to die fighting James than resign.

"Secondly," he tossed the chain to land at my foot. "Lia loves you and keeping you means I have leverage against her." He rolled his eyes. "It's been a long time since I had a way to control her and I plan to take advantage."

"I won't," I pulled back my shoulder, flexing my muscles and preparing to fight.

"You will," he growled. "Because, if you don't, Lia and Nettie are next to pay the price for what you boys have done." This cooled some of my heated anger. "Nettie will be turned over to the authorities-" he dramatically waved his hand in the air. "I can only imagine what they'd do to her. And, of course, when it's clear that her brother has been protecting her, I'm sure he'll face a form of consequence. And sweet Lia," he smiled darkly. "She will not have swift death like your friend."

"She has nothing to do with this," I argued.

He had my face in his hand and my body in the air before I'd seen him move. "But, she does. She knew what you were doing, hid your acts from me and," he threw me against the brick wall, "gave you money to flee." Again, he tossed the shackles my way, letting them strike me as I lay on the ground. "She can endure a great deal of torture, Rhys. A great deal."

I shuddered at the thought of what he'd done to her over the years for him to make a statement like that.

Did I fight and risk that he meant what he said? The look in his eye was that of a man in the midst of madness. I truly believed he was going to torture someone for the crimes he felt had been committed against him.

It was me or Lia.

Grasping the chain, I closed the cold metal shackle around my ankle. He launched the lock my way and it slammed against my temple. When it clicked in place, he pointed at the second chain. I crawled to it, sitting in the middle of the floor and secured it around my other ankle. I snatched up the second lock and put it into its new home before he could strike me with it.

Crouching down, he found my eyes with his. "Soon you will beg to return to the life that I offered, and you sneered at. You'll realize the sweetness of a bed to sleep in, a good night's work and pay that you earned. You will thank me for the glass of blood I offer. I don't think it will be long to break you but know this," he slapped my face in a way that did not hurt but felt demeaning and put me in my place. "You will not leave this room until I am satisfied."

He moved to the doorway, silhouetted in its frame. "Do anything to escape this room, Rhys, and Lia pays the price."

Darkness enveloped me with the shutting of the door.

47

There were no sounds to break the sameness of the days that followed. Seeing in the dark was useless when only the walls and floor met my gaze. I would fall into sleep and awake, the only indication that time marched on. I'd lost track of everything, having no idea how much time had passed since I was left to my imprisonment.

Only the increasing hunger told me that hours turned to days and then to weeks. The gnawing in my gut would have been enough to drive any man insane but it was my thoughts that truly pulled me into madness.

Memories of Collin flooded my mind as soon as I woke each night. The film of his beheading played on repeat when I wasn't being plagued with him as a boy, him laughing, him with Diedre, him as we walked from our village to Glasgow, him when he cradled his dead sister, him after the turning, him... him... him... him....

He would have been better if he'd never met me.

Diedre would have been better if she'd never met me.

Nettie and Alden would have been better if they'd never met me.

Lia would have been better if she'd never met me.

The only respite from my torment was the occasional visit from the mouse. But he just looked at me, nose and whiskers twitching, eye imploring and hopeful. I'd say the same thing, "He's gone, mouse. He's not coming back." Then, the mouse would disappear under the door until his next visit. At first, I was happy to see the rodent, grateful for the company. But each time I had to say aloud that our friend was dead broke my heart and eventually I began to resent the little animal, wishing for it to stop reminding me of my loss.

And, then it stopped coming and I knew in my heart that it too had died, and I was completely alone with my regrets.

The ache in my stomach had spread until every fiber of my body was screaming in agony, begging for sustenance and none came.

When James came, I screamed out into the night, thanking him for coming. Then, I'd seen that what he held in his hand was not a glass of blood or a key but a whip.

I rolled away, giving him my back, unable to rise from the floor and without the energy to cry out when it ripped across my shirt to bare my flesh. The next hundred blows hit skin, sending flames across my body but still I remained silent. Weakness and lack of use had taken my voice from me. When the door shut, I could not even muster tears but only felt aching in my eyes as they tried to weep.

Again, I was left to madness and memory.

Upon waking one night, Collin and Dierdre met my gaze. They stood in the corner of the room, watching me. Immediately, I recognized them as apparitions. The grey of their see-through skin was made stronger by the grey of the walls behind them. Their pupils shined in the darkness with the light of spirits.

"Take me," I croaked. "Take me to Hell where I belong."

They continued to regard me, saying nothing. And there they remained for the entirety of the night, staring at me.

Time became meaningless and felt like a concept I could not understand or remember. There was no time - only hunger, the whip, falling asleep and waking.

Being immortal did not save me from damnation. Hell had come to me.

48

The floor sank away from me.

No, that wasn't right. I was being lifted, held in someone's arms. I wanted to open my eyes to see who it was but could no longer move my eyelids.

The chill of the air slid across me, and my shivers were violent.

Once inside, the sounds of the machines were not immediately recognizable. Fear shot an energy through me that was enough for me to open my eyes and see James' face hovering over me, looking forward.

When he lay me in the bed of the room I'd once shared with Collin, I didn't recognize it at first. Wildly I looked around, waiting for the next blow from a whip or ghost to tell me this was all in my head. Memory returned to me in fracture imagines but I'd long ago lost the ability to know what had been real and what was fantasy.

James sat on the bed and lifted my upper body to sit. He lay a glass against my lips and tipped until the blood touched my lips. I grabbed at it, gulping down the contents through mere instinct. I didn't care about anything but that blood.

"Slow down," James chastised as if speaking to a child. "You will vomit it up at that pace." When the glass was empty, I hesitantly handed it back to him. Only then did I begin to distrust his sudden appearance and kindness.

"I will bring another glass before sun rise," he smiled warmly. "You may need a few days to recover."

"How-" I choked out and swallowed to try again. "Why?"

"I think you've learned your lesson," he arched his eyebrow. "I trust you do not want to return to the chains?"

Shaking my head, I struggled to remain seated up without assistance. "How long?" I asked.

"Only ten years," he answered. When he stood, I flinched. If he noticed it, he didn't show it. He pulled open a drawer on the dresser between the two beds and pulled out clothes. Lying them next to me on the bed, he cocked his head to the side. "This time it was ten years. But if I ever see the need to send you back, it will be twenty. Do I make myself clear?"

I nodded.

"Now if I were you, I'd use this night for a very hot bath and be thankful for these new clothes and a bed to sleep in again. I'd appreciate the blood in my stomach and make this a fresh chapter in my story." I picked up the clothes, clutching them close to my chest, afraid that one wrong move or word would result in my return to the shackles.

He opened the door, walking through its frame and turned to face me. I flashed back to the night he'd locked me up - that same image of him standing in the entryway – and blinked back the terror that was threatening to overtake me. He spoke, "I'll bring the glass to you before dawn. Tomorrow night, you come to my office for it as you used to. My expectations have not changed."

"Thank you," I muttered.

He seemed pleased with that. "You're welcome, Rhys." Then he was gone.

I slid off the bed and onto the floor. My back was braced by the bed as I clutched the clothes like a life raft. I no longer wanted to be lost to my thoughts but couldn't help repeating one thing in my head over and over – ten years.

Ten years.

Ten years.

I'd been locked away for ten years.

Where was Lia? Were Alden and Nettie still at the church or had they fled. Would I blame them if they had?

Was I to just go back to things like the last ten years had not happened? Is that what James expected? I think he did and the last thing I wanted was to disappoint him.

Bracing myself with the bed, I pushed off and stood. My legs shook but held me. I was astonished by my own ability to endure. I'd starved for a decade yet still existed to walk to the bathroom and draw a bath like it was any other day.

Upon entering the quiet, white room, I started the hot water to fill the tub and faced myself in the mirror. What look back at me was a skeleton with skin. My eyes were so much bigger than they should have been, hovering above sharp cheekbones that looked like they may tear through my paper flesh. My shirt was long gone so nothing hid my upper body from sight. Each rib pushed against my grey-hued skin. I turned away from my grotesque reflection, removing my trousers and stuffing them into the rubbish, discarding that last piece of evidence, the last piece of the old me.

The joy I felt when I sunk into the hot water brought a tear to my eye. I could not recall anything in my century and a half existence that had ever been as exquisite as that soak. I remained in the water until the bath turned cold and I knew I needed to return to my rooms before I lost the last bit of energy I had.

Clean clothes on my clean body may have been more wonderful than the bath had been but the blanket over me in my bed was the greatest feeling of the night.

When James returned with the second glass of blood, it was genuine gratitude I felt for him. He was the reason I'd been in that dungeon for a decade, but he'd also set me free. I'd had the time to think about it and he'd been right. He'd given me food, shelter and employment and I'd defied him. It was my fault that I'd been in those chains. As sleep over took me, I felt two things: a profound determination to follow James' rules so I would never be punished again and excitement for the next night. I was acutely aware of the freedom I had and couldn't believe I'd ever thought this room to be a prison.

Laying in my room, I turned away to face the wall. Not wanting the see the ghosts of Deirdre and Collin staring at me from the corner.

49

January 1942

The trick had been to remain quiet. When I took my glass each night, I let James speak first then followed whatever instruction I was given. Working the machines was what I most enjoyed. I got to stay in the familiar space of the basement and return to my room. The men who worked alongside me never wanted to talk to me, so it was easy to remain silent.

The nights he sent me out to scare a man into paying or gather something he didn't want to fetch himself, filled me with dread. It wasn't the city I feared, although it was unrecognizable as the second world war amped up. Human supplies were being rationed and the people would line up in the hopes of getting food for their families. They would sometimes look to me but never begged. I'd stopped seeking out my reflection in the mirror years prior but must have looked like someone in the same situation because no one asked me for help.

No, it wasn't the city or the noises or the tasks themselves that made be dread leaving the factory, it was the worry that I'd be tempted to break a rule and James would find out. I made a point to be back as quickly as possible so he would know I'd behaved while outside the building.

Each time I returned, I stood before him, afraid that he would even wonder if I'd done something wrong and punish me for even the suspicion of wrong-doing.

Although, I'd followed his rules since I emerged from those chains 13 years prior, there were times I'd walk into his office for blood to see the whip was out. I'd take the beatings those nights, not knowing why it was happening or how to stop it from occurring but knowing that fighting was the worst choice for me.

I couldn't have told you a single name of the humans who worked the machines or the upstairs shop. I could not have told you the names of any of the local businesses or the politicians or the reason we were at war. I read no newspapers, listened to no radio and interacted with no one but James. I wanted no more out of life than to just get through each night without trouble. I only knew the month and year because of the calendar that hung in the basement. I didn't even know which human crossed off each day or why it mattered.

As the years ticked by, the ghosts hounded me less and less but still appeared in the corner sometimes, staring wordlessly. I'd whisper into the dark, begging them to tell me what they wanted but they'd stay silent, tormenting me with their lack of expression. I had so many tears for them during my first shackled years. I'd bellowed into the night for my lost friend and his sweet sister. Then, I'd found a comfort in convincing myself that they were together in death, but my kind lie to myself fell apart when I saw the spirits and their obvious lack of peace.

On a cold winter night, I rose as usual. My shirt was in need of a wash, but I worried it would not hold up to it. It had become thin from years of use, and I feared asking James for a new one. Since freeing me, he'd stopped giving me wages. Since I had no day off and no desire to be touched by a woman again, I had no need for money and therefore didn't complain about a lack of pay. I accepted that bed and blood were my salary. But it meant I had no way of buying new clothes. I hoped he would see the state of my garments and offer new ones, especially since he had garments in his very shop above my head.

When I walked into the office, I thought I may say something but quickly lost my confidence when I saw the whip on his desk. He noticed me looking at it and smiled. "Don't worry," he sneered. "I will not use it tonight. It is serving as a reminder only." He poured the blood and handed it to me. "I'm to leave tonight on business. It will only be a few days, but I trust you will do as told while I am gone, or the whip is the least of your problems."

I finished my meal and nodded, returning the glass to his desk.

He began shoving papers into a satchel. "I need you to go to the docks tonight. I'm expecting a very important shipment at midnight. Find a man named Nathan and tell him I sent you. Tell no one else and bring it straight here. Should anyone try to take it from you, you have my permission to kill but do not feed." He caressed the whip as he finished. "Am I clear?"

"Yes," I answered, staring only at the floor.

"Good," he sighed. "I'd hate to lose you for 20 years; you have become very useful to me." He left me in the empty office and a shudder ran through me. I knew that my sanity would not survive a return to the room, let alone two decades in its confines.

I left the building with plenty of time to make it to the docks and be there before midnight. The last thing I wanted was to mess this up. As I walked, all the possibilities for error flooded my brain. What if I couldn't find Nathan? What if the shipment didn't arrive or I missed it somehow? What if someone else got their hands on it? What if somehow carried back the wrong thing?

Anxiety filled me when I saw the activity on the docks. Several ships sat a parade rest, awaiting their next mission. Men pushed against and around each other carrying things on and off the boats, yelling phrases to each other. Some were in uniform, clearly soldiers either arriving or leaving for their part in the war. Women stood outside the mass of bodies, offering pleasures for the night to anyone who would take them up on it. I searched the crowd trying to figure out how to find this Nathan amongst the turmoil.

Behind me a voice whispered into my ear. "There is no Nathan." Slow recognition slid over me, and I turned to verify the words' owner.

Alden grabbed my arm and pulled me away from the crowd and behind a tall stack of crates where Lia and Nettie stood. My anxiety turned to terror that robbed me of speech. I couldn't be seen with them. I must flee.

Then, Nettie spoke. "You're leaving tonight."

50

Panic spread like flame across my senses. My brain screamed at my legs to run, run from the people in front of me. They stood there, allowing me to process the previous few minutes. Logically, I knew more than two decades had passed since I lay eyes on them, but I was still shocked by the aging. Grey streaked through the siblings' brown hair and the years were shown on their faces. But the eyes remained young and were full of pleading.

Lia was the hardest to look at. Her beauty remained unchanged, like I'd seen her only yesterday. The familiarity of her was too much for my shattered mind to handle. Gazing upon her brought it all back – the lovemaking we'd shared, the laughter, the dreams along with the vivid image of Collin's first night at the brothel, Collin teaching me to hunt and Collin's last moment.

"No," I stepped back from them. "No, you must go. I cannot be seen with you. I must find Nathan."

Alden took a small step towards me, hands up to show me he meant no harm. "Rhys, there is no Nathan. We made him up."

The panic was cranking up. If they lied to James, then I had no shipment to take to him. I would be punished.

Alden continued, taking another step. "We've been corresponding with him, building trust and entering into a negotiation of sorts. We've spent years proving Nathan's existence and intentions. Tonight was to be the first shipment to him but-"

Lia interrupted. "I know him and how to play this. He knows that others want this shipment as well. He believes it to be illegal liquors. He knows how dangerous this first meeting and shipment is, how badly it could go. Which is how we knew he'd send you instead."

Alden picked the narrative back up, continuing to close the distance between us. "The shipment is to be hijacked and this will be nailed to his door." Nettie came forward with a paper in her outstretched hand. I took it, realizing it was a photograph.

The photo was of a man, lying face down in the street. Blood pooled around the headless body. To his left was his missing piece and it seemed to look at the camera.

It was me. The corpse was mine.

My wide eyes ripped their gaze from the photo to the three standing in front of me. "Magic," Nettie smiled. "Only magic. But that photo was taken of the illusion with a real camera and that picture will remain for always. Once I use magic to send him the sensation of his progeny dying, he will believe this all to be real. That you died for his business, instead of him."

Lia decided Alden's slow approach wasn't necessary and brushed past him to stand directly in front of me. She pointed behind her to a wooden crate, then ensured I was looking at her. "You will get in that crate. Inside is plenty of blood and several books." She smiled. "You will be loaded on the ship tonight."

Alden came to stand next to her and Nettie joined. They all were a breath away from me. Alden grabbed one hand and Nettie took hold of the one still clutching the photo. Alden continued the plan. "A man

I know well is waiting for this ship and will take you somewhere safe. When you emerge from the crate, Rhys, you will be in California."

"America?" The tears began to roll now. Whether from fear or relief or sadness, I know not. But they flowed and something inside of me seemed to awaken.

"America," Lia nodded. "You are dead to Scotland, my love. And dead you will stay. You can never contact us. No letters, no telegrams-" she lay a hand on my cheek. "Do not even say our names. He can never know that you live."

"No," I began, wrestling to say all the things I'd wanted to say to them since the night in the graveyard. "No. He will find me." Panic threatened to creep in again. "He will know, and he will torture you."

Nettie squeezed my hand. "He'll not. He has a photograph of you with no head. He will feel you die. He will assume an illegal business transaction went wrong and you paid the price. He will shed no tear for you only for the money he thinks he's going to make off this enterprise."

Lia wiped my tears away and lay a kiss on my lips. When she drew back, she shook her head. "Please, Rhys. Please, go. We cannot bear knowing what he's done to you, what he continues to do to you. Please," her breath shuddered.

I searched all three faces. They all pleaded with their gazes for me to leave them forever. My heart swelled and the knowledge of what they'd done for me was painful in my chest. All these years, they'd never stopped fighting for me, helping me. I loved them all so much and would never be able to speak to them again.

But if I stayed, I still would not be able to speak to them. This life I was living was no better than being dead and I knew it. And, if I returned to the factory with no shipment, I'd face punishment or have to tell James the truth. We would all suffer.

I knew this was my only choice but was so afraid to take the next step.

Alden broke through my thoughts. "You must go now, Rhys. We've already lost too much time talking. Please, get in the crate so we may find the man who will load you onto the ship and take you far away from here."

"It's time, Rhys." Lia smiled. "It's time to go to America."

I let them lead me to the large box. Lifting off the lid, I saw the smaller box inside that was to be my companion on the journey. "You will have plenty of time to search its contents once on board," Nettie said.

Looking over those faces, words failed me. So, I pulled each one into an embrace. First Alden, who patted my back as we hugged. He spoke into my ear that he had prayed for me every night and would until he died. He told me to be good to others and never look back on my days in Scotland. When I hugged Nettie, she asked my forgiveness for the part she'd played in Collin's death and thanked me for keeping her safe by taking my years of torment without a fight. She took the photo that I realized was still clenched in my hands and gave it to her brother. I assumed from this that he would be the one to ensure James saw it. Last, came Lia who told me that she'd never forgive me if I tried to contact her and that I must find happiness in the new world. Then she whispered the last into my ear. "I love you, Rhys."

When I stepped into the crate, I had a moment of panic at the thought of being closed in but found I had plenty of room to maneuver. I crossed my legs and was able to sit at the bottom with the smaller box held in my lap. I could see that later, when sleep overtook me, I'd be able to curl onto my side comfortably. As I looked up at the three faces peering down at me, I said all I could think of. "I love you all."

Then, the lid wiped them from my sight. At first, the sounds of the nails being hammered in had frightened me. A broken part of me had been certain that this was a new punishment. The concrete room had been replaced by a crate and I'd be locked in for twenty years or more. However, my heart knew those three would *never* hurt me. I told myself this container was not a prison, but a carriage. I don't know how much time went by before I felt the whole thing lifted and carried but I do still remember the exact moments I was walked off Scotland's soil. The rocking of the water once I was placed somewhere in the ship was comforting.

I had a moment of anxiety while waiting for the vessel to begin its trip. The certainty that James would burst open the crate and rip me from it was so powerful that my breath quickened, and heat washed over me. But the moment passed as they usually did when I began to panic; the ship's horn brought me peace.

Only once I felt the boat pick up its pace and I knew I was in open water did I start to let myself believe that I was free.

51

I was too shaken by the night's unexpected turn of events to focus on the box that travelled with me. I merely sat there, letting tears roll down my face. I cried out of joy. I cried for the people who risked everything to free me. I cried over the fact I would never see them again and they would never know what became of me. I cried for Collin who was not at my side on the journey we'd dreamed of for so long. I cried out of fear that this may all be taken from me, that James would somehow be waiting for me in America, only to return me to the factory. I wondered how long it would take me to believe that I was free, how long it would take me to heal what my maker had broken inside me – or if that was even possible. I wondered if the Rhys that I had been so long ago would ever return.

Perhaps Rhys was truly dead.

Upon waking the next night, I found myself still safely inside the crate on a ship and let out a sigh of relief. It was all real.

Only then did I think to open the parcel that my friends had left me. Inside, I found several large wine bottles of blood. I didn't know how long I'd be at sea but knew well that I could go long without it. I decided rationing it to be the best choice. I pulled the cork from one and drank an amount that I felt was equal to the glasses James gave me each night. Recorking it, I returned it to the box and continued my search. The small envelope of money was stuffed with an amount that humbled me. I knew it was all from Lia and held it to my heart like I could connect to her through it in some way.

As promised, books were included but it was more than I'd hoped. Reading the titles, I could tell who had added which one. Gone with the Wind, The Great Gatsby and Rebecca were clearly from Nettie. The Wind in the Willows, The Adventures of Huckleberry Finn and the Grapes of Wrath were from Alden's collection as I'd spied them in his library many times. The staining on the cover and pages told me he'd loved these books well. Pride and Prejudice had Lia's name scrawled on the inside with her elegant handwriting. But it was the last title that made me laugh and could have been added to this group by anyone of them as I think they all likely found it hilarious – a well-worn copy of Dracula by Bram Stoker.

I was delighted at the idea that I'd be able to read all these books. While I could read and write, thanks to Father Michael, I never actually read a whole book. Now, I had nothing but time and several books before me. However, it wasn't the books or the blood that brought me the most joy. It was the three letters I found tucked within the novels that thrilled me.

Alden's was simple, the way most men write. He told me more of what he'd said on the dock. He told me I was not a damned thing and should not act as such. He told me to use my years left to spread love and help those who needed it most. He told me to use my strength to help those who are weak.

Lia's was written in the same beautiful script she'd used to write her name in her book. She told me that she was content in her captivity and that I was not to shed any tears for her. She told me she'd rather have had the time with me she did and say goodbye than never to have known me at all. She promised me she was safe, and that James had stopped hurting her a long time ago, that he did not care enough for her to hurt her and rather would likely find another boy to make vampire and then abuse. She told me to honor her by finding the most joy I could and finding my place in a new world. She told me again that she loved me but felt I already knew that and didn't need to be told any more.

While the first two were welcomed words and warmed my heart, it was Nettie's that held the most power.

Rhys,

Alden and I have not told you everything. I hope you understand why when you read this. I'm trusting you with much by revealing this to you and it's even more dangerous that I put it in writing.

I fled my village after a plague, this is true. But what we have kept secret from you is that our line continues.

I was married, still am married in the eyes of God, I suppose. But he is far from me. He, like you, had to die. He did this to protect himself and my daughter.

She showed power by her fourth year, and I knew she would be a great witch. But, as you know, those who are different are feared and many want to destroy that which they cannot control.

My husband, Robert, fell ill from the same malady that took our neighbors. I was able to use herbs to cure him, but we took the opportunity to make the village believe that he and my daughter, Lily, had died from the disease.

Like you, they fled in the night while I made a show of burying them and wailing over their graves.

I need not tell the whole tale, but it is Robert who will meet you in America and take you to safety. Only Alden and I know they live. We risked much to contact him and arrange this, but I believe that you and he will care for each other. I find comfort in knowing you will be with those that I love so dearly. I know that you can protect them in a way that no human can.

Please tell Lily and Robert how much I love them.

~Nettie~

I read the words over and over, making sure I understood what she said and what it meant. She had a daughter, a husband. They had fled to America as I was now. I would meet them when I arrived.

This had not been the first time that the priest and his sister had saved someone. This was not the first time they'd faked a death in order to set someone free.

How had I been so lucky as to have the trust of these truly good people? Why had they risked, and continued to risk, so much for someone like me?

Did I deserve this kindness?

I didn't know that answer, but I knew one thing – I would become the man that they believed me to be. I would be a good man and live with honor. I would earn the charity that Alden, Lia, Nettie and Nettie's family poured upon me.

In a plain, wooden crate on an ordinary shipping vessel on a part of the sea that I would never lay eyes on – a new chapter was begun.

PART TWO:
AUSTIN

52

February 1942
California

When I awoke, the first thing I noticed was that I was no longer rocking. All was still and the smells that seeped into my small, safe space were different. It was still the smell of the ocean but there were other scents mixed in. A heard a gull cry out and men speaking on top of each other. Engines revved, horns blared and somewhere in the distance was the definite sound of gunfire. I was confident I was on land which meant two things: I'd been unloaded while I slept, and I was officially in the new world that had been by boyhood obsession.

What was I to do next? I ran the instructions from Alden in my head over and over. I was certain that he'd told me that someone would meet me. But, was I to emerge from the crate and await him? I didn't know.

I decided that staying in the wooden box one more night was the wisest choice. I still had blood to drink and had planned on finishing Rebecca this night, so staying where I was didn't upset me at all. The only downside to my plan was if the man was waiting for me on the dock and when I didn't approach, he'd leave. But, if I arose the next night and did leave the box with no help awaiting, I was still in America with cash and no one holding me prisoner.

It wasn't long before a knocking on the side of my hideout startled me, and man spoke into the crate. "I'm Robert," his voice sounded American with a hint of Scotland underneath. "We're loading you onto a truck and taking you out of here. Don't say anything until I removed the lid. Remember," he chuckled, "you're a package."

Then, that same voice boomed out into the night. "Found it. This one's mine. Load it up." Minutes later, I was raised into the air and walked to a new transport. I knew nothing of vehicles other than their existence and sudden arrival in Glasgow. Most Scottish were not wealthy enough to own one but the well-off and owners of businesses loved them, so they still filled our streets. This engine sounded louder than what I was accustomed too but it may have been because I'd heard nothing but the ship and the sea for two weeks.

Air roared around the crate. I wanted so badly to see what was around me, finally lay eyes on America but knew I must be patient. "Just finish your book," I told myself but couldn't focus on the words. I was too excited, too eager to break free. I still couldn't fully believe I'd arrived, couldn't believe I wouldn't open the crate to find this was an elaborate ruse to test my loyalty, that I was still in Scotland and would be thrown into chains for my attempt to flee.

After an eternity of new sounds and smells, we slowed and stopped. I heard the engine die, a door open and close, then a rap at my wall. "Ready?" this man asked. However, he didn't wait for an answer before wrenching on the lid above me. I saw the pry bar forced into the top and felt the blast of fresh air when the lid lifted.

Once the cover was a removed, only a steel ceiling filled my gaze. I'd have to venture out to begin to assess my new environment. Standing was shockingly easy as I'd rationed my blood and was feeling strong. Rising out of the box, it was clear I was on the back of a pickup truck and in some form of warehouse. I had to turn to see my accomplice.

Robert had a body formed from working hard for a majority of his years. The brown of his hair and beard matched the brown of his eyes. The sun had tanned his skin and smelled of summer despite it being winter. His smile was genuine, as broad as his shoulders. He offered his hand, and I used it to climb out of the crate and onto the ground.

"Welcome to the United States, Rhys. You've made it."

"Where are we?" I asked, hearing the awe in my own voice.

"We're about halfway between California and Texas," he answered. "We need to stop. The sun is coming up and we both need sleep." He gestured to the side of the massive garage that we seemed to be parked in. Along the wall were a dozen cots, all with blankets and pillows. "It won't be warm," he chuckled. "But I don't think you'll mind that and we're safe here. It's a bunker for soldiers on long travels."

"But, you-" I worried.

He lifted his hand. "I've slept in far worse and lived to tell the tale. I assure you these clothes are warm, and this place will heat up when the sun starts to hit it. You got enough blood to last you another night?" He asked it so plainly that I was a little startled. I knew humans were aware of vampires, but it was so infrequent that I met a new one, it was going to take a little time to get used to.

"Yes," I answered.

"Let's get some shut eye then," he crossed to the cots, and I followed. "When the sun sets, we finish the drive. This time, you can sit in the front and see it all. No more hiding for you, son. You're free."

While I awaited the sleep to take me, I thought of that phrase and started to feel it. After all the years of turmoil, grief, crime and hiding, I was finally on the other side. I'd realized my dream. I'd gotten away with my sanity and still had lifetimes ahead of me.

I was free.

53

Just the experience of being in a motor vehicle was extraordinary. We appeared to fly like birds and the scenery whipped past us.

I'd never seen a picture of America, only knew it through stories. I hadn't known what to expect, had no images in my head when I'd spoken of it. What rushed past me as we drove was so much more than I could have hoped for. There was so much wide-open space. I saw desert and mountains and water and towns. It was so different from the packed slums and stink of Glasgow that it felt almost fantastical. How could there be so much space?

Robert was either a man of few words or knew that I needed time to take it all in before I'd be able to speak of anything.

I had no idea what Texas was or why we would end there, I only knew that each minute I felt further and further away from dead Rhys, from James and those shackles.

Intermittently, the thought of Collin would encroach my wonderment. I'd think about how much he would've loved this and then I'd push that thought away.

In my lap, lay the small box of books, money and letters. I'd finished the blood that night but didn't care at all about that. What remained in the box was more valuable than any blood. I would've fought to the death to protect those books and letters.

"We're here," Robert broke the silence just as I was starting to smell the dawn on the horizon. "Just in time, too."

He turned off the main road to a path of dirt, barely wide enough for the vehicle we rode in. To me it appeared as if we drove straight into darkness. Mountains were far off in the distance and seemed to run from us as we drove towards them. Trees on either side of us changed from sparse to thick at a rate that gave me the impression of being swallowed. Suddenly, the density opened like a mouth and I saw lights surrounding a one-story home that stretched into the darkness to the left and right of us. The truck slowed to a crawl, then stopped in front of a great arch of steel over a walkway of sorts, leading to the front entrance.

I thought we must be in the wrong place. At any moment, a man with a weapon would emerge from the vast estate to tell us to be gone.

Instead, the door swung open and a woman ran from house to truck, arms wide open. She was so similar to Nettie that I thought it must be her. But this woman was the Nettie I'd met decades ago, as if I'd stepped back in time. My expression must have startled her because she stopped before wrenching the car door open and giggled. "Have I scared you?" She asked with no hint of Scotland in her words, it was all the sharp syllables of America.

Opening the door, I exited to see her without glass between us. It must be Lily. It was the only explanation for how much she looked like a witch in Scotland. "You look so much like your mother," I gasped. "It's like seeing a ghost."

She clapped her hands together and squealed. "I love the way you talk. I'm so happy to meet you. You have to tell us all about mom and Scotland and my uncle and your trip."

Robert came around the truck to meet his daughter, clearly more in control of his emotions that this girl could ever be. She wore he heart on her sleeve and I was instantly endeared to her. "Let him rest, sweetie," she chastised her. "I know you have better manners than this." He kissed the top of her wild brown hair and led her back to the door. I followed as he continued to speak to Lily. My box of treasures was clutched close to my chest. "Where's Simon?" he asked her.

"Guess he stayed in town tonight," she drawled. "He wanted to be back for you and him but said he may have to stay. He'll be back tonight, I'm sure."

Robert stopped on the porch, turning to me. "As those who live here," Robert grinned, "we invite you into our home."

"Yeah, come in," Lily squealed. Then she and her father crossed into the house.

Inside the threshold was more space that I could fathom. So many places to sit and rest. Painting and drawings augmented each wall. I was overcome with it all and foolishly wanted to return to the comfort of my crate to sleep. I knew I was filthy and smelled of unwashed skin. My clothes barely clung to me. My only earthly possession were a few books and some letters in a wooden box. I worried that merely walking through this home I left remnants of dirt on everything I passed. I did not belong here. Still, I dutifully followed the man and his daughter as she chirped excitedly about what she thought Scotland must look like.

Down a long hallway, we entered a room to my right. In it, thick curtains hung over each window. Two dressers faced us from a far wall and opposite them a large closet was open to reveal it was empty. Between the two dressers was a bed larger than any I'd ever seen. The covers were a deep green, the color of pine trees. I quickly counted six pillows at the top of the bed, against a rich mahogany headboard. "This is yours," Lily chimed. "You can put whatever you want on the walls. Simon doesn't care."

Incredulously, I swept my gaze from the room to her. "Surely not," I said. I pulled back on the harshness in my voice. "It is too much. I can sleep in the servants' quarters. I do not belong here."

Lily looked to her dad and back to me. "What do you mean? Of course you belong here, knucklehead. And we don't have servants' quarters. Everyone here gets a room. This one is yours. It's been empty forever," she crossed to me. "You've got your own bathroom. It's the door next to the closet. I'll find you some clothes and leave them outside the doors. We've got plenty to go around, trust me. See ya at sundown." They left and shut the door to leave me alone. Then I heard her from the hallway. "I want to hear about my mom when you wake up."

For minutes I just stood frozen, certain this was a joke or a test and they would return to take me to my actual chambers. I waited as dawn approached. Finally, I made the choice to strip to nothing and sleep in the bed without bathing. There was not enough time to wash. I could apologize to them when I arose for any filth I left in the pristine sheets.

As I expected, the bed was fabulous. It wasn't just because I was comparing it to a wooden crate but because it was true luxury. I sank into the mattress and the covers enveloped my naked body like a cocoon. I heard the sound of clothes being set on the floor outside my door but ignored it. The curtains were thick enough that I did not need to worry about the daylight but I was too comfortable to move.

I was certain that the night would reveal that I had, in fact, been put in the wrong room so I was determined to enjoy every moment of this sleeping arrangement while I had it.

54

New pants and shirt greeted me as I cracked open the door and pulled them inside. The shower was wonderful enough that I stayed in it longer than needed. Once dressed, I contemplated what to do with my books and letters, afraid to leave them in the room unattended but knew I couldn't continue to carry them around. I pushed the box under the bed and added my old garments to the stash under the bed as well. I never wanted to wear them again but wasn't sure what to do with them.

Following the sounds of laughter, I moved down the hallway and into a massive room. It was like the heart of the home, people moving about and each with a clear task. The left side of the room was a kitchen area with Robert and another man working to cook some kind of meat. Lily was facing a man who held a plate in his hand. She scooped some form of food from a bowl and plopped it onto his plate. He moved to the grill where Robert put the sizzling meat on top of the mash that Lily had given him. The man then moved to the table in the other half of the room. I say table but that word doesn't correctly describe its size. If you'd flipped the wooden furniture piece onto its side, it easily could have been a good start to a small home. A man and woman already sat there, finishing off a similar feast. I was fascinated. It had been so long since I'd seen a human cook or eat, I'd forgotten that they did it.

Lily interrupted my observation. "Rhys. Come get yours." I was going to explain that vampires don't eat food when I turned to see her ladle something from a pot on the back of the stove and pour it into a large glass. To my shock, she crossed to me and extended the glass for me to take.

"Thank you," I managed.

"You can sit at the table," she offered. "Everyone is welcome here."

Looking to the humans at the table, I saw two of them nod and one stare intently at what he ate. Cautiously, I found a seat and began to sip. It was a different taste but welcomed nonetheless. The man who refused to look at me pushed back on the chair and stood to place his plate in a sink, then left through a back door. Lily joined the meal at my side, placing her own heaping dish down in front of her. By the time Robert had completed his duty as chef and sat with his own meal, only he, his daughter, I and the man who cooked with Robert remained. The other two people had finished and left to unknown places.

As father and daughter ate, I finished my drink and sat quietly. I'd no idea what to say. I watched the stranger move all pots and pans to the sink and pour a second ladle of blood into a glass. He crossed to us, placed the drink before me and took my empty glass to place it in the sink. "I don't need more," I stated and realized my rudeness. "I appreciate it, but I canna drink anymore."

The man smiled and came to sit at a chair facing me. "Then I'll have it." He reached for the glass, pulling it to him and lifting it to his lips. I hadn't realized until that moment that he was also a vampire but focusing now, I could feel the magic subtly around him and noticed the lack of heartbeat.

"I apologize," I stammered. "I didn't feel it at first."

"No need to apologize, Rhys." He wiped the back of his hand over his mouth. "You must be overwhelmed."

I laughed. "I am. So many new smells and sounds and faces."

"Oh," Lily clapped. "You haven't met." She pointed at the vampire. "This is Simon. He owns this place." She pointed back at me. "This is Rhys."

"I knew it must be," he extended his hand which I shook. "It's not like Scottish vampires wonder onto the ranch often."

Robert told Simon the story of arriving to the port to find my crate, the trip to the bunker to sleep, the drive to the ranch. Simon was asking questions and Robert answering. But in truth I was not listening. I studied Simon. His hair was the color of straw that has been left too long in the sun, a mix of yellow and light brown. It was short on the sides but longer at the top, brushed to the side and appearing almost wet with styling products. His blue eyes were surrounded by heavy lashes, his jaw was sharp and stubble covered it. His voice was accented like Lily's, a sort of slowing to the words with a melodic cadence that I would learn was how many people in the southern part of America sounded. But every so often, he'd say something and a hint of Britain would intrigue me.

"-my mother." I heard Lily's words and turned to her, trying to focus on what she was saying. It was evident that she'd been expecting something from me when she stopped speaking. Again, I was in awe of how much she resembled Nettie, finding it hard to not be fond of her already.

"Say it again, please." There was no way to hide that I'd not been paying attention.

"Tell me about my mother," she repeated.

"Oh," I glanced at Robert and saw a mix of curiosity and sorrow. Simon remained interested in the conversation without showing any concern for what I may say. I found Lily's hopeful eyes. "She's lovely. She and Alden, your uncle, were my dearest of friends." I stopped but could see she wanted more. "She looks exactly like you but 20 years older. She loves to read and sing and draw."

"She does?" Lily asked. "And what about her magic? Is she very good?"

My head swiveled to Robert and Simon. I didn't know how to answer. I was so shocked by her candidness. Simon nodded. "Go ahead; we in this room know."

I turned back to Lily. "She's amazing. She can bring flowers from the ground and weave a spell with her hands to make you invisible."

Lily grinned like a child being given a candy, looking up at the ceiling and resting back in her chair. "I knew it," she cooed, then focused back on me. "Will you tell me all the things she does so I can try to do them, too? I mean, I can do a lot, but I'd like to practice something new, you know what I mean?"

"I do not," I responded truthfully. "What we can do, vampires I mean, is not like your power. We get what we get and cannot change it or grow it though practice."

"Well," she slapped my arm playfully. "That's sad for you but also you dreamboats get to be young forever, so I don't feel bad."

I barked out a laugh and was surprised by the ability to still genuinely feel glee. She must be 30 by my calculations but had the spirit of one so much younger. She was so honest and real that it was refreshing.

"Okay Lily," Simon stood. "You can interrogate him later. Why don't you go do your chores and I'll give him a tour? If we have time, we can all meet back in the den."

"Deal," she smiled, gathering plates and glasses to move to the sink.

"I'll get to it," Robert stated as he left though the back door everyone else had been using all night.

"Ready to see your new home?" Simon asked.

55

Through the back door, was an expanse of green. Acres of grass and trees spread before us. I smelled flames and saw several small campfires scattered over the vast land. I heard cattle from all around, the sounds coming from far and near. Somewhere in the distance, someone was rapping a hammer against wood in a steady rhythm. Several men moved through the night. To our right, perhaps a thousand or so feet away was a red barn that appeared to be our first stop as Simon spoke.

"We call this place Lost Souls Ranch. Ostensibly, it's a cattle ranch. More truthfully, it's a place for those who have no home, who have to hide, who need sanctuary. Everyone has something to do that keeps this place running. Sometimes they stay for a day, sometimes a year and sometimes they finish out life here."

I nodded, understanding some of what he said but not the scope. I wanted to ask questions but did not want to appear rude or ungrateful. I hoped, if I remained silent, he would answer them without me inquiring.

"You're welcome here. I wouldn't have exposed the ranch if you weren't welcome. However," he pulled the barn door open. "there are rules."

I flashed back to the night James found us: the walk to the factory, the list of expectations, the cruelty. Shaking my head helped push the thoughts back down and away from my consciousness.

Simon entered the barn and I followed to see stables of horses, neighing and shuffling excitedly. "Just like we accepted you, I expect that you accept others. We don't discriminate here. There will be no fighting. That is number one. Understand?"

"Yes," I answered, although I didn't fully understand.

"Everyone pulls their weight." He pulled open a gate to let a large, white mare saunter out. He whispered into her ear and she came to stand at my side. "Do you ride?" he asked. I shook my head. "Then, she's perfect. Sweetest thing you ever did meet. Climb up and wait." I did, although it was quite sloppy compared to how smoothly Simon strolled up to a massive black horse and mounted. "Let's walk the trail," he commanded, and I realized it wasn't to me. I felt power slide through the building.

As the horses obeyed and walked us out of the barn, I turned to him. "You speak to animals," I smiled. "Collin-" my words died in my mouth. I couldn't bear to speak of him and let the sentence go unfinished.

"I do," he admitted, not pushing me to explain who Collin was. "Very handy when you run a cattle ranch."

As we cantered into the night, I saw the campfires waiting for cold men to take breaks by their warmth. I saw small cabins with lights inside, a man working to fix a fence, cows drinking from watering holes or sleeping in groups. I couldn't begin to fathom the sheer size of this ranch and how many residents currently worked it, but I was awed the same.

All the while, Simon continued his speech. "Some live in the main house with us and some choose the buildings out in the property. Some want company and join us for meals and some hunt on the land to make their own meals. And, whatever they choose is all right by me as long as they follow the rules."

"Are not fighting and doing your work the only rules?" I asked, surprised by how simple his expectations were.

"And, keep the true nature of this place secret." He clicked his tongue and the horses stopped so he could look me in the eye. "That's most important. If everyone here aren't safe, then everything we've done is gone."

I nodded. "I'm not sure I completely understand. Why would there be fighting here?"

He cocked his head. "Forgive me. I'm so used to hiding things that I didn't speak plainly." He leaned his elbow onto the strong neck of his mare then held up his hand to point at each finger as he spoke. "We got vampires, witches, shifters, werewolves and the occasional fae. And, not all of 'em are happy about each other being here."

"What?" I blurted it out, making my ignorance clear.

He smirked, sitting back up straight and telling the horses to walk again. "Like Travis back at dinner. The man who pretended his food was the most interesting thing he'd ever seen?" I nodded. "Well, he's been here some time now – a shifter – and he don't like vampires much."

"Oh?" I muttered.

"Yeah," Simon asserted. "See on the surface you'd think 'What a bastard", right? You'd wanna show him he's got nothing to worry about or try to make him accept you?"

His silence indicated he was expecting a response. I chose honesty. "I don't know how I would've handled it if I'd known it was me he didn't like. I mean, he doesn't know me."

"Exactly," Simon agreed. "But," he slowed his horse so we we're side by side. "His wife and kids were murdered by vampires. See? So, no wonder he doesn't like us. Can you blame him?"

"So why is he here?"

"Because he's got nowhere else to go." Simon nodded, wisely. "And, I think it takes a real low time in your life to come to a vampire and ask for work when you hate us so much. So, he gets a cabin on the property and safety in exchange for helping brand the cattle and keep them from being stolen." He clicked his tongue to stop the horses again. "A month ago, he wouldn't come near us. Now, he comes in for dinner." Simon cocked an eyebrow. "I think that's progress."

Simon started the horses moving again and we were approaching one such cabin. From inside, I smelled flame, some kind of human food and something I didn't know. It must have been an American smell because it was unrecognizable. A hint of it had been in the kitchen early so perhaps it was a type of food I hadn't been exposed to yet.

Our ride paused in front of the abode, and I dismounted when I saw Simon had. He approached the door, giving it two strong knocks. I came to stand next to him, that new smell growing stronger. When the door opened, a man stood before me. Simon was the same height as me and this man was two or three inches taller. His skin was brown, not from sun but from lineage. His time in the sun made it hard to guess age but I'd put him at in his early to mid-thirties. His hair was inky black and long, tied back with a string of leather. That smell was so strong now that I knew it was this man. The odor hung under the smells of sunshine and sweat. The fire roared in the fireplace behind him, and pipe tobacco still swirled in the air.

"Pedro," Simon began. "We have a new man. Rhys," he looked at me. "This is Pedro. He works the vehicles and will teach you. We need more than one man who can fix these trucks."

I extended my hand, feeling a ripple of something run down my hand. "What are you, then?" I asked, not sure if it was rude but unable to stop myself.

His laugh was deep and had an edge of roughness to it. "Let me guess," he grinned. "It's your first time meeting a werewolf?"

56

After agreeing to meet Pedro in the dining room after sundown the next night, we continued our tour of the property. It was breathtaking in its beauty and size. I marveled at what Simon had created in this place. I found it both wonderous and sad that this place needed to exist at all. I had no hate for creatures different than myself. Why would anyone care what a person is, especially if they cannot control it? Then I thought of the humans I'd killed and shame made my heart heavy and my stomach ache. I could understand why vampires would be hated. We didn't have to kill, didn't have to be cruel, didn't have to abuse our powers … but some of us did.

Then there were vampires like Simon and Lia, vampires who used their position for good. I wanted to be counted as one of them – the good guys.

Once back in the main house, I learned more of the structure. Simon owned the property and ultimately had a say in who was allowed on the ranch. He was the face of the ranch when going into the nearby city of Austin. Much like James' business, the bankers and such believed the ranch was handed down from son to son. No one asked many questions, likely because they liked the money Simon brought into the city.

Robert was in charge of the workers. He provided assignments, kept the paperwork and helped to create identification for those who needed it when they left. He was a construction man, good with building things and making plans. He was the one who told Simon what supplies the ranch needed when he went into the city.

Lily was in charge of the main house. She made the lists of supplies needed for the house, planned meals and kept beautiful vegetable gardens when the season allowed. It was she who gave me the room I was to stay in. She had names for each room and called mine the forest room. She'd offered to help me pick out art for my room and I promised that, when the time came, she could.

Pedro was the "machine man" as they called him. He handled all the ranch equipment, repairs of any machinery – including automobiles – and the decisions about what to get and what was a waste of money. Simon insisted that if Pedro said a piece of equipment was unsavable, then no one could fix it. He'd learned from his father who had the position before him and had passed the previous year. Pedro was raised on the ranch.

Together, they'd created a combination of business and home that should be the example for so many others, but the secrecy of its full purpose was what made it wonderful.

I sat in the great room I'd first entered the night before, what Simon called his den. The couches and chairs were plentiful and looked equally comfortable. I chose a chair, sinking into its softness. Robert and Lily shared a couch. Simon stretched out across a second couch. I wanted to listen to them talk all night. I loved the rhythm of their speech, loved the joy in their voices and the efficient way they spoke of what the plans were for the rest of the winter.

Unfortunately, the conversation lulled, and all eyes turned to me. "So, how old are you, Rhys?" Lily asked.

"Lily," Robert chastised. "That's none of your business. Rhys, you don't have to answer."

"That is alright, Robert." I smiled, warmly. "I do not mind it and I like that she is so candid. I was born in 1784, Lily."

"Holy mackerel," she exclaimed. "You think I'd be used to it, knowing Simon and all, but we don't get many vamps here and it's always weird to see someone who looks younger than me and then hear they're hundreds of years old, you know?"

"I could see that, yes." I agreed. "There is so much for me to learn and become accustomed to, as well."

"You talk so fancy," she smiled. "We're gonna have to teach you some words. People will know you're from overseas, but they can't know you're from another time."

"Very good point," I said.

"I'll teach you how normal people talk here, and you tell me stories about my mom? Deal?"

"Deal," I nodded.

"Simon is older than you and you'd never know," she glanced over at him. "How old do you think he is?"

"I wouldn't know," I answered truthfully. "Is there a way to know the age of a vampire?"

Simon shook his head. "No," he instructed. "You can sense power, the more powerful the vampire, the older they likely are. Although," ne nodded knowingly. "There are ways to dull a vampire's power." I nodded but didn't indicate that I knew from personal experience. He continued, "I was born in England in 1581."

"Ah," I smiled. "I thought I heard England in some of your words."

"Really?" he arched is eyebrows. "After all these years? Interesting."

"Simon was on the first ship from England to America. He helped build the first settlement." Lily was full of information. I made a mental note to not share with her anything I would not want repeated. I didn't think she meant harm, just that see was a very honest woman.

"They've heard the story before," Simon responded. "Lily loves it. Thinks it's like a storybook tale."

"It is," she exclaimed. "I wish I'd been there."

"No," Simon was stern. "You don't." He turned to me. "The settlement was an utter failure. Men starved, were lost to the wilderness. It didn't last long."

"How-" I started but wasn't sure if I should ask.

"Was I turned?" he clarified.

I nodded but it was Lily who picked up the tale. "He went hunting for food and got lost. He was in the woods for days, starving and dying. Some native people found him and took him back to their village. One of them turned him."

"I would have died," Simon said. "Was dying. The best I can guess, I had an infection from a wound on my leg. The fever was minutes from taking me when I was found. I stayed with them until I had fed a few nights, then returned to the settlement. I thought I'd just turn the remaining men – that a settlement of vampires was a great idea. Thankfully, they were all gone and I couldn't because it was a terrible plan."

"They left him," Lily exclaimed. "Just left him to die in the woods."

"To be fair," Simon responded. "Many had gone into the woods and not returned. I'm sure they thought I was gone for good."

"What did you do?" I asked, fascinated by his story.

"I returned to the people that had saved me. Lived with them for quite a long time. A few vampires were amongst their people and we were accepted as part of the tribe. My time with them was my inspiration for this place."

Wrapping my head around the fact that he had lived this incredible story was difficult. He told it so nonchalantly, like it wasn't the stuff of fiction novels. He was like a hero from one of Nettie's beloved books.

"He's being too modest," Lily interjected. "He also helped create Austin. Came when it was still Waterloo and hunted with the guy the city was named after."

I looked at him for confirmation. He smiled. "We all have stories, Lily. We all have events that lead us to this place. The only difference is that Rhys and I get much more time for our stories, so they seem like more than they are. If you," he pointed at her, "had hundreds of years, you'd also do some cool things. I have no doubt about that. I've known women like you in my time and women like you change history from behind the scenes."

She smiled proudly. "That's true."

"Plus," he continued. "If you'd been alive in those early days, they'd have burned you at the stake."

I saw Robert wince, but he didn't say anything. I didn't know if he'd known how much I'd been privy to of Nettie's history, so I kept my mouth shut.

"That's very true," Lily agreed and didn't seem the slightest bit upset by the comment. "It's a shame, though. Because," she waved her hand over the room and stars sparkled across the ceiling like we'd been standing outside on a cloudless night. "Witches are pretty handy."

"That they are," Simon conceded. "Very pretty."

"Thanks," she beamed. "Been practicing. I get bored when it's this cold out. Can't really be in nature like I want." She lay down on the floor to look up at the sky she'd created. Robert joined her at her side, sprawled across the floor. My curiosity overcame my shyness and I laid on the ground to look up at the starry expanse of the night ceiling. Each star seemed to sparkle, its own part of the magnificent tableau.

"Perhaps," I said. "Someday you can make a summer sky for me. I can't remember the sun."

"Oh," she squealed. "I'll start practicing."

Could she do it? Could I see the sun again someday. Before I could ask, Simon's declaration that the vampires needed to get to bed pulled her focus and the ceiling was wiped clean of magic.

We said our good nights and I headed down the hall to my room. When I was inside it, I made a choice. Pulling the box out from under my bed, I carefully unpacked it. The letters went into the top drawer of one of the dressers. The books were lined up on the top. When I lay down for the day, I rolled to my side to look at the simple line of novels.

Then, I quietly thanked the people who had given me those books and somehow gotten me to safety – to my new home.

57

Pedro was at the table when I came into the dining room the next night. Sat next to him was the shifter, Travis. He was talking to Pedro and grew silent when I entered, staring back down at his plate like the night before. "Good evening, men." I made a point to sound as nice as possible, then crossed to the stove. Lily was the only one there that night, stirring two pots, one large and full of some type of stew, the other small and full of warm blood. I ladled my own blood that evening as she was clearly distracted. She wasn't her usually chatty self and I thought I might know why.

She likely thought she was hiding it well, but I saw the quick glances back to the men at the table. I smelled the heat rising off of her and knew she was attracted to one of them. Since Travis was clearly closer to her father's age, I would've wagered a bet that it was Pedro who was sending her heart raced and stealing her words.

Smiling, I found a place at the table. "Will you join us?" I asked Lily.

"Um," she looked around trying to decide her next move. "Okay." She cut the flame under the stewpot, filled a bowl with the fragrant course and sat next to me, directly in front of the wolf. He slid his eyes from Travis to her, then to me and down at his bowl. I knew then that he felt the same for the witch as she did for him.

Did her father know?

"What will we do tonight?" I asked Pedro.

He took a moment to process my words, likely flustered by the female next to me. "Uh, well," he cleared his throat. "I'd like to see what you already know and then go from there."

"That will be easy," I quipped. "I don't know much."

"We'll see but don't worry. I can teach anyone."

Travis stood, wordlessly placing his bowl in the sink and leaving out the back door. Pedro followed with his own empty bowl, so I downed the last of my blood and placed the glass in the sink. "You good if we leave, Lily?"

"Yes," she answered. "You're the last so I'll just wash up." She was scooping stew into her mouth and making a point to not look at either of us.

When Pedro and I were outside, far enough away from other ears, I turned to the man. "How long have you two been in love, then?"

He jerked, turning to face me. "What?"

"I can smell it, hear your hearts racing. It's more than sheer infatuation."

I saw the calculations in his eyes, knew he was deciding how best to answer. Ultimately, he kicked the ground. "Damn vampires. You're impossible to fool."

"Can werewolves not tell these things?" I was genuinely curious. As far as I knew, he was the first of his kind that I'd met, and he seemed willing to teach. Perhaps he only planned on teaching maintenance to me, and I was pushing too far. I waited for his answer.

"First of all, it's lycanthrope. Werewolf is what humans call us and we allow it, but the proper term is lycanthrope and no, we can't smell love."

"It's not love exactly," I said as we began to walk. "It's sort of a chemical that comes off you when you're truly entranced by someone. It's more than a lust or a want. It's a reaction from your core. The heartbeat is different and when two people are truly in love, that beat syncs when they are near each other. Much like you and Lily."

"We need to tell her dad, but we're scared. I waited too long to tell mine so I think we should do it soon. She wants to wait longer," he spoke to the ground while he led me to a large outbuilding.

"What are you afraid of?" I asked.

"That I'll be sent away or Robert will take Lily. This is the only home we know. I was born here, and she was too little to remember before she lived here. It would devastate us to leave and to be separated." He was being so honest and vulnerable that it made me want to help them.

"Do you think that will happen?" I asked, not knowing Robert or Simon well at all.

"I don't," he said as he opened the door to what I now realized was a large garage. "Simon wouldn't send either of us away. But, I'm not sure about Robert. He's so protective of Lily."

"I see," I followed Pedro inside. The area was packed with all types of machinery. I didn't know what most if it was. Two older trucks were parked in the middle and a space in the back was free, I figured to work in. "What is the other option, though? Continue to love in secret? I hope you don't take offense, but you don't have much time in this life. Why waste any more wondering what could be?"

"I've said that same thing to her." He indicated that we were to cross to the back corner. I headed in that direction. "I don't want to wait. I want to marry her, but we have to tell her dad. I don't want to keep seeing her without his blessing, it's wrong."

The rest of our time together that night was spent on various pieces of equipment. It turned out that all my time fixing James' machines had taught me much more than I realized. Most of what I would be working on was ranch and farming equipment, but it was surprisingly similar when it came to figuring out why it wasn't working. Pedro showed me the pieces that were now for parts only, the ones we were trying to keep working and the ones that were new. He would be with me for the first few months until he felt confident delegating tasks to me. In the beginning we would tackle all the projects together so I could learn. I was most curious about car engines and he assured me we would have plenty of opportunities to work on the vehicles as they were always needing some kind of maintenance.

About an hour before dawn, we returned to the main house. He was explaining that there were people who worked the day time, completing chores while we slept, and we were essentially the night shift. It was a 24/7 business running a ranch, so it took great coordination and participation to keep it going.

When we approached the back door, I heard music. I wasn't entirely unaware that music existed. I'd heard piano playing from the pubs of Glasgow and the occasional radio as I walked the streets at night. Organ music came from churches sometimes. But music had been a peripheral noise to me until that moment. We'd never been allowed a radio in the factory and the last 30 years under James I'd been in such a trance that I'd barely registered anything around me.

This night, I heard something extraordinary. It was as if dozens of musicians were playing in the den, an upbeat piece that made me want to dance. It would be the first time I'd see or hear a record and I thought it to be wonderful.

Inside the den, the band echoed through the room as Lily and another woman danced about. She squealed while Simon and Robert clapped along to the beat. "What is this?" I asked to no one in particular.

"Glenn Miller," Lily shouted gleefully over the sound. "Haven't you heard them?"

"No," I responded.

The box that the music erupted from sat along the wall and I went to it, sitting on the ground in front of it. Spread across the floor where squares of pictures. I watched the black circle spin wildly and the arm that slid across it. I lifted a square picture to realize another onyx disc was inside it. Each of these squares held music. Pulling one of the black circles out of its case, I examined it. Nothing but grooved plastic yet somehow these great sounds were stored inside it. As the band finished, I turned to them. "Is it a spell?"

Everyone froze. Robert answered. "No, it's a record. Anyone can have these. They're sold in stores."

"How is the music placed in it?"

They all exchanged glances. "Honestly," Simon said. "I don't think any of us knows how but we love it the same. Didn't you get to listen to music?"

"I've heard music," I answered, returning the record to its place and laying it back amongst the others. "But none like this."

"Welcome to the new world, Rhys." Simon smiled. "You're welcome to listen anytime you want as long as your job for the night is done."

"You should listen to the Andrews Sisters next," Lily came to sit on the ground next to me. "They're my favorite. I can teach you everything about music, Simon too. We just love music. I bet you will, too."

"Aye," I said. "I think I will."

58

September 1954

Our routine was born that night. We'd meet up in the dining room, go out to work and end in the den with music and stories. I learned so much about the world in 1940s America and the history that built this country. I learned about music from Beethoven to Bing Crosby. Jazz was quickly becoming my favorite and I thought I may learn to play an instrument someday. I learned about the machines needed to run the ranch and was adept at learning how it all worked. Vehicles turned out to be less complex than I feared and by autumn I was the one that they came to with car issues. Pedro was thrilled as he hated the automobiles. I'd also began learning some construction from Robert, who was beginning to feel like a father-figure to me.

It was Robert who'd bought me my own record player. I'd come in one night to find it on my bed. The note had been simple – *I don't know what you have been through, but music heals. -Robert*. I'd then started my habit of borrowing a record from the den to listen to it in my room, returning it and taking another. I listened to every record in the house so when Simon would return from the city with a new one, I'd be filled with joy.

It was around that time that I discovered playing music also kept the ghosts away. They came around less frequently so when I'd look into my corner to see them staring, I'd click on the music quiet enough to not wake the house but loud enough for me to hear. When I'd turn from the record player, the ghosts would be gone.

In the spring and summer, I watched Lily plant and grow the most remarkable vegetables to be used at meals. While I didn't eat, I did see the power of being able to grow your own food. I thought she must be using witchcraft to grow such things, but she assured me she was just very good with gardens. I'd discovered too that she was a healer. Injuries occurred often on the ranch. While the lycanthropes healed quickly it was not like the way we heal and some of the injuries or illnesses were bad. The shifters healed even slower, much like humans. They would come to Lily, and she would combine magic and brews. The next day, they'd be back to work.

During my time with her, I answered her endless questions about Nettie, Alden, Scotland, the church and what life had been like when I was a human boy in my village. I indulged her because she answered my endless questions about music and being a witch. I suspected Pedro had told her that I knew of their love, but she never mentioned it outright and I never pushed.

The night they finally confessed to Simon and Robert, there was nothing by joy and celebration. They were married by Simon under a breath-taking summer night sky, surrounded by everyone who lived on the ranch. We'd watched them ride on horseback to his little cabin before dawn and I saw both smile and tears on Robert.

"I wish Nettie was here," he'd whispered. It was the first time he'd mentioned her since I'd arrived.

"Can you write her?" I asked.

He'd shook his head and looked down. "She made me swear to never contact her, to make sure that girl and I stay hidden. Even the messages about you were between Alden and Simon. They left us out of it until the last moments, to keep her safe."

I was speechless. I'd never fully asked how they knew to rescue me, how it'd all been planned. I knew they'd risked a lot to get me here, that even more had been risked in Scotland, but I don't think I wanted to know the extent of their danger. And months later, it seemed like a dream more than something that had happened. I had so much to say to him. I wanted to thank him, hug him, console him, beg his forgiveness … anything to take away what they'd had to lose. But, looking at the fading happy couple, I knew that Robert felt it was all worth it. We hadn't known if Pedro and Lily would eventually live in the main house with us or stay in the cabin, but we knew that night was for them only.

And, the happiness of that night had been nothing compared to her giving birth to a healthy baby girl that they named Julie. We begged them to come live in the main house, but they loved their little cabin. Pedro and Robert had built an extension to the tiny home, giving the growing family plenty of space. So, they remained out there, coming in for meals and making sure the vampires got plenty of awake time with the little Julie.

To all of our surprises, the little girl's brown hair turned blonde over her first few years and the large green eyes, as Robert explained, came from her grandmother's side. She was a happy baby and toddler, never lacking attention from the inhabitants of the Lost Souls Ranch. There was always someone willing to play with her, feed her, watch her or carry her. I will forever cherish the one full night of rocking her while she slept so her poor parents could have some alone time.

That night, in her exhaustion, Lily had referred to me as Uncle Rhys. She sounded so much like Nettie that I had to catch my breath. I thought her to be delirious with fatigue and wrote it off as a slip of the tongue. But the title stuck, and the first time Julie called me Uncle Rhys, an army couldn't have kept the smile from my face.

Julie's favorite thing was to walk in nature. She loved the trees, the cattle, the deer, the bunnies, the birds… whatever she could see or feel outside. We all took turns walking her around the property only to have her cry when we took her inside. Pedro and I were on one of these nature walks with Julie when she was five and first showed power. She stood at the base of a tree and lifted her little hand into the sky. We watched as a branch seemed to lower itself to her hand so she could touch the leaves. Then it returned to its previous position. She laughed and turned to us like a moving tree was the most common of things.

When we told Lily, she paled and had to sit. "I don't know if I'm happy or scared." She said. "I want her to have a normal life, you know? But I also didn't want the magic to die with me."

"That is completely understandable," I assured her. "I think we always knew she was special," I laughed.

But none of us knew how special she was until her tenth year and her first shift under the full moon.

When Pedro tells the story he says he always knew she was a lycanthrope. I call that recollection into question. He may have hoped she was one but did not know for sure until that full moon called to her and we saw her eyes change. I'd been there and he'd been as shocked as I. Thankfully, he'd moved fast and gotten her into the trees. He'd shifted too and been able to stay with her all night while Lily paced the room, watching out the windows of the main house. It wasn't until we'd heard two distinct howls in the distance that we'd known she would be changed but okay.

I'd been in my bed when she'd returned but was told that night that she'd slept all day and was thrilled to find out she was both witch and lycanthrope.

My story picks up two nights after this when I woke to find the back door open with Robert and Pedro just outside it, facing two men I didn't know. Their smell told me they were like Pedro and they didn't look happy.

"She stays here," Pedro said. "You have no claim to her."

The two strangers exchanged glances then faced Pedro. "You're right, we don't but we can insist that a trainer be sent to her. Her uniqueness is wild and may endanger the pack. We will send a councilman to stay here and report back to us."

"Fine," Pedro said. "Send him. But she stays here."

One of the men looked over Pedro's shoulder to me. "Vampire," the distain was dripping off that one word as the two men turned and left from our view. I heard a car door shut and the sound of their vehicle leaving.

"What was that?" I asked.

"The pack my father left," Pedro answered. "They have concerns about Julie being part-witch and part-wolf being raised among vampires and shifters. They think our way of raising her is radical."

"And?" I questioned.

"And," Robert growled. "They thought they'd just come take my granddaughter back to the pack lands and we would be okay with that."

"They can't," I exclaimed.

"The pack doesn't believe in human law," Pedro explained. "They think anything lycanthrope is theirs to take."

"So, we fight?" I clarified.

"No," Pedro turned. "No fighting. They'll send someone to be sure we're teaching her how to be discreet and safe. Once their representative is satisfied, he reports back and they leave us in peace."

"It's the best way," I heard from the open doorway and spun around to see Simon. "They've left us alone all these years, they don't want a war as much as we don't." He placed a hand on my shoulder. "I fought alongside their ancestors to get them here and onto their own land. They might not have been there, but I know their grandfathers and great-grandfathers have told them. They may not like vampires, but they know they're here partly because of one and I think it eats at them." He addressed all of us. "When this representative arrives, we treat him as we treat everyone who comes here."

"Rhys," he faced me, handing me a basket. "Can you take food out to Travis? He's still ill and I'm sure he'd like the company."

"Sure," I said.

59

Over the decade I'd been on the ranch, Travis had warmed up to me and we'd built a friendship as only two men who've overcome horrors could. The years were not kind to Travis and either sadness or his tendency to imbibe had aged him. He'd taken to bed a few days ago and had been excused of his chores for the time. We'd all been giving him less and less these last two years as we could see he didn't move as well as he used to and was slower than the tasks often needed. Simon had said many times that he'd wished Travis would just come to the main house and end his days in comfort, but Travis was too proud to take the charity. He wanted to earn his keep.

I'd truly learned the strength of this man when he'd come in one day to tell us that he'd caught a gang that had been stealing cattle all over Texas. Ranchers had lost so much to this gang of men, and we knew our ranch was the next to be hit. We'd doubled the watch and every man who went out to find the criminals had been armed.

Every man except Travis that is.

Unbeknownst to us, Travis had shifted into a cow every night and stood amongst the herd, waiting for the thieves to show. After weeks of doing this, three men had slipped onto the property with cattle prod and truck, ready to steal some prize steer. Instead, they'd heard the screaming of a wild man and saw Travis, naked as the day he was born, running towards them. He'd chased them into their own truck, locked the door with them in the back and driven the truck to the main house so we could call the authorities.

The thieves had been so shocked by the events they'd all told a different story with one consistent theme – yes, they were the cattle thieves. Ultimately, they were so embarrassed by being bested by a naked, unarmed man, they would all plead guilty.

I have many stories like that about Travis but that one was my personal favorite. So, when I saw age and abuse begin to take his strength and zeal, I started helping with the things he could no longer do. At first, he swore at me but eventually he looked forward to my help and companionship. After a few weeks, he'd even started having full conversations with me. He never talked of his family or asked me about anything vampire related but we talked of music and places he'd wished he'd visited. One night, I'd walked him to his cabin when he'd had too much liquor by the campfire and seen the guitar. When asked, he'd picked it up and played. Before I knew it, he was teaching me to play, and we were truly friends.

This night, I used my knuckle to knock and entered into the one room of his cabin. He lay in his bed at the back and the smell of rot was strong. Whatever malady was taking him had worsened in the day since I'd last checked on him. I crossed to him, placing the basket on the end of the bed and opening it. I pulled out the water first, lifting him to seated and bracing him so he could drink. I didn't know if he would and was relieved when the muscles of his throat pulled the water in. His eyes fluttered opened and he smiled weakly. "Hey," he slurred. "Got food?"

I figured it was good that he was asking to eat. Stacking all the pillows, I lay him against them so he could remain seated. I brought the sandwich to him and he was able to hold it himself, taking small bites. While he did that, I pulled the next thing from the basket. It was a drawing by Julie of cattle in a field of flowers. *Get well soon, Travis* was neatly printed in crayon above one of the cows. I handed it to him, and he smiled. "Oh, that girl."

"I know," I agreed. "She's better than medicine."

"Yeah," he slurred between small intakes of sandwich. He lay down the meal with so much of it still uneaten. "I can't eat anymore."

"Why don't I leave it on the bedside table in case you change your mind?" I asked, re-wrapping it and laying it where I said I would. "And, I'm going to get Lily."

"No," he grabbed my arm. "No. I don't want healed."

"Why?" I asked.

"It's natural to get sick," he said. "Natural to either get through it or not. And," he winked. "My time will come whether we want it to or not."

"But it doesn't have to be now," I said, knowing from the smell that he would not recover from this one.

"Rhys," he said. "I've got a beautiful welcoming committee waiting for me on the other side. Don't you worry about me, boy. You may be sad when I go," he leaned back. "But, I won't be. I'm ready."

"I'm sorry for what happened to your family," we'd never broached the subject but if this was to be the last time we spoke, I wanted it to be honest.

"Hey," he said squeezing the arm he still held. "It wasn't you that done it. You don't hold the weight over everything that every vampire does and you know what?"

"What?" I asked.

"I was full of so much hate in my heart for so long and you took it from me. You pushed through all that hate, and you're my friend. You showed me that not everyone is bad and judging someone because of one part of them is wrong."

Shame threatened to overwhelm me. He didn't know the things from my past, didn't know that I too had taken lives. Would the family of my victims have had the same hate in their hearts that he was describing? Would someone have helped them through their loss like I had for Travis?

"I want to do something, and you best not argue," coughing robbed him of words and a wheeze hissed through each breath. "Don't deny a dying man, it's rude."

I rolled my eyes. "What is it?"

"Take my guitar," he sank into the pillows, exhausted from struggling to breathe. "I want you to have it."

"No," I started.

"Christ boy," he groaned. "Just take the damn thing. It's not my virginity, it's just a guitar and I want you to have it."

I raised my hands in surrender. "Okay, okay. I'll take it."

"And bury me out with the cows," he laughed. "I love those stupid animals."

Those were his last words and they were perfectly Travis. We followed his wishes. The guitar was now in my bedroom, as well loved as my cherished books and treasured record player.

The funeral was the next night. Travis was laid in a simple wooden box with the drawing Julia had made him, in the pasture that the cows grazed most often. We told stories about Travis and laughed at the uniqueness of the shifter that had become family, whether he liked it or not. Lily and Julie had painted a wooden cross to serve as his headstone. Flowers in every color clung to the greenest vines. They seemed to wrap around the cross and looked so real I thought I may be able to touch them. I knew Travis would have hated the fuss but felt we all needed it. He was with his family again while we had to return to the running of the ranch like nothing had happened.

That night was our way of preparing ourselves to move on.

It was also the last night before the lycanthrope representative would arrive and none of us knew what it would mean for the future of our little sanctuary.

60

We had known to expect a man from the pack to arrive at sundown. What we weren't prepared for was two lycanthropes on our front porch moments after sunset.

Flavio was the older one. Again, I'm not good with human ages and know that the wolves age slower but I would have guessed him to be in his mid-twenties. He filled the doorway, broad shouldered and several inches above me. His hair, like Pedro's, was dark and long. Unlike Pedro, his eyes were amber, like dark honey. The brown of his skin was a shade darker than Pedro's making those eyes dazzle with the contrast of light against dark.

Michael was young, likely grade school aged. He shared the older man's skin and hair color but his eyes were a deep blue. They looked very out of place. His hair was cut short to his head, leaving nothing to take away from his gaze.

When they were inside and sitting in the den, it was explained that they were half-brothers with the same father but a different mother.

"I'm sorry," Simon explained. "We didn't expect two of you or for you to be younger. I had prepared a cabin for you, but I think, perhaps, you may want to sleep in here. We can get a couple rooms ready."

"A cabin is perfect," he said. "Thank you."

"So," I asked. "What exactly do you need to see or do?" I knew we were all wondering but no one was asking.

"I'm here to teach the little one," he said. "The ways of the wolf."

Pedro interjected. "I can do that," he insisted.

"Listen," Flavio raised his hands. "I'm not here to step on toes. I'm here to help you guys and help him," he pointed at his little brother who was excitedly grabbing a third cookie and dipping it into the glass of milk he held. "You've never been on pack land or learned from us. You learned from your dad, right?"

"Correct," Pedro was still tensed but listening.

"So, I can teach her the updated stuff, you teach your stuff and your wife teaches them her stuff," he shrugged his shoulders like he was giving the simplest of instruction.

"What do you mean? What stuff can my wife teach?" As if conjured by her mention, Lily came through the back door with Julia's hand in hers.

"My mom was a witch," the little boy said between mouthfuls of cookie. "I'm a witch and a wolf, just like her." He pointed to mother and daughter then went back to his dessert.

I don't think we could have been more shocked if a parade had burst through the side of the house to march through the den. We stared at the boy, mouths agape. Lily froze next to her husband as Julie snatched up a cookie and sat next to Michael. She looked around at us, confused about why we all stared.

"What's wrong?" she asked.

"Nothing," Flavio answered. "Just my brother spitting out information despite him being told to wait until the timing was right."

"Is it true?" Lily asked.

"Yeah," Flavio answered. "My dad was so torn up after my mom died that he had to console himself with women. This" he tilted his head towards his brother. "Is the result. He did the right thing and married her. It wasn't until they were man and wife that she let us know she was a witch. We knew you could pass on the wolf in the blood but didn't know about the magic until recently. By the time he was doing the witch stuff, his mom had already left. We don't know where she is."

We all looked at the boy to see if he'd react negatively to the mention of his mother abandoning him, but he just sat the empty milk glass down and leaned back. He was merely listening to the adults talk with a full belly and seemingly had no cares in the world.

"So," Flavio continued. "The pack didn't know what to do. Then," he looked over to Julia. "We heard that another half-witch-half-lycan was born and not far from us. So," he smiled. "You got stuck with us until we know that he and the girl can control their beast and magic."

Simon scoffed. "They could've just told us the truth, you know? Instead of the show they put on here."

"Yeah," Flavio smirked. "But they don't want to ask a vampire for help. They'd be seriously mad if they knew I was telling you the whole truth but I'm not good at lying. I lose track of the story."

"Well," Lily let out a breath. "I think we have a lot to do, then. As far as I know, they're the only ones of their kind. It's not like there's a book on this."

"What can I do to help?" I asked.

Simon, Robert and Pedro all looked to each other. It was Lily who spoke. "Why don't you help them get the bags to their cabin? I'll think of a place to make a kind of classroom and start to gather supplies, make a lesson plan. Pedro?" He turned to her, probably eager for any task that would be of assistance. "Can you write down all the things you think you should teach them? I think it wouldn't be a bad idea to ultimately put something together that others could use."

"Others?" Pedro arched an eyebrow.

She sighed. "Just do it, please." He left to follow orders before he turned this stressful situation into an actual argument. Lily pointed at Flavio. "You too. Use tonight to get comfortable and write down anything you think is helpful for a young wolf, things you find useful, things you wish someone had taught you. We meet back here next sundown for food and our first lesson."

"Why do we have to be on their time?" Flavio jerked his head towards myself and Simon. "Wait 'til sundown?"

"We don't always," she chastised. "But for the most part, we like to have them included. They don't have the privilege of going outside anytime they want like we do." She reached her hand out for Julie to take. "Remember that we're here because of Simon. So, the same way we adjust for you when you shift, we can adjust for their needs."

With that, mother and daughter were gone from the house and on to start creating a classroom for witch-wolves. Flavio raised his eyebrows and looked to us. "Does she always get her way?"

We answered in tandem. "Yes."

61

The next night Lily led a group to Travis' cabin. It was clear when we walked inside that she had spent all day turning his one room home into a school. Where his couch had been, two small desks and chairs stood. His bed was gone and the wall it had been up against now held a large chalkboard. Next to it was a shelf filled with books. My heart ached for a moment seeing the remnants of his life gone and his home repurposed. But I knew Travis would have loved the idea of kids in his little cabin and had to believe he was with his own children now.

Lily sat the children in their desks as the adults stood behind them. We all listened to her plans. She'd already been teaching Julie at home and would include Michael in the basics of reading and mathematics. After these lessons, they would switch to specialized education – rotating between Lily teaching witchcraft and controlling magic and Flavio or Pedro with lycan teachings. I volunteered to be with Lily and the children when it was just them, so they were not alone in the cabin. When one of the men was teaching, I would get my chores done.

Simon and Robert praised Lily for her hard work, Pedro made her promise she would rest well the next day to recover from her lack of sleep, Flavio thanked her for accepting them so quickly and the children grumbled that they didn't need extra school.

That hour in the cabin was a perfect example of how the ranch operated, everyone jumping in and helping no matter what the need was. The first week, we rotated through plans smoothly with each person stepping in when it was their turn to teach or just be present to support Lily and the children. We learned that the students needed to break after two hours to run around outside, or their unspent energy made it impossible for them to focus. Their favorite game was racing one of the vampires, knowing full well that they could never truly be faster. The first race, Simon let them win and they were angered that he treated them "like babies." So, from that night forward, we would make certain to leave them in the dust and make a dramatic show of waiting for them at the finish line. It was in the midst of one of the races that the pack representatives showed up unannounced to see our progress.

"This is your training?" one of the wolves called from behind me and I turned to see the same men who'd sent Flavio and Michael.

"They're taking a break," I informed the lycans as the kids skidded to a halt next to me.

Flavio jogged up to stand between us and the pack. "Elders," he spoke with a hint of fear. "We are letting the children take a small recess and then they go back in for lessons."

The two wolves exchanged a glance then responded to Flavio, making it clear they were not addressing me. "Show us then."

Flavio laid a hand on Michael's shoulder. "Let's show them your school room."

We led our guests back to the cabin where Lily was erasing the chalkboard in preparation for new material, she looked over a journal in her hand then reached up with chalk in had to start writing. I cleared my throat and she spun to face us, clearly surprised to see the visitors. "What are you doing here?" she asked.

"We are making sure the young ones are being trained," one answered in a tone that said he didn't think he should be questioned. "What are you teaching them tonight?"

"We just finished math," Michael blurted out. "Now we're gonna do magic."

The elder arched his eyebrow. "Are you?" He looked to Flavio, and I was certain I saw fear in the older brother's eyes now. The elder locked his gaze onto Lily. "Well then, teach."

The children sat at their desks and Lily didn't move. "No offense," she shut the book in her hand. "You don't need to hear this. You can't do magic and one of the things we're teaching the kids is to keep these lessons secret. I'm sure you both understand why."

"Excuse me?" the older of the two visitors was turning red. "You will tell us what you're teaching our young pack member. You don't keep secrets from us."

I felt the power in the room start to grow. It wasn't clear if it was coming off Lily, the wolves or all of the above but I knew it was bad. Flavio jumped in front of the representatives. "She doesn't stay for the wolf lessons; we keep it among the wolves. But I stay for the witchcraft lessons. I swear to you she teaches them well."

The calmer of the two men looked at Lily while he responded to Flavio. "If you can hear her talk about magic, why can't we."

Lily answered this. "Because, every witch needs someone protecting them. Julie has me and Michael has his brother. His brother needs to know how to help him control his power. It's not like a bunch of witch-wolves exist."

"Witch-wolves?" The still red elder asked.

"It's what they call us," Julie giggled. "Isn't it cool?"

The elders looked horrified. Flavio tried to calm them. "You know that I would never do anything to jeopardize him or the pack. If I say she's doing what we asked, then you have to trust me."

"Why can the vampire be present?" At least the older visitor was losing his ruby complexion and seeming to calm down, but I didn't like the way he asked.

"Because I also have magic," I answered, trying to not sound irritated. "It may not be exactly like a witch's, but should the children struggle to control their magics," I cocked my head. "I have over a hundred and fifty years of practice."

This appeared to quell whatever fight was rising up in the two older wolves. They may have not liked me, but I was certain they did not want to enter into combat against me. At least for that night, they didn't think it worth a fight. The older one sharply raised his hand and pointed at Flavio. "Remember the consequences, boy." They stomped out of the classroom and minutes later we heard the vehicle speed from the property.

Lily asked the children to quietly read whatever book they like from the shelf while the adults moved outside to speak. Once away from the very good hearing of Julie and Michael, Lily rose up on her toes to get into Flavio's face. "What does that mean? The consequences of what?"

Flavio appeared to wrestle with what to say next. He let out a breath, turned and began pacing, hands in his hair. "It's not going to happen."

"What?" I asked. "What's not going to happen?" Flavio continued to pace around.

"You better answer," Lily angrily whispered.

He stopped, slowly turning to face us. "I won't let it," he tried to assure us.

Lily's eyes widened in the kind of anger only a mother can muster. "I have no problem using magic on you. You've got three seconds to tell the truth."

Flavio marched up to her and pulled me in. "They'll kill me if they know I told you," he began, barely audibly to human ears. He bounced his eyes between her and I before sighing in resignation. "If we can't prove to them that the witch-wolves aren't a threat, I've been told to take them to pack lands while you all sleep."

"What?" Lily raged.

"Shhh," he grabbed her arm. "Don't scare them." He pulled her further from the cabin and I followed. "I would never do it." He assured us. "I'd rather take him and run. I've got no idea what the pack would do with them, but I won't even risk it."

"Why?" I asked, trying to understand.

"Because," he answered like I should've figured it out. "The pack is scared of anything different. And these two kids are unlike anything else. The lycanthropes were mad enough when they realized my dad married a witch and brought her into the land. But he didn't know so they forgave him. Once she had a kid, they weren't going to do anything to her. The pack loves children and women who continue the bloodline are respected above anyone else. But," he shoved his hands in his front pockets and looked down. "When he started doing witch stuff, they all freaked out. They threw him in a cage." Flavio looked up and tears glistened in his eyes. "If he hadn't shifted, I think they were going to kill him. Being part wolf saved him."

Lily covered her mouth with her hand, I think to stop from screaming.

"What about his mom?" I asked. "Why didn't she take him when she ran?"

He shrugged his shoulders. "They all say she ran away and abandoned him to save herself." He swallowed hard. "I don't think that's true. I think they killed her."

Lily put her hand down. "But, your father?"

Flavio shook his head slowly. "I think he knows and he's protecting the pack. I think he'd protect the pack over his own son, too. I know it's awful to say about my own father, but I don't trust him to save us."

A flash of James filled my mind's eye – a creator who won't protect his own.

"So," I stepped in. "We ensure they have no reason to fear the children." I turned to Lily and made sure she was looking in my eyes.

"Your ma was good but you're even better. Teach those kids how to control the magic and they'll be okay."

"What if they aren't?" Worry filled her eyes. "What if the pack lets their fear of something different control their actions?"

"Then we protect them. Those kids have lycanthropes, vampires and a witch on their side." She nodded, resolution and determination filling her eyes. I continued, "There is no safer place for them than this ranch."

As we returned to restart the lessons that now seemed the most important thing in the world, I looked up into the sky and prayed that I was right. Sadly, I knew more than most how quickly things can go terribly wrong.

62

"Controlling your magic," Lily began, showing no worry despite me knowing that she now felt immense pressure to teach this very thing. "It's the most important thing you can ever learn. Having magic abilities means that you have a big responsibility to know when to use it, how to use it and when to hide it." She looked over at Flavio and I standing in the back then to the children again. "There are people out there that will be afraid of you if they know you're witches. This is why you not only need to control your magic but also keep it secret. Do you understand?"

The children exchanged looks and nodded.

"You do?" Lily asked.

"We do," Michael answered.

"But we can do magic on the ranch, right?" Julie asked.

Lily nodded. "If you need to but just because you can do it on the ranch doesn't mean you always should do it."

"So," Michael asked. "How do we know when we should?"

Lily smiled. "When it helps."

"Simon uses magic with the animals," Julie told Michael. "He's a vampire."

Michael turned back to look at me. "Do vampires have magic like witches?" I realized that the boy may never have spoken to vampires before us and likely had never been taught about them.

I stepped up to join Lily, addressing the boy. "Vampires have *some* powers but not like witches. We only get one or two abilities, and we cannot grow it like you can."

"Have you tried?" Julie asked

I paused for a minute, thinking over her question. I had played around with my power but knew it was more about the type of blood I was drinking and not something I could grow over time. But did I really know that? James would never have told me the truth about my magic and all I knew came from small pieces of information. I knew we drank cow's blood each night as we lived on a cattle ranch, but I hadn't even tried using my powers since leaving Scotland. On the ranch there was no need to mask or to mesmerize anyone so I'd no clue if it was strong or not. I made a mental note to talk to Simon.

"I haven't," I told the children. "But I will try along with you as you do your lessons. Good?" The kids nodded excitedly.

"How come they don't talk about vampires at home?" Michael asked his brother.

Flavio came and joined us at the front. "First," he glanced between the two pupils. "You both need to swear that you don't talk about what we learn in here to anyone else?"

"What about my dad? My grandpa? Or Simon?" Julie asked and I smiled. The girl knew herself well enough to not agree to keeping secrets from those three. I was proud of her for asking questions and not blinding swearing allegiance.

Flavio grinned. "You can tell them. What you learn from us about being witch-wolves stays amongst us, Pedro, Robert and Simon. Deal?"

"Deal," the kids shouted in tandem.

Flavio sighed. "Follow me," he waved and we did.

Once in a clearing, next to a roaring campfire, Flavio stood dramatically. "Since the time men were drawing stories on cave walls the wolves and vampires have been at war. Deadly fights between the two break out all the time, leaving destruction and sorrow in their wake." The story sounded rehearsed like it had been heard and spoken hundreds of times. "Over the centuries, on this land, the many battles have left our numbers dwindling and their numbers rising. And while they grow with ease, our women give birth less and less. So, we hide on our lands, among our packs to protect our ways and save the future. We do this so we may rise up one day to finally send the undead into their own form of hiding – returning them to the shadows and graves they should remain in. We will sit in our rightful place at the top for we are born and not made. We are from nature, and they are unnatural."

I was speechless. What do you say after a monologue that calls you unnatural?

Thankfully, Flavio was not done. "That's the speech I've heard a thousand times, the speech they tell all the lycanthropes every time we meet." He sighed. "They believe that the vampires have cursed our women with their powers to slow our breeding and that defeating the immortals will break this curse."

"That's ridiculous," Lily snapped, taking the words right out of my mouth.

Flavio raised his hands in submission. "I know but it's what they all believe. And," he looked at the kids. "They think that this is a sign of the blood being further tainted, our species being wiped out."

He squatted down to be eye level with the kids. I looked to Lily, unsure if we should let him continued. She stared at him, the concern on her face as well.

"You two are special," he smiled warmly. "You're not the problem. The hate and fear that the pack teaches, the way they pass on their prejudice to their children is the problem. We" he waved his hands to include myself and Lily. "We should be having each other's backs, protecting and helping each other. The humans don't care if we're witch or wolf or vampire or what. They only care that we aren't human and most of them would kill us before learning our names. Which is why we gotta look out for each other. Why places like this are so important." I glanced at Lily and saw the pride in her face. "So," he continued. "You guys gotta learn how to control your magic and your beast so the pack doesn't have a reason to worry about you. And, so you can stay here and help the different people who stop here for protecting, even the vampires. Because you two," he wagged his fingers between boy and girl. "You gonna be able to help so many folks. You're going to help us spread love not hate." He held out his hand. "So, promise me you keep the secrets and be careful and listen to us, alright?"

Michael shook his brother's hand. "Promise," the little boy said.

Flavio moved his hand to Julie. She shook it. "Promise," she mimicked.

"All right," he stood, looking down to the kids and then to us. "Let's get to work then."

63

While Flavio was teaching the children something about lycanthropes and puberty, I excused myself. It didn't take long to find Simon. I followed the sound of his humming and tracked him to the barn. He often serenaded the animals while he cared for him. He reminded me so much of Collin when he spoke to the livestock like pets. I couldn't help but picture the mouse whenever I watched a mare or duck or cow dutifully follow Simon around.

"Rhys," he greeted me and went back to his task.

"Simon," I started but then stopped, wondering if I should proceed or leave my questions unanswered. I worried that he would be angry with me for prying or think less of me for not knowing these things.

"Yeah," he stared at me, curiosity filling his gaze.

"Can I ask some questions?"

"About?" he went back to brushing the mare.

"Well," I crossed to sit on an old bench, facing his back as he worked. "About being a vampire."

Simon stood up and turned. I wished he'd continued his brushing, so I didn't have to see his face as I spoke. To my dismay, he came to sit next to me and gave me his whole attention. "All right."

I searched his face and saw no judgement, no sign that he thought me foolish for my lack of knowledge after so many years of being on this Earth. I still couldn't face him and looked to the floor. "Our powers? They are strong when drinking fresh human blood and weak on animal blood. Can we be strong without drinking human blood?"

"Hmmm," he processed and answered with a question. "What powers do you have?"

"Masking and mind control," I answered.

"Do you need to look into someone's eyes to control them or can they just hear your voice?"

"I have to catch their eyes," I responded.

"That's called glamouring." He said. "If you could do it without them looking at you, that's called melody. You can kind of use your voice to make people feel a certain way."

I thought of Lia and the tinkling bells in her voice. I missed her in a way that made every muscle in my body hurt. I wanted more than anything to send her a letter while knowing it could never happen. I would've given anything to hear her voice one more time.

"And who taught you about your powers?" he asked. I searched his eyes, saw the earnestness in them. I didn't think he would ever betray me, but old wounds were ripping open. My disbelief that I could trust anyone was powerful and came with experience.

"No one really," I answered. "I manifested the masking quickly, the glamour-" the word felt weird in my mouth. "It came much later."

"And," he was obviously being careful when he chose his words. "The one who came before you? Who made you?"

"He could also mask."

Simon smiled. "I mean did he teach you about your abilities? Explain how they work and how the blood affects them?"

"No," I admitted. "It was humans who taught me that old animal blood weakens you and fresh human blood makes you strong." I held back the part about how I killed humans and became strong after.

"I see," he scratched the back of his head and thought. "Well, I can't speak for why your maker didn't teach you anything, but I can tell you this. There's a lot of humans out there that think they know a lot about us. But you see-" he smirked. "Most of what they know was taught to them by us, in the hopes they'd believe it and not know the real facts."

"Is that true?" I cocked my head.

"Yeah," he cocked an eyebrow. "I mean fresh blood from humans will help kick your powers up but it's a short-term answer. When the blood is outta your system, you gotta find more, right?"

"Aye," again I held back the confessions, but the flashes of memories were making it hard to concentrate. My mind threatened to fill up with images of the humans I'd killed in the streets for my own gain.

"But that means if a vampire had to fight in between meals, he wouldn't be at his strongest, right? Do you think we'd have lasted this long if we always needed to be full of fresh blood to fight?" He paused so I could think about what he said. He had a point. It wasn't always easy to get out and drink from a human, even in the city. So, what about vampires in the country or from long ago?

"So," he continued. "Yes, some fresh human blood will boost your powers but Rhys, you can learn to grow your power on your own. You can practice and practice so in a time of need, you can pull that magic out at full blast."

Was that true? I sat in silence, processing what he'd said and thinking about the meaning of it. Simon didn't move, waiting for my next question or thought. If he'd just told the truth, it would mean that I'd spent a century and a half not knowing my potential or even knowing what that potential was. I was weaker and less knowledgeable than a vampire my aged should've been. A newborn with a supportive maker would've been stronger than I was at that moment. The reality washed over me, a fine trembling beginning and threatening to overtake my reason. A warm tear slid down my cheek, removing any possibility of me pretending I wasn't affected by this new information.

"Rhys," Simon said cautiously. "I don't know what happened to you before you got here but I have a good idea. I saw what walked into my kitchen that first night I met you and know a broken spirit when I see one. I've also seen the horrible things men do to each other and vampires aren't excluded from cruelty." He lay his hand on my thigh. "I can't change the past for you. You never have to tell me, or you can tell me everything when you're ready or you can just tell me what you need, and I'll help."

Swallowing back more tears, I answered. "Teach me."

"Done," Simon slapped my thigh, standing to find the brush he'd set aside. "I'm gonna finish up with these horses and call it a day. From now on, when the kids are learning the wolf stuff, you come find me and we will work on vamp stuff. Fair?"

64

Rest did not come quickly for me that night. Instead, the information from the previous hours rolled through my head at a dizzying pace. The idea that the lycans were teaching each other to hate us with the ultimate goal to go to war with the vampires was horrifying. How could a group who'd never met me, hate me for being something I didn't choose to be? How could they be teaching others to hate without any concern for what that could create?

Then, there was the knowledge that they'd told Flavio to kidnap the children in the night if they couldn't control their magic. How could they ask a young person to do something so awful with no thought for the children or the grieving mother left behind? Would they come for the kids if Flavio didn't listen? If he ran with Michael, would they come for Julie? Could we protect her? How many wolves were there?

Sadly, what tore the largest path of destruction through my brain was the knowledge that my own maker had never cared for me. Obviously, I'd known him to be brutal and harsh when not obeyed. I knew that he made me to be a work horse, treated worse than the cattle on this ranch.

I was nothing more than another one of his machines. Still, I'd never suspected that he'd purposefully not taught me how to be a vampire so he could keep me weak. I'd believed that it was the blood that gave and took my magic. To find out that it was always within me- it made me feel naïve and foolish. I'd been strutting around for so many years, thinking I was a powerful god but had been no more than a daft child.

Rolling to my side, I saw the ghosts.

Collin was more visible than Diedre this night. She was so faded that I feared a single blink would take her from my sight. Her hair moved around her like a slight breeze caressed it. It danced around a sorrowful face that was so similar to her brother's it broke my heart. His eyes held disappointment and locked onto mine. Neither moved a muscle, made no attempt to communicate or leave. I'd gotten into a routine of using music to dispel them but on this occasion, I felt like I deserved to stare at those spirits. It was a punishment I'd earned to look upon my lost loved ones.

For minutes, I lay on my side with the dead as my audience and it was only once I closed my eyes to darkness that I felt them leave.

When the sleep lifted and I arose, I was still facing that corner. Like every time I'd opened my eyes since moving to the ranch, the corner was empty. The specters only came at the end of the night and never left the corner. A few times I'd thought about putting something in that space to see if it would stop them from arriving but never followed through. While their unplanned presence always filled me with sadness, the idea of losing the spirits of those two, the last reminder they'd ever existed, was too much to consider. Even though I knew deep down it was my own imagination, that real ghosts did not exist, I needed to believe that those two visited me.

Rising to pull on my pants, I started my usual path to wash my face only to freeze in my tracks. Something was different in the spirits' corner. At first, I thought it must be a trick of shadow and light as my imagining of ghosts could not actually leave real evidence. Crossing to examine, I ran my fingers over it to be sure and had no explanation for what now lay there.

The letter H was carved into the wooden planks where a dead brother and sister had stood in the dawn.

65

Simon stared at the single letter etched into the boards. I'd found him immediately and asked him to follow me. "Do you see it?" I asked.

"I do," he looked confused. "I'm not angry but why would you do that?"

"Simon," I started and then the words dried in my throat. I'd never told anyone about the visions of Collin and Diedre. Until that moment, I'd been certain that I imagined them for my own comfort when James had locked me away and then for a sort of self-punishment once I'd been safe in America. Would Simon think me mad? Was I mad? Had I done this in my sleep somehow?

"Do you believe in ghosts?" The words were out so I couldn't take it back. Depending on how Simon reacted, I could adjust what I followed it up with.

"Of course I do," he answered to my relief. "But I didn't think you had the power of seeing ghosts."

Now I was the one confused. "Speak plainly."

He rubbed his chin. "It's a vampiric power," he explained. "The ability to see and talk with spirits. Most of the real mediums you come across are vampires. Although I think witches can do it too. You'd have to ask Lily."

I held up my hands. "Hold on. It's one of my powers? How? I thought vampires only get one or two?"

Simon land a hand on my shoulder. "Let's get Lily."

I stared at the H on the floor while Simon found her and brought her in. He must have filled her in on the information because she didn't seem shocked when finding the wood scratched. "That's it?" She asked, pointing at the message.

"Yeah," Simon answered. "Rhys was just going to tell me about his visitors."

I cleared my throat. I hadn't occurred to me that I would have to talk about Collin and Diedre once I'd brought the carving to their attention. I'd been so overwhelmed by realizing they were real that I'd not thought it all through. Looking at the two people next to me I knew I needed to trust them to get to the bottom of this. "Collin and Diedre. I grew up with them in my village. Collin and I ran away to Glasgow together, we're turned by the same maker. Diedre was never made vampire, she was murdered too young when she was visiting us." I swallowed hard. Saying it as fast as possible with little detail made it easier to get out. "Collin was killed before I came here. He broke the rules, and our maker punished him for it."

Uncomfortable silence filled the room. I didn't want them to ask any more questions. I'd shared what I needed to and hoped it as enough.

"You knew them," Simon said. "I don't think this is a vampire power. Vampires who commune with spirits are visited by many ghosts and it's usually for a purpose. They can call on specters to help or inform them."

"It sounds to me," Lily said. "Like they're coming to you. You're not calling on them or bringing them out."

"But, why?" I asked, the pain in my heart threatening to steal my voice. This whole time I'd been trying to ignore them or get rid of them, thinking them to be my own troubled mind. Instead, it had been *them*.

My dearest friends had come to me, and I'd shunned them. I sat on the bed, unable to look at the message on the floor anymore.

"I don't know," Lily sat next to me. "We're going to find out. I don't know a lot about ghosts, but we can work on this together. They scratched that into the wood for a reason. Think about anything with the letter H that could apply to them. How often do they come to you?"

"I never know. Sometimes it's months, even years without them and sometimes they come every night for a week."

"Okay," she sighed. "Well, we need to focus on the kids for now. When I have some free time, I'll work on a spell to try to help them communicate with you. Or we can try a séance one night."

"When you're ready," Simon added.

"Yes," Lily agreed. "When you're ready to make contact."

When I was ready to make contact with my best friend and woman who were both dead because of me? I didn't think I could ever be ready for that.

It didn't matter anyways because – as we have all learned – life has a way of laughing at your plans and telling you what your next steps will be.

66

I heard the screaming from the woods and ran towards the shouts. Several men surrounded something on the ground. Pushing one out of the way, I saw Robert who was clearly struggling to breathe; his right hand clutched his left shoulder.

"Go for help," I wasn't aware of Simon arriving, but he was shouting orders and sending the men away.

He dropped to the ground next to Robert and I joined him.

"Please," Simon begged. "Please let me save you."

"No," Robert yelled through gritted teeth.

"What's going on?" I asked, not knowing what to do.

"It's his heart," the other vampire answered. "He's got a bad heart and there's nothing the doctors can do. I want to turn him, but he refuses."

"When it's time to go," Robert grunted and sucked in a breath, clearly in pain.

"Please," I beseeched. "Think of Lily and Julie."

The human groaned. "I am," he relaxed. The pain was subsiding, but it didn't mean he was out of the woods. "And I'm thinking of my wife, my family who have passed. We all get to be back together on the other side."

Before I would have asked him how he knew that for sure, but with my recent discovery about the existence of ghosts, it didn't seem crazy that an afterlife was possible.

Robert cried out again and squeezed his left shoulder tighter, hyperventilating and clenching his jaw. "You swore," he demanded in between ragged breaths.

"I did," Simom acknowledged.

I couldn't ask for specifics because Lily came running up to throw herself over her father. "They're bringing up a truck and we're going to the hospital."

She looked up to me. "Finish the kids' lesson tonight for me?"

"Of course," I agreed.

The pickup slammed to a stop next to Robert. Pedro jumped out and scooped the man up off the ground with ease. A ranch hand in the back of the truck was ready to tend to Robert while they sped to the nearest hospital. Lily joined him in the bed with her father, tears rolling down her face and onto the now unconscious patient.

Helplessness was not a new feeling for me but was particularly difficult to experience as I watched the vehicle retreat. Humans are so vulnerable and their lives so short. The reality that Robert could never again walk the ranch was so clear. He was the man who shuttled me to this ranch, who saved me from Scotland and put himself at risk for a complete stranger. He was the love of Nettie's life. She'd protected me and gotten me away from abuse and I couldn't save the father of her child.

I thought of Julie, sitting in her school room with no idea that her grandfather may have breathed his last breath.

"What did you swear to him?" I asked Simon.

Simon was still staring in the direction of the receding truck. "That I would care for his family as my own, allow them to continue to live in safety on the ranch." He sighed. "And that I would make none of them into vampires."

"Have you?"

"Have I what?" Simon asked.

"Ever made someone into a vampire," I wanted to know how and why it was done, and he was the first vampire I'd felt safe asking questions so candidly.

"Once," he answered. "They didn't survive the turn."

"Oh," I said. "I'm sorry." I wasn't sure the appropriate response in a situation like this. "I never will," I added.

"Why do you say that?" Now, all his attention was on me.

"I just can't," I didn't know how to put it into words. "I can't do this to someone. They could never possibly know what they're saying yes to, and I would never do it against their will."

"Is it so bad?" he asked, looking genuinely curious.

"To forever be in the dark? To continue to meet people that you cherish and then lose them? Be so close to humans but never a part of them?" I nodded. "Yes, it is."

"Not everyone dies," he argued.

"Yet, we still lose them somehow. To circumstance, distance, time. So," I looked up to the night sky. "I will never make another."

"And that it alright," Simon agreed. "Not everyone should be a maker."

"That's true." I fought back comments about my own maker, tempted to release the whole story into the woods that night and tell Simon what I'd come from. In the end, I couldn't muster the energy to even start.

We made our way into the classroom where Flavio was leading the children in physical activities. They giggled through jumping jacks and pushups, clearly needing to expend energy. Flavio looked to us, aware that something bad was happening and I gave a slight nod to let him know it was being handled.

Clapping my hands together, I drew their attention. "All right children," I smiled. "How about we catch frogs? It's beautiful outside. The one who catches the most gets to ride on my back while I run as fast as the wind."

For the rest of the night, the kids found frogs and brought them to Simon, Flavio and I as we waited patiently to hear news. In truth we did not keep count, so in the end we declared it a tie and swore that each child would ride the back of a vampire the next time we ran through the woods.

Flavio had taken Michael back to the cabin for bed and Julie was asleep in hers when the truck slowly pulled up to the front door. I only needed to see Lily's face to know that Robert had left this world.

We agreed to let Julie enjoy her sleep and tell her when we all arose. Lily left to curl up next to her daughter and begin to grieve her father. Pedro made a bed on the floor next to his daughter's bed so he could help either one should they need anything.

For the 100th time I hated my inability to help someone during daylight hours, hated being bound by the sun and loathed my uncurable condition.

67

We buried Robert two days later. The hospital had asked several times if we were sure we didn't want him in a "proper cemetery" but Lily had been unyielding. He came home to the ranch and was buried next to Travis. We could visit him anytime we wanted and knew it was what he would have wanted.

Julie wouldn't cry in front of us. The first time she stood up without explanation and ran from the school room, we found her sitting next to her grandfather's headstone. I smelled the tears on the air before we reached her and encouraged Lily to let her grieve alone. The girl returned to the classroom an hour later, sat down and asked what the next lesson would be. She didn't mention where she'd been, and we didn't bring it up. Whether that was the right way to handle it or not we didn't know but we were all lost in our own pain, and this felt like the best way.

We continued like this for months, going through the routine of eating, teaching the children, tending to the ranch and going to bed. It was like the heart of the ranch had stopped beating when Robert's heart had done the same.

Lily threw herself into training the children. I think she'd seen how tenuous life is and wanted to ensure Julie would be safe if something should happen to her mother. Flavio and Pedro showed the same intensity and focus. The first time they all shifted after Robert's death, the howls from the woods were sorrowful and haunting.

I'd end each night playing records on the player Robert had given me, staring into the corner and watching for ghosts who never came.

It was the spring of 1955 that snapped us out of our funk. The blooming flowers and the bird songs reminded us that things restart. Planting the garden helped us focus on creating new things instead of what we'd lost.

The summer brought night swims in the lake and fireflies. The autumn brought harvest and spooky stories by the campfires. That Christmas, we bought our first television and the fall of 1956 we watched a young Elvis Presley on the Ed Sullivan show. It was the beginning of Julie's love of the singer – an obsession that lasted years.

On a full winter moon's night in 1957, we had an unexpected visit from a pack representative. He insisted on shifting with Flavio, Pedro and the children – who were now teens. Lily, Simon and I tried to stay busy and distracted while the wolves ran. We knew our own lycanthropes were able to control their beasts and not attack our cattle while in animal form but didn't know if the pack member was the same. We also didn't know exactly what he was watching for or judging so we used our anxiety to fuel our chores until they all came from the woods.

Simon and I had little time to assess the situation before we had to lay down for the day, so we had to trust Pedro, Flavio and Lily to talk to the pack rep and tell us at sundown what the outcome of the night was.

It turned out that he was happy with them as wolves but still very skeptical of them as witches. They'd been too exhausted by the shift to perform any magic for him, and he'd been disappointed. However, he'd said he understood and would be back. In truth we didn't want to demonstrate magic for anyone in the pack since we didn't know how they'd take it but at least we'd bought ourselves more time to decide how to handle future requests.

This interaction had brought up old worries for me as well. Since our talk in the barn, Simon and I had completely forgotten about our plans to teach me the ways of the vampire, all that my maker never had. I didn't need my powers at the ranch, so it'd gone to the bottom of the list of priorities when Robert had died. Then, the wolf had shown up and I'd remembered that I may need to fight some day and didn't know if I was at full potential or how to even test it.

I hadn't seen the ghosts since that night, so they too had gone forgotten. I hadn't wanted to ask Lily about contacting the dead right after her father passed away and as time went on, it had seemed unnecessary.

I did, however, often ponder what the H on the floor could have been for. Was it "help"? Did they want my help? Or was it "hello" and they only wanted to greet me? Or had they been trying to carve "heart" since Robert's heart attack had only been hours later? Which would explain why they hadn't come back, because I hadn't saved him.

There was no way to know without them returning or Lily finding a way to communicate so until one of those things happened, I was only driving myself mad when I sat in that corner and ran my finger over that letter H.

So, I stopped. I stopped staring into the corner at dawn or pondering the meaning of the letter. I stopped worrying about the dead and put all my energy into the living.

I asked Simon to start training my powers. I took over all of Pedro's duties as he'd taken on all of Robert's. I watched the children turn into teenagers and started to tour all the new arrivals to the ranch. I learned to drive and went into the city with Simon sometimes to look at records and even caught some concerts.

As the 50s gave way to the 60s, we all watched Michael and Julie fall in love. I think we knew before they did. It was Lily that caught them kissing in the barn and verified for all of us that we'd been right.

"I think I'd rather her continue to dream that Elvis will sweep her away," Pedro had mumbled when Lily told us what she'd seen, choosing to busy himself with chores rather than accept his little girl wasn't little anymore.

In 1963, in the same spot that Lily and Pedro had wed, the two witch-wolves exchanged vows. We celebrated until the vampires had to call it a day and the newlyweds made their way to their own cabin and the start of their new chapter.

I should've suspected that we were all too happy. It's dangerous when everything is going so well. It means you have a lot to lose.

68

February 1965

"It's a girl," Micheal burst into the main house where we all waited for news. Lily had been with Julie all day as she labored to turn pregnancy into a baby. "Julie is doing great, and the baby is healthy with ten toes and ten fingers." The room erupted into cheers and Pedro dropped to his knees on the floor from sheer relief.

"She doesn't want visitors yet," he continued. "She's exhausted but-" he pointed at the elder wolf. "She would like her dad. Go on, grandpa."

Pedro jumped to his feet and ran through the backdoor before anyone could stop him. Flavio crossed to embrace his brother. "You're an uncle," Michael laughed.

"What's her name?" I asked.

He squared his arms and puffed out his chest with pride. "Victoria Grace," he beamed. "We're calling her Tori."

"Let's hope she doesn't look like you," Flavio joked.

"Thank goodness," he laughed. "She's the spitting image of her mom. I'm gonna head back but you guys are all welcome to start stopping by tomorrow after sunset, deal?"

"Can't wait," Simon said. "Second generation to be born on this soil. Wouldn't miss it for-" A pounding on the front door brought silence to the revelry. We must've been distracted by the joy because we'd been unaware of someone arriving on the ranch.

Three men stood on the front porch when we opened the door. One I recognized immediately as one of the pack members. The years hadn't been kind to him, yet the eyes remained as cold as the first time I'd seen him. He stood a few feet behind the other two. The power that radiated off of him felt vaguely like a threat. "Gentlemen?" Simon began as cordial as he always was to visitors. I heard the hint of concern under his words, but he wasn't calling power, so I didn't worry yet.

The two other men were equally broad, and their arms told me they worked out in a gym or lifted heavy things on a regular basis. The dark stubble across their jaws made them feel ominous but it was the dark eyes that told me they meant business. "I'm Antonio," the one to my right said. "This is Ramon," he gestured to the man next to him, then cocked his head backwards. "You already know Luis." I hadn't know the older wolf's name, but I did now.

"Hello, I'm Simon and this is Rhys. What can I do for you?"

"We want to talk to Flavio," Antonio was brief and got right to the point.

"About?" Simon asked.

"Pack business," Ramon said, crossing his arms in front of his massive chest.

Flavio came to our side before Simon could say anything else. I didn't know if Flavio sensed that Simon was about to put up a fight, but I had and knew it wasn't the best choice until we knew these men meant trouble. "Hola, Luis. Can I help you?"

Luis looked uncomfortable. "Can you come outside?"

Flavio looked to us and nodded that it was okay. He knew we could hear anything they said outside, and we'd years ago established the word *lilac* as a code word for needing help. Flavio and Michael were family and we trusted them to protect us above the pack. This was one of those times we had to let him be in control. Even if Pedro had been in the room, the pack didn't see him as one of theirs, so we had to put our faith in Flavio.

Michael crossed to join his brother, but Flavio gave him the kind of nod that tells you now was not the time. "Go to where you're needed. I'll find you later." Michael turned and followed his command, heading to his wife and new daughter so his big brother could handle whatever had been brought to our doorstep.

Once outside, with the door shut, Ramon spoke in a harsh whisper. "Tell me you didn't allow your brother and that girl to marry." The directness of the words and the growl that edged them told me he already knew the answer.

"Sounds like you already know that answer," Flavio responded, taking the words right from my mouth.

"How could you?" Luis inserted. "We sent you to train him and bring him home. We need offspring in *our* pack, not more mongrels and half-breeds."

"You will bring him back to pack lands to impregnate one of ours, to start bringing the wolf blood back to pure. Do it tonight. The marriage is not true until they sire a healthy young one."

The growl that emanated from the front yard was one of warning, not to the pitch of a fight yet. "They've had a healthy girl this night," Flavio snarled. "My niece will not be called a mongrel or half-breed." His voice dropped an octave. "And you will honor and protect my sister-in-law as she has given us a new generation."

"Lies," Ramon snapped. "You lie to protect them."

"He does not," it was Micheal from the front yard. He'd not listened to his brother after all but had waited in the shadows to see if he would be needed. "I have a daughter, protected by every creature on this land, so I suggest you return to your home and forget all about us."

You didn't need vampire ears to hear the snarling that rose from every wolf outside. Simon and I were poised, ready to move with a single word.

"We raised you," Luis growled, no longer trying to keep his voice low. "You would turn your back on your own? What should I tell your father? How would you have him hear of this shame?"

"My father," Michael barked out a dry laugh. "Lost my loyalty when he allowed my mother to be sacrificed."

Simon and I exchanged looks. This whole time we all believed Michael to be unaware, blissfully ignorant. But he'd carried that knowledge with him and now had a family to protect. The weight of the world rested on 20-year-old shoulders.

"What's to stop us from taking the bitch and drowning the pup?" Antonio sneered.

Flavio answered, "Lilacs."

Antonio's neck was in my grip and Ramon's was in Simon's hands before they'd registered the door opening. Flavio and Michael each had one of Luis' arms. Simon leaned in so close to his captive that spit slapped Ramon's face while he snarled "This is my land, wolf. I allowed you on it in the hopes of peace, but you've abused your invitation." Simon's face twisted into one of rage. His fangs gleamed in the moonlight, and I was reminded that he was much older than I. "You tell the whole pack, if you step foot on this property, I'll see it as a declaration of war and drain every one of you. Do you understand?"

"You can't do this," Ramon sputtered out. "They're ours."

"We are not yours," Michael snapped. "We speak aloud to you with witnesses to hear-"

Flavio picked up what his brother was saying and they spoke in unison. "We break our ties to the pack and declare ourselves lone wolves."

Luis shook free from the boys, and they let him. He backed up, away from us all, eyes wide. "You will lose our protection and can never return."

"We have protection," Michael answered. "This is our pack now. My daughter, my wife, my brother, my father-in-law are my pack. The vampires, the shifters, the fae that live here-" He raised his arms out wide. "They are our pack." He dropped his left arm and used his right to point at Luis. "You are just the fucked-up family we were born into."

Simon and I let go, allowing our wolves to gasp for air and mirror Luis' walk backwards to the car. We four moved back up to the porch, forming a line between them and our home. As they slammed the car doors and started the engine, Luis rolled down the window. "If the new pup is a threat," he wiped the back of his hand over his mouth. "It will be taken care of."

Before I could get to the car and rip the door off to extract Luis, they hit the gas and were tearing up the driveway to get off our land.

"Go back to your wife and daughter," Simon laid his hand on Michael's shoulder. "They won't be back any time soon. I think we made our point." This time Michael did listen. We heard him heading back to the cabin and his scent faded. Once we knew he was gone, it was Flavio that asked the question we were all contemplating.

"What shitstorm did we just start?"

69

We'd all chipped in to get the new parents a color camera and a dozen rolls of film. Julie had been thrilled and the first roll was filled before Tori was two days old despite the fact that the baby basically slept 22 hours a day.

I was holding the tiny thing so Julie could sleep when Pedro came in and sat next to us. "I heard what happened." He looked at the baby, but I knew he was talking to me. I glanced back to make sure the new mother was sleeping before I answered. "They'll be safe."

"Will they?" Pedro asked, locking eyes with me. "How can you be sure?"

"Because every being on this ranch would die to protect her and Simon is the strongest person I know," I smiled down at the sleeping child. "And her mother and grandmother have more magic than all the vampires I've ever known combined."

Pedro laid his head back against the couch, staring at the ceiling. "I wish Robert was here. I don't like being the oldest male of this line. Feels like too much pressure, you know? Too much responsibility."

"You don't carry it alone," I assured him. "We are all in this family and I'm much older than you."

He laughed "Yeah, I guess you are."

The door opened and Lily stepped into the cabin. I knew without being told that she'd want to hold the infant and knew better than to argue, so I held the baby out for her grandmother to take when I heard mother awake.

"I'm so sorry," Lily apologized to her daughter. "I didn't want to wake you but needed to see this little angel."

"It's okay, Mom."

Crossing to Julie's bed, Lily sat on the mattress, one arm holding the little one and one hand holding her daughter's. I snapped a picture of that moment – three generations of witches and a powerful female line.

That picture is a treasured possession of mine and still in my bedroom to this day.

SIDE NOTE

November 2020

Katie-

I'd like to take a moment to pause in the telling of my history. The next part will contradict a story I told you, one that is well documented in your first journal, the one you published under the name "Bite Shift".

I'm sorry that I wasn't completely honest with you when I first told you about my past. After I'd turned you, I was hesitant to share everything. While I knew you well and believed that turning you was the right choice – I was terrified to expose my past. My fear that I cannot trust anyone, my shame over some of my choices and my desire to exist unnoticed was so ingrained in me that I still have to make a conscious effort to tell the whole truth.

Please forgive me for my lack of complete honesty until this point. Furthermore, as you meet people in my retelling that you now know in your life, I ask that you forgive their lack of complete transparency as well. They were honoring a promise to me, a promise to protect my secrets until I was ready to admit them.

This journal is my way of sharing every single part of me with you, my progeny and family. You may come to me once you've read this and ask any question you like. I will answer with honesty. And should you need time to process the information before talking to me – need space – than I respect that. I am here when you are ready and will love you always.

Now, I would like to share the honest recounting of the first time I met Sorin.

70

March 1968

The night couldn't have been more beautiful, and the moon was one of the fullest I'd seen in a while. While the wolves ran, Simon and I watched Tori look for frogs. I didn't know if all children loved nature or it was the witch in them but the three-year-old searching for amphibians reminded me of her mother and grandmother, always barefoot and talking to wildlife.

We didn't know if the baby would ever turn but knew it was too early at this stage, so the vampires were on nanny duty every full moon. Much to the chagrin of her mother, the plan this evening was to teach Tori about s'mores. I was working on making the fire while Simon was bringing up the supplies from the main house.

To my shock, along with crackers, chocolate and marshmallows, Simon returned with another man at his side.

I felt this vampire before I saw him. Over the years Simon and I had been training my abilities, I learned to sense the power of another. Simon, as a master, was very strong in his magic. But this vampire was on a different level, something about him pushed against me. I would always assume immortals did not do it on purpose before taking offensive to someone's magic brushing against me. It was the same with this new arrival - until proven otherwise, I believed he was not purposefully throwing his power out.

Taking the moment before they were close to observe him, I first noticed the utter fairness of his skin. All vampires lose a shade or two over the centuries, but the alabaster of his skin made him the palest of his peers. In contrast, the blue-black of his hair shimmered in the light of the full moon. He was taller than Simon by an inch so taller than me by two. While I'd become accustom to the grace with which immortals moved, this new vampire traveled in a way that took me aback. His muscles seemed to ripple under that perfect skin to transport him in a way that didn't actually look like walking, more like floating. The eyes that locked onto mine as he spoke to Simon were a grey that reminded me of winter dawns. It was like looking into his gaze made me chilly.

"Rhys is my right hand and can help you if I'm not available," Simon was saying seconds before they were in hand-shaking distance. "If he says it, you can be sure it's me saying it to."

"Pleasure to meet you," the visitor said, hand extended. An accent that was unfamiliar hinted under clipped speech. He wasn't from America, England or Scotland and was working hard to make his words sound unaccented.

I took it and the grip was strong. "You are?"

"This is Sorin," Simon answered for him. "He was rockin' in a chair on the porch when I walked up. He'll be with us for a little while."

I dropped Sorin's hand when I heard Tori run up. The frog extended in her little grasp ribbeted, clearly annoyed by being found. "He's fat," the girl exclaimed, then promptly dropped it to the grass when she saw the new vampire. The frog hopped away like his life depended on it and Sorin dropped down to a squat.

"Hello, little witch," he smiled, and the words sounded like music on the air.

Tori giggled as Simon and I exchanged glances. We didn't know how this new arrival knew but were well accustomed to supernatural guests saying unexpected things. Tori didn't seem to mind. She giggled and threw her arms around the visitor.

Simon chuckled. "Tori's our official welcoming committee."

"Hello, Tori," Sorin pulled back and stood with the tiny toddler's hand in his. "Shall we go find your runaway toad?"

The two made their way to the pond and I could almost feel all the frogs slide deeper into their sleeping places to avoid the captors. While we made a habit of trusting every being that arrived on the ranch for help, we both kept an eye on Sorin since he was with Tori.

Simon placed the s'more ingredients on the ground and brushed his hands together. "So?" he asked.

"He feels old," I said.

"Yes, he does," Simon agreed.

"What's the story?" I asked, knowing full-well the vampire by the pond could still hear us.

"Heard about this place through some other supernaturals," Simon explained. "He didn't say much but I think he's trying to get away from something or someone." Simon stoked the fire. "Like most of the folks who come here."

"Yeah," I recognized. "It makes me sad how many of us need a place like this."

"I know," Simon echoed. "I'm so proud of what we do but every day I wish that we weren't needed, you know? That everyone was accepted and happy and safe and the new arrivals stopped."

"It's a good dream," I smiled, opening the bag of puffy, white sweets. Yelling out, "Tori." She looked up and I waved her over.

Sorin allowed the tiny lady to pull him back to the fire and her babysitter for the night. When they reached the fire, Simon and I exchanged devious smirks. "Ready to try a new treat?"

71

When we arose the next night, we found the wolves sitting around the dining table. The hot blood smell told us our meal was ready. Simon and I poured our drinks and joined the discussion. We needed to tell them about the new vampire that had been assigned a room and gone to bed before they'd returned. However, they were clearly in heated debate, so we listened.

"We need to be ready," Pedro fumed. "Let's hope it never happens but if it does and we're caught with our pants down-"

"We don't know the whole story," Michael interrupted.

"Yes, we do," Flavio exclaimed. "Why wouldn't we trust her?"

"I'm just saying that scaring everyone and living in fear isn't the answer," Michael argued.

"Time out," Simon finally jumped in. "What's going on?"

Pedro sighed, stabbing his fork into a piece of meat and shoving his plate forward. "Another wolf found us last night. It happens sometimes; there are wolves everywhere, you know? So, we let her run with us, hunt with us. But," he took a big swill of a waterglass. "When we shifted back, she informed us she was from the pack. She'd been looking for us to warn us."

"Of what?" I asked.

"She said," Michael continued. "The pack is divided about the witch-wolves. Half of them think this is a sign of the wolf blood dying and that they should all go out and find non-wolves to breed with. The other half thinks our existence is a curse on lycans and a test."

"What kind of test?" Simon asked before I could.

"One on the faithfulness of the pack," Pedro shook his head. "They think it's a test from the gods and they need to kill the mix-breeds to prove their worthiness, that 'sacrificing the mongrels will return favor from our ancestors and offspring to the pack.'"

"What?" I snapped.

"It's crazy," Flavio jumped in. "Even for the pack. I don't know if we can trust this girl. We don't know her."

"Why would she lie?" Michael asked. "Risk so much?"

"What do you know of her?" Simon queried.

"Nothing," Flavio responded. "She came to us as a wolf, ran with us and after shifting, told us this and then ran away. We don't even know her name."

I was speechless. I'd learned the horrors that many beings are capable of but even this felt a little crazy. Would they really try to attack on our soil after the last time? How many were there that believed killing a kid would bring them fertility? It felt preposterous even in a world of the unbelievable.

"I've been too long away and there're new wolves in charge," Flavio said. "I just don't know what they're capable of."

"I do." Every gaze shot to the man in the entryway. Sorin was still, not completely entering the room but making himself known.

Simon stood. "Gang," he held out this hand to invite Sorin into the conversation. "This is Sorin. He came last night and will be with us for a while."

The men stood to welcome him. Lily crossed to pour blood into a glass and returned, offering it to the newcomer. He stood, sipping on the blood. I could see that he was deciding what to say next or if he should speak at all.

"I fought in a battle with the wolves," he started, cautiously. "This one was to assert vampire dominance over lycanthrope." He sipped again. "Which I do not believe in. I sided with the wolves and brought the anger of my fellow immortals against me." You could have heard a sigh from across the ranch, we were so silent as he spoke. "In the end, the vampires still won. But it was not for the lack of power in the packs, it was because they cannot remain united." He locked eyes with Pedro. "No one species should reign supreme above all others. Vampires are not perfect. I've known many nocturnal to engage in horrific acts but," his eyes seemed to drift away like he wasn't really with us anymore. "At least vampires stick together. I cannot say the same for the wolves. They fight within their ranks, betray one another, hold to old ways and superstitions. They have no unity." He shook his head, clearing his thoughts and returning to the moment. "You cannot underestimate the insanity that comes with blind belief in anything."

We remained unspeaking, unmoving as we processed what he'd said. It was Simon that finally ended the lack of sound. "We want the opposite on this ranch. I made this place for every species to be safe and welcomed. Whether they are pure breed," he smiled and tilted his head towards Michael. "Or mixed. I want everyone to have a home."

"Forgive my forthrightness," Sorin finished his blood is a large gulp. "Do you find that being mixed makes you stronger?"

Michael and Flavio exchanged glances. Since Julie and Tori were not at the table, he was the only one to answer that question. "I don't know. Why?"

"I met the young witch last night," he arched hie eyebrow. "I've known witches before, am naturally gifted at gauging ability. You," he pointed at Michael. "Feel stronger than most witches and most wolves. I believe this is because you're the best of both. I'm sure your wife will feel the same. It's only natural for your child to also be the best of both," he smiled. "However, your daughter is something I've never felt before. Her ability is practically too much to even breath around." He shook his head, almost like he couldn't believe the words coming out of his own mouth. "I think that she will be a force beyond what we've seen before, that mixing the species creates stronger blood not weaker like these pack members are trying to tell you."

We were hanging on every word this man was saying. His voice held a kind of certainty that assured us, like he had knowledge beyond what any of us could. His presence was wisdom-filled and confident, yet the set of his shoulders told me there was a dark history behind those eyes. I think that those of us who've survived abuse and neglect have a way of recognizing each other. I had the impulse to reach out and hug him, like I needed to tell him everything was going to be okay. I didn't know where it came from, but it was there. Almost every entity on this ranch was coming from something or hiding from something so I was used to the hint of sadness in the eyes around me, but Sorin's were more than that. I'd never ask him what had led him to us, but I knew it wasn't good. And, while I'd had my own dark years to repress, I somehow knew that what he'd experienced was far worse.

The downside to eternity is that it's a lot of years and opportunities for us to be damaged in some way and no ticking clock to countdown the moment the suffering ends.

"What do you recommend?" This was Simon. Despite being the owner of the ranch and older than most, he often asked the opinion of others. It was one of the things I admired about him.

Sorin took a breath and let it out, "Do not underestimate a zealot. If they truly believe in something, no matter how illogical or superstitious, they *need* for that belief to be true and will do anything to protect it or act on it. I would prep your ranch for a siege," he looked at Simon. "Then pray it never comes."

72

Sorin was on the ranch until the beginning of summer. He helped us fortify any gaps in the fencing or security. We were all surprised to see how handy he was at manual labor. Something about him presented like an artist, someone graceful and higher class. Yet, he was clearly comfortable with hard work. The first time he took off his shirt, I saw the evidence of difficult labor in his back muscles. His ease around the largest of the cattle told us he was familiar with livestock.

The females on the ranch adored him. They almost seemed to drift towards him whenever he arrived, hanging on his every word. As vampires, we know that there is something about us that can draw anything non-vampire towards us, but Sorin was on a different level. And, the males didn't appear to mind since they too loved to get his attention.

One night, as the fires roared and we all enjoyed our post-chore discussions, Sorin asked me to walk with him in the woods. My duties on the ranch and our determination to prepare for any movement from the pack had kept me too busy to spend much time with him so I was thrilled to have a few minutes to get to know this intriguing immortal.

The first fifteen minutes of the walk into the trees was silent and serene. If Sorin just needed to walk and wanted company, I was okay with that. I let him lead. In the distance, the sound of a guitar and everyone singing *Bridge Over Troubled Water* danced over the night breezes. He found a fell tree and sat so I joined him at his side. We listened to the joyous sound of all the ranch singing together. It was one of my favorite things, when we all sat and sang. Some people knew how to harmonize, and others couldn't carry a tune in a bucket but we all gave it our fullest souls.

"It's the universal language, music." Sorin's smile was genuine, he was truly enjoying the sounds and it endeared him to me.

When the song ended and the familiar strumming started, I heard the crowd start into *Pale Moon Rising*. It made me chuckle since I knew it was one of the lycans who requested it. They all insisted it must be written by a werewolf.

"You have a very special thing here on this ranch," Sorin said.

My chest filled with pride. "We do."

"I must confess something to you and forgive my bluntness since there is no easy way to say it."

I turned to see his eyes fixed on me. While I was becoming accustomed to his grey gaze, this night it was so intense that it took me off-guard. "Go ahead," I invited.

"I know James and Lia."

All of the air was sucked out of my lungs. The pain in my chest was so strong that I had to remind my tilted thoughts that I was not human and could not be having a heart attack. I repeated in my head *You're safe, James isn't here. You're safe, James isn't here. You're safe, James isn't here.*

"Rhys," Sorin grabbed my hand. "I am sorry. I should not have said it so plainly. Please, forgive me."

"Why?" was all I could muster.

"Why say something?" Sorin clarified. All I could do was nod. "Because I want you to know that I'm certain of the cruelty you've suffered. I didn't say this to upset you or expose your past in any way and I apologize if it felt like a threat."

"Does he-" I couldn't make myself ask.

"Know you are not dead?" Sorin asked, finishing my thought again. And again, I could only nod. "I do not know. I met them long before he sired you. And, I've heard through others that all of his progeny, save Lia, have died. If he does not believe you dead, I could not know that."

I just kept nodding, trying to process.

"Rhys," he waited for me to look at him. "I told you this for two reasons. First, I too have fled something and someone cruel." He waited for me to indicate that I'd heard the first part. "Secondly, I am leaving tomorrow at sundown for a city called Pittsburgh in Pennsylvania. If for any reason-" he paused again for emphasis. "Any reason, you must run from here, come find me there. I will protect you."

My ridiculous nodding just kept happening, like I couldn't control my own neck muscles. It felt like my functioning was no longer in my control, fried by one piece of information, and the nodding head was all it knew to do. I fought back tears, refusing to cry in front of this strong male.

"If you need to stay dead," he reassured me. "I will help you stay dead out there. I'm not telling you to leave Simon. I think very highly of him. I simply want you to know that you have a second safe place to go."

"Thank you," it was all I could make myself say. As the song ended by the campfire and the family I'd built started to sing *Hey Jude*. "Must you leave tomorrow?" I was growing fond of him and enjoyed having more vampires around.

"I must," he answered. "I've already stayed longer than I intended to."

"When will you tell the others? I think little Tori will be heart-broken," I managed a weak smile.

"I'll tell them at first meal and then leave," he shrugged his shoulders. "No point in dramatics. That little one," he looked at the ground just as sadness filled his eyes. "She's special. I think she, her mother and her grandmother together," he returned his gaze to mine. "They are the weapon you may need someday."

He stood, unceremoniously leaving me to ponder his last statement. He had a habit of speaking in a kind of riddle sometimes and this one was more curious than anything else he'd said while he was with us.

It was twelve years before I'd know what he meant.

And, the ghosts returned to give me a similar warning.

73

September 1980

We were all in the den of the main house, enjoying our last two hours after chores. Everyone was there, laughing and talking on top of each other. We we're talking about decorating the ranch for Halloween. Some of the ranch residents felt the holiday was one of the reasons supernatural creatures would never be accepted while others thought it was good fun. Tori wanted to host a "haunted house" and invite all the townspeople to come for a scare. She was always asking for contact with the city, desperate for interactions with new faces and anyone her age. The argument was a common one recently and we all told her for the 100th time that we couldn't have an open house for all the city of Austin. She stomped, crossed her arms and told us all how unfair we were but we held strong.

Yes, the pack hadn't made a move since we'd first been warned but we still didn't trust anyone outside the ranch, especially with the safety of Tori. We still walked the perimeter nightly to ensure no one was trying to sneak onto the land. We still ran drills to practice what we'd do if a siege occurred. We still trained our magicks to be certain we were at full power.

And Tori believed we were all unnecessarily paranoid and hated the way we lived.

"It's Halloween," she argued. "We can all just be ourselves and they'll think it's just us getting into the spirit of the holiday."

"It's not that," Simon explained. "It's too many people here in a chaotic situation that we can't possible control."

"You don't-" her retort was cut short by music down the hallway.

I'd been listening to *Pink Floyd's The Wall* for a few weeks. I enjoyed the album, so left it on the turntable. *Mother* played from my bedroom, obviously at full volume. As far as I knew, everyone was in the main room. That left no one back there to start the record, let alone move the needle to that song in the album.

Simon and I exchanged concerned glances. I shot my hand up in the air to stop anyone from speaking or moving. The silence allowed for me to hear every lyric and was an eerie soundtrack to my walk down the hall and into my room. Opening the door revealed my bed with the player next to it, the record rotating and no one in sight. It wasn't until I stepped in and turned that I saw them – the spirits standing in their usual spot.

I hadn't seen them since Robert died and fully believed they'd moved on, or I'd never actually seen them.

"Lily," I was afraid to speak, that any sound would send the ghosts fleeing. I kept them in my sights as I heard Lily come down the hallway and into my room. She followed my gaze and I held my breath, waiting to see what she'd say.

"I see them," she whispered.

Collin and Diedre continued to stare only at me, not indicating that they knew another was in the room or not caring. "What do I do?" I asked Lily.

"Talk to them," she said.

"Why do you appear to me?" It was all I could think to ask. Expecting no answer, I dropped to my knees on the floor, no longer able to hold myself up. For a century I'd been haunted by these specters, and they'd only stared. I believed it was all they could do.

Until that night, when Diedre moved her finger to her lips and tapped them.

"Talk?" I asked. The ghost nodded.

"How?" I asked.

Collin repeated the motion of his sister, tapping a finger to his lips.

Lily rushed from the room, and I heard rustling in the den. Several voices asked what was going on and if we needed help. I heard the witch ask them to please stay where they were. When she returned, a spirit board was clutched to her chest. "I've been waiting," she gasped. She held it out to the spirits and my friends both nodded. A thrill shot through me as I realized my ghostly visitors were about to communicate.

Lily dropped to the floor beside me, laying the board down and pulling my hand to the planchette. I was shaking but her hand over mine gave me comfort.

"Tell us, spirits," she begged them. "Why do you come to Rhys?"

Diedre and Collin each reached out an arm towards the board and the planchette shook under my fingertips. I gasped. Would I be hearing a message from my departed friends? What would it be? Was I prepared to hear what they had to say? Tears began to roll down my cheek from the overwhelming emotions of the moment.

"W" Lily said next to me. I forced myself to focus on the board so I wouldn't miss the words my loved ones had come from the other side to give to me. "O" she spoke as the ivory piece glided across the board. "L."

"Wolves," I shouted and looked up for affirmation. Diedre and Collin's faces were filled with hope and desperation. It was the most emotion I'd seen on them since they'd begun visiting me. "What about the wolves?"

"C" Lily spoke but the planchette was noticeably slower. "They're losing their energy."

I could see it in their forms, they were fading. They were losing their energy and may not be able to manifest again for some time. I had an idea. "Julie. Tori," I shouted. "We need you." They appeared in the room seconds later, both wide eyed to see ghosts in my bedroom. "Focus," I begged, desperate for this to work. "Combine your energies and give it to them."

Lily stood so her daughter could take one hand and her granddaughter the other. Their eyes closed in tandem, all three mumbling something. I felt the power rising in the air, wrapping around me and reaching for the spirits.

The planchette vibrated, then shot around the board. I called out each letter as it paused. "C-O-M-I-N-G. They're coming to the ranch? YES. Why?" The witches continued to mumbling, showing no signs of hearing what I was saying. "T-A-K-E-T-O-R-I. Take Tori? Why? S-A-C-R-F-I-C-E." I didn't need to ask why, I already knew. I guess after a decade, the crazy ideas of the pack had won over and the majority had a plan. "When," I asked. "D-U-S-K." The needle skidded across the record, turning the music into shrieking. The planchette was sliding around erratically. "S-A-V-E-H-E-R." Every lightbulb in the room exploded. The witches dropped to the ground, covering their heads with their hands. The rest of the group ran from the den into the bedroom to fight whatever threat we we're facing.

Only when the music gave way to silence did we look to see an empty corner.

74

"Spirits don't cross the veil to tell tall tales," Lily was explaining to the group what'd happened and what it meant. "They came to warn us, and I believe them."

We'd pulled every single person living on the ranch into the main house to let them know what was coming. They listened intently and no one had questioned our story. They'd all been a part of preparation in some way and knew this day may come.

"I believe them too," Simon took over. "That means we have twelve hours to be ready."

"We are ready," I reminded everyone. "We've been preparing for years, and we have the upper hand, they don't know that we were warned."

"There's one problem," this was from Michael. "If they're coming at dusk, it could be minutes or even an hour before you two can wake up and help."

Flavio jumped in. "I say we run, take Tori and be halfway to the ocean before they even pull into the ranch."

Tori spoke up. "No way. I'm not spending my life running."

"She's right," Julie agreed. "If we run now, we run forever. We'd lose our home, our family, it's too much."

"But," Flavio argued. "If we stay, we could lose it all anyways. I don't want to risk anyone's life."

"We vote," Simon declared. "All in favor of packing and running." Only one arm shot in the air – Flavio's.

"Fighting?" Simon asked and everyone else rose their hands. "That settles it," he continued. "We don't need to plan because we've gone over this so many times. The only difference is that this isn't a drill anymore. Everyone knows their part."

"As soon as they arrive," I pointed to one of the newer females, the one that hadn't really had time to prepare. "Your job is to wake Simon and me. We can wake when the sun is still up, but you may have to work hard, slap us if you have to." She nodded, eyes wide. "Then, you get to the barn and make sure they stay safe." She looked relieved. While it was a very important task, it was by far the safest assignment. She was a zoological fae, not much help in a battle but she'd be able to keep our beloved animals calm and protected.

"We will be fighting at your side as soon as possible," Simon said. "If you're able to hold them off 'til we awake, that's best. See if they'll talk, try to postpone any fighting, buy us the time to rise."

Pedro nodded. "Flavio and I can do that."

"Everyone needs to get sleep if you can," Simon pleaded. "I can't thank you all enough for this. Some of you are new to us but you're still willing to stand by us and I will never forget it."

After a few minutes of hugging and reassurance, only the core groups remained: Pedro, Flavio, Michael, Lily, Julie, Tori, Simon and I. We exchanged silent glances and long embraces. No one wanted to say it but we all knew that some of us may not be alive a day later.

For almost 40 years, I'd lived on that land, helping build the family that now stood in a circle. I'd never imagined living anywhere else but had to face that it may all be gone soon. I silently wished for more: more time, more runs in the woods, more campfire singing, more frogs... just more.

I shook my head, clearing it of doomed thinking. I couldn't go into battle with such negativity.

"You okay, Uncle Rhys?" Tori asked.

"Yeah," I smiled. "Of course. Just so grateful for you all." The next part came out without thinking. "I wish your great-grandmother was here to meet you."

Lily jumped on that thought. "Tell us a story about her?" she asked. I don't think any of us were ready to separate.

Normally I'd fight it, not wanting to risk slipping back into those dark days and the memories that may come with it. But this night, I felt it appropriate. "Well," I flipped through possibilities and landed on one. "Did I ever tell you about her poetry?"

And that's what I did until dawn, recounted the poems of Nettie, the terrible attempts her brother had made to also write verse and the way they'd compete with each other as only a brother and sister can.

As I lay down, I hoped to arise to a false alarm or that the lycans would change their minds. Even as I prayed for it, I knew it was a fool's wish.

Ghost don't rise from their rest to warn you of nothing.

75

Gasping for air, my first thought was that I was wet. My second was the observation that the fae above me was holding a bucket and looked panicked.

"It's already begun," she said through tears. "You must hurry."

I leapt from bed. "Where's Simon?"

"You were the first I woke," the bucket hit the ground with a thunk. "You wouldn't wake up. I had to throw water on you."

"I'll get him," I commanded. "You get to the barn."

Obediently, she turned and fled from the room. Across the hall, Simon slept. When I crossed to him, I took a brief second to register what we look like while resting. He could have been a corpse, utter frozen and bluish tinting to his lips. Slapping his face, he thankfully inhaled air and bolted to sitting.

"It's happening."

He jumped from the bed, and we cautiously moved to the den, unsure how much sun was still out and if any windows were uncovered. While it was dimming as we watched, it was still too much for us to join whatever was happening outside. A chorus of grunting, bodies colliding, something snapping and bestial roars filled the air around us.

"We can't just listen," I begged.

"We must," Simon answered. "If we go out, we only become flames to do more damage. We won't be able to help them."

A women cried out and the cry was cut short by a squelching. A male bellowed. Scuffling on the dry dirt. A howl.

Then, whimpering in the midst of growls and a woman cried "No." It was Julie.

Before I could move, the front door burst outward and Simon was on the porch. The last rays of the sunset were receding into the horizon. I joined him at his side to assess.

Dozens of lycanthropes had arrived to steal our youngest and were clearly winning the fight. Several bodies lay scattered around but I'd no time to identify the fallen. Simon ran into the fray, pulling a man off of Julie and throwing him into a tree. The resulting crack of sound when his back broke sped across the darkening sky, pulling the attention of many of the wolves to the vampires who'd joined the fracas.

Paralysis overtook me. My brain screamed for me to run down the stairs and into the battle, but my muscles wouldn't respond. I could only move my head to take in the entirety of the siege.

I watched a male lycan snap the neck of one of the shifters who'd raised his hand the night before to volunteer his life for Tori, a vow he'd now fulfilled. The wolf moved to the one-on-one battle nearest him to make it a two to one fight.

My breathing was erratic. I couldn't focus my thoughts enough to draw power, let alone charge into battle.

Pedro struggled under a lycan, slashing at him with a knife but the wolf was too big and seemed unphased by the cuts. He knocked the knife from my friend's hand and pinned his arm to the ground. Wrapping the other around Pedro's throat, I watched his forearm flex and heard a sound like crackling fire. Then Pedro stopped fighting and the wolf hopped to his feet to find another one of my friends to murder.

Heat came over me and an electricity filled my core, thawing my freeze response. Running to Pedro, I saw how limp he was, his still chest and knew he was dead.

Looking up, I found Julie and Tori, back-to-back with three females circling them. The witches were mumbling, and I knew their magic was keeping the wolves from touching them, but it wasn't going to last forever. Sorin's words filled my head, and I flashed back to the three of them with the ghosts. Clarity washed over me.

Running to them, I threw one wolf at the side of the house. Grabbed the other two with a throat in each of my hands. Screaming backwards to the witches, "The three of you must join power. Together, you're a weapon."

I wouldn't have had time to explain but thankfully didn't need to. As the wolves in my grasp struggled, I locked eyes with one. "Leave and don't return." She went limp and I let her go to begin her long walk off the property and to her car. I repeated this with the other. Some of the lycans screamed at the departing females to get back to fighting but I knew they'd never set foot on our ranch again.

Behind me, I heard the chant begin and allowed a moment to find them - three generations of witches on the porch, holding hands in a circle. Then the weight of someone slamming into me took me face-first to the ground. A sharp pain ripped through my side as a lycan tore out a chunk of my shoulder with his very human teeth. Before he could go back for seconds, the weight was gone and I rolled to see a blood-soaked Michael holding out his hand to pull me up.

The bite meant my right hand was useless until it healed and while it would be fast, it wouldn't be until after the fight had ended.

From my periphery, I saw the sun began to rise and shielded myself only to realize it was not the sun. The light was coming off the chanting witches and growing to envelope the battle. One by one, the wolves began howling and walking backwards from the fight, pushed back by the witches' spell. What remained of our people dropped to the ground, hyperventilating and exhausted from combat. Simon and I began a march up the driveway, becoming the back-up plan if the magic somehow began to fail. If the wolves stopped retreating, we were an arm's distance from them. Every lycan snarled but couldn't stop their bodies from moving away from the fight. I found Ramon in the group and locked eyes with him. "We will return," he snarled, and I refused him the satisfaction of a response.

We watched them climb into vehicles and fill the beds of pickup trucks, speeding from the grounds in clouds of dusts.

I felt the spell pull back before I heard a scream.

Simon and I sped to the sounds of Julie and Tori sobbing. Between them and on the ground, was Lily. Her black dress had meant none of us had noticed the blood seeping from her side and down her legs. Because of the corpses now scattered around the property, the smell of blood had been everywhere. None of the vampires had noticed her blood mixed in with the rest. Lily's slow exsanguination had just been a small part of the whole. It wasn't until the chanting stopped and they'd opened their eyes that Julie and Tori had seen the crimson pool at Lily's feet and known she was gravely wounded.

"Take me to Pedro," she begged.

Without question, I scooped her up to lay her next to her husband, ignoring the fiery pain in my right arm as the muscles of my shoulder tried to repair. She pulled herself up to sit and brought him into her lap, cradling his head. The wail of grief that erupted from her was heart-wrenching. She rocked him and the blood continued to spread out from her back. "I'm coming," she whispered over and over. "I'm coming, *mi amore*."

"No, Mom," Julie dropped to her knees beside them. "No, please. I can't lose you and dad on the same day. Please, Mom."

"I love you," Lily smiled at her daughter then granddaughter. "Dying for you is the greatest honor I could have. I need to be with my mother now, with my husband. But I will watch over you." Her eyes fluttered, her skin growing pale.

"Turn her," Tori begged, yanking on my arm and trying to pull me closer to the dying woman. "Make her a vampire, please Uncle Rhys."

"I can't," I shook my head and took a step back.

Tori ran to Simon, pulling his arm but he was statue-still and unmoving. "Please, Uncle Simon. Please. Make her a vampire. You can."

"I can't," he whispered, looking at the dirt. "I promised."

"No," she screamed at him. "No," she screamed at me. "Why won't you help her?"

"Tori," Lily's word were weak. Her heart was slowing in my ears, and I hoped the child would not waste these last few moments. She crossed to her and collapsed to the side of her grandmother. "I want to go. I'm 70 years old. I've lived longer than my father and been blessed to meet you. Don't cry." She opened her mouth as if to continue, then let to fall shut. Slumping over Pedro, her heart attempted a few more feeble beats then ceased.

I spun away, unable to witness the grief of daughter and granddaughter. I couldn't bear to face the corpse of the girl who'd played me a record for the first time and taught me about gardens. I grabbed fistfuls of my hair, dropping to my knees on the ground and raged into the night. My mind's eye saw flashes of young Pedro and Lily smiling at each other over the dinner table, attempting to hide a love we all saw. I saw their wedding, their little cabin, pictured them holding Julie for the first time. I filled my thoughts with them while they lay dead feet from me.

Rage replaced my sorrow. Rage against the wolves, rage at my fear which paralyzed me as my family died and rage at the unfairness of life. I punched the ground over and over. Simon joined my side, wrapping his arms around me. I embraced him in return, allowing the family behind us to have their own mourning. Only he and I understood that we'd seen too much death already and were doomed to experience it over and over.

How many people would we love and lose in the remaining years of eternity that we faced?

76

The row of headstones that started with Travis had become one of two rows as we had to add a second line of dead family members. The cattle bellowed as we stood over Pedro and Lily's freshly covered coffins. It was like the beasts grieved along with us.

Julie and Tori stood with Michael and Flavio on each side. Each took a turn telling a story about the fallen parents.

We'd had a memorial the night before for the others who'd died at the hands of the wolves and protected the ranch to their last breath. Too many had been lost. Only the fae from the barn and two shifters remained. But each had asked to move on, and we couldn't fault them.

Now, we took part in a second funeral and only the four of them and we two vampires remained. Running the ranch was going to be difficult and we would have to rebuild while also completing our normal chores, but this could all wait for another day.

For now, we needed to mourn.

After saying our goodbye, Simon and I walked away to give the family some time alone. He'd been uncharacteristically quiet since the siege. While I didn't fault him for losing some of his spark, I worried that he was disappointed in me. The need to address my concerns was growing every hour, making it hard to breathe or focus on anything but my failings.

"I failed you," I blurted out and Simon halted to slowly turn and face me.

"What?" he asked.

"I froze," I couldn't look at him, I needed to get it out without seeing his reaction. "I froze on the porch and just watched. I *watched* Pedro be killed and did nothing. If I'd moved as soon as you did, I could have saved him. Julie wouldn't have lost both parents at the same time. Hell," I slammed my chest with my fist. "If I'd saved Pedro, maybe he would have saved more people."

Silence followed. After a while, I found the courage to face him. Simon only shook his head. "You can't take this all on. The blame falls on those zealots and their plans to kill innocents." He crossed his arms and arched an eyebrow. "You did what you could. None of us are perfect, Rhys. I was scared shitless. If we peed, I think I would've wet myself."

I chuckled and the sound surprised me. "You're being kind."

"I'm not," he pursed his lips and gave his head another shake. "Every day I carry around a bit of fear. I'm afraid I won't live up to my promise on this ranch, that the pressure and responsibility should fall on someone more capable than me." He reached out to rest a hand on the same shoulder that had been ripped open two days prior. "But when you act *despite* being scared, that's courage. You showed courage when you came here, when you let that wall down to let people in, when you fight and when you love."

I thought about that. Was he right? Was I braver than I gave myself credit for just by pushing through fear?

"Let's go make them some food," he gently pushed my torso towards the back door. "When they come in, we'll have some chili and cornbread for 'em."

"That sounds like a job for an American," I laughed.

"Hate to break it to ya, buddy. But you are American, we both are now."

77

March 1981

New arrivals to the ranch, fresh paint, taller fencing and patched holes are nice but they don't really erase what happened. As spring arrived, I hoped for a true renewal. I wanted to plant a garden in honor of Lily, watch the vegetables grow and bring them in for dinners just like she did.

Julie and Tori were starting to seem a little more like themselves. For weeks after, they didn't laugh, didn't do magic, didn't come in for dinner. I knew Tori was angry with us for not turning Lily but hoped she'd see that it was the right choice eventually. As the weeks went on, Julie joined us again at the table. Then, with time, Tori did too. They restarted her lessons, getting her ready to take the exam to make her an official high school graduate.

Christmas brought a little more joy back. We watched holiday specials on the television and decorated the enormous tree that Flavio had chopped down and brought in. I'd never forget awaking for the night to the wonderful smell of pine. I think I purposefully walked over and smelled that tree a hundred times before New Year.

As we welcomed 1981, Tori started to talk about leaving the ranch for college. We all knew it wasn't possible but let the teen fantasize about a normal life and request brochures from universities all over the country.

It felt like we were on the other side and reaching the light at the end of a long, dark tunnel. I was creating the lists for the next trip to the city. Newcomers weren't as frequent as they used to be and moved on quickly, but we had a few extras that night, so I wanted to be sure the food was adequate. On top of that, I wanted to be sure to get some extra work done on the property while we had the extra hands.

Drums started down the hall, freezing my hand mid-stroke. The pen fell from my weakening fingers to roll across the table and onto the floor. I was undoubtedly alone in the house; I knew it with complete certainty. So, the only way that the Rolling Stones could be emanating from my room was if the ghosts were back. The last time, they'd come with dire warnings. What were the odds that they came with good news this night? Since they'd chosen *Sympathy for the Devil* to announce their arrival, I was sure it was not a happy visit.

Standing, I started a journey to my bedroom that felt impossibly far. Mic Jagger was singing and telling the story of Lucifer himself, adding to the sense of foreboding. I felt detached from my own body, watching my hand reach out to turn the knob and open the door like it had a mind of its own. The spinning record twirled under the undulating needle arm next to my unmade bed. A few steps into the room and I could feel them at my back.

Summoning all my strength, I turned to face my own personal portents. Diedre looked sad, her eyes wet. In contrast, Collin's face showed desperation. His mouth was moving frantically, no sounds emanating from the rapid movements. "I don't know what you're saying," I begged. "Hold on," I yelled, diving to the floor and pulling out everything under my bed. Years of collecting had led to a cluttered space and under the bed was no exception. Finally, I found it, retrieving the spirit board. My thoughts were racing and I fought to slow them, focusing on the planchette under my fingertips. Raggedly, I pulled in air and let it out, looking up to the closest thing to a brother I'd ever had. "Tell me."

Without any of the witches, the planchette crawled across the wood at a frustratingly slow pace but it moved. "J" I shouted when it stopped the first time. Minutes passed before it could reach another letter. "A" I looked up to Collin and saw pleading in his eyes. I didn't know how much longer they would last without magic to feed them. The planchette vibrated, starting its weak push across the alphabet. As it approached the next letter, I think I knew what it would land on but didn't want to be right. "M" My voice quivered. Finding Collin's eyes, I silently begged to be wrong.

"James?" I asked weakly.

He nodded and I felt heat rush from stomach to face as my heart dropped into my bowels. Reality started to fade at the periphery of my sight. I worried I'd lose consciousness. "He knows?" I didn't want the answer but knew I had seconds to ask.

Brother and sister nodded in tandem.

This time when Collin's mouth moved, I could read his lips and understood the one word he was trying to say before they both faded from sight.

Run.

78

When I came to, I was on my bedroom floor and the sound of the record needle bouncing against the center rod greeted me.

Standing, I stopped the player. My possessions still scattered the floor where I'd thrown them from under the bed and the spirit board lay in the middle. I hadn't imagined it. It had happened. Which meant the message was still pertinent.

James knew I was alive. James was coming for me.

Everyone on the ranch was in danger. We we're only six months out from the last attack and still recovering. We didn't have the same numbers, the benefit of practice or any idea of when he'd arrive. For all I knew, he was minutes away.

I could pack and run, telling no one. If they didn't know where I was or when I left, they'd have no information for James. He'd chase after me and leave them all alone.

But he'd probably torture them to be sure they told the truth. He'd burn down the ranch to send a message or to just hurt me. After all these years, I knew he was livid and likely ready to make anyone and everyone pay for what he saw as a disrespect against him and his property.

I had to tell everyone, give them a chance to run.

Moving as fast as I could, I rang the dinner bell, calling everyone to the main house. Simon was first, asking what was wrong but I begged him to wait until we were all together so I could be sure the message was consistent for everyone.

Once they were gathered, I took a deep breath. My hands were shaking and my voice quivering while I told them an abridged version of my time with my maker. I ensured that I was very clear about his cruelty and complete lack of morals. A myriad of emotions crossed the faces in front of me as I spoke. If I focused on any one face, I wouldn't be able to finish so I kept my gaze moving.

"He knows I'm alive. He knows I'm here. He's coming for me and I think you should run. I can fight to protect the ranch. If I can't win, I'll surrender." I gulped.

Without pause to digest, Tori stomped her foot into the ground. "Absolutely not. We're not leaving you here alone."

"She's right," Michael took a step to be between his wife and daughter. "No way would we abandon you."

"Thank you," I said. "But, it's out of the question. You've all lost so much only half a year ago. We can't withstand another assault and I refuse to lose anymore of you."

"Too bad," Simon crossed his arms. "We stick together, or all of this is for nothing, meant nothing."

"I don't think you understand," I pleaded. "We have no clue when he'll arrive, and I can assure you he's more powerful than you realize. I only know that he masks and as Simon has explained, that's pretty common for us and not always counted as a power. He could have two more abilities I don't know and he's not like us. He doesn't care about killing."

"We're wasting time arguing," Flavio insisted. "We aren't leaving, Rhys, so let's put this energy into getting ready."

Simon took over before I could throw out another reason for them to leave me behind. "Julie and Tori, start working on a spell that will hurt or send vampires away."

"We can't," Julie shook her head. "Not without it effecting you two and without Mom, I don't know if we have the power. We haven't done much since she died."

"Work on something," he said. "If he doesn't know we have witches, then we have the upper hand." Julie grabbed Tori's arm and they ran back towards their cabin and spell books. "Flavio," he continued. "Take a horse and walk the perimeter. Make sure we're good. The new barbed wire means they would have to come from the front and that helps. Does he fly?" Simon was asking me but again I didn't know.

"I don't know," I admitted. "He never showed me what he could do."

"Let's hope not," Simon cocked his head and rubbed his chin. Flavio was already halfway to the barn. "Michael," he sighed. "Sharpen the sickles. Hide them in places we can get to them. It's crude but if one of us can get close enough to cut off his head, I wanna take that shot."

"You got it," he jogged after his brother to find the tool shed and his mission.

Our two newest male residents exchanged glances. They were twins and travelled together but we didn't know much about them, only that they were supernatural beings and in need of work. They didn't feel like anything I'd met before. They hadn't been there long enough to ask deeper questions, so their species remained a mystery. "You can leave or hide if you'd like," I said. "I've certainly not earned your loyalty or would expect you to lay your life down for mine."

"We will fight for you," the one named Samuel said plainly, like he was ordering a meal.

"We will fight for this place," his twin Isaac echoed.

"We need torches," Simon instructed. As many as you can have ready and fuel soaked. Stack them by the front door.

They moved like they'd rehearsed it, turning together and jogging towards the garage where our gasoline was stored. I should have been filled with gratitude or awe but I was numb. One phrase repeated over and over in my head, *James is coming. James is coming. James is coming.* If he got me, I'd be lucky to live a century chained up in a hole. My punishment would be legendary. He wouldn't just kill me. He'd make me watch all my friends die and then torture me for eternity. Unless he broke me and made me his soulless slave again.

"If we start to lose," I said out loud. "I'll end my own life." I didn't say it for shock or pity. I just wanted Simon to know my plans. "If he gets me, please kill me." I waited for Simon to look into my eyes. "Promise me."

"No," he said.

"I cannot live under him again." I grabbed his biceps, shaking him. "You have to promise me. Kill me, Simon, please. Do not let him have me."

After a moment, he nodded furiously. "Okay."

"Okay," I said into the night. "What do we do?"

"I'm making a call," he said. "You go gather enough wood for the biggest bonfire you can make. Pile it in the front yard. Then soak it in gasoline."

"Done," we embraced and broke off. Without knowing if we had minutes or days, we couldn't waste any more time.

79

The attack didn't come that night. We gathered in the den with half an hour before dawn to regroup and discuss next steps.

"We know he can't approach in the day so that helps," I explained. "His waking habits will be similar to ours. But we don't know how close he is. He could show up minutes after sundown or may need time to get to us. We just need to be ready at any moment."

Simon spoke next. "We know he's strong but he's alone, so we have the advantage of numbers, and we know he's coming. Our supplies are set up for easy access and we all know our parts."

I picked up the speech. "I can't thank you all enough for your willingness to help. It means so much to me."

"Wasn't even a question," Michael smiled.

"So," Simon finished. "We all need our rest. We'll meet back here the second the sun is down. I want you all fed by the time we rise. We can grab some blood as soon as we're up and we'll all be fueled for battle. This is what we're gonna do every night until it happens – prepare for a fight but hope it doesn't come."

Michael, Flavio and the twins left for their beds as instructed, leaving Julie and Tori behind. "We think we have an idea," Julie said to Simon and I. "We need a little time to work on it but with our magic combined, I think we can do it."

"Great," Simon winked at them. "If anyone can do it, it's you two. Now get some shut-eye."

They left through the back door to join Michael in their cabin, hopefully to get actual rest and not continue to work on spells for me.

"Rhys," Simon sounded hesitant, not something he normally portrayed. "I'm so sorry for what you suffered. I figured it was bad, but no one should have to go through that and you we're so young. A maker should protect their progeny not be the one they need protecting from. What he did was wrong and none if it did you deserve," he laid his hand on my shoulder. "You know that, right?"

"I'm working on it," I admitted.

"And Collin's death? Rhys, you can't take the blame for that either."

But, I could. "There's a lot you don't know," and that was the closest I was getting to a confession that night.

"I'm sure," he tilted his head. "Maybe some night you'll tell me everything but Rhys," he waited for me to make eye contact. "We all got secrets and things we are not proud of. But, whatever you did, Collin was not your fault."

I nodded, trying to show him I agreed even though I didn't. I just wanted the conversation over. I want to be alone to process the newest predicament I found myself in.

As I lay in bed, I thought of all the people who'd suffered or been hurt or close to danger because of me. I'd broken the hearts of my parents and Diedre. I'd gotten Diedre murdered. I'd gotten Collin turned and killed. I'd put Nettie, Alden, Lia and Robert in danger to get me out of Scotland and here. I'd gotten Pedro and Lily killed. Now the rest of the only family I had was facing an immediate threat.

I couldn't help but stare at that empty corner. "Please" I whispered. "Please tell me where he is, what to do."

Unfortunately, that corner stayed barren and silent. I couldn't blame them. They'd already done so much. They didn't owe it to me to do anymore. I felt guilty, knowing part of me never wanted to see them again.

But I would see them once more – with one last warning.

80

It was the screaming that woke me. Someone was screaming my name. I fled from the room to the den, kicking open the front door to find the person begging for help. Simon arrived at my side, back on the porch and eerily reminiscent of the night of the werewolf siege.

Much like that night, the fighting had started while we we're asleep. I recognized many of the lycanthropes that had been pushed back by magic six months prior. They were struggling in hand-to-hand brawls with the tiny group we had left to protect the ranch. In the midst of the fighting, a truck was parked, and a large wooden crate filled its bed. Before I could remark, it shattered outward into flying splinters and broken planks. Ice water filled my muscles, freezing me in place as the familiar paralysis cemented me in place.

My own personal nightmare stood proudly where the crate had once been.

We'd known he was coming. But what we hadn't planned for was him bringing the pack with him. What we'd failed to think of was how foolish he'd have to be to come alone. And, James was no fool.

Each one of my family was held tight in the grip of a wolf, scattered around the truck. The twins lay broken on the ground, side by side. They'd been reaching for each other when death took them.

James stepped off the truck with fluid ease, each step he took towards me pulled more air from my lungs and sent my body shaking. Simon contracted every muscle in his body, ready to pounce.

"Ah, ah, ah," James waggled his finger. "You move, cowboy, and I signal every lycan to snap the neck of their captive." He outstretched his arms and twirled. "How many would you like to lose tonight? What price would you like to pay for keeping my property from me?"

Simon relaxed beside me. James stopped at the beginning of the walkway. A sensation filled my gut, pulling me to him. He was calling me – maker to progeny – and I couldn't resist. Even my paralysis was no match for the call. I stepped forward, my brain begging my legs to stop. Down the stairs, I went. The smile that crossed James' face was wicked, a smile that would convince you he was possessed. A foot from him, I stopped. He reached for me, laying his hand on my cheek.

"My, my," he lightly slapped me. "You look very good for a dead man." Then he chuckled at his own joke. "The years have been good to you." I remained silent despite his pause for a response. "What?" he asked. "No greetings for your maker?"

"Hello," I said dryly.

"Now," he smirked. "Say goodbye to your friends. I'm taking you home."

"No," Simon bellowed. "You're not."

"Oh?" James arched an eyebrow. "But I am. And," he looked around. "The wolves will be taking your ranch. I told them they could have it if they helped me."

"Never," I spat.

"Here's the thing, boy." This last word was emphasized by a slap that was no longer playful. "We can kill everyone and take the ranch, or they can give up the ranch and leave. Either way ends with you in Glasgow and this ranch belonging to the animals." He leaned in to whisper in my ear. "Except the mixed ones. They'll be killed. Seems the pack is non-negotiable on that."

His face so close to mine sent my fine tremoring fear into full-blown shaking. I could feel the beatings on my body, the tearing at my flesh, the dampness of the dark room and the chains on my ankles.

He leaned back, smiling. "And in case that isn't incentive enough, I brought a gift." James raised a hand in the air. A single crack filled the air and mingled with the sounds of my friends' pounding hearts. It was the crack of a finger snap.

From the bed of the truck, I heard a slither and a saw her emerge from the back. Except for the blood dried down the front of her white dress, she looked exactly as I'd remembered.

"Lia."

81

She crossed to James, standing by his side and directly in front of me. I could have reached out and touched her but was too scared to move. Her eyes begged for something, but I couldn't be sure what she was asking. Did she want me to return with them? Fight him? Kill her? I didn't know and she couldn't say.

"Reunited," he cooed. "And doesn't it feel good." He wrapped his arm around her waist and pulled her into him. "I can't believe you'd leave her, Rhys. I thought you loved her."

"I do," I choked out.

"But," he clicked his tongue in disapproval. "You left her. And when I found out you were alive, well I knew she had to have helped you." The smile became more sinister. "She had to learn a lesson, didn't you?"

"Yes," she whispered, dropping her gaze to the ground.

"Until I could get my hands on you," he met my eyes. "She had to take the punishment for all of you, since the priest and his sister are long dead."

"Take me and leave her," I offered.

The laugh that barked out of him was a mix of amusement and anger. "I'll take both of you. You are my creation, and she is my wife. You belong to me."

A commotion pulled our attention to the left, as a blur slammed into the wolf holding Julie. As he flew into the air, his fellow pack mates looked around them to follow the new arrival. Julie took the opportunity to tackle the wolf holding her daughter and Michael smashed his heel down onto his captor's foot.

Simon grabbed Lia and ran to the right, disappearing behind the huge pile of wood I'd built only a day before.

Our newest arrival skidded to a stop behind James. Sorin wrapped his arms around James in a bearhug. My maker's face was filled with shock. But it didn't take him long to recover. He disappeared from Sorin's arms and reappeared standing on top of the truck. "Kill them," he bellowed. Only one of us remained in the grasp of a wolf. With a fluid, practiced motion, Flavio's neck was snapped, and he dropped to the ground in a heap.

"No," I screamed, reaching out for him but knew I was too late.

James' arm extended to the pile of wood Lia and Simon hid behind, fire erupted from the fuel-soaked timber. Lia and Simon ran from their hiding place, slapping their clothes to stop the flames that flared up to eat the fabric.

The pull in my stomach returned, ripping at my insides. I knew the only relief was to go to James. Lia doubled over, clutching her stomach and screaming no.

Michael ran for his brother's body only to be grabbed by two lycanthropes. I couldn't find Tori or Julie and hoped they'd continued to run as far as possible.

I couldn't withstand the pain any longer, shuffling to James to alleviate the cramping. Lia was in my periphery, using the same disjointed gait to reach her husband and abuser.

"Stop the fight," James roared into the night. "Or I kill Rhys in front of you and you all still die."

Simon shouted from behind me. "Rhys, you have to fight it."

"I can't," I groaned. "Remember what you promised," I yelled back to him through gritted teeth.

When I reached the truck, I climbed up into the bed with Lia following me. James loomed above us, watching us helplessly lurch towards him and his plans for us. I could see everyone from this vantage point. Sorin stood next to the pyre, a torch lit in his hand and ready to move when opportunity struck. Simon was pinned to the ground by a lycan on each arm and each leg. They'd ripped open his shirt and scratches covered his abdomen. One of the wolves was lapping at his blood. Michael was between two lycans, an arm held by each as they kicked the back of his knees to sent him into a kneeling position. The girls were gone, not having to witness this. It was the one relief I had in all of this.

It was too close to the previous fight, too much blood for one piece of land and it all felt so useless. There was too much death for not a good enough reason.

James was going to win. He was going to take me back and Simon couldn't put an end to my misery in the position he was in.

A tear rolled down my cheek.

"What a disappointment you are," James' face twisted into one of disgust. "You're just as pathetic and useless as I remember." He kicked out, his boot connecting with my chin. "Stop that mewling."

The blow had sent my consciousness reeling, I saw stars and heard whispering. My vision swam, then returned to focus. But the whispering didn't cease. I spat out blood and turned to find the sounds.

From behind the house, Julie and Tori walked in tandem, their mouths moving in a chant. On each side of them was a transparent but clear specter. Lily flanked them on the right and Nettie on the left. Four generation of witches approached in a line and whispered a spell.

The lycans twisted and shrieked, releasing their captives and dropping to the ground to writhe in pain. Their flesh rippled and the sound of tearing fabric filled the night as each man ripped open to allow a wolf to climb out and also writhe on the ground. They were being forced to shift; their beasts were being pulled from within them.

Simon and Sorin released their torches to run to the crying wolves, grabbing them up to throw them into the fire one by one.

Michael crawled to his brother, shaking him and wailing.

The witches continued to chant, giving the vampires the time they needed to slaughter each incapacitated wolf.

I screamed within my brain to run but was held in place by the call of my maker. Even in all of this, he would not release us.

Sorin and Simon had finished their task, leaving James as our only foe. They stood, side by side. The slices on Simon were already healing and Sorin had taken no injury. James may be powerful but those two together might be able to stop him.

If I could get Lia away from him, we might stand a chance.

The witches had stopped their spell. I felt the magic die down, felt the ghosts leave and heard the two living women run to Michael, pulling him off his brother and to the safety of the backyard.

It was a vampire showdown.

James grabbed Lia by the throat and pulled her in front of him. "Let us leave," he demanded. "You killed the wolves, so you get to keep your farm. But, these two are mine."

"No deal," Simon debated.

"You'd rather lose him to death than to distance?" James asked, attempting to sound innocent and confused.

"I promised," Simon answered, like it should explain everything.

"So be it."

The next few moments would haunt my dreams for eternity. James whirled Lia around, grabbed each side of her face and pulled her in for a kiss. She froze, not fighting but not participating in it either. Then he'd yanked up in a swift movement. It wasn't until her body dropped and her head remained in his hand that I'd realized what he'd done. As he tossed her head into the fire, I registered her long, ruby hair flying out behind it like wings.

I'd no time to respond before he grabbed me and pulled me in front of him. He'd replaced me with her like it was nothing, using us as shield or threat or bargaining chip but never seeing us as anything but his property. To my shame, I still did not fight him, did not allow Lia's death to rally my strength. My years away from him had not undone his programming and my well-learned obedience to him held me in place.

"He can be next," he explained.

"Okay," Simon reached up his arms in surrender. I felt power surge off of him and didn't know what he was doing until I saw the bull emerged from the back of the house and barrel for the truck. I braced myself, ready to take advantage of any moment where James wasn't holding me.

When the beast slammed into the vehicle, we were airborne and flying backwards. The impact as I hit the ground was jarring but not enough for me to not roll to my right and away from James.

I crawled towards a shine in my periphery and wrapped my hand around the base of the sickle as James was grabbing my feet and pulling me to him. Someone had stuck it in the tree in case it was needed. The yank at my feet and my grip pulled the weapon from the trunk. I rolled onto my back, extending the curved blade. James let go, standing and smiling. "Oh, scary. You've got a knife." He cocked his head. "What a shame that you don't have balls."

I heard the chanting behind me again, the witches were back and working up a new spell. It distracted me just long enough, that I turned to see them, and the blade was yanked from my grasp.

Returning my gaze to the now-armed James, I had no time to reach for him before he brought up and flung it over me. A scream erupted and the chanting stopped. I followed the course of the blade to find it in Julie's chest, her eyes wide and Tori screaming.

James grabbed me from behind the same way Sorin had grabbed him earlier. He turned us to face the approaching vamps. "Freeze," he commanded, and they did.

"Get Tori out of here," I begged. Sorin gave me a nod, turned into a blur and the teen was gone from her mother's side.

"Now you," James instructed Simon. "You leave with the last of your people and I take Rhys. I'm done with your tricks and games."

"I'm out of tricks," Simon raised his hand in surrender. "You bested us. You win."

"Fuck your flattery," James spat. "I win nothing. My wife was worth a thousand times more than the pathetic piece of meat in my hands. Now, it's a matter of principle, of respect. He will pay for every moment he was away, for turning her against me, for making me look like a fool. I'll do things to him that no one has imagined, then he'll heal and then I'll do it again."

The trembling was back, the icy fear that froze me in place. My brain shut down, losing its ability to process anything. Simon and I locked eyes. "You're not worthless," he reminded me.

Faces flashed through my mind as James laughed behind me. I saw all the people I didn't fight for – Diedre, Collin, Alden, Nettie, Pedro and Lia. *Fight for yourself,* I heard Simon's voice screaming in my mind.

I drove my head backwards and felt James' nose crack against my skull. He stumbled backwards, losing his grip.

For the first time in my entire life, I would not be a coward. I owed it to everyone who protected me to fight or die trying.

Courage in the face of fear.

"I didn't deserve any of it," I raged, swinging and connecting a fist into James' jaw, then repeated it over and over, left and right, blow after blow. Years of fear and wrath were poured into each punch. Shock filled his eyes as he stumbled backwards, away from me. He raised his hand to throw power.

Before I could give it a second thought, I hunched, drove my shoulder straight into him and ran us both into the roaring fire.

82

January 1982

It had taken weeks for me to heal the burns I'd suffered throwing myself into that fire. Simon had injuries to his hands and arms from pulling me out but my whole body had taken damage from the flames.

Michael had needed more time than that to recover from the extensive internal damage. Lycanthropes heal fast so he had that advantage. But nothing could help him with the pain of losing his brother and wife in the same hour. That was going to take a lot more time.

Tori was at his side the whole time, creating healing potions for him to drink, wheeling him to the gravesides each day and showering him with love. She grieved in private, refusing to tell any of us how much pain she was in.

It was Tori that had thought of conjuring her ancestors' ghosts to use in the spell. She'd thought about it one night while pondering the purpose of my own spectral visitors. She'd figured that if non-witch ghosts could communicate, then witch ghosts could probably chant. And, she'd been right.

Sorin had stayed for a week to help us rebuild and bury. He had been Simon's call the night before and immediately boarded a private plane for Austin. He'd slept nearby, planning to visit us. He never could've expected the attack would happen the very next night. He'd heard the struggles as he approached the ranch, smelled the blood and wolves, knew he had to act.

And it'd been Sorin who'd known what the twins were when we'd buried them. They were djinn, something very rare, especially in America. The idea that we may have caused the end of an endangered species sat heavy with me. It somehow made the whole night so much worse. It also made me wonder how many other species were out there, hiding and feeling unsafe. I'd reinvigorated my desire to get the ranch fully back up and running again.

It had also cemented my plan to move away from Lost Souls Ranch.

When I'd told everyone, they'd begged me to stay. They'd told me that it wasn't my fault, that the ranch would fall apart without me, that I didn't need to leave. But it was all untrue.

The ranch would not fall apart without me. I did need to leave. And it had been my fault. I could no longer stay in Austin and put the people I loved in danger.

It was time to leave.

Over the years, I'd invested all the pay that Simon had given me. I was wealthy and didn't need to worry about money. I'd tried to give some to Simon, but he was even more financially successful than I and refused even a penny. He only made me promise to send letters and call every once in a while.

Sorin had a small house for me in a rural area outside of Pittsburgh. I'd be alone and no one would get hurt because of me. I could spend the remainder of my days in solitude, never caring for anyone again and that felt like the perfect plan for me.

So, I celebrated the new year with everyone, then loaded up a moving van for my trip. I would drive at night, sleep in motels during the day and be in Pittsburgh by February. Tears were shed. Promises were made.

As I pulled away from the ranch, I allowed myself one look in the rearview before I vowed to never look back again.

PART THREE:
PITTSBURGH

83

February 1982

Sorin let me buy the cottage off him for a ridiculously low price. He was now master of the city. I didn't know how, and he wasn't exactly forthcoming with the information. I'd noticed a change in him from his first visit at the ranch to when I moved. He was harder, colder. But, as someone who was trying to heal a lot of unseen damage, I wasn't in the place to try and help another. So, I let him keep his secrets and I kept mine.

He'd implemented a pledge since coming into the position of lord of the city. All vampires had to pledge, or they were not welcomed. He didn't ask me for the full pledge but did insist I promise to ask him before telling a human what I was and that any vampire I made would come to him to pledge within a day. I didn't plan on making another and I owed him my life, so I didn't hesitate to promise.

Then, he left me in my solitude as I'd asked, telling me I can visit his home whenever I needed.

For twenty years, I didn't visit. I used the time to heal and get to know myself. I read, planted flowers down my walkway and built a home. I lived off the blood of the animals in my surrounding woods. My calls to the ranch started as daily, then weekly, then monthly before they became a holiday only duty, then fell off completely. I felt like I couldn't move on or recover if I kept holding onto the past.

My hatred of lycanthropes had become well-earned and cemented in my soul. If I heard a howl or inadvertently flipped on a werewolf movie or found my book of choice including lycanthropes, my rage would well up in my gut. I'd chalked up the kindness of Pedro, Flavio and the beautiful half-lycan children I'd helped raise as anomalies. I believed all lycans were my enemy. I'm ashamed to admit that I vividly imagined ripping werewolves apart to comfort myself on my darkest days.

It took several years for me to feel safe. A snapping branch outside or a burst of wind would convince me that James was out there, back from the dead and here to throw me in a crate bound for Scotland. I'd sometimes stand guard at my window, looking out into the trees, watch for a vampire or wolf who came to hurt me.

It took a decade for me to stop thinking about Lia. I cried more tears for her than for anyone else I'd lost. It had been hard enough to leave her in Scotland, but I'd comforted myself with thoughts of her joy. But now, I knew she was gone and there was no way for me to lie to myself anymore.

When she'd faded from my thoughts, I found my libido returning. I believed with my whole heart there was no way I'd ever fall in love again, but eventually began to crave the touch of a woman again. I ventured out into the city to find companionship whenever it was too much to bear. In hindsight, my sex drive returning was a good sign, a sign that I was healing and finding my spark again but in the midst of it, my needs just felt like an inconvenience.

84

April 2002

After twenty years of living this way, I recognized that I couldn't continue as I was. My latest project had been creating the jungle room in the basement. The lower level was without windows, what I obviously needed to be safe during the day, but it felt too much like the empty room I'd been locked in as punishment. So, I'd given it life with running water, colorful murals and all the music I could ever need.... And, I still felt bored.

I needed more. I needed to interact with others, have something to do and get out. I had the internet at that point, but chatrooms couldn't replace real-life conversations. I'd learned everything I could about computers and was able to use them to their fullest potential, but it was never going to replace the world of the living. So, I took Sorin up on his offer to visit his manor and tell him what I needed.

The manor was impressive, alive with music and lights. Vampires moved about the grounds, parting for me when I pulled up and stepped out of the car.

A tall, African-American woman stood in the doorway to the beautiful home, eyebrow arched, and arms crossed. "Can I help you?" she asked as I approached.

"Um," I stumbled over the thoughts in my head. I'd gotten out of practice with others, forgetting basic conversation skills. "I'm here for Sorin."

"Do I know you?" she asked.

"Do I know you?" I repeated, slightly offended by her tone.

"Tamela," she smirked. "His head bodyguard. So, again, I'm going to ask who you are since I've never seen you."

"Rhys." Did I shake hands? Bow?

"The recluse?" She asked.

"The what?"

"Sorry," she put her hands up in defense. "Didn't mean to be rude. I know about you, of course, I know every vamp in the city. I just never saw you and didn't think I ever would. You're better looking than I imagined."

"Really?" I could feel how awkward I was but couldn't stop it. "What did you imagine?"

She shrugged her shoulders. "A hobbit, I guess."

The snort that erupted from me was likely the most embarrassing moment of my life. "That's a good book," I blurted, trying to save the conversation.

"Follow me," she said, turning into the parlor and heading for the stairs. I followed, glad to end the torture of trying to be cool around this new female immortal.

At the top of the stairs, she turned right and disappeared into a room. I hesitated, knowing I could still turn around, run to my cottage and return to the safety of solitude. But, the idea of returning to the loneliness was unbearable so I followed her into the office.

Sorin sat in a large, leather chair with a massive desk between him and another vampire. The second man leaned over the wood, tapping on the papers on the desktop. The vampire appeared older than every other vampire I'd ever met. His hair was white and pulled back into a ponytail, the skin around his eyes and mouth showed aging, yet he still held an air of distinction. "So, you're happy with the seating chart and moving the banquet to a bigger venue?" he asked Sorin.

"Yes, Will," Sorin sighed. "Go ahead."

The vampire named Will popped up, rolled up the papers they were examining and strode from the office like a man on a mission.

Sorin looked to Tamela in the corner who popped her chin up and in my direction. Sorin followed her gaze to land on me; a small smile crossed his lips. "Rhys," he stood, coming around to offer me one of two merlot-colored chairs. I sat and he took the other. "To what do I owe the honor of this visit?"

He was different. In the twenty years since I'd moved here and last seen him, his shoulders appeared heavier, his face less expressive. The sparkle had left his grey eyes and he didn't feel like the same person. He'd created some kind of wall around him, shut down.

"I'm just going a little crazy all alone," I admitted, trying to start the conversation.

"I can imagine," Sorin nodded. "Isolation is fine for a while, but we are not creatures whose nature is to be without others." I nodded, unable to say anything. "So, what do you ask?"

"Um," I thought about it. What was I asking? When was I my happiest? "Work," I said. "I can work around here if you need help."

"That's a kind offer," he tilted his head. "But, I've more than enough help here."

Disappointment filled my gut. It'd taken a lot to come to him and ask for help. But, what had I expected? For him to just have an answer for a predicament I got myself into?

"I do know of something, though," he continued. "I don't know if you'd like it, but you'd have work and still remain under the radar."

"Sounds great," I smiled.

Sorin reached for a notepad and pen, wrote something down and handed me a phone number. "How do you feel about the hospital?"

85

June 2009

The CD for the evening was one of Radiohead's. It had taken a few years for me to convince administration that it was okay to have music playing since I worked night shift and no one came down. They'd relented and stipulated that it needed to remain at a professional level, so I followed the rules to not lose the privilege.

I was in a good mood since that night was delivery night and I'd get a fresh supply for my home fridge. Drew, the delivery guy, hadn't been hard to convince. The first time I'd met him, the smell of marijuana was so strong, I figured I couldn't lose anything to ask. If he was appalled, he'd probably not even remember it the next day. If he asked about it, I'd deny him and ask him if he was smoking anything.

But if he agreed, I could stop living off squirrels and racoons, which would be nice. My first month in the blood bank, I'd gone half-insane trying to ignore the smell of the human blood bags all around me. I wanted to steal them or open one, but I knew I'd be caught. Since Sorin had gotten me the job, I didn't want to do anything that would jeopardize him. I would need to get ahold of bags *before* they were part of the inventory.

When I asked Drew if I could pay $100 for a bag, I held my breath. Without pause, he'd asked how many bags I wanted and how often. And so began a beautiful arrangement. I didn't ask where he got the bags, and he didn't ask why I wanted them.

Going back to human blood helped me continue to feel like myself again, the self that'd been so happy on the ranch. It made it easier to mask, too. Since leaving Austin, I hadn't been practicing my magic so when I needed to mask at work, it'd been hard at first. The human blood made the masking easier. So, the nurses could see shy, awkward, dorky Rhys.

I heard the door and thought it might be Drew but he didn't come down the stairs, he came through the side door. So, whoever was approaching wasn't coming with blood. I checked my computer and didn't see any new orders for units, so they weren't coming for blood, either. The smell hit my nose before I heard her chittering. The perfume and tobacco meant it had to be Monica.

I rolled my eyes. She was fine, as humans go, but could border on an annoyance. Her hair was the kind of blonde that only came from a box, and I was sure would lead to hair loss. It was hair-sprayed half to death, in a way that made her smoking more dangerous than she realized. Every time she lit a cigarette, she risked her hair erupting into a pyre. Her makeup was always too heavy. There wasn't enough cosmetics to cover up the scowl that crossed her face whenever she saw me.

She hated me and I was okay with that.

As she bounced towards my room, I mentally prepared myself for her arrival. She was telling someone the history of the hospital, so a new employee must've been getting the official tour. I gathered my energy to ensure I had my masking in place. Sometimes getting irritated could pull effort from my powers and Monica had the tendency to irritate me so I upped my power.

It wasn't Monica that caused my focus to waiver, it was the new nurse with her. Her ebony hair framed sapphire eyes on a face I knew well, a face from my past. My vision waivered when she shot her hand towards me for a shake. She could have been Diedre's twin.

"Hi," she beamed. "I'm Kate."

86

May 2014

It took more than a few visits from Kate before I stopped shaking at the sight of her. She was so like Deidre that she was instantly endeared to me. That was before I even got to know her.

So many of the staff avoided me. They thought I was weird, which was fine. I was different from them and they probably sensed it. I didn't take it personally. But Kate wasn't like that. She stopped by sometimes on her shifts, bringing me coffee and asking me about myself. We talked about music and the bands we'd seen. She told me about her two daughters and showed me pictures from their different events and trips. My favorite were the beach ones. I'd never seen the ocean during the day or felt the heat of sun-soaked sand. I'd stared at one so long, Kate had given it to me. I'd tacked it onto the office wall, imaging the sounds and smells of that beach.

We'd talked about her divorce and how she wanted to just live under the radar, unnoticed and quite certain she'd never love again. This resonated with me.

To me, she was like seeing what Diedre could have had if I'd sent her away that day, sent her back to my mother and the village and her wedding. She could've told stories of her little ones with the same radiating pride and love that Kate did. Maybe she would've become a healer like Kate. Lord knew the girl was smart and knew every berry and plant that grew around the village. Perhaps she would have cared for others and saved lives just like this nurse did.

Sometimes, I imagined that Diedre was reincarnated in Kate. Her spirit had last come to me two weeks before Kate's birth. Did it find its home in the body of a Pittsburgh baby, starting from scratch with no memory yet looking and feeling so much like her? Or could Kate's family have descended from Diedre's own family? While Collin was her only sibling, she'd had cousins in other villages, as far away as Ireland. Could Kate be a distant relative of the ebony haired girl I'd grown up with?

This particular night, I was pondering the reality of it and considering doing some genealogical research when a man strode into the blood bank. His white coat meant he was a doctor, yet I'd never seen him.

"Can I help you?" I asked, checking the computer for any orders. "I don't have an order if you need blood."

"No," he shook his head. "I'm just here to introduce myself and get the lay of the land."

The new physician was tall and broad enough that the back of the lab coat strained to wrap around his shoulder. Either he'd borrowed the coat or had bought it before bulking up. I knew from talking to other doctors that residency could pack on the pounds from stress eating anything you could get your hands on. But this guy didn't look like his coat was now too small due to fat. The size of his arms told me he lifted weights to manage the pressures of medicine instead of reaching for snacks in the breakrooms. The sharp jawline was shaded by stubble, a shade darker than his brown hair. Between the darkness of his unruly locks and light beard were the bluest eyes I'd seen. I glanced to Kate's ocean picture and back to the doctor's irises. They were near identical.

His hand shot out and I grasped it. One pump and he froze, looking me up and down like he was just seeing me. Those well-trained eyes were assessing me like a cell under a microscope. I didn't like it, scanning myself quickly to be sure my masking was in place. He looked suspicious of something, but I had no clue what. After an uncomfortable few moments of staring, he released my hand. "Dr. Alex Kitchner, new hematologist on nights."

"Rhys, blood bank guy, also on nights," I chuckled and shrugged, trying to appear more awkward than usual. "What can I do for you?"

"Uh," he still looked like he wanted to say something but wasn't. My anxiety was getting the best of me, convincing me that he knew. But how could he? He'd just arrived. And, people who'd I worked with the last twelve years didn't suspect anything, despite my age not really changing, so why would he?

"Tell me the process here," he was back to business. "What happens once the order is in?"

So, I explained to him everything that I did, how the blood was tracked and checked, how the nurses handled it and what the protocol was for emergencies.

When he left, I let out the breath I'd been holding and flopped down to my chair. He'd really rocked me for some reason, and I was uncharacteristically nervous.

That's when Kate came in, coffee in each hand and a look of annoyance. "I passed the new doc on the way down." She rolled her eyes, handed me the coffee and sat on the couch. "Did you meet him?"

"I did," I swiveled my chair to face her. "Thoughts?"

"He seems like a jerk," she blew a piece of hair out of her face. "However, Monica is in L-O-V-E."

"What happened to Chet?"

"Brett." Kate clarified, taking a sip of the coffee. "Dumped her. She was devastated, as she usually is. But Dr. Hot Stuff is a good distraction."

"Do I know this Dr. Hot Stuff?" It was Dr. Kitchener from the doorway. He'd returned and I'd been so distracted by my act of fake drinking coffee that I'd missed it. Kate jumped to her feet.

"Nope," she said. "Guy from my last hospital." She brushed past him, and I heard her run up the stairs to return to her unit.

I gathered myself before turning the chair to face him. "Did you forget something, Doctor?" I tried to sound polite, and made a show of looking at the computer like I had important tasks to complete.

I felt him approach the desk and look down at me. "Forgive my bluntness," he cleared his throat. "Does anyone in the hospital know they have a vampire in the blood bank?"

87

I stared at him, unblinking. My mind raced with the options I had. I could glamour him, deny it and call him crazy, pack up and quit my job then relocate to a completely different city. I'd need to start again. Should I change my name?

"I don't know if you have mind control," he continued. "But I ask that you don't use it on me. I can assure you; I won't tell anyone."

"I'm confused," I stood. "Vampires aren't real. Is this a joke?"

"Hear me out," Dr. Kitchner sat in the place Kate had just vacated, then indicated for me to return to my seat. I did, waiting to see what he could possibly have to say. "I ask that you keep my confidence as I will for you." I nodded, still not admitting anything. "I've been studying vampires since I was in high school. I guess you can call it my life's work. It's why I went into hematology. You see," he leaned forward. "I want to find the cure."

"For what?" I didn't think I was following.

"Vampirism," he said, like he couldn't comprehend why I wasn't understanding.

"That's-" I thought about it. "I mean, it's impossible."

"Is it?" He arched an eyebrow. "Think of how many treatments, procedure and cures we've found. Why not this?"

"Why?" I was curious, wanted to know more but had to be careful not to give anything away.

"Before I tell you this," he crossed his arms and leaned back. "I need you to come clean."

This was way out of my league, and I needed advice. I stood, holding up a finger and excusing myself to walk down the hallway and out the side door. Once I was standing by the cemetery, I retrieved the cell in my pocket and dialed a number I hadn't ever needed until now.

"Yes?" Sorin asked after one ring.

"I have a bizarre situation," I cleared my throat, the nervousness I was feeling amped up.

I'd visited the manor many times since the first time and heard stories of Sorin's leadership. He'd become not cruel but strict. It was clear he had expectations and had no problem handing down punishment when those expectations we're met. It was best to just say it.

"There's a new doctor here who knows about vampires, apparently he's made them his life work. He's recognized me as one and is asking. I haven't said anything, I can still deny or glamour him. What do you want me to do?"

To my shock he wasn't angry or surprised. "I've been forewarned about him," Sorin answered. "He's looking for a cure and seems to be exactly as he portrays." I was speechless. If Sorin knew Kitchner was coming to my hospital, why wouldn't he warn me? "You can tell him, Rhys and help him if he needs. Finding a cure would be a huge success for us. Could you imagine, shortly after your turning, if you could have taken it back and returned to human?"

The line went dead, leaving me to think about it. Would I have taken the cure if it had been available? Would I take it now if the doctor could pull it off?

When I returned to my office, I shut the door behind me. Dr. Kitchner remained where I have left him, showing no signs of impatience.

When I sat, I inhaled and exhaled. "I was turned in 1807."

He leaned back, crossing his arms again and processing what I'd revealed. "My sister is a vampire."

88

May 2015

I t had become clear that I was going to have to do something big to be
able to keep my job at the hospital. I'd heard two of the older nurses
in the stairwell, talking about how I never seemed to age. I didn't think
either of them truly thought I was a vampire, but they knew something
was not right.

I'd spoken to Alex and he'd become my eyes and ears for a few
nights. His report back was what I'd expected, rumors were starting.
Thanks to a high turnover rate, there weren't really that many people
that worked at PMC who'd been there long, but there were enough that
it was a problem.

Sorin's counsel had been clear. I was to glamour a hospital full of
employees or resign and find a new job. Obviously, one option was less
labor-intensive than the other. It wasn't my job that I didn't want to
leave, really. And, I knew Alex would visit me wherever I was. There was
one thing that made me choose the riskier of the two choices.

I didn't want to leave Kate.

So, a plan was made. Alex and I decided that I'd glamour anyone who'd started at the hospital prior to 2015, convincing them I'd started in January and was a new employee. The goal was to get to everyone before the new batch of medical residents started in the summer.

It took two weeks, but we did it. Alex had made a list and marked off each person as I wiped them of their memories of me so I could introduce myself as a new hire.

I feel shame admitting that it didn't bother me at all to mess around in the heads of so many of my coworkers, but it is truth.

Kate was last. I cried after I wiped her memories of our first meeting, our coffee talks, our building friendship. I knew that there was no guarantee that she would feel the same way about me the second time around. So many little magical moments create a friend and any change in the process could result in a different outcome.

Looking into her eyes, it broke my heart to say it. "You've never met me before. Forget me and every minute you've spent with me. Instead, an older man worked down here. He was gruff and you rarely spoke. You just got your blood and left."

Alex walked her out of the room before the trance had left her gaze. Like he had with so many before her, he returned a minute later.

"Nurse Kate," he cleared his throat. "This is Rhys. He replaced Owen in January and I thought it time you meet. He'll be running the blood bank now."

I froze, waiting to see if the glamour would hold. Her hand shot out. "I'm Kate. I work on five. Let me know if I can help you with anything. I think you'll like it here." I took her hand, gripping it and pumping it up and down. Before I could say anything, she looked at something behind me. "Oh," she smiled. "Beautiful picture. I love the beach, too. Take my daughters all the time." She squinted. "Is that Myrtle Beach? It's our favorite."

I chuckled, cursing myself for not taking down a snapshot that she'd taken herself. But she didn't appear to recognize it as hers and I thanked the universe for her habit of taking more pictures than even she could remember. The glamour was clearly working, which made me equally sad and happy.

It had been a huge risk to take on this mission but having her in front of me made it all worth it. We'd get to build our friendship again, have those same talks and she'd tell me about her daughters all over again. It'd even be able to use this fresh slate to work on my speech, make it more modern and make a point to be less awkward. It had all been worth it and I could return to a safe, boring life in the blood bank.

No one would ever have to know what I did.

89

September 2019

Alex and I spent a great deal of time at the hospital and outside of work compiling information. Alex scribbled in his journal whenever I talked about other vampires. He wanted to know it all: abilities, the oldest vampire I'd ever met, what the turning was like, what it felt like to sleep and wake, what I thought about, what blood tasted like and how vampires mate. He was a mix of scientist and detective, trying to unravel the mysteries of my kind so he could break it down. He was like a kid who took apart appliances to see what was inside and then rebuilt them to ensure he understood all of it correctly.

More than once I'd commented that he'd perform an autopsy on me if he could know for sure I'd heal.

He thought I was being dramatic.

I didn't.

He'd taken so many vials of blood that I'd lost count. Each time he'd return to tell me it was another failure and I'd reassure him that if anyone could figure it out, it'd be him.

Sometimes, when he was in my office, Monica would find a reason to page him. I knew it was for nothing important and shake my head when he'd call, listen and thank her for the unnecessary update on his patients. He tried to play dumb and insisted she was just a very thorough nurse. I knew better.

It was clear that Alex's heart was for his work and nothing else. He was so desperate to save his sister that he'd neglected his own needs to the point of them going into hibernation.

I'd heard the story of Sheena so many times I could repeat it back. He kept hoping I'd catch some tiny detail as a vampire that would reveal where she'd gone. I'd vowed to him that once the cure was ready, I'd use my prowess online to track her down. Until then, he needed to focus.

Kate stopped by less frequently. It was evident she didn't like Alex. Once, when she'd popped in and saw the good doctor was already there, she'd dropped my cup of coffee on the desk, turned and walked right back out. I offered the beverage to Alex, hoping I wouldn't have to dump this one down the sink like I always did. It felt wasteful so I was thrilled he took it. "What is the deal with you two?" I asked.

"With the nurse? What do you mean?" He shot a glance to the now empty doorway and returned to his reading.

"Why do you hate each other?" I prodded.

"I don't hate her," he pulled off his reading glasses to stuff them into his jacket pocket and shut the book. "I don't think enough of her to hate her. She's a work colleague, that's all."

"Well, she's clearly not your biggest fan," I chuckled.

"She doesn't have to be," he shook his head. "We're here to do a job and that is it. As long as she cares for my patients, if she doesn't like me, I'll won't lose sleep over it."

"I don't get it," I sighed.

"Get wait?" He asked.

"Why the women fawn over you," I explained. "Whenever we go out, they all drool when you pass them. I'm supposed to be the one with the supernatural allure but when you're around, I'm invisible. Perhaps they like the whole brooding, off limits vibe you put off."

He stood. "I don't have time for a relationship," it sounded rehearsed. "And, a one-night stand comes with too many risks."

"Ah," I nodded. "Are trying to convince me or yourself?"

"Neither," he snorted. "If you'll excuse me, I've got lives to save. Boone's gonna order a couple of units for 502. I've got to find out why the man's H&H won't hold. Going to check on him after I test my latest theory. If you don't see the order in 30 minutes, just put it in for me, will you? Boone's getting forgetful."

"Deal."

90

Kate had been more like herself when she'd returned for the bag of O Neg that Dr. Boone had ordered. Well technically I'd ordered them, but as long as the patient was getting what he needed, I didn't care about how it happened.

After she'd left, I'd returned to watching a man rebuild a motorcycle on YouTube and contemplating if that should be my new hobby when a cold wind swept through the office. I'd thought someone had opened the outside door at the end of the hall, but it didn't make sense that the wind would've made it this far when I looked up.

Standing in the doorway of my office were Collin and Diedre's spirits. I stood, blinking to be sure I saw what I thought I saw. They'd not come to me in almost 40 years, not even a knock on the wall. I'd truly believed they'd moved on.

They shimmered in the entry, both waving for me to come towards them. I shook my head. "No," I said. "No more. Haunt me no more."

They continued to motion for me to join them.

I walked around my desk, facing them but not approaching. "I'm sorry," I whispered. "Sorry you died but it was not my fault, I know it and have found my peace."

Someone came down the stairs. I froze, waiting to hear the sounds of approaching steps but instead the outside door opened and shut with a thud. A minute later, the faint sound of classical music floated back to me.

"Please go and cross over," I begged. "Find peace."

Collin's waving became frantic, and Diedre looked angry.

The scent of blood hit my nose.

Then, Diedre yelled, her voice booming against my eardrums. "Save her."

I ran down the hallway, not certain what was happening but knowing immediately who was out there. I prayed I wasn't too late.

A blur ran from her body when I burst through the door.

She was crumbled on the ground, frantic wet gasps becoming too much like agonal breathing. I was at her side in a flash, on the ground and cradling her. I had seconds to think, listening to her weak heartbeat slow. I couldn't do it, couldn't lose anyone else.

Before I could talk myself out of it, I tore at my wrist with my teeth and shoved it into her mouth. "Drink, Kate, drink it." Her throat remained still. "Kate, please don't be dead. Please, please, drink." I hated myself for not listening to the ghosts as soon as they'd arrived, not following them to this place. "Please don't let me be too late."

Relief rushed over me when the muscles of her throat started to pull at the wound and gulp down the blood. I didn't know if it would work since I wasn't the one to bite her, to drain her of blood, but I had to try. We needed to get away from this spot before we were seen. "You have to stop," I pushed her mouth from my wrist, ready to move but she began to sob. I didn't have the heart to yell at her, trying to comfort with words and song but knowing full-well that we needed to move. "Rhys?" she asked, and I shushed her. Every moment we stayed there was increasing our risk.

"I know you're scared, and you have no idea what is happening, but we have to move." I lifted her off the ground to return to the office.

Once we were in the car, I moved as quickly as I could to get us back to the cottage without getting pulled over. She lay quietly in the back. While I wanted to start asking her if she was okay or start telling her what I had just happened, I needed the time to think.

What had I done? I'd fed her my blood, the thing I swore I'd never do. I'd started the process of pulling her into eternal night without her blessing.

How was I going to tell her? What would she choose? And, what kind of maker could I be? I knew nothing of being someone's sire.

I needed to make some calls before anything else.

I got her inside and sent her to the bathroom for a shower before stepping outside to dial Sorin. He was quiet while I told the story. I left out the ghosts, but the rest was a second-by-second recounting of the events. When I finished, he was quiet. I waited for reproach or more questions.

"Bring her tomorrow night to pledge," he said, colder than ever. The line went dead.

The next call was to Alex. The retelling for him was more abridged. He expressed his sorrow for the events but applauded me for saving him. "How sure are you that you'll have a cure to offer her?" I asked.

"Nothing is definite, Rhys. You know that. But I vow to work harder than ever. Do you want me to do the same thing for her that I've done for you?"

"Could you?" I asked. "She's going to have it hard, Alex. She's got kids."

He was silent for a moment. "I didn't know. I saw her earlier and was so shitty to her. I didn't know."

"You couldn't have known," I assured him. "The important thing now is that we help her."

"That's if she survives the turn," he clarified, bringing forward my biggest fear in all of this. Not every vampire survived the turn and until completed it and came back, she could still die.

"She'll survive," I said more to myself than him. "She's strong."

91

The next night, I opened my eyes to the weight of her on the bed next to me. "Thank you," I whispered into the dark.

A fine trembling overtook me, not fear like I'd experienced before but release of fear. I think a deep part of me had been certain she wouldn't make it through. That I'd have to lose another, say goodbye to another. That I'd have another death on my head. But she'd made it through and lay next to me.

While I knew logically, she wasn't Diedre or Collin or Lia, I felt like I'd finally somehow saved them by saving her.

Without needing proof, I knew the ghosts would never return to me. They'd finally be at peace. I rose from the bed, opening a hidden door in the wall, to see my most-valued treasures. Travis' guitar leaned against the back wall, next to the stack of books that had traveled with me from Glasgow to America. Inside one, I found the picture of Lily, Julie and Tori, lightly laying a kiss on it then returning it to book. I ran my fingers over the case that held Robert's record player which had stopped working by the end of the 90s. These things no longer brought me pain but felt like little pieces of a path that led to this moment.

It was time to stop holding on so tightly to my lost family and start building a new one.

I closed them back into their safe space and returned to my spot on the bed, lying on my side to face her. I needed to take her to see Alex and Sorin tonight but wanted to take care of her first. She would need to clean up and eat.

I could fix up the room next to mine for her. She deserved a place to feel safe like I'd been given by Simon. I wanted this home to be for her what the ranch had been for me. I could take her for clothes, order her furniture, whatever she needed to start this part of her life as comfortably as possible.

But for this moment, she had peace and I wanted her to have as much peace as possible.

For a man who swore to never make another, this moment felt destined to occur. I'd been so against making another vampire and had believed nothing would ever make me do it. But the previous night, with her on the ground, I hadn't even questioned it.

While she looked like Diedre, she'd become her own, wonderful person in my eyes. She treated everyone with the same warmth and kindness, making the least of us feel worthy and seen. Losing her from this world was unthinkable and I'd been there to be sure it didn't come to pass.

Why had the spirits come to save this one human? How had Diedre been able to create a voice to send me running?

As insignificant as I was, I felt like I'd played a role in a greater purpose. I believed Kate would go on to do something brilliant, even though I couldn't be sure what it was. She felt special. Turning her had felt like the universe lined up perfectly for this to happen, like so many things had to fall into place to specifically lead me to be there to make her a vampire.

Or, perhaps all makers feel this way when they've turned someone.

Her eyes popped open and immediately searched for me. When she found me, she relaxed.

The best part of my life had begun.

Epilogue

Katie,

I know you must have questions, which I'm open to. I've skipped over some things in the interest of time. I cannot write out centuries of material. But, if you want more detail, have questions about anything or need to hear a specific event in my words, I'm happy to do this for you.

I cannot apologize enough to you for wiping your memories. I hope you understand why I did it but wouldn't fault you for being upset. I should have told you as soon as I turned you.

I'd like to repeat that some of these things did not line up with what I told you in the beginning of our time together. Alex and Sorin were protecting me, doing what I asked of them by letting me tell you when I was ready to.

And, I'm ready to.

They've both been told that I'm doing this and will answer any questions you have with my blessing.

I've reconnected with Simon and he knows I am telling you all of this. He's hoping you'll want to visit so he can meet you.

I accept you may see me differently after this. While, yes, I've told you what I did in Glasgow, I left many details out. Now, you know the whole truth.

More than that, I'm ashamed for the vehemence I held for the lycanthropes. I know now that it was prejudice, a blind hatred against an entire species. I've admitted all this to Diana, told her my history and she's helped me grow. For this, I will be forever indebted to her.

I was entirely honest in this journal. You are the best thing I've ever done. I know I compared you to Diedre but please know that she is not the reason I turned you. **You** *are the reason I turned you. You being made vampire, being a Maiden was and is fate. I don't know why the universe chose me to bring you over or how I earned that honor, but I will be grateful until I take my last breath.*

I look forward to seeing you again after you've read this, with no secrets and untold stories between us.

I love being Uncle Rhys again, seeing the girls grow. I love sharing music with them and telling them stories of my home. They've healed something inside of me.

I love seeing the way you've changed Sorin and Alex. They were both so closed off, slowly extracting themselves from the world and their own possibilities. You've brought them out of their shells, given them reasons to live again.

Most of all, I love you, my daughter. I can't wait to see what the years bring you and the powerful woman you continue to grow into. You never stop amazing me.

You have a piece of my heart - forever and a day,

Rhys

The End.

Made in the USA
Middletown, DE
11 June 2024